FLORENCE GRACE

Also by Tracy Rees

Amy Snow

FLORENCE GRACE

TRACY REES

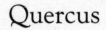

First published in Great Britain in 2016 by

Quercus Editions Ltd
Carmelite House
50 Victoria Embankment
London EC4Y oDZ

An Hachette UK company

A CIP catalogue record for this book is available
from the British Library.

PB ISBN 978 1 78429 617 9
EBOOK ISBN 978 1 78429 618 6

10 9 8 7 6 5 4 3 2

Typeset by Jouve (UK), Milton Keynes

Printed and bound in Great Britain by Clays Ltd, St Ives plc

For my wonderful parents, as ever, with all my love
and for all the Old Rillas and Laceys who have
helped make my life magical

Chapter One

The damn pony had bolted again. It had to be the most wicked, contrary creature in the West Wivel Hundred. We had been only half an hour on the moors when a pigeon flashed up in front of us, one foolish, startled creature before another. The pony plunged and vanished from under me, sending me sprawling in the mud. From there I watched his hairy white backside disappear into the distance.

'Coward!' I yelled. 'It were a *pigeon*!'

A sea mist had come up sudden and swift. Peaks and dips, track and rock, wholesome ground and steaming, stinking bog were all cloaked alike in the same milky vagueness. Only someone very intrepid or foolhardy would proceed. I considered myself neither but I did not have time to waste waiting out a sea mist. It could last minutes or days and I was already late. A whole day late, in fact.

I wasn't even sure why I had stayed the night in Truro. Lately, life seemed to have become a tyrannical series of irrational impulses I felt compelled to follow – and a consequent series of exhausting questions to which I had no answers. Is this what womanhood was? If so, I begged I might put off the honour a few more years.

I did not doubt that I would find my way home – the moors were home to me in a way that nobody else could understand – but the mist was a dod-blasted nuisance, clammy and cold and snaking. Stephen would certainly say he told me so. Damnable pony. Let it slip on a rock and break its neck or stumble into a bog and drown in thick black mud, the flighty creature.

So I fumed, stomping along, thirteen years old and knowing I was in the wrong. I wouldn't have cared *how* long I was out there with the mists and the mud and the moor spirits, but for knowing that Nan would be worried. Last night was the first we had spent apart since Da had died.

The previous day I had gone to Truro with Stephen and Hesta for an exciting opportunity – so it seemed to us then, young and inexperienced as we were. This opportunity had come from the most unlikely of sources: my old schoolroom enemy, Trudy Penny.

She had sent me, of all things, a note! I do not believe any inhabitant of our tiny hamlet had ever received correspondence before. It was written on white paper and enclosed in an envelope with a waxen seal. It read thus:

Florrie,

On fifth September coming, my uncle and aunt, Mr and Mrs Beresford of Truro, are having a party to celebrate their son's engagement. They are short several staff due to household changes — bad timing, says my aunt, who is losing her mind over it. They need hands and I thought you and your friends might like to earn a little money. They will pay sixpence each person for the day. You would be helping the housekeeper at their house in Lemon Street. If you are interested, please let me know by the end of the week and I will tell them you will come.

Regards
Trudy

I immediately knew I would go. This wasn't one of my 'premonitions' — no special intuition told me it was so — it was simply that I desperately wanted to. It would take time, however, for reality to catch up with me. Hesta and Stephen were unadventurous souls who required much persuading: I said 'sixpence' many times. Nan, who had nothing in the world but me, needed even more convincing. Again, I said 'sixpence'. I patiently argued away every worry and doubt, but suffice it to say I eventually bent them all to my will. If obstinacy runs in families, I have a double share.

I thought it was to be an isolated adventure. If I had known what that gentle party in Truro was to foreshadow, I might never have gone. Then again, that wouldn't have made any difference to anything.

And so we went to Truro, Hesta and I on Stephen's father's pony, and Stephen walking by its side. I had seen towns before – I had been to Lostwithiel and Fowey – but I had not imagined such an air of gentility and prosperity. I had never seen a place like Lemon Street in Truro. It was cobbled and broad and there was no mud. Horses and carts and even *carriages* rattled up and down. Gentlefolk strolled its length, smiling at each other and saying 'good day'. It was a pleasant, sunlit afternoon in early summer as though even the weather had been arranged with gracious intent.

The houses were built of grey stone and adjoined each to the next as though stuck together. They would never blow away in a gale. Their residents would never have to worry about the roof holding up in heavy rain. The three of us stood in the middle of the street, gawping, until a carriage nearly bowled us down. Stephen pulled us onto the pavement, a thing we had not seen before, and we stood before a splendid house. It seemed impossibly audacious that we should enter.

'Is Trudy Penny sure about this?' demanded Hesta. 'Is this some sort of mischief she's playing? Mayhap they'll throw us out and back we go to Braggenstones tonight.'

'Well, we can't stand here all day,' I said, tugging my arms from my friends' and climbing the steps to seize the lion's-head door knocker. Of course, we should have gone to the back, but we did not know – we had no experience of houses large enough to warrant two entryways.

4

We were shown to the kitchens and told what to do. Everyone was kind enough and I think the housekeeper was sufficiently flustered to see us less as muddy, inexperienced waifs from the country and more as angels of salvation.

The next few hours passed in a flurry of orders and there was no time to do anything but respond to them. If that were my life, if I had been a servant in such a place, I do not think I could have borne the endless direction. But for that once, because it was all so new and lively and different, I flew about with a bright eye and endless energy, earning myself more than a few words of praise. I caught glimpses of Hesta from time to time. Her beautiful white-blonde hair was tied back and her tiny face looked resigned and a little miserable. But then she had orders enough at home. I only caught sight of Stephen once and he looked confused.

But I was happy. It was a new challenge and I was doing well. I was helping, making a difference. I had imagined I might feel lonely or homesick so far from all I knew, but I loved being a new Florrie, a Florrie who could turn her hand to anything and thrive in a completely new place. And when the housekeeper popped her head through the door to announce that the guests had started to arrive, a ripple of excitement ran through the servants.

Suddenly everyone was dipping hands in a pail of water to lay cooling palms on flushed cheeks, and tucking wisps of sweaty hair back under their caps and wraps. Aprons were untied and skirts smoothed. Then, two or three at a time, the staff were permitted to creep out to 'the nook', a hidden space from where one could see the gentlefolk coming to the dance.

'Come on, Florrie, our turn,' one of the kitchen maids said after a while.

'Me?' I was thrilled. I had thought perhaps only the regular staff of the house could expect such an indulgence. I followed Vera along the passage and up a small flight of stairs to the side door of a large dining room. It had a sort of outer area, curtained off from the room by heavy, thick drapes of plum velvet; this was mostly filled by a table bearing a spare bowl of punch, crystal glasses, white china plates and other things that the guests might need replaced in an instant. We squeezed into this hidden space and peeped our noses past the curtain to see a world of colour and light.

I watched, spellbound, as the gentlemen bowed and the ladies sparkled. I feasted my eyes on pink and peach and ivory gowns. I had never seen such things; even my schoolteacher's pretty pastel dresses were simple compared with these. I longed to touch them and absorb their lustrous sheen. And the jewels! I did not even have names for what I saw then. Deep green, blood red and clear as sunlight in dew; they looked like something from another world, no world that *I* knew.

And then, to watch the people! This, more than the spectacle, was what enthralled. To see disdain concealed behind a smooth mask of politeness, the mischievous sparkle in the eyes of the demure younger ladies, the self-importance of the moustachioed gentlemen – I could have watched all night. When the band struck up I was in seventh heaven. The way they curtseyed and whirled from partner to partner was nothing like the heavy-footed, red-faced country dances I had been to once or twice in Boconnoc.

And the *music*! I could hardly believe my ears. All my life had afforded me in the way of music so far was Rod Plover sawing away at his fiddle, or occasionally the lusty voices of my neighbours raised in a chorus of country songs. But sometimes in my mind I had heard something I couldn't describe – a tinkling rise and fall of notes, whole passages of music that danced on and on like the wind . . . I had tried to describe the experience to Hesta more than once but all she did was screw up her little face in confusion.

'What can it be, Hesta?'

'It just be your fancy again. You're strange, Florrie Buckley, for all I love you.'

But I knew it was important, just as I knew many other things I could not explain and for which I had no proof. And that night, squashed into the nook next to the punch bowl, I heard for the first time 'my' music in real life.

'What is that?' I asked Vera, tugging at her arm and pointing.

'Why, that be a piano, child,' she said.

'Pi-ah-no,' I breathed in wonder, as though she had said 'Elysium,' or 'Olympus'.

Vera must have seen something in my face for she patted my arm and said, 'Stay a while.' She was soon replaced by another maid, who crammed herself in beside me and stood breathing heavily in my ear while we watched.

I tried to impress the sights on my memory, for I could imagine no way that I would ever see them again. As my eyes roved over the crowd they fell on a young man and I felt a little tug at my heart, another moment of uncanny recognition . . .

It was the kindness of his smile that caught me first. He was attractive, yes, with curling hair like yellow gorse, clear brown eyes like moorland pools and a lovely face caught somewhere between manhood and boyhood. That drew me, for I felt so in between myself at that time; from the sunny smile on his face he looked as though he were handling it far more gracefully than I. His patient expression, the way he looked upon each person as though he were truly interested in what they had to say, impressed me in a room full of masks and formalities. As I watched, a number of proud mamas and papas introduced their young daughters to him. At last he caught one by the hand and led her into the dance.

I stifled a giggle. That was the most ungainly girl I had ever seen! And my hero, though moderately graceful, was not so skilled a partner that he could compensate for her. Together they stumbled gamely through a gentle waltz, bumping into pinch-faced couples and sending them staggering. They were a liability on the floor. When the waltz finished and a lively polka struck up they should have known to retire, but they started leaping and skipping with all the poise of a pair of new-born calves. I covered my eyes briefly, then took my hand down just in time to see them hurtle off-balance. Inevitably the young lady tripped in her skirts and tumbled to the ground, knocking into a trio of chairs upon which were perched more circumspect young ladies – and sending them flying.

I was about to roar with laughter when my companion in the nook flew to her aid. I remembered that I was there to work after all, so I chased after her. The girl's father was at her side in a trice, shooting a fierce look at the young man and helping his daughter to her feet.

'Here, girl, help me,' he said to the other maid. 'Take her arm. Come, Fanny, lean on us. Let us seat you somewhere quiet.'

The little cluster limped off, leaving me standing without purpose in this sparkling room full of people who weren't like me. I noticed one, however, who was doing as I had longed to, and rocking with laughter. He was another young man, sitting in the farthest corner of the room. He shook with a wicked mirth. I grinned, then looked away.

'Be *you* all right, sir?' I asked the golden young man, since no one else had. Everyone seemed to hold him responsible for the catastrophe.

'*Really*, young Sanderson!' muttered more than one portly gentleman, and 'Sanderson, you *must* take more care!' admonished a number of ladies. It seemed hardly fair.

He looked at me in great surprise, but before he could answer a forbidding-looking woman with a sweep of dark hair bore him off. His mother? I could see no resemblance, and yet she behaved very proprietorially towards him. I took advantage of being universally ignored to slip back behind the curtain and continue my evening's entertainment.

A dance or two later, I was thinking that I really should get back to the kitchen when I spied the hapless Sanderson standing alone near my alcove. On a mad impulse I tweaked back the curtain and hissed at him. He turned to me in astonishment and I beckoned him in. Casting a quick look around, he ducked behind the drape and I let it fall again, concealing us.

'Hello,' I grinned, well pleased with my prize. When we were six, Stephen had proposed to me inside a hen coop. This was better.

'Hello,' he said, terribly politely. He was older than he had looked from a distance, I saw, almost grown-up really. I should never have accosted him so had I realised.

'I saw your young lady fall,' I observed. Perhaps it was not my most tactful moment.

He coloured, red as a farm boy. 'She's not my young lady, she's a family friend. I'm afraid I'm not the most accomplished at the polka.'

'*Pish*. It were her. She were terrible. You done well to keep her upright that long. Why is everyone blaming you fer it? Why are *you*?'

'It's the gentlemanly thing to do. One does not admit that young ladies have, er, faults of any description.'

'Truly?' I was intrigued. 'That's stupid, en't it? Of course young ladies got faults. They be people, like everyone else. I got faults. I got heaps of 'em.'

He looked amused and confused both at once. 'Oh, I'm sure you don't.'

'Oh, I do! Heaps!' I fell silent, realising it was not the most impressive introduction I could have made. 'I got heaps of things I do well, though, too.'

'I am certain of it. Like what?'

'Like reading. I can read very well. And I can write. And I can make medicines out of wildflowers and recipes and *spells*.' The last claim was not entirely true but I wanted to impress this pleasant, sweet-smelling young man.

'Spells! Gracious. How clever.' He looked a little nervous but smiled that good-natured smile again.

'Would you like some punch, sir?' I pressed on, trying everything I could think of to keep him from going. I gestured at the spare bowl on the table and ladled him a glass before he could answer me.

'Thank you.' He took it and peered round the curtain. 'Goodness. This is a splendid hidey-hole, isn't it?'

''Tis, aye. I should get back really. They let me come up and watch only I don't think I was meant to be so long.'

'You work for the Beresfords?'

'Oh no, sir, I'm from Braggenstones.'

'Bragg . . . ?'

'You wouldn't know it. It's in the middle of nowhere. I'm just helping out here for this one night. I never been anywhere like this before.'

'And do you like it?'

'Very much, sir. Do you live in Truro?'

'I live in London. I'm here with my aunt and my brother, representing the family.'

'Which is your brother, sir?'

He smiled even wider and beckoned me to his side so that I could peep out with him. I could feel the warmth of his clean, exquisitely clad body next to mine and relished the feeling of comradeship with someone I considered must walk two feet above the earth.

'Over there, by the punch bowl.'

It was the wicked young man I had spied earlier.

'He be nothing like you!' I exclaimed. It was true. The brother was a funny-looking thing. He didn't have the erect posture and serene expression of the other gentlemen, but sat hunched over like a troll, scowling. People gave him a wide berth. He had a wing of smooth silky hair, as dark as his brother's was fair, which fell across half his face, and his skin was sallow.

'Younger or older than you?' I asked, guessing younger.

'Older by two years. He is the heir and I am the insurance,' he laughed.

I didn't understand him. 'I never seen a boy so miserable,' I observed.

'Oh, Turlington's not miserable. He's resentful. He generally likes to do whatever he pleases and he did not want to come here. My grandfather blackmailed him, so he's sulking.'

I looked again with interest. I liked to do whatever I pleased as well. 'I like your name. It suits you.'

'Why do you say that?'

'Sanderson. Sand. You're all golden like sand.'

He blushed a little. 'Well. Thank you. You're the first person who's ever said that. Normally they ask, "Why do you and your brother have such extraordinary names?"'

'Well, why do you? Sorry, but I must ask now you've said it.'

'It's because my family is so very proud that they'll only marry women from other fine families. Then, to preserve the name of those families, they confer the surnames as Christian names upon us boys.'

I must have looked confused, for he elaborated.

'My mother's name was Isabella Sanderson. I was their first-born son, so I was named Sanderson. Turlington's mother was called Belle Turlington. It's a way for my family to brag about their excellent connections.'

'How odd. Only, don't you and Turlington have the *same* mother, if you be brothers?'

'A good question. The Graces are a complicated family. You see—'

But I did not come to see, for his fierce aunt swept past in that moment. 'Have you seen Sanderson?' she demanded of the gentleman at her side. 'Where has that boy got to? Between his clumsiness and Turlington's appalling manners, I don't know what the Graces are coming to.'

He pulled a face. 'I had better go. I mustn't be found in here. But first may I have the pleasure of knowing your name?'

I would not have wanted to be found by that witch either. I curtseyed. 'Florrie Buckley, short for Florence, sir.'

'A pleasure to meet you, Miss Florence.'

I liked being called Florence. She sounded like an altogether different girl from Florrie Buckley of Braggenstones.

'Thank you, this was a welcome respite,' said Sanderson. And he vanished, back to the world whence he came.

When I got back to the kitchen there was a fine hurrah going on, and Hesta was at the centre of it. She had fallen and cracked her head on the stone floor, bled all over it and fainted. She had been tended to and deemed unfit to continue working by the doctor. Mr Beresford had been summoned. He was stooping with his hands on his knees in front of Hesta, who lolled in a chair by the fire. He offered to send the three of us home in his private carriage, or else to put us up for the night.

'Hesta! Are you all right?' I cried, rushing to her side. Her sweet face was wan and her blue eyes vague.

'I be all right, Florrie.' She took my hand bravely. 'Only I do feel queer and I should so like to be at home in my own bed.'

'Of course, dear, of course,' I soothed her, though my heart sank. 'That be very kind of you, sir, thank you,' I added to Mr Beresford.

'Naturally, child, naturally. I feel terrible that such an accident occurred when you have come all this way to help us.' I thought what a kind man he was and wondered how he could be related to horrible Trudy Penny. 'There were three of you, I understand? A young man?'

'Aye, sir, Stephen Trevian.'

Mr Beresford nodded. 'Mrs Chambers, please fetch Stephen Trevian at once. I am sending these three children back to the moors. Wallace, fetch the carriage. Now, young ladies, I must return to my guests but I wish you a good journey. And a speedy recovery to you, poor child.' He sloped off and I held Hesta's hand and murmured words of comfort until Stephen appeared, all concern.

'I'm concerned enough myself,' muttered Mrs Chambers. ''Tis a long night ahead and I needed the hands. You do *all* have to go, I suppose?'

'Aye,' said Stephen at once. 'We came here under the promise we'd stick together. We can't let Hesta go in a carriage alone, and she's not fit besides.' He stood over Hesta protectively, so stocky and serious, so sure of right and wrong, that Mrs Chambers looked resigned.

But I had glimpsed a shred of hope. Hesta was looking pinker already. Stephen was as staunch and reliable as anyone could wish in a friend . . .

'I would stay, ma'am,' I ventured, 'but that I couldn't travel back over the moors on my own at night. My grandmother would skin me, and that's a fact.'

My hope was reflected in her face. 'If you were willing, child, you could stay the night. You could share a room with Sarah, there's a spare bed. You could help in the morning with the tidying and I'd pay you another sixpence besides the one that's promised. You're a good worker, you've been moving like lightning all day.'

'Florrie, no!' said Stephen at once. 'What would Nan say? She'd skin me, leaving you here all alone. We must go together.'

'But Stephen, how will we get the pony back?'

'Well, he can run alongside the carriage, I expect.'

'He'd never keep up with Mr Beresford's fine horses. No, I'll stay, and help out here and earn another sixpence for Nan. I won't be on my own –' I waved my hand around the crowded kitchen – 'and I've somewhere safe to stay. I'll ride back in the morning, when I've done all that Mrs Chambers wants.'

'Oh, child,' she said wistfully. 'If only you would!'

'She can't,' said Stephen.

'I will,' I said.

'Florrie, *no*,' added Hesta. Always agreeing with Stephen she was. 'This en't home. You don't know what will happen. You can't stay without us. Nan would *burst*! Come in the carriage with us.'

A boy stuck his head around the door. 'Carriage ready,' he called.

'No,' I decided. 'We said we'd do this and I want to see it through. Hesta, you can't help, you're hurt and you're better off at home. Stephen, of course you must go with her, she needs someone. But I'm fine and I like it here and I want the sixpence. I'll be back in Braggenstones before lunch tomorrow. Nothing to worry about. Off with you both now. Hesta, be well, my dear.'

I gave her a hug as she wavered to her feet and Stephen cast me a very displeased look. It was his nature to look after people and by splitting us up I was putting him in a very uncomfortable position; he could not take care of us both. But Mrs Chambers was bustling me off and I was put to work washing plates. I looked over my shoulder to see my friends walking out slowly, Hesta leaning on Stephen, his arm fast about her shoulder. Then I turned back to my dirty suds.

*

Secretly I'd hoped to see that strange pair of brothers again, but in the end it was an unexciting evening. I washed dishes, I peeled vegetables. I ran back and forth, a thousand miles or so, I reckoned, carrying trays and stacks of crockery and towers of linen for the overnight guests. I dropped into the spare bed in Sarah's tiny attic room at three in the morning, so tired I could not sleep.

'I saw that dark-haired Mrs Grace tonight. She looks fierce,' I said, hoping for conversation.

'Ooh, that nephew of hers with the golden curls!' Sarah murmured at once. 'What a fine-looking gentleman. Mind you, I wouldn't go with him no matter his pretty face. He's a Grace, you know, and that means trouble. Oh, *he* may be nice enough but the rest of them? Trouble.'

'Really? Why so?' I asked, yawning, as if my insides were not sparking to know. But Sarah was already asleep, flat on her back as she lay, and not another word was to be had from her.

I lay on that unfamiliar mattress, every muscle aching, my head spinning. My body was fizzing like cider. I had never had such a feeling of being so incredibly alert, like an animal ready for anything, yet so tired, tired, tired . . .

At half past five Sarah was up, exactly one minute before a loud bell clanged through the attic. She was halfway into her dress before I had managed to sit up, let alone muster any questions. I did not have to change, for I had slept in my dress, but

I would have to wash and see to my hair before appearing in front of my temporary employers.

I resumed my duties – though at half the pace of the night before. A lavish breakfast was already being prepared for the guests, despite there being no sign of any of *them* so early.

When everything was ready and there was a lull before the guests descended, Mrs Chambers took pity on me. 'You've worked well, especially considering you've never done it before,' she approved. 'We can manage now. Go home, child, you look fit to drop and you've a way to go.'

By then, I was ready to come away. I thanked her – and thanked her again when she placed not a shilling but a florin into my hand. I could not wait to hand *that* over to Nan. That would surely button her nagging about my staying overnight in Truro. A footman showed me to the stables.

I was saddling Stephen's father's pony when I heard a rustle in the straw made by something much larger than a mouse. I whipped round to see a young man sit up, straw in his hair, looking around in confusion.

I jumped, but recovered myself quickly. 'Morning,' I said tartly, smoothing out the girth.

He frowned and scratched his head. 'Morning. Is this . . . the *stables*?'

I snorted, looking pointedly at stalls full of straw, horses and steaming heaps of dung. 'What makes you think that then?'

He rolled his eyes. 'I *mean*, what am I doing here?'

I shrugged and took the reins. 'How should I know?'

'Too much champagne,' he groaned, getting to his feet and looking all around him. I recognised him then. Turlington Grace. Brother of the delightful Sanderson.

'I know you!' I exclaimed. 'At least, I know who you are. I met your brother Sanderson last night. I'm Florrie Buckley. Florence.'

He squinted at me. 'Ah! You're the one he told me about. I wish *I'd* been kidnapped by a beautiful girl last night. But my biggest adventure was drinking too much. And ending up here.'

'Don't sound much of an adventure to me. And aren't you too young to be drinking? You don't look much older 'n me.'

'How old are you?'

'Thirteen.'

He looked thunderous. 'I'm almost twenty! Everyone thinks I'm younger but I'm not. For the love of God! I'm a grown man.'

'If you say so. Well, I must be off. Say hello to your handsome brother for me.'

'Where are you going?'

'Home.'

'Where's home? Truro?'

'No. I live in Braggenstones. A tiny place way over on the moors. Long way from here.'

'And you're going to ride there alone?'

'O' course. I do it all the time,' I lied.

'Won't you be afraid? I heard the moors are full of restless spirits and vile marshes.'

'Aye, that they are, but that don't worry me. I'm no city girl.'

He came over to me and stared into my face. 'I can see that,' he said, and I sensed that it was a compliment. I could smell the alcohol pouring off him.

Turlington Grace had brown eyes, darker than his brother's, dark like moorland peat, fertile and precarious. I could see a thousand conflicting thoughts doing battle there. I wondered what his life was, his history, and I was suddenly acutely aware that his body was near to mine. Even huddling close to his brother in the nook had not felt like this. Last night, Turlington had looked so shrunken and hunched I was surprised to realise now that he was taller than me, much taller, and everyone in Braggenstones called *me* a young birch tree. He was slender, where his brother had been robust. I felt suddenly sorry for him, and I did not know why. The moment stretched on and there was an intent silence between us.

Sad. Sorry. In need of a friend. The words sprang to my mind unbidden.

'Turlington Grace,' I murmured, for want of anything else to say.

'Grace,' he agreed bitterly, which I thought was strange. Then he did an even stranger thing. He dipped his head and rested his forehead on mine so that we stood, brow to brow, for a minute at least. Impatient, the pony butted us and we stumbled. I fell against him and he caught me in his arms, stronger than he looked. I suddenly wished I was not wearing a dress I had been working and sleeping in. He set me back gently to the vertical, for which I felt grateful, since my legs failed me in that moment and I could not do it for myself. His nostrils, I noted, were slightly flared and his eyes were quite lovely. He still had straw in his wing of dark hair and I reached up and picked it out.

'I'd better be off,' I said, wishing he'd detain me, but he stepped back at once. 'Are you all right?' I added, for he looked lost and lonely. A strange way for a girl of thirteen to feel for a grown man. But then my soul was hundreds of years old, they told me.

He nodded. 'I'm fine. Thank you, young witch of the moors. And will *you* be all right, out there with the ghosts and ghouls? Can I offer any assistance? I or my brother?'

I imagined the pair of them, in their fine suits and clutching a champagne glass each, escorting me over the moors, and giggled. 'No thank you, Turlington. You stop drinking so much now. It can't be good for you, not knowing how you come to wake up in a stable.'

I led the pony outside then leapt aboard and clattered off down Lemon Street. I was soon lost – I could find my way much better with trees and stars and rivers for landmarks than amid streets and houses and crowds. I was distracted, too, by my encounters with two such different, beautiful boys. Funny how, even then, Sanderson was *sir* – a young gentleman – but Turlington was always Turlington.

Half an hour on the moors and the pigeon flew and the pony bolted and now here I was. Walking through the mists towards home. It was a devil of a fog; I couldn't see more than six inches ahead. But I had been walking these moors all my life. They had been my refuge through every trial and tragedy. I felt an affinity with them that I could not explain to the satisfaction of Nan or anyone I knew. Only Old Rilla – our local wise woman and charmer – understood. She said the moors were my soul-home: the place I could never be lost. When I couldn't see I simply relied on my other senses – I could feel the thudding or squelching of my boots, the tussocks or smoothness of the way, and I knew what sort of land I was on. I could hear the trickle of the streams and knew which way they were flowing. I could smell the trees on the slopes and the sea from the peaks. My senses were unfailing guides, along with the spirits Turlington had spoken of.

Marsh spirits were widely acknowledged to thrive in this

lonely place. They were held to be malcontents who liked to lure, torment and otherwise play havoc with humans. And it *was* true that people died on the moors every month. The people of Lostwithiel and Boconnoc swore it was a diabolical place. Even the Bodmin folk avoided it and they knew something of desolate moorland.

But to me these spirits were only ever friends. I felt them all around me and it would no sooner occur to me to fear them than it would to fear my neighbours in Braggenstones. The moors were their place, and somehow also my place, and that made us kin.

While I walked that day I thought long and hard about the two Grace boys. It had all felt so momentous – going to Truro, making a good impression on the housekeeper, meeting those strange brothers. It seemed certain that it would not be the end of the story. But common sense said that it must and would be. For what did I expect? That the ambrosial Sanderson would remember the outlandish village name he had heard just once and come cantering over the moors on a white horse to claim me? It was clearly impossible, yet somehow my imagination sought about frantically to *make* it possible. Or perhaps that the rebellious Turlington would come striding out of a storm, billowing smoke, and snatch me by the hand and throw me down in the heather? Even while I blushed at my own inclinations I knew that was not about to happen either.

It seemed clear to me that I had fallen in love with at least one of them, that I would certainly never see them again and that my life would be the poorer and greyer for it. It was agony. I longed to go straight to Old Rilla and tell her everything; she could always help me understand, she always helped me see a bigger picture than I could conjure alone. But I knew that today, at least, I could not go. As I neared home, I could feel that Nan was worried, so I picked up my feet and hurried at last.

Was it a gift or a curse, my ability to sense so acutely what others were feeling? I have never been sure. I couldn't always do it from a distance, and sometimes it came only in small, barely comprehended flashes. But that day I could feel everything Nan had endured since the previous night when Stephen and Hesta had returned to Braggenstones without me and she had cuffed Stephen's ears for leaving me behind.

I knew that the stupid pony had trotted into Braggenstones, halter trailing, legs coated in thick white mud like columns of clay. I knew Nan was even now pushing away thoughts that I might be lying with my head broken on a rock. I knew that when she saw me appear on the horizon, her heart would lift in relief. So I could not tarry, not even to go and see Old Rilla. No, I could not keep Nan in her anxiety any longer.

At last, I mounted the last ridge above Braggenstones. It was late afternoon. The sun burst forth brilliant and brash, mocking my journey, mocking the expanse of moor that lay behind, still shifting and sifting in mist. It was like two different worlds, me standing on the threshold between them. Truro lay behind me and Braggenstones, all familiar and solid and safe, lay ahead. I paused for a minute and closed my eyes, feeling the sun on my face and the clammy mist still cold and clinging to my back. Then I stepped forward into the sunshine.

Chapter Two

Nan was furious. She showered me with so many chores that it was two days before I could go and see Old Rilla. As I worked and sulked I turned over the events of that night in Truro endlessly, and the strange feelings they had engendered within me. I dwelled, too, on my life before that night. The two worlds were utterly different; it was impossible to see how they might be linked and yet my feelings told me it was so.

My life began in Nan's small cottage on a dark night. There was a storm. Inside the cottage, my mother had laboured to give birth, attended by thunder and lightning and howling winds – but no physician. The door burst open, blown by the gale, and hung like a staggering drunk from just one hinge, banging and banging against the stone wall, as if intent upon making itself understood. *Death is coming*, it seemed to say. *Make ready, make ready. Death is coming*.

And indeed my mother did die that night, though she held me for some half hour and nursed me and named me, before she slipped away. Thus I understood from my earliest days that death and life are intertwined. Most of us do not carry that knowledge so near.

My father was away at St Ives, for it was pilchard season. A short one that year – only four or five weeks long it transpired to be. Long enough, nevertheless, for him to return home to find his wife gone and a small daughter in her stead. It was Nan who grieved for my mother and tended me in those first hours after the storm took her. Of course, it wasn't really the storm that did it, it was a too-hard labour and a breach birth, but I persist in thinking of it that way. It was midsummer. The storm brewed up like something concocted by a demon, swept over the moor, destroying two homes and damaging others, then blew off again, taking my mother with it. I like to imagine that her spirit was carried off on that mighty gale, riding a flash of forked lightning. I like to believe that she is always with me when the wind blows. Stephen said that was blasphemy, but why should I not imagine freedom for my mother's spirit? It gives me no comfort to think it confined to a casket, sunk in the ground.

I grew from baby to girl in the usual succession of small miracles that are so commonplace we easily forget they are miracles at all. I adored my father. As a baby I reached for him as soon as I heard his voice, Nan told me, and as soon as I could toddle I would run after him wherever he went. He was a lion to me, with long auburn curls and a beard. He would hoist me up on his shoulders where I would ride, imperious as a rani on an elephant. I saw him too little, and my memories of him are too few; he spent such long hours and days at work – *hard* at work, on the land and in the mines and sometimes out at sea. But when we were together the world sang. He was a man gifted with the ability to love deeply. He had loved my mother so, and now he loved me.

We lived in a close community, small and remote; farmers of sorts, in a gentle valley, a smooth green ribbon in an otherwise uncompromising expanse of weatherswept, treacherous, boggy moor. Eleven cottages were strung along the valley floor like standing stones. There were squares of carefully tended garden; this was a tiny pocket of balmy, gentle land and we took full advantage of it. There was nothing there that would make any of us our fortune, but at least we could grow our own food. We would never starve, not quite. We grew vegetables and barley. Occasionally one family or another would have a cow, which meant milk for us all. And sometimes there were a few chickens scratching around. We grew produce to sell at market – vegetables, fruit and even flowers, which we tied in bunches to delight the townsfolk. In a good year we loved to live so simple and remote, self-contained and free. In a bad year we gnashed our teeth and wept bitter tears over it.

Observing us all from high up on the moor was Heron's Watch, an old, empty farmhouse which held a strange lure for me. I would often walk miles out of my way just to linger in its tangled grounds and peer through the windows into shadowy rooms. It was yet another odd inclination of mine.

Nan could remember when Heron's Watch was inhabited. Then, men and women from Braggenstones would go there to do odd jobs in exchange for a few coins, or resources we didn't have in the hamlet, like cheese or beef. It had been a life-giving stream running through the village. But the family had died out and the farm had passed to a Falmouth relation who didn't care for it. The land was sold off piecemeal to local landowners until only the house was left, crouching at the edge of the moor, reflecting on all the things that people forgot and ways of life that had passed away.

When I was young, Da, Nan and I were the best of friends. Nan was as small and pinched as he was large and expansive. Well might she be pinched – she had already seen two sons die; one had fallen from a tree and the other drowned at sea. The occupations available to poor Cornish men were hazardous, but money had to be earned and families supported. She used to say it wrung her heart to see my da setting off for the coast at pilchard time, and for the mines most other days, but she had no choice but to wave him off and welcome him back as though ignorant of the dangers he faced, as though life were a manageable thing.

She wore her iron-grey hair in a plait that reached almost to her waist. I used to tug it when I was a baby, and brush it when I was a little girl, though plaiting it was too deft a job for my small hands. I watched, mesmerised, as Nan did that herself.

I called her Nan because she was my nan. Everyone else called her Nan too, for that was her name. I used to like that double layer of meaning. I liked having the extra claim on her.

As for my mother, they told me she came from Launceston and met my father at a great dance for the West Wivel Hundred (more than one Londoner has decreed this an outrageous name; nevertheless, that was the area in which I grew up). They told me of her grace and the mischievous light in her eye as she twirled under a summer moon. How could my father not have been captivated? She had soft dark hair, dark brown eyes, pale skin and a dreamy glow about her, like morning mist. They told me that she sang like a lark, that she was kind and good.

I was a determined child with hair that was brown, but confused about the fact: it also bore thick strands of honey-gold and glinting copper. Nan used to say I had Cornish hair. I had my mother's dark eyes and I was too tall.

I had two special friends in Braggenstones: Hesta Pendarne and Stephen Trevian. Like me, they came from families that had worked the mines thereabout for a century and the land even longer. Stephen had hair like damp straw. He was stocky and ever so slightly cross-eyed. He was serious, a little ponderous at times, and Hesta and I delighted in teasing him. Hesta was half my height, a little white-haired fairy with blue eyes and a great gift for laughter. We were not the only children in our hamlet but we were closest in age, only eight months between us all.

We were six when Stephen came to find me one day, led me by the hand into the hen house and said, 'I want to talk to you, Florrie.' To this day I don't know what had possessed him.

'I been thinking,' he began with no ado. 'When we be grown-up, I think we should be married. What do you say?'

What *could* a girl say to such a proposal? I had no wish to marry but it was what people seemed to do. 'All right then,' I decided. 'Thank you, Stephen.'

'Good. My da says I'm to clean the pony's shed. Want to help me?' And with this romantic tryst in place to celebrate our union we scrambled out of the hen house. I returned to this memory now, in the light of the two young men I had met in Truro, and smiled, a little scornfully.

So, I had two special friends. I had a father and a grandmother, who both loved me. I had a roof over my head, and that roof rarely leaked. I had food fresh from the ground, glistening with raindrops, almost every day. I had the freedom to explore the moors from a young age, where I commanded the spirits that everyone else feared. I thought that a girl could wish for nothing more.

I was also . . . special. My grandmother said it from the start. She said it so often that I was three years old before I was completely sure that my name was Florence – Florence Elizabeth

Buckley – and not Nan's Special Girl. Perhaps I was at that. I had no money or distinction, and no beauty that men would launch ships for (though Stephen continued to declare stoutly throughout our childhood that he would marry me and no other come the day). The things that made me special were those that just came naturally to me.

Like never getting lost on the moors. And sometimes I knew things before they happened. I could often understand what people were thinking and feeling, sometimes before they knew themselves. Sometimes, too, I knew facts, like, *You hate your mother*, or, *You've travelled a great deal*, before they even opened their mouths. Once it was, *You love your pretty grey cat*. I asked how the grey cat was before it had even been mentioned, prompting a suspicious stare from the lady in question and a reproachful scowl from Nan. I learned not to say what I knew because it disconcerted people, but it didn't stop me from knowing it.

Nan was very proud of me, which caused her grave upset, for pride was a sin. But she called me her greatest comfort, her guiding star, and her Special Girl when we were alone together and she was sure that no one else could hear. I wondered if Sanderson, or Turlington, had thought me special.

When I was seven, a tall, tangle-haired girl with eyes more often than not fixed on the horizon, my father told me he would very much like me to attend lessons in Tremorney, a small village three miles away. He was a poor man with big dreams and those dreams extended tendrils that grew gently around me. He had nothing, yet he wanted me to have the best of everything. I have always admired generosity of spirit more than any other kind.

My education was quite an irregular affair, with a syllabus indiscriminately composed of whatever reflected our teacher's interests. That teacher was a young woman of just eighteen years old. Her name was Lacey Spencer and she hailed from Penzance. She had a connection with Tremorney in the form of an aunt whom she had visited regularly from earliest child-hood. When she grew older, and realised the extent of the poverty and ignorance in our area, she longed to start a school there. She had little idea of how to manage such a scheme but her intentions were good. Her doting parents, two kindly middle-class people with the money to indulge her, gave her their blessing. The costs were low as she taught from her aunt's front room.

Lacey Spencer had a slim figure and bouncing brown curls. She wore a different colour every day – lemon, lilac, peach, turquoise, apple; it was like looking at a rainbow. When I first saw her, I thought, *Daylight. Laughter. Determined.* Young as I was, I could not yet appreciate what a remarkable undertaking the school was, but even then I knew Lacey Spencer was going to be important to me.

It was at school where I met the aforementioned Trudy

Penny. Trudy, with her pink satin ribbons and ballet shoes, and her cousins who lived in Truro. Trudy was two years older, a Tremorney lass, whose parents could have afforded to pay for her to have proper schooling but didn't see the point.

She was a mean little thing, Trudy, and her constant tormenting hurt my feelings more than I ever let her know. She said I smelled like a pig. Since we had no pig – we could not afford one – I doubted that was true, but the expressive wrinkle on her round nose whenever she sat nearby did make me fret about my cleanliness. It was hard to keep clean when I had only one dress that I walked in, tended the garden in and rode in (when Stephen's father would let me). And although I disliked Trudy, I did love to look at her ribbons and her clean pink skin.

For weeks, therefore, I tried to be her friend. I daydreamed that she would see beyond the dirt and realise that I was special, that she would invite me to her house and show me her books and toys and ask me to show her the magic places on the moors. I used to take her gifts – a few strawberries in summer, a hawk feather, an unusual stone with a pretty green pattern. Her scorn on being presented with these humble offerings knew no bounds.

'What do *I* want with *that*?' she'd sneer, throwing the feather out of the window into the street, where it looped its way to the ground to be broken under the hooves of the innkeeper's horse. 'A *stone*?' she taunted, cocking her head and pretending hilarity. 'You've given me a . . . *stone*. 'Cause there aren't any other stones in all of Cornwall, so I couldn't see one if you didn't fetch me one?' and she tossed the offending object back at me, none too gently. She ate the strawberries, though.

Miss Spencer's 'school' was a strange affair. Nine children, mostly very poor and dirty, packed into her aunt's front parlour on the main street in Tremorney. We perched in vast, straight-backed armchairs stuffed with horsehair to listen to stories of knights and Greek gods and learn what Miss Spencer knew of geography and mathematics. School was just five hours in the middle of the day, on Mondays, Wednesdays and Thursdays, including a break for mutton broth, tea and cake. I believe this latter feature accounted for the continued attendance of much of the class.

Homework was entirely optional, in recognition of the fact that most of the pupils had miles to walk home, work to do when we got there, and more still to do before first light the following day. I do not know what benefit the other children derived from the school – besides good fresh meat three times a week – but I know what it meant for me.

Even before I was exposed to Lacey Spencer's ragbag of educational material, I had known there were worlds outside of Cornwall, outside of growing vegetables and darning the same old dress, outside of everything I had ever known. I could feel them as I wandered, which was often. ('Feet with a life of their own,' Nan would say in wonder and exasperation.) Then Miss

Spencer taught me to read and suddenly those worlds were between my hands, written down in words. I loved the Greek myths best: those old stories of Chaos and creation, of the Titanides and Centimani, of gods and mortals and the capricious patterns of life. The outrageous behaviour of the gods and the sly tricks they played on each other made me smile. I knew they might not be true . . . yet still I paid those gods lavish compliments whenever I remembered, just in case.

My supplications did not work. One day, when I had been attending school for almost a year – I was eight years old – I was reading to the class from *Tales from Shakespeare* by Charles and Mary Lamb. I did so haltingly; although I was quick enough when it was just the book and me, transferring that skill to speaking aloud did not come naturally. It was *The Tempest*, I remember. Suddenly, a chill ran through me, so drenchingly cold and shocking that I dropped the book. Charlie Mendow tittered. Trudy Penny made some hoity remark. Miss Spencer rushed to my side and asked if I was unwell. I could not speak. I stared out of the window, at the street and the normal human world, and I knew for certain that once again death had come upon us to take someone I loved. I saw my father's spirit flash before me, as red and bright and fierce as his beard, all free and exulting. I pulled my hand from Miss Spencer's and ran for home, bolting through Tremorney like a thief on the run. I only stopped once the whole way, though my breath came in grating gulps like a rusty hinge.

When I reached Braggenstones I saw the mine captain outside our cottage and I knew it was true.

'Da!' I wailed, hurtling through the door, but Nan caught me and held me fast. I learned in later years that she wanted to save me from seeing his crushed and bloodied body. And although I am grateful that my last sight of him was that sunburst of living orange-red outside the classroom window, my arms have ever afterwards ached for the lack of holding him that one last time. It is an emptiness that refuses to leave me.

He had been killed in a collapse, of course, along with six other men, though none other from our hamlet. One out of every five miners died in an accident in those days and despite occasional attempts at reform, I doubt the situation is very much better now. From time to time the government mutters something about innovative new safety measures and the gentleman mine owners look into it and get quite excited for a while, then decide they are too expensive to install. Meanwhile, men keep dying.

When Nan barred me from the bedroom that day, I fled outside, pushing past the gathered neighbours to throw myself on the ground outside the cottage. The rough earthen path seemed unbearably significant: I would never see him take those last few strides to our door again. I sobbed and beat the ground and rubbed my face in the dirt. It was Hesta who came and sat with me and wrapped her arms around me and rocked me. Moments later Stephen joined us, pacing around us while I sobbed into

Hesta's shoulder. She had loved my father too; her own was small and mean and too busy coughing and spitting to give Hesta any love. Eventually Stephen, too, sat down on the ground and reached his arms around us both.

The days that followed were full of numbness and mist. My da was gone. I knew it, yet I couldn't accept it. I couldn't find a way to be in the world without him. Even though he had been absent for so many of my waking hours, there had always been the possibility of him to shape my days. There was his smell in the cottage and the glimpses of him working in the field and the rhythm of his comings and goings. When I was asleep and he came home from work, his voice in the downstairs room would float up and enter my dreams. I loved him dearly, deeply, dreadfully.

I wandered a great deal on the moors, looking for Da among the spirits. I walked the four miles to the mine, hoping, in some part of me that believed in miracles, to meet him coming back along the track, swinging his lantern and his pick. Sometimes I did pass groups of men homeward bound and I would shrink to the side of the path and search their faces. But though they were loud, and they were vivid and they were living, they were not my da. Not once was I stopped; no one demanded to know what I was doing out on the hills alone at my age. It was as if my unhappiness had made me invisible – as if *I* had somehow entered another world.

A week turned into two and Nan grew frightened. I would eat nothing and I was thinner than ever. I had ceased my roaming and spent my days on the bench beneath the window, staring across the valley. Neighbours came: Hesta's mother Bertha, Billy Post the preacher, Stephen's father Adam. Bertha brought me soups she had made specially, but nothing could tempt me.

So Nan at last sent for Old Rilla. She came late one autumn afternoon. The air was clear as a yellow diamond with great violet-black clouds massed on the horizon. A thin crack of melting gold ran along their top and I could not tear my eyes from it. I had always fancied I could float up to the light on the clouds and step through that crack into a magical kingdom where all was gold and glory. I wondered if that's where my da was now and wished I could go and see him, but I felt too leaden to float.

I had never set eyes on Old Rilla before then, though I had heard plenty about her. She was a wise woman, a medicine woman, a charmer. Among our people she commanded greater trust than either the doctor or the preacher. She lived in a little hut high on the hill at the edge of the moors but she roved a great deal from village to village, going to the people who needed her. She had the reputation of being hard to find, hard to please and if she decided she would not work with someone, nothing could sway her.

She was older than Nan, with long hair that was snow-white,

rather than grey. She wore it loose around her shoulders like a young girl. She had on a blue dress and her eyes were blue too. She was not easy to look upon, though. Her nose was sharp as a hawk's and her eyes were like flint.

'Child, child,' she chided when she saw me. 'So you're trying to join them, are you?'

A great silence fell upon the cottage and her words seemed to hang in the air.

'Who?'

'You know who, child.'

I nodded. Though I never did know, really, who she meant that day. Did she mean my parents, both gone from me and together in God's love, if the preacher was to be believed? Or did she mean the shadow beings on the moors? Did she think I was trying to waste myself away until I became an insubstantial spirit because being a human child was too hard? Perhaps I was.

'Do you want to live a life?' Old Rilla demanded, with none of the brow-furrowed sympathy I had seen on every visiting face lately. Her clear eyes shone like a rain-washed, scudding sky. Such light burned in them. It made me want to sit up a little and think.

Did she mean did I want to *live*, rather than waste away and die? Or did she mean did I want to live a *life*, rather than anything else?

I wanted to tell her that I *did* want to live a life, but had forgotten how, that knowledge having departed with my da. As to living any old how, just getting through the days as a person not – yet – dead . . . well, that I could happily dispense with. But I couldn't frame the words; I was very weak. Instead I reached for her, feebly, to keep her attention. To my surprise she immediately snatched at my hand and placed something in it. It was a smooth stone of about three inches wide and almost the same depth. It was a deep orange, the colour of sunset, the colour I always associated with my father, the colour of the flash I had seen in the sky the day he died.

'Keep it near you always. Touch it and hold it whenever you can. And when your feet start roaming again, come and see me. Do you understand?'

I nodded, feeling tears come to my eyes, tears of relief that I had not been told to eat, to look to the future, to count my blessings. Holding a stone was something I could do.

'Look, child!' she gestured to the window and a peachy glow flushed her face, making her look, for a moment, like a young woman. I turned my head. It was one of the most magnificent sunsets I had ever seen. Orange and gold and bright pink all bled one into the other and floated in an ocean of purple cloud. I cried in earnest for the first time since losing Da and then I fell asleep, aware that Rilla was muttering something above me.

Old Rilla saved my life; we all acknowledged it. I learned to sit up again, and eat, and accept the kindness of neighbours. Sometimes that was difficult, for as good as all these people were, it was still *Da's* kindness I missed, *Da's* company I wanted. I came to understand why Nan was so sour to outsiders: the people she really wanted around her were gone – all but me. How then could she find genuine enthusiasm for anyone else?

Nan and I grew closer to one another. I did not go back to school. Sitting in a room with other children, reading stories, didn't seem quite right for me any more. Instead I helped more around the house and land. I went with Nan to market at Lostwithiel or Liskeard and occasionally to the famous market at Fowey in Pyder Hundred. A magical kingdom, that seemed to me, by the side of a glinting blue river. The seasons turned, the sky grew light and dark over the moors and I slowly began to leave childhood behind.

I sometimes wonder what the texture of my life would have been in the usual way of things – a penniless orphan in Braggenstones. Nan loved me dearly but I was her last treasure and she clung to me fiercely. All too easy to imagine a life with no outlet for my unusual tastes and abilities, my sensitive nature bruised and blunted by so early a tragedy and an unremarkable continuance. But instead, my life continued luminous and rich with learning and for this, I accredit two people: Old Rilla and Lacey Spencer.

Chapter Three

Miss Spencer came to see me two months after Da's passing. I was so happy to see her when she came bouncing along the valley in a pretty green dress and cape.

I admired her. The route from Tremorney to Braggenstones was not a walk that every well-brought-up young lady might take, especially in winter. Yet she arrived, flushed and hair escaping every which way from her bonnet. She appeared delighted with everything she saw, which endeared her to me the more, for I knew how roughly we lived.

'Hello, Florrie!' she hailed from some way off and I ran from the cottage to greet her. 'I am so pleased to see you.' She kissed my cheek and held me in her arms. 'And so very sorry about your father. He was a wonderful man.'

I nodded. 'Lance Midden gave me your message, miss, thank you. I weren't myself when it came. I'm sorry I didn't send one back, I didn't mean to be rude.'

'It never occurred to me that you did. Now, Florrie, is it a terrible intrusion or might I visit with you a while? I've missed you in class and a dear friend gave me all these biscuits and this elderflower punch for my birthday Thursday last. I shall never finish them, so I wondered if you would help me.'

'We should be pleased to have you, miss. Come in.'

She was so tactful. She knew we had little to offer. My eyes gleamed at the sight of the biscuits, all wrapped in a transparent white paper inside a thin white box and presented with a cheerful blue bow; I was feeling better indeed.

We walked to the cottage and I saw Nan lay down her hoe and shield her eyes against the December sun. I could tell from the set of her shoulders that she was not pleased. But I would not let her be gruff with Miss Spencer, who had come so far with such good grace to see us. I nudged her hard in the ribs when she spoke curtly to Miss Spencer, willing her to muster a grudging hospitality.

When punch and biscuits had been distributed, Nan got to the point.

'I suppose you've come to ask Florrie to go back to her lessons,' she said disapprovingly, as if Miss Spencer had come to draft me into the navy. The two women sat side by side on the bench and I sat on the floor with my arms around my knees and my back against the rough wall.

'In part, yes,' Miss Spencer answered, setting down her cup on the bench beside her and smiling at me.

'Well, she can't. It's different now her da's gone. I need her here. It be kind of you to think on us, Miss Spencer, but Florrie were lucky to come to you when she did – it's more than most children round here can get. She can read and count and she knows such stories! On that Promethis and Zoos and all on 'em. It's set her up good, and we thank 'ee.'

'I understand. I truly do. I haven't come to disturb your life together, especially at such a time. I had heard that Florrie was back on her feet and wanted to visit anyway, and I wondered . . . Florrie, how do *you* feel about it? Given that your father was so keen for you to grasp all the learning you could?'

'She's not interested,' said Nan.

'She's askin' *me*!' I retorted, indignant.

'But you en't. You said so.'

I scowled. 'It en't that I'm not interested, Miss Spencer. I loved school and I know that Da wanted me to go. It's just that . . . it don't feel right now.'

'In what way, Florrie, can you tell me?'

'Da's passing changed everything. There's just me and Nan now. I'm needed here. And I *do* want to learn, only I can't feel the same about it now. It were nice coming to be with the other children, only it were . . . it were –' I cast about for inspiration – 'it were for childhood. I know I'm only young, but I've gone beyond it now.'

Miss Spencer nodded slowly. 'I think I understand. It would be hard, I'm sure, to be in a room full of other children all going about their days in the usual way. Well, not to worry, I have another idea. Why don't I come here to give you lessons? Oh, it would only be one day a week because that's all I have spare, but I'd be very happy to do it if you'd like. I could lend you books and perhaps you could study in whatever little time you have to spare and . . . well, it would be something, perhaps.'

Nan and I looked at each other.

'We couldn't pay,' said Nan, looking fierce at having to voice what was patently obvious anyway.

'I couldn't have you come walking all this way every week, just to teach *me*!' I added, though my heart had leapt when she said it.

'Well, I wouldn't walk, Florrie, if it makes you feel any better. My father's buying me a pony, so I'm a very lucky woman as you see. If I can extend a little of that luck to others, it would make me very happy. And that would be quite payment enough, Mrs Buckley, be assured. I wouldn't expect anything else, except perhaps some fresh strawberries come summertime. I do *adore* fresh strawberries.'

'Oh, Nan, can she? I'd like that very much.'

'Mrs Buckley, I hope I don't offend you by offering. It's just that Florrie's very bright, as I'm sure you're aware. I often felt at school that the class was holding her back. This way she could learn at her own speed and in her own way. I'm hardly the best teacher in the world and I know my approach wouldn't find approval with any official college in the country. But I suppose I'm all that Florrie's got and for as long as I know more than her, I'm happy to pass it on, that's all.'

I could see the excitement in her eyes. I recognised her offer for what it was: the impulse of a generous spirit. And I think Nan did too; at least, she gave a reluctant nod and muttered, 'We thank 'ee, teacher.'

I felt a fizz of good cheer for the first time since Da had died: something to look forward to.

Miss Spencer set down her cup. 'Well, good!' she exclaimed, clapping her hands. 'Shall we start on Tuesday?'

With one agreement in place I knew it was time to honour another: with the wise woman who had saved my life. We had seen no sign of her in the interim.

Nan was both impressed and unnerved that Old Rilla had asked me to visit once I was better. Proud as she was of my 'special' ways, she wanted to keep my feet firmly on the ground, and close to her at that. I think she was half afraid Old Rilla might turn me into a toad, or apprentice me to a lifetime of strange practices. Yet she was so deeply grateful to the charmer for bringing me back from the brink of starvation that she felt an agonising mixture of wariness and devotion towards her. She wanted to come with me.

'Florrie, I'd best come along and have a proper word with her so she knows how grateful we are.'

'She knows how grateful we are. I'll tell her how grateful we are.'

'So you don't want your ol' Nan coming along with you then?'

'Not really, no. Well, Nan, you know how she is. She'll probably send you back and then we'll both have to walk back alone anyway. Waste of time, is what it'd be.'

'All the same, I'd feel better if I came.'

'Nan, no.'

'Yes.'

'No!'

By this point I knew we would get nowhere. So the following morning I rose even earlier than usual, even earlier than Nan, and stole from the cottage while she still snored in the chilly darkness. She swore she never snored, but she did.

It was good to head for the hills again. It had been too long since I'd done so. The sky was black as ink and the stars were a milky trail about its arc. There was a full moon that shone down its rivers of pale light and the air was cold and sharp; no wine I have ever tasted was as heady. I ran the first while, in case Nan should wake and come after me, stubborn old boot. When I had gone far enough I walked, relishing the springy grass beneath my boots and the wild smells and the drifting wing of an owl – not quite seen, but sensed, somewhere nearby. I felt myself expanding as if my sides would burst.

At the top of a hill, I saw a solitary rowan tree, standing

guard a little way from Old Rilla's cottage. There were still berries on the slender purple-brown branches. I slowed my steps. Everyone knew that rowans grew where witches lived. Everyone skirted the places where a lonely rowan grew. Were they true, the stranger things that were said about Old Rilla? I steeled myself to find out – a promise was a promise.

A few twigs had fallen from the tree in the winter winds. In the paradoxical way of all things, rowan wood was also used to protect against witches. I picked one up and tucked it in my pocket. It couldn't hurt.

The sun was just coming up; the sky was palest pink, swirled and swathed with lilac, the clouds were the grey of a dove's wing, and brimming gold edged the land.

I reached the cottage. What kind of hours and routines might a wise woman – a witch – keep? Should I knock on the door and risk waking her? I decided to sit on her doorstep and watch the sunrise, my orange stone warm in my hands. I had kept it close by, as Old Rilla had instructed; it had become my talisman. It made me feel calm and its colour was always a comforting reminder of Da.

There Old Rilla found me some while later, when she returned from over the hill. She'd been out all night attending a difficult birth, she told me. The mother had wanted her to stay longer but she had set off right away as I was coming. I did not ask how she could have known it, more than two months after her invitation; it frightened me a little. Her face showed no sign of weariness and she did not appear to need breakfast.

'We'll go to the garden,' she said.

I was mildly disappointed. I had plenty of garden-tending to do at home, and I would not have been averse to learning a bit about how to turn people into toads instead (Trudy Penny sprang to mind). It seemed things were not to be so interesting.

However, I was wrong. Old Rilla's garden was nothing like ours. It covered a large stretch of hillside behind her cottage, but some way down. I wondered why she didn't make it closer to save herself the walk.

'This is where it wants to be,' she said.

As it was December, the branches were mostly bare. But even stripped and tangled as they were, it was easy to imagine the profusion that would dazzle the senses in spring and summer. I recognised a few plants – raspberry and sorrel and meadowsweet – but there were many others that I could not guess. They all grew together in comradely accord; it looked as if there had been no order to their planting but I guessed that was not the case. The early morning light flowed through them, glinting off twigs and stalks that were not all brown but purple, green, red and silver. Anyone who thinks a garden in winter is dead is not looking. It was sleeping, perhaps, but very much alive. It was waiting.

It was not fenced like the gardens in Braggenstones where

the precious crops of flowers and vegetables that brought us our little money were grown. There were merely white stones at intervals around its edge. Coming to it from higher up the hill, in the half-light, they looked like a constellation of stars. I asked why she had no fence.

'You fight a losing battle when you try to keep out what has the right to be in,' she said. 'And to keep in what needs to be out,' she added.

Here and there were lengths of string, caught between posts and hung with clusters of shells that rattled in the breeze like fairy footsteps. I half expected to hear a silvery giggle. The garden ran up to and into a wooded copse, and there we went. The branches were hung with hollow wooden pipes of elder that swayed and blew melancholy notes like an elfish summons. I shivered as I looked around me. It felt like a serious place; you couldn't imagine children climbing these trees and laughing and throwing conkers at one another, as they did at Braggenstones.

''Tis a wondrous place, Old Rilla,' I said in honest rapture.

She nodded. 'It likes you too,' she said.

We had come to what I reckoned to be the heart of the wood and stopped walking, standing in a friendly silence for some time. I rested my hand on a slender trunk of hazel. Together we breathed.

I don't know how long we stood there. I had never met another grown-up who would just stand in a wood, letting time slip by, in that way. Life was always such a press of chores waiting to be tackled, such an urgency of action and purpose. I was unusual enough in that I spent what time I could contemplating ancient times and gods that probably never even existed. Now I was standing in a wood in December, thinking about nothing at all, while the cold trickled under my cloak. But oh, I felt calm. And I felt strong, almost as if I was taking something in from the old hazel tree. Was I to become half girl, half tree? Would I find, when the time came to move, that my feet had sunk into the earth and extended roots downwards? That my hair had turned into rustling leaves?

'So you've chosen the hazel. I am not surprised,' said Old Rilla at last. I was not aware of having chosen anything at all; the tree simply happened to be beside me. ''Tis the spirit tree, the tree between worlds, did you know that?' she asked me.

I shook my head.

'It grows in the place where our world meets the other. You will be a bridge between two worlds, Florrie Buckley.' I shivered, though I had no idea what she meant.

At last we walked back up the hill and I found that I was still a girl, not a nymph, after all: I still had feet, not roots, and my hair still blew about my face in its annoying way, snaking into my eyes and mouth, forcing me to spit it out. I saw Old Rilla casting me a glance from time to time, though we did not speak until we entered the cottage and she set about making food.

Old Rilla's home was very like mine and Nan's. A single

room downstairs and, I guessed, just one more upstairs. Built of old stone, greyish-white and rugged. A small fire was burning, as though it had been entrusted with staying home alone, thus she could quickly set water to boiling. Soon we sat with a cup each of blackberry tea and a bowl of porridge made thick with chopped hazelnuts and flavoured with an explosion of tastes that I simply could not name. The final flourish was a lavish spoonful of honey from, Old Rilla said, her own bees. I could hardly believe my luck.

'So, Florrie Buckley,' said Old Rilla at last, when we set down our bowls. 'Here you are.' I nodded, wiping my mouth and looking all about, hopefully, for more. 'Were you afraid to come?'

I shook my head, swallowing my last, delicious mouthful. 'Did you want anything of me? Can I help you with anything, while I'm here?'

But she answered with a question of her own. 'Do you like your lessons, then?'

'Oh, very much. Lacey – Miss Spencer – she's so nice and pretty and she tells me all I want to hear about the old gods, the old legends—'

'You like to think. You like to learn.'

'Aye.'

'What else do you like?'

I thought about it. 'I like eating, when I have the chance. I like my friends, Stephen and Hesta. I like Stephen's father's pony. No, I don't like it. It's a wicked brute and none too

54

clever. But I like the feeling of riding it. I like to walk up on the moors and be alone there. They mostly think me odd for that, in Braggenstones.'

'Why alone? Why not with your friends?'

'Oh, they never want to come. They think the moors are ghostly. I don't mind, though. I like to play with them in the village, but up there I can hear better on my own, and feel things better. They'd get in the way.'

'And your father? You miss him still, I s'pose.'

'Every day, Old Rilla. He were the light of my life. Do you know what's curious, though? I can remember my mother far better, though I only met her once when I were newly born and too small to see, I expect. How can that be? Nan says it must be wrong. But I can see her face and hear her voice, but Da – I had him 'til I were eight, and he's smudgy now. The memories en't clear like I want them to be. It's the feeling of having him around me I remember the most, and his colour . . .' I was aware that I was saying things that I had said to others and that had been met with no comprehension. 'It's like this, his colour,' I finished feebly, holding up my stone.

But Old Rilla only nodded as though I'd said nothing out of the ordinary. 'He is gone, and so it is his soul you see.'

'But my mother's gone too.'

'But not completely. She still has a part to play in your life.' I frowned but before I could ask her more, she said, 'Are you very busy, Florrie, with your lessons and helping your nan?'

I nodded again, swallowing my last draught of tea. It was going cold. It had a clear, sharp taste and was the purple of twilight. Then I had a thought. Was I going to miss out on something? 'Not too busy, though,' I qualified. 'Not as busy as Hesta. Her parents never let her do anything interesting. She says she don't want to but I think she has to tell herself that or she'd go mad. Nan lets me do things, so long as I'm not away from her too much. No, I'm not all that busy really.'

'Well, I'll let you get back to her now.' I was disappointed. 'But would you come again, Florrie?'

'Oh, I should love to.'

'Would you like to learn with me? About the plants and herbs, and the things you see and feel?'

I had a sensation like a door being wrenched open and fresh air pouring in. Until she said it I had not realised how much I had been longing for just one soul to understand what I was talking about when I spoke of those things.

'So very much,' I said in a low voice. 'I thank you.'

Old Rilla got up and started rummaging around on a rough wooden shelf. She took a few things down then laid them before me on a length of old cotton that might once have been a petticoat. A small jar of honey – I hardly dared to hope. A clay bottle with a stopper.

'Hawberry brandy,' said Old Rilla, smiling – for the first time – at my avid expression. 'A gift for your grandmother. I believe she will enjoy it. Tell her only a thimbleful at a time.'

Three scraps of what looked like birch bark, containing dried leaves, roots and flowers. 'Angelica,' said Old Rilla, twisting it up securely, 'for your grandmother's stomach.' How did she know Nan complained of her stomach? Perhaps she had heard talk.

'Sow thistle. It'll make you strong, both of you. Brew it as a tea. And borage to make you brave.'

'Are such things in store for me that I'll need to be strong and brave then?' I said it as a joke but as soon as the words were out I didn't want to know.

'Everyone needs to be strong and brave.' She added six brown eggs and a brownish-grey bar of something dense and glistening that I had never seen before.

'What's that?'

'I call it beech mast sticky. It's a sweet treat. I sell it to the gentlefolk and they like it well enough.'

'Is this really all for me and Nan?' I had to make sure. It seemed like such improbably exotic bounty.

'Aye. Perhaps it'll go some way to making your nan happy that you are to visit me again. When will you come?'

I shrugged, my eyes still glued to the beech mast sticky. 'Whenever you want me to.'

'Come next week then,' said Old Rilla, tying the cotton into a bundle around the goodies. 'Be off now, child, and don't break those eggs on your way.'

Chapter Four

This was the life I had led by the time I met the Grace boys at the party in Truro. It couldn't have been more different from the genteel world I glimpsed that night. By then I had been visiting Old Rilla for five years. No one – including me – knew why Old Rilla wanted to teach me what she knew but I never had a moment's doubt that I must learn it.

I had come to take for granted her knowledge of impossible things, even to depend upon it, and she took seriously, and discussed with me, ideas and sensations of mine that everyone else dismissed as mere fancy – or downright strange. Coming to understand the world in a different way felt so good. I would trip back down the hill after my visits, joy bubbling in my heart and, I feel sure, a light shining off me.

Then I'd get back and it would be, 'Oh, Florrie, you're back. The pony got terrible wind, I be thinking he's et some cabbages.' Or, 'There you be, Florrie. Ma says we're scrubbing floors this evening, so I can't come to see you.' Or, 'Ooooh, Florrie, my back's powerful stiff, I'm done in. There's soup if you want.' Small wonder that it was Old Rilla I turned to if I needed a really satisfying conversation.

So as soon as Nan forgave me for staying in Truro that night I raced off to find the charmer. I was wild to know what it had all been about, that chance meeting that felt so little like chance.

Up the hill and past the old rowan I went, the way so familiar now I could have done it backwards and in my sleep. She wasn't at home and I thought I would burst with impatience. Unwilling to go home frustrated, I went onto the moors, pushing through ferns that had been head-high to me when I first started roaming. Now they only reached my waist. I went up to the giant stone that balanced on top of the hill overlooking her cottage. It was taller than me, and grey as the rain, surrounded by a scatter of smaller stones, like courtiers. It had no name that anyone remembered. Whether some earlier civilisation had somehow hauled it there or whether nature had placed it there in one of its many ineffable finishing flourishes, I did not know. Either way, there it perched, and up I scrambled to survey my kingdom, and to wait.

It was a perfect morning of late summer. Swathes of early morning mist lay in the folds between the hills. To the west lay the shifting sea, threaded with golden light. Before me, Tremorney lay in the distance. Heron's Watch was half a mile east of here. My fascination with the old farmhouse had not lessened over the years and I loved to imagine myself living there, the grand lady, with rooms full of books and a herd of cows. It had a peculiar hold on me, that house.

Behind me was nothing but moorland, rising and falling in an endless, languorous lilt and roll like the ocean. I lay on my back listening to the rippling chirrup of sweet little birds and the frill and flurry of their wings. I gazed up into the wide blue bowl of the sky. In that moment the Grace boys were forgotten. Truro was forgotten.

I rolled onto my stomach and watched a beetle clamber with thin-legged precision along a crack in the stone. When it came to a patch of white lichen it stopped, considering. I liked insects. They were always so undemonstratively, humbly occupied. They didn't grimace and groan and stretch their aching backs. They didn't, so far as I could tell, worry about what the future would hold. They just clambered about, falling off things and picking themselves up again, then crawling off in a new direction. I felt there were lessons to be learned from that.

When I turned over again I saw smoke rising from Old Rilla's cottage: at last she had come home! I jumped off the rock and ran. I hurried inside without knocking and she looked up without surprise.

'A big night you had in Truro, Florrie Buckley,' she said.

'You know! You can sense it! Oh, what does it all mean, Old Rilla?'

'Nonsense. I saw Lance Midden yesterday. He told me your nan was that furious with you. Stir this.'

I took her ladle while she made tea and then we went to sit on the doorstep while I told her of being a servant in Lemon Street for a night, of hiding behind a velvet curtain with a young man from a different world, of standing, brow to brow, with his brother in a stable. I told her I was certainly in love with them both. I told her it had felt unbearably significant, as if my life was about to change, but now I was back, and it was over, and it had just been one night after all.

Old Rilla smiled. She did it so rarely that the big rock on the crag appeared emotional in contrast, but she smiled now.

'I was young a hundred years ago or more now,' she said and I was *almost* sure she was teasing, 'but I remember the first time I thought I was in love. I have learned a lot about it in the meantime. Don't be in too great a hurry to rush towards your destiny.'

'So they *are* my destiny!' I gasped. 'Oh! Which of them am I to marry, Old Rilla?'

'Marry, child? What are you talking about?'

'But you just said—'

'Florrie,' she said, taking my hand. 'Listen to me. These feelings you have, yes, they are important. You are right to think it. But they do not necessarily mean what you think they mean. Love is a strange and mystical force. It leads you down avenues you would never otherwise tread. It is always – *always* – about so much more than the coming together of two people. When life wants you to . . . take a step forward . . . when it wants you to learn something . . . it sends you love as a way to make sure that happens. If we want to live a life, we listen. But it is not for the faint-hearted. Love is no pretty storybook emotion. It is like the sea. It is the most beautiful and powerful thing there is. But it also has the potential to destroy everything. It takes lives, changes lives, beguiles us and lures us and disappoints us. It breaks hearts. It can send you mad. To think of love and marriage as one and the same thing is like thinking that the sea and a bucket of water are the same. Only humans could mistake themselves so. Life is calling to you now, through these two boys, and I say to you, beware. You are but thirteen. Let yourself have a little peace before all that begins. For once it does . . .' She trailed off and gazed into the distance, her blue eyes far away.

I felt my legs fizzing, which always happened when she told me something that transformed my understanding of the world. I didn't know whether to feel disappointed or relieved. 'Well, it's not as if I have any choice, is it?' I huffed. 'They'll be back in London now and I will never see them again. Whatever life wanted me to learn, it only gave me one night to do it.'

'Perhaps,' murmured Old Rilla. 'Perhaps.' If she knew something then, if she saw something of my future, she would not tell me, though I begged her. So I went back to my life and soon enough summer drifted into autumn again and it felt as though life would go on like that forever. It seemed that the wind would blow through Braggenstones and the rain would fall upon it and the mists come down to stand between it and the rest of the world. That we would grow older and marry and die and tend the earth and sell its yield and so on and so on until the end of time. But there is no such thing as forever.

Chapter Five

I was fifteen when everything changed. I had grown up a little and become calmer, more patient. I suppose I was preparing myself, in some instinctive way, for the approach of adult life. Another three or four years and I would be married. I would have children, and then I would be the one responsible for dreaming up ways to afford small necessities, to keep a home as clean and warm as possible in that wind-blasted spot. When that time came, it comforted me to know that Nan would be nearby when I needed advice; that even when I no longer shared a cottage with her, I would be just footsteps from her door.

One Monday, Old Rilla was called away, so I came home early. I was astonished to find Nan entertaining Lacey Spencer, as if it were the most natural thing in the world. Lacey had realised that they rarely conversed, she explained, so she had taken it into her head to remedy it. I was sceptical. They rarely conversed because of Nan's patent dislike of anyone who did not come from Braggenstones.

Two weeks later, Lacey appeared again, spontaneously. Apparently she had come to bring me a book by the poet John Clare. I needed to apply myself to his verses without delay. I was very pleased to have the book, but I could by no means address it over the next two days and well she knew it. Then Nan decided to offer her some blackberry cordial, saying Lacey looked peaky after her ride, although I thought she looked as rosy and well as always. Nan bade me finish the peas alone, so the two of them hobnobbed indoors together for the second time. It was vexing.

Then one morning I woke to find Nan gone. Just gone without a word. I couldn't help myself, I was worried. I set off to see what Old Rilla thought about it. And when I got there who should I see *with* Old Rilla, sitting outside in the sunshine, but Nan. Their two faded heads were bent together like a pair of old silver birches. I felt a surge of irritation – it was as though we were changing places: Nan taking off without explanation and talking to my friends, and I fretting and chasing about the countryside after her. I marched towards them ready to give Nan the choice words she would have given me in such a situation. But as I neared, Old Rilla looked up. She saw me and very deliberately shook her head. She gave Nan no indication that I was there and her message was clear. I must leave.

My stomach turned. Nan must be sick. Why else would she be talking with Old Rilla without me? I walked slowly home and sat on our step looking up at Heron's Watch, full of questions.

The afternoon was at its height when I finally discerned a small figure moving over the familiar land, casting a sharp, spiky shadow in the sunlight. I went inside, put a kettle on the fire and threw some leaves in two mugs.

'Have you been idle all this while?!' Nan cried when she came in. 'I see no baskets filled, and those windows look no cleaner to my eyes.'

'Yes, Nan. I done none of it. I been waiting for you.'

'Oh, idle child. Just because I got a little business to see to don't mean there isn't still work to be done.'

'Business with Old Rilla?'

Her dark eyes grew darker.

'I saw you, Nan. I went to see her this morning because I was worried about you.'

Her nut-brown face grew pale. 'What did you hear?'

'Not a single word,' I answered, thrusting a hot mug into her hands and closing the cottage door, 'which is why you need to tell me everything.'

'Can't an old woman have any secrets? Can't I have a drop of privacy after all I've endured in my life? There's work to be done, Florrie! It's no time for confiding and tea drinking.'

I shook my head. 'There's always work to be done, Nan. That don't ever change. I won't take no for an answer.'

She was always so obstinate I was prepared to argue a good while longer but she slumped onto the bench beneath the window.

'Florrie, my lovely child, sit down.'

I did so, and I knew this was nothing small. 'You're sick, aren't you, Nan?'

'Yes, child, I'm dying.'

I bowed my head, useless to say anything – such a truth could not be understood immediately. The grief of it, though, hung heavy between us. I looked up to see her watching me. I moved closer to her and wrapped my arms around her.

'Don't, Nan. Don't go.' The plea of a child.

'I must, my love. I'm sorry. I wouldn't leave you if it were for me to decide. But be strong, Florrie, for you know I love you dearly and you've had that love for fifteen long years. It will be with you always.'

Fifteen years. It did not feel long to me. I saw the seasons come and go and the skies change over Braggenstones without my nan beside me and it was a cold and empty prospect. I had come to accept a life of planting and reaping and selling and cleaning and digging and planting again, but I did not love it so well that I could relish the idea of it without her. I breathed her in, held her brown hand tightly, tried to soak her up. At least we had time; she would not be snatched away as Da had been.

'How long, Nan? Can't Old Rilla help you?'

She hesitated. 'Old Rilla has helped me already, a great deal, though the illness has gone beyond even her healing. I have a little while, Florrie. Perhaps a month. But it's best you made me tell you today for I've been a coward over it and Rilla helped me see how to explain things to you, things you must know now, before I go.'

A month! Autumn would come again, and Nan would not be here. How should I bear it? 'And Lacey. She knows?'

'Yes, Lacey knows. She has been kind. I should always have respected that young woman more.'

'But how could Lacey help? She knows nothing of healing.'

'No. But . . . there is more besides, Florrie.'

I lifted my head from her bony shoulder and frowned. Besides Nan being fatally ill? More?

She took a very deep breath. 'Florrie, I need to tell you something that will . . . change everything for you. I don't know whether you will hate me for telling you now or hate me for not telling you years ago. Rilla says you will not hate me at all, it is not in your nature.'

In the pause that followed, the birdsong soared and the roof creaked. I finally attended to what she'd said a few moments ago: *Rilla helped me see how to explain things to you.*

There was a secret then, and I was about to learn it, and my life would change.

She fussed herself into a comfortable position, leaning

against the thick stone wall, and held my hand as if she were about to tell a fairy tale to a child.

'Your mother and father were very much in love,' she began, to my surprise. 'I'm not a sentimental woman but even I have never seen love like it. It shone from them like moonlight off water.'

I waited. I already knew this.

'Your mother, Florrie, didn't come from Launceston.'

'She didn't?' It seemed a funny thing to lie about.

'She came from London, and she was a lady. Well, not a lady by title, but a lady compared with us. You know what I mean. A gentlewoman.'

My mother? A *gentlewoman*? Out here in Braggenstones? A *city* girl? Nan was playing a prank. But why joke at such a time?

'She came from a family that be . . . well, they be rich, Florrie. And, and . . . *notable*, and quite . . . *notorious*.'

I could see her struggling to produce the right words to help me understand, words which were never needed around here. I knew that she had heard them from someone else, Lacey perhaps. Notable? Notorious? How?

'It used to be a very large family, though there are not so many of them now. They are a proud lot and given to feuding. When your mother fell in love with your da, they cast her out. They saw him as no better than an animal. They said he was sweaty and . . . ill . . . ill . . . illiterate and they said . . . that for her to marry him would be like mating with a pig.'

I gasped, but Nan's brown hand held me fast and bade me listen.

'So your mother ran away. When your da turned up here with her, Florrie, you can guess how I felt. I don't like strangers, as you know, and suddenly there was this beautiful little creature with a white dress and a London voice in my cottage, clutching your da's hand. My last – my best – son, telling me that he would marry her. Not a sturdy Cornish lass who would bear him ten children and work hard all year round, but a foolish girl with romantic notions – so I thought – and a head turned by a handsome face. I was not warm to her, at first.

'But I changed my mind, Florrie. That don't happen often, I know, but it den't take me long. They told her, her family, that if she married him they would never see her again, she could never go home, she'd never have a penny from them. She weren't a stupid girl, and your da were an honest man. He told her what our life is. She came here, she saw us. And she chose your da. Sure as I was that she'd made a fleeting choice, she were a good wife to him. She loved him. She learned what was needed and she set to doing it. She never complained. And she was a beautiful person to have nearby, like you. She fitted this life, this family. Don't ask me how – I've never understood it, but that's how it was. So you see, she may as well have been from Launceston. It made no difference.'

I couldn't bite my tongue any longer. 'But, Nan! How did

they meet? Where on earth did Da meet such a fine lady? He never went to London! Was her name really Elizabeth Wade?'

'She was Elizabeth, yes, and you are named after her as we have always told you, Florence Elizabeth Buckley. They met when she was in Truro. Her family have connections there and there was a wedding that some of the fine London cousins had to attend. But no, she was not called Wade. Her name was Elizabeth Grace.'

'*Grace?*' I exclaimed.

'Why yes, Florrie, what of it?'

Memories swam through my brain. 'Nan! Them boys I told you of in Truro, the brothers with the funny names, they were Graces! They be *related* to me!'

I could hardly believe it. Old Rilla had told me life was calling me through those boys. But I had never imagined *this*! I shook my head in bewilderment. I remembered riding away from them feeling crestfallen, thinking, *This can't be all there is to it*. Well, it wasn't.

'Of course,' mused Nan, 'of course. Down from London you said they were. Well, Florrie, they are your family, one way or another. Most of the family were too proud to visit the wilds – that's how they thought of Cornwall – but your mother was happy to see a new part of the world and meet a new branch of the family. She had plenty of brothers and sisters and she came with one of each.

'Your da was helping in the stables that night. One of the Graces' carriage horses had tekken sick. He tended it, and she came out in the middle of the fine party to see how the poor beast was, and that is how they met. She was to stay in Truro for two weeks. They spent all the time together that they could. When she went back to London it was only to tell them that she had found her husband. Oh, I could tell you more about how they progressed, how they came to understand each other, but first let me tell you the important part, the part that concerns you.'

My head was spinning. There was still more? It was hard to imagine what could concern me more nearly than the identity of my mother and the sacrifices she had made to come and *be* my mother.

'Elizabeth had a forgiving nature. When she fell pregnant she wrote to her mother, even though they had not spoken for more than two years by then. She told her that she was very happy and that her husband was the best of men. She said she was expecting a baby and that if her parents would like to see their grandchild, she and your father would be very happy.

'Their reply broke her heart. They wanted nothing to do with her after such a shameful match. They wanted nothing to do with an uncouth man like your father and they wanted nothing to do with his child.'

'Some loss!' I snorted.

Nan looked thoughtful. 'So I've always felt, Florrie. Even so . . .'

'Even so what?'

She looked shifty. 'I . . . I've done something, Florrie. I don't know if you'll be pleased – most likely you won't. But 'tis done now and I wanted to do it in case you told me not to.'

'What did you do?'

'I wrote to them.'

'You did *what*? But you can't write!' I exclaimed, directing my attention to the least important fact of the matter. I was not thinking straight.

'Well, all right then, Lacey wrote it for me. But I told her what to say. That's how she's helped me. I explained everything – that you are an orphan, that I'm dying, that you will be all alone, living in poverty, a child. I told them that you are beautiful and gifted and a credit to your mother. I just felt, Florrie, they're your family, like it or not, and when I'm gone you'll have no one.'

'I'll have Stephen. And Hesta.'

'But who will Hesta marry in Braggenstones? Most likely she'll move away to one of the villages and you won't see her so often. And Stephen? Yes, he's a good boy . . . but Florrie! This *life*! Look what happened to your da. Look what happened to his brothers. All gone. Stephen's in the mines now and there be only one of him. What if you lost him too? What would become of you out here alone with no one, and no money? Florrie, your da wanted you schooled because he wanted a better life for you than this. He wanted you to have . . . opportunities. This is one.'

The room was shifting around me. The people who had condemned my family to a life of poverty and struggle through their intolerance; the people who had scorned my father and turned away my mother and wanted nothing to do with me . . . How was that a family at all? And yet, what Nan said was true. I had already thought it: I did not *want* this life any more without her. Through the haze of thoughts I realised she was still speaking.

'They answered my letter, Florrie.'

'They did?' I sat up straight, astonished. 'What did they say?'

'They want you, Florrie. They want to come and get you. At once.'

But *I* did not want *them*. Why should I pretend to feel privileged to be sought by such people? People who had insulted my father and turned their backs on my mother? I considered them not only deeply unpleasant but also dangerously foolish. My temper flared up with all the self-righteous indignation and axe-like judgement of adolescence.

'I will *not* go with them!' I declared in horror.

'But you must, Florrie! Think of what they can give you, what your life would be. Think how happy your da would be to know you would never want for anything. Think sense! You got no choice, girl.'

74

'If you think that, then no matter what else ails you, you be losing your mind!' I cried.

I ran from the cottage and slammed the door. I ran to the moors. It was the only safe place. I stayed out for hours. I did not think about where I was going, I just pressed forward, until I was as deep in their boggy, confounding depths as it was possible to be. When it started to rain, cold and shocking through my dress, I welcomed it: a grey sky and veils of silver to make the way even more inscrutable. I think I hoped I would get lost there after all, maybe perish and never have to think of losing Nan or coming half from a family I had never known. But, of course, I could not get lost.

I dragged myself home after dark, received the predictable hiding from Nan and stood in front of a meagre fire, unclothed and shivering, while she wrung my dress out of the window and spread its sodden expanse over a chair, muttering her ire all the while.

For days we went on arguing about what I must do, wasting our precious time left together. Our rows were fierce and Nan enlisted Old Rilla and Lacey both. They urged sense upon me too but I would have no truck with sense at such a time.

But all along there was a part of me that realised the truth of what Nan was telling me: I needed those awful people. Proud and free-spirited as I was, I hated to think of it. But she was right, though for other reasons besides her pragmatic arguments of security and comfort.

It was as if, with the news of Nan's illness, the path along which I had been travelling had come to an abrupt end. The doors I had expected to step through had all been slammed shut – and locked. I remembered how I had been when Da died and I could not face going through that again. I had some idea that if I could only get away, my grief would not crush me as fully.

Then, too, there was the part of me that was quite simply bored at the prospect of my expected life. I remembered suddenly – and guiltily – the dance in Lemon Street. I remembered how I had rejoiced in becoming a new Florrie for a night – Florence. I remembered how I had always envied Trudy Penny her pretty clothes and fripperies and not because I was avaricious but because I loved beauty and the deliciousness of the fabrics and ornaments. I thought of what I could *learn* if I moved to this other life, and it made my stomach flutter. I told myself that no one *needed* books or teachers or new experiences. But the truth was that I did. When I thought about staying forever in Braggenstones there was nothing to make my stomach flutter, just a dull, trudging weight.

I might rage all I liked but in my heart of hearts I knew the truth: for private reasons all of my own, I needed the Graces. And I hated them for it.

Chapter Six

I would not be rushed, however. They may have wanted me at once, but I would not leave Nan. That they could even propose it was typical of the heartless monsters I had decided them to be. I would go when I was good and ready.

I could not even bring myself to tell Stephen and Hesta at first. It seemed preposterous, disloyal, that I would choose to leave our trio and start a new life far away. I would have every advantage, and they would not. Meanwhile the Graces were shadows in my imagination, as insubstantial as ghosts. I felt as if Nan had made up a fiction as to how things were to end for me and we were all going along with it as a kindness to a dying woman. I couldn't believe I would *really* be going to London when it was all over here.

And yet I grew thirsty to know all there was about them. I was to be a *Grace*! That pull, that sense of rightness I had felt with those boys – it was because they were *family*. I wasn't sure whether I was pleased or horrified. I asked Lacey, Nan,

Old Rilla, even Trudy Penny, for every last snippet they knew about the Graces – and it amounted to this:

They were very much talked about, in London, of course, and apparently in many more places besides. They had never been the richest family – though rich enough to get into plenty of trouble and vastly rich compared to us – but they had been prominent. One Morden Grace of antiquity had made his fortune in shipping. There were rumours of piracy. He married a great beauty and fathered ten children. The line flourished and Graces were everywhere in the early years of the last century.

The family commanded an unusual share of good looks, rash tempers and blind luck. Society was uncomfortable with them – their rakish origins, their suspect morals – but they had money and sheer numbers, so they demanded a place. There was a different tale for every Grace: two had been gaoled; more than one went on the stage; there was a decent sprinkling of philanderers and black sheep; their ranks included a famous painter of nudes, a fabled gambler and even a minor composer.

When a male Grace married (as I had already learned from Sanderson), their first sons were given the family names of their mothers as Christian names. It was another thing to set them apart, that they must advertise their difference through a collection of outlandish names. It was generally considered to be in very bad taste, as though the clan was collecting other fine families, hammering home the great network of connections – and therefore power – that they enjoyed.

But in recent generations their numbers had dwindled. Where once the Graces had stuck together (Grace blood being thicker not only than water but than any other blood in existence) somewhere over the decades their proud, fierce spirit had led to quarrels and feuds. Several (like my mother) had been banished. Several, in the way of things, had died. Others had remained unmarried or moved abroad. The current patriarch, Hawker Grace, apparently sat in an echoing house in Belgravia with only a scant handful of heirs and heiresses about him. He was determined to return the clan to its former glory.

It was not an encouraging history, but I reassured myself that they could not possibly be *that* bad. I remembered how gentlemanly I had found Sanderson to be. Then I remembered his aunt, with the crow's hair and furious face. I remembered Turlington, hunched and scowling. Turlington again, exuding debauchery in the stable. And Turlington once more, resting his forehead against mine, and that strange feeling of the world coming apart at its edges. I had not shared *those* memories with my loved ones, not even Stephen and Hesta.

When I finally told them I was to leave they stared at me in dull shock and told me I could not go – *must* not go. Hesta cried every time she saw me for a week after that, and Stephen swore he'd marry me at once, to stop it happening.

'But it *must* happen, Stephen,' I told him gently. I tried to explain the long days of agonising I had undergone, that I had arrived at my decision through a roundabout mental exploration and that, now that I had done so, it was firm and unchangeable.

'But shouldn't you have talked to me?' he asked. 'I'm to be your husband.' It had never occurred to me. And we were fifteen.

'I shall wait for you,' he added, confused.

'We were children when we said that, Stephen. You are my dear friend is all. You are under no obligation to me. I never foresaw this but now that it has come, all is changed.'

'You'll be back. You'll come back in a year or two and we'll be of age, or p'raps you'll be too fine for me then, Florrie. Is that it? You'd rather a gentleman. Well, I can't blame you for that.'

'This en't about gentlemen nor any kind of man! That en't where my thoughts are, Stephen, do you not understand? It's about losing Nan, and not being who I thought I was and having a future my da would want for me . . . maybe.'

But he didn't understand and nor did Hesta. 'You have the love of a good man, Florrie,' she scolded me later, when we were alone. 'What a thing to walk away from. You might find richer, but you won't find better.'

'I *know* that. But he's *not* a man, Hesta, he's a boy. He was a boy when he asked me to marry him and he's a boy still and he can do nothing for me when Nan leaves us, but the Graces can. And here's another thing, he *don't* love me, at least no more than he loves you, or I love you, or you love me.' I had never questioned Stephen's attachment to me, but as the words left me I knew that they were true.

When Nan died, much though I grieved for my own sake, I could not be sorry for hers. Those last weeks in August she had suffered more than seemed fair. It was a hot summer, which only added to her discomfort, and she said that the pain twisted in her stomach like a bag of eels. I heard her cry out, once or twice, at night, though for the most part she kept her agony to herself, with the same stoic endurance with which she had battled through life.

She would not let Old Rilla do very much for her. It made me cry with frustration and rage, but she remained, to the last, suspicious of all that was not worldly or familiar. Still I slipped the occasional leaf of angelica into her tea, or placed certain stones under her bed, whispered certain words over her when she was asleep and I do not know whether it was thanks to these measures or the grace of God (and to this day I am not convinced they are not the same thing) that a week before she died, things grew easier for her. Then there was nothing for me to do but hold her hand and talk to her. She liked to hear me speak of the great things my new life would hold. I was too heartsore to dream in earnest, but I made up pretty things, to ease her mind. I think Nan died firmly believing I was going to marry a duke.

Nan slipped away, all gentle and calm, on a Sunday morning. By Thursday I was on a coach to London.

Chapter Seven

Of course, it was not quite so simple. Between Nan's passing and my leaving, there were two events of note, one expected and one quite astonishing. The first was, of course, Nan's burial, in the churchyard at Tremorney. All from Braggenstones and many from Tremorney attended. My nan was one of ours, through and through. The priest intoned words that soothed me, though my faith had by then been coloured by many years spent with Old Rilla. The world is bigger than any set of words spoken by a man of the cloth, and bigger than any wealth of country lore. It is bigger than any individual experience. Therefore all can fit inside it quite comfortably. I think I have always known this.

I had been to many a funeral in that small church – ours was that sort of life. I think that a collection of those dreary scenes has condensed into one that presents itself as a memory of Nan's, but in truth is no more than a general representation of loss: the dark mourners around an open grave, white flowers, brown coffin, burnt sky, a sense of absence at the very heart of it.

There was a weary trudge home, I do remember that. Those familiar miles were like ash under my boots, the landscape leached of colour and texture and scent. It was as if I had eaten a meal and licked the plate clean, then continued to lick until there was no trace left of flavour. That would be life in Braggenstones without Nan.

We had sent a note informing the Graces of Nan's passing but had heard nothing further from my new family. I felt nervous, I confess: what if they had had a change of heart? People who could disown their own daughter for her heart's choice could not be relied upon, it seemed clear. So relief ignited, even in the dusty grate of my gloom, when the cottage came into sight and before it stood a fine black carriage with glinting gold trim. I wondered what route *that* had taken to get here.

A disconsolate driver lolled atop, plumed hat hanging from his drooping head. As the approaching tramp of the mourners roused him to wakefulness, the carriage door sprang open and out stepped an unexpected person. She was a young woman, older than myself by some years, to be sure, but I had been anticipating they would send the intimidating raven-haired aunt of my memory, or perhaps Mr Hawker Grace himself. Even so, there could be no doubt that this was a Grace, and she had come for me.

She was dressed in a silver-grey dress so tight-fitting of bodice and wide of skirt that she looked like a pewter bell I had seen at the Beresfords' party all that time ago. She was as slim as a twig, as poised as a bird. She had dark brown hair, strange silver eyes and skin so moon-white she could have been made from china clay. Her dress was adorned with black jet buttons and braiding. A jaunty black hat with a black feather sat at a certain angle on her coils of hair and a shiny black boot peeped from beneath her skirts, appearing perturbed to find itself resting on mud.

The crowd of mourners stopped dead, like a bunch of bullocks, to stare.

'Good day,' I said, stepping forward. 'I expect you be looking for me.'

She gave me a look that I can only describe as 'narrow'. 'You're ... *Florence*?' she surmised, as though I were as likely to be a Robert. I became aware of my thin black dress hanging from my bony frame like sacking.

'Aye, m—' I just avoided calling her 'miss'. 'Florrie Buckley. I be glad to make your acquaintance. And what might your name be?'

'Oh Lord!' she tittered, glancing about her as though she might have two or three elegantly dressed friends gathered nearby. There was no one to share her mirth, however, but for a passing hen. 'Mama *will* have her work cut out for her! What an outlandish, ragbag old thing you are. You're *Florence Grace* now, dear, you'd best get used to that. I am your cousin, Annis Grace.'

'Cousin Alice, pleased to meet you.' Though I wasn't.

'Annis! Annis! Not *Alice*. Lord!' She rolled her eyes. If she hadn't been my only link to my new life, I would have kicked dirt all over her glossy dress.

'An-nis,' I repeated like a slow pupil, unsure of the name. I had not heard it before.

'Yes, Annis! For heaven's sake, it's not Scheherazade!' (Scheherazade I knew.) 'Well, come along then, in you get, we must go.'

'What, *now*?' I squawked, forgetting my manners.

'Oh, charming! Yes, now. Or were you expecting us to enjoy a light tea, a little parlour entertainment before we embark? Do you have any keepsakes? Then gather them, please! I cannot imagine you have much.'

Her undisguised scorn, her patent disregard for my feelings on what was clearly a difficult day, and – let me be fully honest – something about the smug upwards tilt of her haughty little nose, drove me to bedevilment.

'I be sorry, Cousin *Annis*, but I cannot come with you today. 'Tain't convenient. Please come back for me tomorrow.'

I heard a little gasp from the Braggenstones onlookers and I heard Hesta mutter, 'Oh, here we go.'

It was true that I had not expected to leave so abruptly. It was true that I wanted to be present for all of the traditions to mark Nan's passing. Certainly I wanted to say a proper and emotional goodbye to Lacey and Rilla and Hesta and Stephen.

But the fact was, all four of them were right there and there was nothing to be said that was secret. All I would miss by leaving was a few speeches and the chance to watch Rod Plover and Dick Pendarne drink themselves slowly and lavishly into a stupor. But I disliked my cousin *Annis* and I wished to annoy her, just for the sake of it. I have that streak in me.

'Not *convenient*?' she marvelled now. 'I suppose you have somewhere better to be?'

'Aye. Here. There be feasting.'

'I'm sure! It all looks *most* abundant. However, I've been sent by Hawker to bring you back with me and that is what I shall do.'

Old Rilla, knowing me well, stepped forward and took my hands. 'Go, child,' she said, her blue eyes boring into mine, saying silently, *Stop being a stubborn beast and give in for once in your life*. ''Tis time, and lingering won't change anything.' I knew it was true, but a stubborn beast I was so I shook my head and turned back to Cousin Annis.

'What time tomorrow be convenient for you? Any time after ten of the clock would suit me well.'

Her alabaster brow creased in disbelief. 'Have it your own way,' she retorted. 'But I will not be back. Believe me, once is quite enough to visit this place. You are a most ignorant and inconsiderate young person.'

I shrugged. 'G'day then, Cousin Annis. Safe journey.'

Her face darkened and I actually shivered. I had been

marvelling at her disdain, her unsympathetic manner, but now I saw something darker still.

'Very well,' she said in an icy tone and turned on her elegant heel to walk back to her carriage. We had not so much as shaken hands.

I honestly believed that I might be watching my new life stalking away from me before it had even begun. Since my old one was now buried in the graveyard, I felt my knees start to shake – it was as though the earth had split beneath me and I had no foothold on either side. But just before I fell through, she turned about and stalked back towards me, her face the very portrait of resentment.

'Here,' she said, rummaging in her purse, bringing forth a few coins and flinging them at me. I missed them all and they landed in the parched grass – glinting silver amid dusty gold. 'If it were up to me, you could stay here 'til you rot, but old Lucifer is set upon you and I cannot be the cause of you not coming to him.'

'Lucifer?'

'Yes, Lucifer. It's what we all call him – not to his face, of course. Hawker. Your new grandfather, dear. I will not stay in this godforsaken ditch a moment longer. Follow when you will – that will pay for a conveyance. 'Tis you who have turned down the offer of company, comfort and respectability. But join us you must. Rest assured *I* shall do nothing to make you welcome when you reach us.'

She climbed into the carriage and from the way it shifted under her negligible weight I suspected a wheel shaft had been wrenched on its transit across the moor. Rod could have put it right in a moment. I said nothing. The fairy tales all speak of love at first sight. Less is written about enmity at first sight, but it was born that day nonetheless.

As we all stared after her, I sank to the grass and picked up the coins one by one. As little as I liked taking her money, she had clearly disliked giving it to me even more. And all because she must not fail in a task set her by Hawker Grace. I knew then that she was afraid of him and wondered what manner of man could strike fear into a woman like that.

Chapter Eight

Thus I came into my new life: with an enemy waiting for me, a threat hanging over me and all at the behest of a man considered to be a match for the devil himself. 'Twas not the most promising of beginnings.

It was 1850. The Cornwall Railway was still almost a decade away, so I travelled by coach, and in the opposite direction from the many young men from my da's mine, which had closed down by then. At that time they were all heading south to Hayle and leaving Cornwall in their droves for Bristol or Liverpool. From those towns, so exotic-sounding to us, they embarked for New York or San Francisco. Some joined the California gold rush; some were bound for the copper mines of Michigan. It was a trend that only increased over the following years, but even then the stream was steady enough that I felt myself a lonely traveller voyaging against the tide.

My memory of the journey is hazy and vague. Stephen and Hesta roused me while it was still dark and escorted me to Liskeard so that I might catch the first stagecoach, for it was a full two days' journey to the great city of London. Hesta and I clung together, sobbing, until her pale little face was blotchy and shining. Never mind learning or adventure – at that moment I felt I would give anything just to be able to stay with Hesta and never say goodbye. Stephen kissed me goodbye, a proper kiss, which took me by surprise so I handled it badly, shrinking away and hurting his feelings, I know. Was he trying to change my mind? Re-establish his claim upon me? Comfort me? He achieved none of these. Cornwall saw me off with inscrutable indifference and a miserable wash of rain.

I passed the hours in numb disbelief that my life as I had known it was over. The seeming impossibility of it insulated me against any fear I might have felt as I undertook the longest journey of my life, all alone. Similarly, any sense of adventure I might have felt had been quashed by meeting my fine cousin the day before.

We left Cornwall. We must have passed the broad and gleaming Tamar but all I really saw were my own memories. I had stayed for the feasting – and hated it. It was melancholy and riotous in equal measure and there was no comfort to be had in it. I had, as they say, cut off my nose to spite my face.

I had said a tearful goodbye to Lacey the night before. She was only content to return to Tremorney because Old Rilla had undertaken to spend the night with me in Nan's cottage. Lacey promised to write and I held on to that promise like a limpet during that journey and through the many years that followed. For all that the others loved me and vowed never to forget me, Lacey was the only one who could write. She was the only one who could reach into my new world and make our friendship a tangible, comforting thing.

Old Rilla had bid me farewell in Nan's cottage in the darkness of early morning, with only the moon and stars to see by. She cupped my face in her warm, strong hands and gazed deep into my eyes. 'May all that is good and true go with you, Florrie Buckley,' she said. 'Always remember that life is more powerful and mysterious than anyone on this earth can fathom. There are always deeper paths pulling us and stronger winds blowing us than we are able to grasp. Take comfort in that, when you need to, and remember that you are a gift.'

'I don't want to go now, Old Rilla,' I sobbed, clinging to her bony frame. 'Can't I stay with you? I would help you, learn with you. I don't eat much.'

'Now that last bit is a lie,' she said, but there was no humour in her blue eyes, only sadness. 'As for the rest of it, do you think I haven't thought of it? If it were my place to be your refuge at this time, it would gladden my heart for I've no wish to lose you. But it isn't. I have looked deeply into it. Your destiny takes you away from Cornwall now and I cannot thwart that for sentiment.'

'Will I ever come back?' I wailed.

'That I cannot see. I only see a fork in the road for you,

many years hence, and you will be pulled equally in two directions for a time. I cannot see the circumstances, nor the choice you will make.'

'But will I be happy, Old Rilla?'

She did not answer, merely wrapped her arms around me, then said, 'You are strong and brave and free, Florrie Buckley. Always remember that.'

'Deeper paths and stronger winds,' I whispered to myself now as I left my life behind. People joined me in the rattling conveyance and then got out. It was crowded, then empty. The day wore on and the horses wore out; they were exchanged for fresh beasts.

Late in the evening we stopped at a place called Norton St Philip, where we were to spend the night. I had known – I had been told – that the journey must be broken, but I was in no state of mind to enjoy the novelty. My fellow passengers bubbled into the inn like a brook spilling into a pool. I followed more slowly, like an ooze of mud.

I shall not write of my night in the George Inn. I cannot remember it and it bears not the slightest significance upon my story. Likewise, the early rising and long journey of the following day. Suffice it to say that I arrived in London at last. Then and only then did I come back to myself and look about me, aware that I must take some sort of interest after all in what awaited me.

*

Let me skip with all possible haste to my arrival at the house that was to become my new home, and my first evening there, if only to be done with the telling of it. It is not a happy memory. I was hungry and stiff. I longed to breathe the clear air of the moors, to run free and shake off the confinement of the last two days, but, of course, that was not my world any more. I was escorted thither by a kindly gentleman, a fellow traveller.

Looking back, I know how lucky I was – a young girl alone with a gentleman in a strange city – but at the time I took the assistance of neighbours for granted. He did not talk to me much, merely led me along at a great pace, repeatedly delving into his waistcoat to consult a shining pocket watch with a hopeful expression as he went. I scurried after him, agape at the boil and bubble of the city, the noise and the confusion and the buildings . . . buildings everywhere. How would I ever have found my way without assistance? My foolishness in refusing to go with Annis impressed itself upon me anew.

And thus, on a late August evening, the sun simmering somewhere behind a haze of dirt and activity, I found myself standing on the front steps of Helicon, the home of the Grace family. I know now that it had been built but thirty years earlier, but at the time I thought it must have been there forever, growing like a tree from unshakeable roots.

Helicon was a large white stuccoed villa near Belgrave Square. It gleamed faintly in the evening sun. It was not joined on to other houses, like the Beresford home in Truro, but stood quite alone, like the cottages in Braggenstones, except far, far bigger. Twelve, maybe fifteen times bigger! I saw at once that there could be no place for Florrie Buckley of Braggenstones there, and that I had better become someone else as soon as possible.

I hesitated on the street, for I sensed something else too; it was stronger than intuition. I knew, for a certainty, that I was never going to be happy in that house. Given that I was only fifteen and likely to be there years, it was a dismaying prospect. I didn't want to go in, but I had nowhere else to go.

My legs, always so strong and sure, trembled as I climbed the steep steps. My hand, which had grasped spades, reins, sacks of grain, faltered to lift the black iron knocker, fashioned in the shape of a sea serpent, bristling with teeth. What manner of welcome might I expect here, in this family of feuds and grudges?

A squinting housekeeper opened the door.

'No work here,' she declared. 'Graces don't hire.'

'I be Florrie Buckley, ma'am,' I said, then hastily corrected myself. 'That is, I be Florence Grace – granddaughter to Mr Hawker, who said I was to come.'

Her eyes grew round and she stepped aside to let me in. 'So *you're* the cousin from Cornwall! Come at last! You took your time, didn't you? The last person who took this long to answer a summons was a solicitor called Draycott. An' guess wha' happened to him?'

I cocked an eyebrow. 'Lost his position?' I hazarded.

'Drowned.'

I could make no sense of her familiarity, nor the watery fate that had befallen Mr Draycott. I mustered myself.

'Well, I be certain my grandfather don't plan to drown me. Be the family at home, ma'am?'

'Some is, some ain't.'

'Well, may you be so kind as to let those as is know that I be here?'

'Yes, yes, come with me.'

I bent to untie my bootlaces. My boots were, of course, my only pair, caked with good Cornish mud, dried now and powdery. The floor — black and white tiles — was certainly the cleanest I had ever seen and coming from a world where cleanliness was hard won, it seemed the only considerate thing to do. She did not correct me.

I stood up to take in my surroundings properly. The hall was vast, and dominated by a giant staircase that parted after a dozen steps or so to rise in two separate branches, both of which reached the same landing high above. A large mirror hanging on that landing reflected back both stairways, confusing me. Dark panelled walls bore paintings with gilt or wood-and-lacquer frames, portraits of Graces of yore with satiny bosoms or curling grey wigs.

I followed her up the staircase in my threadbare woollen stockings through which my big toes poked out, both right and left. I could not help but run my hand over the length of the mahogany rail as I went. I had never felt wood so glossy and smooth, so free from splinters and weather stains and the nibblings of small, many-legged creatures. It hardly seemed wood at all.

At the top of the stair we gained a long corridor, which led to another staircase at its opposite end. There were many doors, one of which my guide knocked upon and opened. I felt myself looking around gingerly, as if too much observation might overwhelm me.

'Florence Grace has come, ma'am,' she said to someone within, then vanished.

There I stood in my stockings, in the biggest room I had ever seen. It must have run half the length of the corridor. Six windows spanned its height, floor to ceiling, in a row, letting in the waning summer sunlight that spread about the room like honey. It was not a beautiful apartment, exactly – it was too stark, too ostentatious – but I thought that perhaps I would not find anywhere in London beautiful until my eyes grew more educated.

There was one thing, however, that thrilled and captivated me at once. In the very centre of the room, like a drifting island, I saw a huge instrument – a piano! I knew it at once – the black and ivory keys were just like the piano I had seen in

Truro two years ago. But this one was far bigger, and made in a different shape, curved and carved, with a sort of lid standing up in the air. The wood was glossy and warm. A tiny gasp escaped from me, barely audible. I couldn't imagine how it would be to play something so splendid. I stared and stared, while a clock behind me ticked away the disapproving seconds until I remembered why I was there.

Three ladies sat about this lofty space, the distances between them just a little greater than I would have expected. Perhaps they were trying to fill it up. Two young women sat on the farthest extremities of a pale green chaise longue. One was my Cousin Annis. Sitting on a high-backed chair of black lacquer was the woman I had seen two years ago at the Beresfords' party. Sanderson's aunt. *My* aunt? I had no idea how all these people fitted together. I felt a pitiful disappointment that Sanderson and Turlington were not here to welcome me. Where were they? In my imagination we had been a trio of friends from the first moments of my arrival – I had been rely-ing on it, I realised – but instead there were only these cool, perfect ladies to greet me.

It was clear that the two young women were sisters. They were alike in all but the colour of their eyes: where Annis's were that strange greyish-silver like the sea, her sister's were button-black, making her less striking, more appealing.

At the sight of me, Annis muttered something and her mother silenced her with a hiss. Quite literally, she hissed at her. Not, 'Shh,' or, 'Hush,' but a sharp, dry, 'Ssssst!' that would have made a snake reconsider striking. This imposing matron rose from her black seat and came to greet me. I was tall, but she had some three or four inches on me, I noticed, looking up at her. There was the gorgeous coil of black hair that I remembered, the proud face, the perfect nose.

Hard, I thought suddenly as I stood before her. *She is a hard woman*.

Her posture was exquisite; she was so composed and vertical that she might have been a statue. She wore a dress of lustrous dark purple silk and a huge silver and amethyst buckle glittered at her waist. From this arresting ornament fell several silver chains and thence hung the most unexpected objects. I saw a pair of scissors, a small bottle, several keys, a thimble and even a watch face.

And she likes to be in control of everything.

I realised I was staring at her waist so I raised my eyes determinedly to meet hers once again, though it was not comfortable to do so. Her opinion of my appearance was written there most plainly. I became aware again of my old black dress hanging like a rag, my wild hair straggling almost to my waist, my sunburnt skin and overlarge hands and feet.

'I am your Aunt Dinah,' she said, looking as though it pained her slightly to admit it. Nevertheless, she extended her hand to shake mine and led me to the little cluster of gentility in the centre of the floor. She must have noticed something, some absence of footfall behind her, for she darted a quick downward glance at my feet and frowned, more in puzzlement than displeasure.

'Girls, this is your cousin Florence. Please bid her welcome. Florence, these are my daughters. Annis I understand you have met. This is Judith, my younger girl.'

'Pleasure to meet you, Cousin Judith. Pleasure to see you again, Cousin Annis.'

'Why, *greetings*, Cousin Florence,' gushed Judith like a moorland brook. She was younger than her sister, close to my own age perhaps. 'I have been in a *fever* to meet you all these long weeks since we heard of you. Fancy. A long-lost Grace, living in obscurity in Cornwall. Now to be restored to her rightful position. How very picturesque! What a grand tale it does make! We shall all be watching you with bated breath to see how you flower, you may be sure. Indeed, most of London may very well be watching you!'

'Judith! What nonsense you speak. When will you learn that one or two well-chosen words are superior to a foolish flurry? Florence, you will excuse my daughter. She is excitable. She imagines that London takes a great deal more interest in us than is truly the case.'

'Sorry, Mama,' Judith subsided. *Bubbly, biddable and friendly*. I imagined that here at last was a softer heart, a warmer nature. I *needed* to believe it, though I received no specific impression of her, no actual *knowing*.

My Aunt Dinah gestured me to a chair that stood some little way off from the group. I did not know whether I should move it closer to them and, if so, how close, or whether to sit where it was and hail them from a great distance. I chose the latter.

'Cousin Florence,' said Annis. 'I am sure that when we last met, you were in possession of some sort of footwear. Have you lost or sold them on your way to London? I do hope you were not set upon by vagabonds and robbed?' Her syrupy tone made it clear that she would have been delighted to learn that I had been set upon and robbed.

Her mother shot her a sharp glance but said nothing. Perhaps she was curious herself.

'No, Cousin Annis. I removed them myself and left them in the hall.'

'Good heavens! And may I ask, I hope you do not think me impertinent, why on earth would you do such a thing?'

'How could I imagine *you* impertinent, Cousin Annis?' My tone was equally sweet. 'I took them off because it seemed polite. They were very muddy, you see, and the floor very clean. I did not wish to make work for others.'

She giggled, a silvery little cascade of laughter, and Judith chimed in like a jolly golden bell. 'But, Cousin Florence, here in London, you see, floors are meant to be *walked* upon! Is the arrangement somehow different in Cornwall?'

'No, it be quite the same. Only I was not used to visiting grand houses in Cornwall.'

'Oh, I see! It *be* the same in Cornwall, Judith. Fancy! It *be* quite the same!'

'Why naturally, Annis, I'm sure it *be*!' But Judith laughed so blithely that no one could have taken offence. She smiled at me and I smiled back.

'That's enough, girls. Well, Florence. There is a very great deal to be done now that you are here. You are not just to be a Grace in name, you know. Therefore we must make you presentable, teach you to speak – properly, I mean – educate you, show you around London – though perhaps not quite yet – and we must teach you about the family so that you know who you are and where you come from. Do you understand?'

I understood perfectly but I wondered if this process of refinement was to begin there and then, before I had had supper. 'I do, Aunt, and I thank 'ee. Can I ask, in what way are we connected? You are my aunt, I know, but . . . ?'

'Your mother was sister to my husband, Irwin. He is dining at his club tonight so you shall meet him tomorrow. He and your mother Elizabeth were two of seven brothers and sisters.'

I nodded, seizing upon this information. Tomorrow I would meet my mother's brother! Then, I realised suddenly, my aunt was not a Grace, not by birth, though her daughters were. And *I* was! I wanted to ask whether one of those other brothers or sisters might be a parent to Sanderson, but I remembered how he had hidden from her that night in Truro. It would not do to reveal our encounter now.

My aunt showed me to my room. She led me to the end of the mahogany corridor, holding aloft a brass candlestick with three branches and three wavering lights atop. We mounted the second flight of stairs. As we walked my aunt pointed out her own chamber and the girls' adjoining rooms. I saw yet another small, steep staircase climbing still higher into the dusky roof of the house but my own room was here.

Aunt Dinah held the door for me to go in before her. I saw a high, dark bed and a tall dresser bearing a pitcher and basin for washing. I saw an even taller cupboard, which I came to learn was called a *wardrobe*, and all of this tall furniture leaned in upon each other and frowned down upon me so that I wondered how a person might think or breathe in here. There was one thing, however, which encouraged me: a desk. A *bureau*, I learned to call it. This was not a lovely piece of furniture. It was dark, with bulging legs and carved leaf patterns bearing no resemblance to any leaves I had seen. It had clawed feet like the paws of Cerberus. But it was a desk. It answered something of the hopes I held for my time here.

'I thank 'ee, Aunt,' I said, turning to her. She looked rather fabulous herself, standing there at the threshold brandishing that restless light. 'I do think I shall be happy here.' I was only trying to be polite.

'Happy?' she echoed, with that same perplexed wrinkle on her lofty brow. 'Do not set your sights so high, child. If you can get by, that shall suffice.'

I was dismayed by her lack of faith in my future, though I was of the same mind myself.

'Aunt, where may I take a walk?' I asked. I knew there were no moors to run upon but . . . I raided my brain for the little I knew of cities. 'Be there a . . . *park*? Or even . . . a *garden*? Somewhere close enough that I won't get lost.'

Lost. A possibility for me for the first time in my life. The very thought made me feel diminished.

'*Walk?*' she exclaimed as though I had said 'slaughter a babe'. 'Child, it is almost nine o'clock at night!'

'Aye, Aunt, but there be light yet and I be cramped and aching from the coach.' She looked uncomprehending. 'I been sitting. All the long day.'

'Well, yes, child, of course you have.' She shook herself slightly. 'I will ring for Benson to bring you a little supper, then go to bed, for we have much to do in the morning. I have put aside an old dress of Judith's for you to wear until we take you shopping. You are not fit to be seen yet. Well then, goodnight.'

I decided to abandon the walking idea for now. 'Oh, Aunt! Before you go. May you tell me . . .' I hesitated. 'How do I find the outhouse?'

'*Outhouse?*'

'Aye, the, um . . .' I racked my brains for a polite word but I couldn't find one. 'Privy. If I should need to, um . . .'

'Oh! Good heavens! Child, what are you thinking? These are not suitable topics of conversation at all! You use the chamber pot, of course, and Benson will dispose. Now let us have an end to it.'

'I en't trying to make conversation,' I explained, feeling I was being judged most unfairly. 'I'm trying to learn how things are done here. It be very different from what I am used to, Aunt, and likely I'll make a lot of mistakes but pr'haps not so many if I ask questions.'

'Questions.' She shuddered again. 'That is quite enough now.'

She withdrew, shutting the tall, dark door on me and leaving me with just the three writhing candle flames for company. I sat on the high bed and waited for Benson, whoever he or she might be. It could not have been more different from home, where I could have found my way around our tiny cottage blindfolded. Where Nan was rarely out of earshot.

In the brief time I had been at Helicon, I had learned that three of the most natural things imaginable – questions, bodily functions and walking – were considered contemptible. I stared around the forbidding chamber and waited.

Like that long ago night in Lemon Street, I was exhausted but could not sleep. Then, my wakefulness had been borne of excitement; now it was caused by heartache, intense physical discomfort and a brain all scrambled with the horror of a dawning reality. 'Oh, Nan,' I whimpered more than once, 'what have I done?'

I had taken my orange stone from my small pack and tucked it under my pillow. I clutched it now as I tossed and turned. I had always kept it, and though I had not relied upon it for comfort in many a long year, I did so again now. 'Take me away,' I whispered, as if it were enchanted. 'Keep me safe.'

The bed was hard, the mattress lumpy. At home I had not had a proper bed at all, merely a straw-stuffed pallet on the floor and blankets, yet I had not once lain awake feeling every ache in my body as I did here. After a full day's work or walking, it had offered comparative softness and dear familiarity. Here my body's aches were of an altogether different sort from that created by hard physical exercise and I wondered, if walking were frowned upon, how I might ever find ease again.

I had hazarded to ask Benson where I might walk when she had brought me my supper. She was not much older than me, but had already been at the house for six years. I think she saw the loneliness in my face.

'I hope I don't offend you, Miss Florence,' she said, 'but downstairs we've been saying how brave you must be, to come here and start a new life. We admire you.'

I learned later that she was rather editing the truth and there were quite as many servants who thought the improvement in my financial expectations could and should reconcile me to anything. Still, it was the first kindness I had been shown.

'I'm glad *I* don't have to be a part of that family,' she mused to herself then, which was less comforting.

But when I asked her about walking, she too looked confused. 'I could not walk if it were to save my sister's life, after a day's work in this place,' she said with feeling, and I realised it was late and I was detaining her.

The food she brought me differed vastly from what I knew. There was a meat pie bursting from thick, golden pastry, dripping in flavoursome gravy. There was water and sherry and a small round cake, which I could not recognise but which dripped with syrup and burst with unfamiliar spices. I confess it was delicious and I devoured it all – it went against my upbringing to waste food – though eating such rich fare so late surely contributed to my sleepless night. But these are the reflections of hindsight. At the time I merely snatched at nourishment when it was before me, whether in the form of a pie or a few warm words.

Chapter Nine

The next day, Benson woke me at seven. But I had not long fallen asleep. I tumbled from bed and my feet reached an unfamiliar floor. Instead of the cold stone of the cottage, I felt wooden floorboards and a silky rug.

Benson was there to wash and dress me, she explained. I almost laughed. I had been washing and dressing myself since I could remember; mine was not a life given to cosseting and babying, like that of my hothouse cousins. Still, the smile withered on my lips when I saw the confusing array of garments that Benson had laid out for me.

But first a methodical washing must take place. It was conducted standing up. Benson preserved my modesty by leaving me in my nightgown to wash and lifting it one section at a time to work on the exposed area. I had never given any thought to my modesty until Benson went to such pains to respect it! But the water was hot, that was delightful.

Then Benson applied herself to the undergarments. Chemise, drawers, corset. *Three* petticoats. The first was of cotton, with a stitched border that ruched the fabric and gave it the bell-like shape I had noticed the day I met Cousin Annis. The second was of flannel and the third was made of some bizarre woven matting, springy and abrasive. Benson told me that it was horsehair. I later learned that five petticoats were preferred, but my aunt would content herself with three until my own supply could be purchased.

There were stockings – green and blue paisley silk on that first day. A woollen vest. A frilled and embroidered camisole . . . And at last, just was I was losing the will to live, the dress.

Naturally it was finer than any I had ever worn, and finer even than any I had seen Trudy Penny wear. At last a lustrous fabric with a jewel-like sheen was mine to caress. It was the most wonderful colour: a sort of pale yet rich blue-green. It must have looked striking with Judith's dark hair and black eyes and it was becoming on me with my brown-gold hair and brown eyes. The reason for the petticoats then became clear, for the dress was heavy yet my petticoat army withstood its weight to swell the skirts outwards in that shape that is so pleasing to the eye. I had the feeling of being some tiny, precious artefact that had been carefully wrapped and re-wrapped in my protective layers for fear of breakage, a most unaccustomed sensation for me. (In Braggenstones – one petticoat, stays, one dress. And liberty.)

I was given blue shoes to wear and my hair was brushed

thoroughly. I am not ashamed to say that it made me cry. It was not that Benson was ungentle, but the tangles were long-term residents and her battle with them was mighty. I am not well-suited to taming.

My hair was then rolled and folded and when I looked in the glass my mouth fell open. I looked quite unlike myself. The smooth hair gave my straight dark eyebrows an uncompromising look. With the wild strands all tucked away, my hair appeared a uniform dark brown; the gold and copper were hidden away. My clear blown eyes, slightly curved at the corners like those of a deer, looked dramatic. The sheen of the dress emphasised the brown of my skin – I saw how dark it was compared with Benson standing next to me, all indoor-white like my cousins.

Benson showed me to a large dining room for breakfast. I prayed to every god I had ever heard of that at last I would see Sanderson and Turlington. There, seated at the table, devouring kidneys, were Aunt Dinah and Judith and Annis. There was also another young woman, and I almost gasped when I saw her. All the Graces I had seen were good-looking. At worst they were striking, at best arrestingly handsome. But this girl was beautiful in a way that I yet struggle to put into words. Think of a girl from a fairy tale, so golden of hair and sweet of smile, so blue of eye and peachen of skin that she should rightly have been clad in diaphanous silver and found amongst blossom groves with leaves scattered through her hair. (In fact, she was wearing the same bell-shaped skirts and restrained yet elaborate hairstyle as the rest of us.)

And there, at last, at the sideboard, helping himself to eggs and salmon with silver tongs, was Sanderson. I felt a leap of joy to see him, yet also a little fear. Our previous meeting had predisposed me to think of him as a friend but perhaps it was otherwise for him. It might make him uncomfortable. He might look down upon the cousin he had first met as a servant. *Will he even remember me? How will he greet me?*

Sanderson was murmuring with a portly gentleman who I guessed to be my uncle Irwin. He looked mild, and a little overwhelmed by the abundant choice of food. I liked him on principle because he was my mother's brother, although I worried how he coped with his viperous wife and daughter if he could be taxed by breakfast. Yet he turned with a warm smile when Benson gave a light knock to announce me.

Kind, I thought. *Easy to persuade. Likes to please everyone.*

'Well, this must be my niece!' he cried, abandoning the sideboard with some relief. He lumbered to my side and clapped my hand in both of his. 'Welcome, my dear! It's Florence, isn't it? I am glad to know you.'

Here at last was the welcome my heart had been craving. I clung to his hand and bobbed a half-curtsey, not knowing the etiquette for meeting long-lost, wealthy uncles.

'I thank 'ee, Uncle. Aye, 'tis Florence. I be so happy to meet you.'

He was a tall man and heavyset, yet with a slight softness to him. He did not look as though he minded his girth. It must be a delightful ability, to accept life as it comes at you and not be always chafing and querying and challenging, as is my wont.

'You are not much like your mother, Florence, except for your slenderness and something about the eyes, I think. Perhaps you take after your father?' Uncle Irwin was the only Grace who ever allowed the existence of my father. 'She was dear to me, Florence. A good sister. I was heartily sorry to hear that she died though we had not seen her for so long.'

'Thank 'ee, Uncle. My nan never did say a bad word of her. I wish I'd known her. I'm told I'm a little like her and a little like my da but mostly I think I'm just me.'

'An original! Splendid! Well, come in, my dear, don't stand there on the threshold. Come and know your cousin Sanderson. Come and have some breakfast. Oh, you've met my wife and daughters, I believe?'

He towed me this way and that, uncertain where to start me off. It made me smile. It helped me greet my aunt with a greater cheer than I might have mustered otherwise.

'Good morning, Aunt. Good morning, Cousins. I hope you be well this morning.'

Two frosty nods responded. Judith, however, leapt out of her chair and kissed my cheek. I was quite disarmed.

'*Quite* well, thank you, Cousin Florence, though the air in my room is stifling in August even *with* the windows open and Annis, you know, talks in her sleep even though she swears she does not — I hear her through the wall — therefore I am ill-rested and out of sorts, although happier for seeing that you have not run away from us, with or without your muddy boots. And you, Cousin, I trust you slept well? Were you quite comfortable?'

'Judith.' Her mother recalled her to her seat with but a word.

'Ah, my lovely daughters! My divine wife!' Irwin stood behind them proprietorially, his hands resting heavily on Aunt Dinah's shoulders. 'You may count yourself fortunate, Florence, to have such mentors to guide you in your new life. There are none better qualified.'

'I be certain of it, sir,' I murmured.

I thought it odd that he did not introduce the other young lady at the table. In fact, the whole little family seemed to be angled slightly away from her. I kept trying to catch her eye over their shoulders, but she gazed down at her plate with a faint smile. Perhaps some etiquette said that I must meet Sanderson first.

'And this,' continued Irwin, beaming and stepping away from his flock, 'is your other cousin, Sanderson.' I tensed and held my breath. 'Quite the fine gentleman about town, you know! But he would not be from home when he heard that Cousin Florence had arrived, would you, Sanderson?'

'Indeed not, Uncle.' He looked exactly as I had remembered him and I felt such relief.

'Cousin Florence, a true pleasure to meet you,' he said warmly, shaking my hand. 'It must feel very strange, but rest assured we are all very pleased to have you here. I am *exceptionally* pleased to have you here for perhaps a new cousin will excuse me for a while from the endless round of engagements my aunt subjects me to!' He gave a golden smile to Aunt Dinah, who rolled her eyes. I breathed out at last. Perhaps, between Judith and Irwin and Sanderson, I should find a way to be happy here after all.

'Pleasure to meet you, Cousin Sanderson.' Since he had given no indication that we had met before, neither did I. *Did* he remember me, I wondered? How I longed to ask him so many things. For instance, where was his brother? When would I see *him* again? I thought it curious that they did not mention him: *Sanderson's brother Turlington had to leave early this morning but you will meet him this afternoon*, or some such.

'Truly, though,' Sanderson continued, 'if you need anything at all, please feel you can count on me. I wish your transition to life as a Grace to be as easy as possible for you.'

'I should be careful, Sanderson, if I were you,' said Annis bitingly. 'Don't encourage her to ask you *anything* she needs to know or she will take you at your word and you may find yourself in some *very* uncomfortable waters!'

Judith giggled again and I knew that their mother had told

them every word I had said the night before. I burned with hurt.

'I thank 'ee, Cousin Sanderson. Having left my home and all who loved me, I have great need of a friend.' I could not hope that my words would soften the hearts of *those* women, but I wanted him to know how I valued his kindness.

'I am sure of it, Cousin, and so it shall be. Now, will you take some breakfast?'

He guided me to the heaped sideboard and piled a little of everything onto a plate for me. I was glad not to have to choose. Food could not command much of my attention while last night's supper still lay heavy in my belly and so many questions went unanswered.

Even Sanderson, with his charming manners, did not introduce me to the beautiful young woman. I threw her glance after glance as a seat was pulled out for me at the table, but still she looked away. I wondered if she were a servant, but then why would she be sitting there, gorgeously dressed and breakfasting with the family? It seemed wrong to ignore her as the others appeared to be doing, yet I felt so unsure of everything in this strange new world.

The family fell upon their food and ate as though they had not done so for weeks. Most of what was upon my plate I could not recognise but that was not the pressing concern now.

'And are there other Graces living here, Uncle?' I asked,

breaking into the concentrated silence of the epicures. 'I heard you – we – be a large family.'

'We *are*, not we *be*,' snapped Annis, pushing her plate away as though bad grammar made her feel sick. I flushed.

'Oh, not so large as once we were, Florence. Not nearly so large. This is about the sum of us now, I'm afraid. Is that not so, my dear?' He applied to his wife as though she might have a few relatives hidden about her person that he may have overlooked.

'It is.'

I was puzzled. 'But Mr Hawker Grace, do he not live here too?' I remembered seeing the letter from him, in Lacey's hand.

'Oh yes, to be sure! To be sure! Father lives here!' beamed Irwin, volunteering nothing further. Then where *was* he? And why was no one mentioning Turlington? Was he now married and living in another family's home? Was he *dead*?

'You were one of seven brothers and sisters, my aunt told me, Uncle Irwin?' I tried again.

'Quite so, my dear, yes,' he agreed, piling his fork with scrambled eggs. 'Your mother was one, of course, God bless her. Ah, dear Elizabeth.'

'And you, Cousin Sanderson? Do you also have a great many brothers and sisters?' I persevered. I wished I had not when I saw a deeply uncomfortable expression shadow his face.

'Sadly no, Florence.' Which was not to say he had *none*, I noticed, but I could not ask more.

'Grandfather rarely eats with us, Cousin Florence,' piped up Judith. 'No doubt you're wondering when you shall meet him. You must be very anxious to do so. He may be away on business – I never can keep track of his comings and his goings. When shall she meet him, Mother? Shall it be soon? Shall it be today?'

'She shall meet him when he sends for her, Judith, and young ladies are better seen than heard at mealtimes as at all other times.'

I understood the criticism was also aimed at me and fell silent. Clearly the order of the day at breakfast was to apply oneself to food, even when one was not hungry, and to stifle curiosity, even when it threatened to overwhelm. My confusion grew.

I tried a bite or two of everything on my plate. Some things I liked, some I did not. Servants flitted in, without speaking, and flitted out again with empty dishes. I took to staring steadily at the blonde beauty opposite me so that every time she peeked up at me I might smile. After the fourth or fifth attempt she smiled back. At last, breakfast was concluded and my uncle got to his feet.

'I must leave you now, I have a great deal of business this morning. Florence, I shall see you tonight at dinner and you must tell me all about your first day at Helicon.'

'I shall, Uncle.' I was sorry to see him go but took the broken silence as permission to speak again. 'You mentioned a plan for me, Aunt? I wonder what I am to do today?'

'Come with me, child, and curb that curiosity of yours. You are to do what I tell you to do, one thing at a time.'

Sanderson threw me a sympathetic glance as I followed my aunt from the room.

'Goodbye,' I said very directly to the young woman, who sat like a ghost at the table. She smiled at me again and her lips moved. No one clapped their hand to their brow and exclaimed, 'Good Lord! How rude! We forgot to introduce you to Such-and-such.'

Was she a fairy, seen only by me? I thought not – I knew something of beings from other realms, and I could have sworn that she was human.

My aunt bore me off to her study. It was a compact, square room with thick green drapes of a hue so sappy and strong it made my eyes dance. There were three equally green armchairs, for cosy mother-and-daughters tête-à-têtes, I assumed. And there was a desk of the ubiquitous dark mahogany, on either side of which stood two hard mahogany chairs, clearly intended for more businesslike interviews. This is where we sat, facing each other like associates. She placed two sheets of paper between us, one covered in writing and one blank.

'I have made a list,' she said without preamble, tapping the written-upon sheet, 'of all we need to address to make you presentable. Speech, of course, appearance, deportment, education, accomplishments, manners, *table* manners,' she added, scribbling something next to an item on the list. 'Finesse, the art of conversation . . . Oh, there will be more, but this is where we shall start.'

It seemed a daunting curriculum to me. I truly would be somebody different by the end of it.

'Then,' she continued, moving her finger lower down the page, 'we must consider all the things you will need to know, about the family, for example. If you are to be a Grace, as my father-in-law insists, then you must know about the Graces. Also which literature is fashionable, which artists and musicians to like, which plays and poetry. You will need to know London, of course; we shall have to take you to theatres and restaurants and amusements so that you may speak knowledgeably of them when asked.'

She appeared joyless, as though theatres and amusements and the rest were an unspeakable tedium. I wondered how I would be feeling now if there were some affection between us, if it were Lacey who was to take me to all such things. I might very well have felt that all my dreams had come true. As it was I was only sensible of a great many challenges at which I was almost certain to fail.

'And the other page, Aunt?' I asked faintly.

She drew it towards her and dipped a quill into an ink pot. Then she wrote two words at the top of the sheet. *Florence Grace*. 'If we are to become family, then we need to know you also. That is to say, the factual details. Let us make a start right away. Do you have a middle name?'

'Elizabeth, after my mother.'

Elizabeth, she wrote upon the page.

'When is your birthday?'

'Midsummer's Day. The twenty-first of June.'

She scribbled again.

'You are fifteen years of age, I believe?'

'Yes.'

'And I suppose you have no schooling at all.'

'You are wrong, Aunt. I went to school for nearly two years when I was young, and after that I had private schooling. I can read and write and count. I know the myths of Ancient Greece and Rome, I know Shakespeare and a number of poets . . .' I fell silent before her disbelieving expression.

'Well, a rudimentary education is something, at least. We shall see about engaging a governess for you . . .'

She trailed off, tapping her nails on the desk and frowning. My aunt appeared at a loss to know where she might begin to address all that was distasteful about me. My hair was dreadful, I looked like a heathen, my posture was disgraceful, my accent reprehensible, my manners appalling. Aunt Dinah estimated two months at least before I could be introduced to anyone outside the family. 'What was Hawker *thinking*?' became her repeated lament throughout that interview.

When it came to an end I was relieved.

'Helicon be an interesting name,' I said as we left the study, careful not to frame it as a question. 'I wonder what it might mean.'

She closed her eyes as though she had a headache. 'Helicon *is* an interesting name,' she corrected. 'You cannot use the infinitive form of a verb after a noun. Helicon *is* large. The book *is* red. The drapes *are* green.'

I did not understand. 'I . . . I . . .' I began, but could not guess at what came next. How had something so natural as speaking suddenly become so foreign? 'Sorry, Aunt,' I tried. 'Helicon *is* an interesting name. What does it mean?'

She favoured me with a scornful smile. 'I should have thought you, with your extensive knowledge of the mythologies, would have known that.'

'No, Aunt, I never came across it before.'

'Helicon was a great river, part of Poseidon's realm, gifted to him by Zeus himself. The house is named as a tribute to our family's great shipping history; that is how we came into our fortune, you know, centuries ago. Like Poseidon, the Graces are not easily satisfied and when we want something we claim it.'

But Poseidon was always ultimately thwarted by Zeus, I thought. *I know that much. His schemes to rule over the land were always thwarted.* It came upon me suddenly that the Graces would be similarly disappointed. I knew it as certainly as I had foreseen my own unhappiness. I said nothing, however. Had my aunt only known it, I was already learning.

Chapter Ten

Luncheon. We returned to the dining room, where we had eaten breakfast only hours before. I had already eaten more that morning than I would have eaten in a whole day in Braggenstones. Now I was to eat again, though I did not want or need to, and although I *knew* I should not, I couldn't refrain from asking why.

'*Why?*' My aunt's long look of exasperation was almost enough to make me feel sorry for her. 'It is the hour for *luncheon*, child, therefore, *luncheon* is what we shall have! There are many in London, even in this area, who cannot eat as we do. We strive to be the most fashionable household in Belgravia, Florence. This privilege is clearly lost on you. Nevertheless, rest assured, we shall not alter our dining habits to suit you.'

'No, Aunt,' I murmured. Eating, *fashionable*? Cornwall had never seemed so far away. 'Are you hungry, Aunt?' I asked, honestly curious.

'*Hungry?*' she echoed despairingly, in a tone that suggested

I was being truly cruel to her. At the table she sat as far from me as possible.

Uncle Irwin and the beautiful girl were not there; otherwise we were the same assembly as at breakfast. Annis was as silent as her exhausted mother but Judith maintained a cheerful prattle and Sanderson made good-humoured conversation. I took advantage of his presence to learn what it was I was eating.

'Why, Cousin Florence, this is hashed hare,' he explained, waving a spoon at a silver tureen. 'This is cold roast pheasant, pea soup, cod in oyster sauce, stewed carrots, mashed potato with, I think . . .' He poked at a white mass in another silver bowl with the spoon. 'Yes, it's the one with bacon in it, my personal favourite. Oh, and I think there's a damson pudding for dessert. Is it damson pudding, Judith?'

Apparently it was. It seemed that once again the thing was to try everything. Even with just a small serving of each it amounted to an enormous plate. I felt guilty, eating such fare when everyone I had ever loved was almost certainly eating bread and ale (and at this time of day not even much of that) but I overcame my scruples to fit in, to satisfy my curiosity, and because it tasted so very good. The result was that I left the table with a painful feeling in my taut belly.

I was resigning myself to the prospect of an afternoon with my aunt when Sanderson asked her if he might show me the garden. To my astonishment she agreed.

'So long as you don't keep her above twenty minutes, Sanderson. We have so much to do today.'

'Certainly, Aunt, twenty minutes will suffice to take a turn about the garden, if you're agreeable, Cousin Florence?' I was, of course.

So Sanderson led me through a side door into a pleasant square garden with a small stable block at one end. It was walled and fringed by trees on both sides, providing privacy from the side aspects of the neighbouring houses, and a mulberry tree stood at its very centre.

'Oh, it's so good to see *grass*!' I groaned in relief, bending without thinking to remove my shoes and stockings. All I craved was to feel cool, soft grass under my feet, instead of silk stocking and wooden floorboard. To feel the air on my skin. There was not very *much* grass, just ten neat wedges divided from one another by paths of white gravel. Nevertheless, I was outside. A robin sang its pretty song in one of the trees and a small breath of air stirred the branches. The sun shone on my face and I closed my eyes.

'Um. I hope you don't mind me pointing it out, Cousin,' said Sanderson hesitantly, 'and I don't mind for myself, of course, but, well, if our aunt were here . . . that is not something she would approve of, taking off your shoes and your, well, you know. Oh, I know you mean nothing by it. But *she* would say . . . well . . .'

His words clipped the small wings of my heart, which was

just beginning to soar a little, and it tumbled back to earth with a bump. I opened my eyes.

'I mean nothing by it,' I echoed sadly. 'Thank 'ee – *you*, Sanderson, I should have realised. It's just I miss it so much.'

'Grass?'

'Well, yes. And all of it. The land. Cornwall. Home.'

'Will it be *very* hard for you to feel at home here, do you suppose?'

'Oh, Sanderson, I don't know that I ever shall! 'Tis a world all new to me, where every little thing that is most natural to me is shown to be wrong! Thank 'ee for bringing me outside. Thank 'ee for your kindness. Promise you'll be my friend here, promise!' I forgot my speech again and found my lip trembling with fervour.

Sanderson hesitated, as if he, too, could not trust his words. 'Why, of course I will, dear Cousin. Heavens, I am so very sorry that you are so . . . uncomfortable. I am not used to such . . . well, we Graces do not often speak from the heart, you know. I shall contrive to secure us these short intervals alone whenever possible. Perhaps they will be a comfort.' At once he looked aghast, as if he had made a terrible faux pas. 'I beg your pardon. I mean only that it is easier to speak truly . . . away from the others. I hope you did not think I meant any disrespect towards you.'

I had thought no such thing, and to be able to speak openly with Sanderson was what I coveted the most.

'And when I cannot,' he went on, 'please do not think my friendship withdrawn. 'Tis only that Aunt Dinah has such very precise ideas on what must be done and when, and I can do more for both of us if I do not incur her displeasure. *That* is a thing that has never helped anyone. And I would like to help you if I can, though I am no expert on young ladies, as you may remember.' He lay a consoling hand briefly on my arm, then withdrew it at once. 'They may be watching, you know.'

I glanced up at the long windows of the drawing room. The sun shone upon them so that all I could see were great yellow rectangles of glass. 'So you *do* remember meeting me in Truro,' I smiled. I had been right about him. Here was one Grace, at least, who would be kind to me no matter what dress I wore or what family I hailed from. It made me feel, perhaps, that I could tolerate the rest of it.

'Of course I do. When Hawker announced that a long-lost cousin was coming to us, that she was living by the name of Florence Buckley in a Cornish hamlet called Braggenstones, I remembered you at once! You can imagine my astonishment. But also my delight! Being beckoned from a dance to hide behind a curtain doesn't happen to me every week, you know. Of course, best not to mention *that* to Aunt Dinah.'

'I know that. But it's so frustrating when there is so much I want to ask you. Most of all, where is your brother Turlington? Why does no one mention him? I longed to ask you this morning but, of course, I could not without showing that we had met.'

'Thank you, Florence. I appreciate your tact.' His handsome, sunny face darkened. 'Here at Helicon, it truly is best to let things lie and not upset them. As for Turlington . . . you're quite right, we don't talk of him.'

'But why? Is he dead? I'm so sorry, Cousin, I do hope he be – *is* – not dead.'

'Not dead. Disgraced. Completely and utterly disgraced and sent away. He is alive, Florrie, but to us he may as well not be.'

I was caught between horror, disappointment and delight at hearing my old familiar name. 'You called me Florrie, how wonderful,' I said, while I was trying to work out what to say about the rest of it. I had been enchanted when we first met in Lemon Street and Sanderson called me 'Florence'. Then, I had liked feeling ladylike and different. Now nothing in all the world could be more comfortable than to be Florrie again; but she was already disappearing.

'It's how you first introduced yourself in Truro. How Turlington and I referred to you after we met you.'

'You miss him,' I realised suddenly. 'You're saying he be – *is* – disgraced because that is what *they* say, but *you* don't feel like that. You wish he'd come back.'

He sighed, such a deep, shadowy sigh. 'You're very perceptive, Florrie. Oh, I shouldn't call you that, Aunt Dinah would have a fit. She says it's a name fit for a . . . well, never mind. Sorry. Only perhaps when we're alone together we can be ourselves. You can be Florrie and I can miss my brother. I would like to be as honest with you as you have been with me. It would be a welcome novelty.'

'I should like that.'

'Well then, you're quite right. I love my brother dearly, and I don't much care what he's done. If it were up to me, I'd welcome him back tomorrow, but I'm the only one who feels like that, I think. Apart from our grandfather, perhaps, but then that's . . . complicated.'

'What *has* he done? Would he *want* to come back do you think, if he could? Do you know where he is?' Oh, the luxury of asking questions – a luxury quite as great as stretching my toes in the grass.

'Let us walk,' he said quietly, taking my arm in a gentlemanly fashion. 'I am supposed to be showing you the garden after all.'

'Let us walk,' I repeated. I was trying on his elegant phrases the way I had slipped on the blue shoes earlier. They were just as uncomfortable.

We began a sedate amble up one side of a grassy wedge and down the other, me barefoot on the grass, Sanderson crunching on the gravel at my side.

'Look there, Cousin Florence!' he declaimed for the benefit of an imaginary audience. 'A fine apple tree! And there is a splendid fig tree! You have come a little late for the white roses but over there . . .'

'Yes, yes, it's a fine mulberry tree. And those are fine raspberry canes and there are splendid lilies by the wall. I *know* gardens, Sanderson. I want to know about your brother. My cousin.'

'We don't have much time but I'll tell you quickly. He's always been in trouble with the family, even when he was very young, for drinking too much, for gambling and generally behaving like a law unto himself . . .'

'But I thought that's what Graces *did*! I beg your pardon, I mean, I heard some stories about the family—'

'It's what we *used* to do,' he corrected, gesturing at the stable block for the benefit of our supposed audience. To ease his discomfort I turned my head with an expression of great interest. 'But not for the last ten years or so. Now we are trying very hard to be respectable. It was the timing of it that hurt my grandfather the most. We were starting to get somewhere, to receive invitations into homes where we had not previously been welcome. Graces can't stay still, you see. We must always advance, else we think we are going backwards.'

I remembered my aunt saying that the Graces were never satisfied.

'People could see that we were changing. Grandfather kept trying to impress upon Turlington that as the eldest grandson he must live an exemplary life and raise up the reputation of the Graces, but Turlington didn't want to raise anything except . . . well, except hell, pardon the language, Florrie.'

'I've heard worse.'

'One night at a ball he got so drunk he smashed a huge floor-to-ceiling mirror that our host had imported from Persia. There was a whole legend about it, it was indescribably precious. A week later, he stole a horse from a guest of our neighbour, who was staying in London. That gentleman left town without his white mare, and two weeks later Turlington came home with a black horse he claimed he had bought in a country sale. But the dye had been applied very poorly and everyone recognised Mr Blount's mare.'

'Why steal when you are so rich, when he had so much?'

'No one knows, though we are not so rich as we wish to be, Florrie. We live an expensive life.'

'What else? You haven't told me the worst of it, have you?'

'No. You really are uncanny, you know. We went away for a month, to let the fuss die down in London. We stayed with friends in Hertfordshire. Grandfather and Aunt Dinah *promised* them that Turlington's bad behaviour was a thing of the past.'

'But it wasn't.'

'Not by any means. He seduced our hosts' daughter! When it came to light there was *such* a rampage. Grandfather and Aunt Dinah were beside themselves. The Padfords demanded redress. Mr Padford and Turlington came to blows . . .'

I burst out laughing.

'It's not *funny*, Florrie! He disgraced a young lady of good family. A good, sweet, virtuous girl who can never be married now.'

'Well, she obviously weren't *that* sweet and virtuous, were she!' I chuckled. 'I'm sorry. I know it en't funny, Sanderson. Your brother be – *is* – a wicked man. It only sounded funny in the telling. So, they demanded redress. There was *such* a rampage . . .'

He smiled at my attempts at genteel speech. 'Yes. And Grandfather has banished Turlington. He's in Madeira. I do have an address for him but I keep it hidden like a buried body. We're not supposed to correspond. I believe he's lonely and wishes he could come back but –' he spread his hands eloquently – 'what he *did*, Florrie!'

I shook my head in wonder. How could two brothers be so different? Then I remembered something Sanderson had told me that long ago night in Truro. They had different mothers. I wanted to ask him about that but here was Judith, stepping delicately along the gravel towards us.

'Coo-eee!' she trilled, waving her little hand frantically. 'Coooo-eeeeee, Cousin Florence! You're wanted back inside. Annis and I are to share the task of instructing you, so I am to be your mentor. What delightful fun! I promise you shall find me benevolent. Oh, you've lost your footwear again, I see. Are your feet so tiny that shoes keep simply sliding off, I wonder?'

I gave Sanderson an imploring look and he shrugged. Then we both arranged smiles on our faces. 'I en't used to such beautiful shoes, Cousin Judith.'

'*Am* not,' she chided. 'I *am not* used to such beautiful shoes.'

I gritted my teeth. 'Indeed. I am not. They pinch my feet and I wanted to feel the grass. Let me put them on again and I shall join you.'

Judith gasped, her pretty black eyes wide with horror – and a little delight, I thought suddenly. 'Your stockings too! Oh, Cousin, whatever would Mama say? Thank heavens she did not come to fetch you herself. In front of *Sanderson*! Oh! I don't know where to look!'

'I'm sure Sanderson's seen feet before,' I muttered. I sat on the grass, intending to pull my stockings on, then I realised I could not do so without lifting my skirts, something I felt sure would be even more horrifying.

'Of course he hasn't!' said Judith. 'Not a young lady's feet, anyway. For you are a young lady now, Cousin Florence! Ah, you see, I begin my gentle tutelage already.'

'Truly?' I frowned up at Sanderson.

'Truly,' he confirmed.

I gave up on the stockings, aware still of the mighty windows above us. I got to my feet again and slipped on my shoes, clutching my stockings in a ball in my fist.

'You had better find somewhere private to put those on,' said Judith. 'I'll go and tell Mama you'll be along in a minute otherwise she'll get impatient and come looking for us. Make haste, Cousin!'

She turned and hurried inside. As we followed, I looked up again. From this angle the sun was oblique and I could indeed see a face at the windows. But it was not my aunt or Annis.

'Sanderson!' I grabbed his arm and pointed. 'Who is that?' But she was gone.

'Who is who?'

'The beautiful young lady with the golden hair who was at breakfast this morning but nobody introduced her. You know who I mean, surely?'

'Of course I know who you mean, Florrie. That's Calantha.'

'Calantha?' It was another name entirely new to me.

'Yes.'

'But who *is* she? Is she a Grace? Why does everyone ignore her?'

'Oh, we don't ignore her, it's just that it's *awkward*. She's sort of a Grace, but not really. She's Grandfather's nephew's daughter . . . what does that make her to us? I can never work it out.'

'*Why* is it awkward? Quick, before Aunt Dinah comes and finds me without my stockings.'

'Oh, because it's so very sad. You see, the poor girl is insane. Utterly insane.'

Chapter Eleven

I shall never forget my second day at Helicon.

It began, as all days did and ever shall in that household, with breakfast. This was a simpler repast than the day before: boiled eggs and toast and numberless platters of breads bejewelled with nuts and fruits and I knew not what. Bread had always been such a simple affair at home. There was a great brick of butter, glistening and creamy, seated nobly atop a mountain of ice, and an array of preserves which looked magical and tempting but not one of which tasted as good as Old Rilla's elderflower jelly or plum jam.

There were also steaming pots of tea and coffee, a disappointment and a row.

The disappointment was that Calantha was not there. I had decided during the long, sleepless hours that when I saw her I would greet her in clear and friendly tones. I was so excited at the prospect of my daring that I quite slumped when I saw her empty seat at the table.

'Posture, dear!' sang Judith sweetly.

'Never mind that, Judith,' said my aunt in tongues of flame ('tis the only apt description). 'Can you explain to me, Florence Grace, what you were doing running around the garden in your nightgown in the middle of the night? What new disgraces have you dreamt up for us today, I wonder? What fresh humiliations are we to suffer at your hands?'

My fingers twitched. My hands held a silver butter knife and slices of bread bristling with cherries. I laid them on a sprigged china plate and turned to my aunt.

'What were you doing *watching* me in the middle of the night?' I asked, affronted and bewildered.

She dabbed at the corners of her mouth with her napkin as I had been taught to do yesterday then laid the napkin on her plate and stood up. She crossed the room in six easy strides (I always did admire her elegance) and slapped me hard across the cheek. The sound rang throughout the dining room. My eyes smarted and through the haze I saw Sanderson looking troubled, half rising. Our uncle, beside him, shifted in his seat.

'If you learned only one lesson yesterday, I might have thought it was not to answer back,' she seethed. 'If I want to watch you all the round of the clock's weary march, I shall do so. In point of fact, however, I have better things to do. I couldn't sleep last night. Small wonder, between your recalcitrance and the Sisyphean task ahead of improving you. It did not ease my mind when, looking out of the window, I saw you, *en déshabillé*, running about on the lawns! Now explain yourself at once and hear me when I say it shall not happen again! Go on, child, I am waiting.'

'I apologise, Aunt,' I muttered, though I longed to fling the butter in her face. I held myself very tall and still, like a cat. 'I could not sleep either. I be – *am* – accustomed to a great deal of fresh air and exercise. I understand that we have much to do during the daytime so I thought I would take a little air at night, when it would cause no trouble, nor delay. I did take my wrap, Aunt, I was quite decent. I only wanted to feel the grass under my feet and breathe the night air.'

'If you miss your heathen ways so very much, perhaps you had best go back to where you came from.'

'I would like that, Aunt, but I believe my grandfather will not allow it.'

She turned away from me in disgust. 'It's as though you're speaking a foreign language,' she said, returning to her rolls and coffee. 'Feel the grass? Breathe the air? I assure you everyone else in London gets by very well without such things and so must you. A respectable young lady of good family does not go barefoot! And yes, I know you removed your stockings in front of Sanderson yesterday.'

I looked at Judith in surprise and she coloured slightly. I imagined she had been pressed by her forceful mother into honesty and felt guilty about it. She was so pretty and slight and eager I could not resent her.

'You are a disgrace, Florence!' continued my relentless aunt. 'I know you are a country girl – I was prepared for cloddishness, ignorance – but I was not prepared for the wanton flouting of every decent stricture. You behave like a trollop. You are just like your mother.'

'My dear!' interrupted Irwin at last. 'A care, if you please! You speak of my dear sister.'

'Well, Irwin, but it's true. Elizabeth left her family because of her lust for a brutish peasant and this is the result of that union!'

And then I did fling the butter. And not only the butter, but the dish in which it sat, upon its dragon's nest of ice chips. My aim was true – the butter hit my aunt squarely in the chest with a most delightful sound. Ice chips rained around my relatives like falling stars and the glass bowl was so solid and chunky that it did not break but bowled along the dining table like a boulder sending forks and cups scattering. Two cups shattered. The bowl rolled off the end of the table and hit the ground with a loud clunk.

'How dare you speak of my parents that way?' I raged. 'My da was not brutish! He were a kind man, he were good. If *you* had found yourselves among *our* folk, struggling to learn *our* ways, he would never have been so grand and unwelcoming, he would have tried to *help* you! He were honest and clever and he didn't pretend to be something he weren't! You make me sick with your airs and graces! You turned your back on my mother!

You spurned my father without even knowing the man you scorned. You look down on *everyone* but you are no better, I tell you, you are *worse*! You are the very worst people I have ever known and I am *ashamed* to be one of you!'

My voice had risen throughout the length of this impressive discourse. By the end of it I was shouting and tears of fury were running down my face. I could feel myself shaking with the outpouring of pent-up tension.

'You little witch!' screamed Annis, who had ice in her hair and ice in her lap and ice – I deduced from her uncomfortable wriggling – in her collar. She leapt from her seat and *ran* at me – I had never thought she could move so fast. She seized and shook me, so I pushed her and she shrieked. She pulled my hair – hard – so I ripped hers loose from its coils and she shoved me so forcibly I fell . . . and then she was upon me, surprisingly strong for such a respectable young lady. But I had not yet turned into a drawing room flower and I threw her off in no time, giving her a hard slap for good measure.

At that point Sanderson and my uncle caught hold of us and pulled us apart, holding us until we subsided. Gradually we turned back from writhing, hissing vipers into young paragons of womanhood. Judith was screaming, so her mother slapped *her* and Irwin murmured, 'Ladies, ladies,' in placating tones as if there might yet be some way to make everything right.

'You see, Irwin,' said my aunt in a low, menacing voice.

'She is a danger to our family. She will tear us apart, you mark my words. She has been tainted and it can never be undone. No matter what polish or refinement we try to teach her, it will always be superficial. We must manage using the strictest possible measures.'

'Perhaps you are right my dear, only . . . do consider how she has been raised and she has been here but a day. This must all seem very difficult for her.'

'It is difficult for *me*! You cannot imagine the dumb resistance of her, questioning *every little thing* that is natural and right. It would try the patience of a saint, Irwin. Well, child, come with me. I shall lock you up for the rest of the day and perhaps that will teach you to appreciate the liberty of meals and comforts and walking from room to room.'

'Room to room?' I echoed faintly, thinking, *How is that liberty?* But then her words sank in. 'No, Aunt, please! I could not stand to be locked up!'

'Ah, you have her, Mother,' said Annis with a satisfied expression. 'Now we know her true fear. You will rule her now.'

I was speechless. How could people *think* like that, one about another?

'No truly, Aunt! I have come from a place where I have walked – *run* – for miles each day! I am already suffocating from . . . so much clothing, and sitting down all day and so much *food*! I am sorry, I am truly sorry for throwing the butter

138

and I won't do it again, only do not lock me up! Please! Please! I would die!'

It was the first time I had ever begged anyone for anything. It would be the last.

My aunt did not hesitate. She hauled me off to a small space leading off an attic room, little more in size than a closet, and lesser in height. Inside, there were two packing trunks, one stacked upon the other, and a small straw pallet which suggested that someone had slept in there at one time. There were no windows and, when I was locked in, it was totally dark.

A few moments later I heard the key in the door once more and my spirits were all flooded with relief. It was over. She had only meant to frighten me, to teach me a lesson. But I was to be released after all and I was so grateful.

'Oh, thank you, Aunt, thank you!' I was ready to fall upon her weeping and throw my arms about her when the door opened, mistaking my feelings and thinking perhaps, in that moment, that I loved her. But she had only come to thrust a jug of water and a chamber pot into my small prison.

The door was slammed shut, I was plunged into darkness once again and I heard the key turn. Her footsteps retreated. I was alone.

I lost myself entirely. I began screaming to be let out, pounding on the small door with my fists. I could not stand up under the low roof so I lay down and kicked and kicked at the door with all my strength but the wood seemed to have the solidity of a castle keep and I wore only Judith's delicate indoor shoes. I don't know how long it was before I gave up but I howled and screamed curses all the while. When I realised I was trapped indeed, I kicked at the chamber pot and I smashed at the wooden crates and generally effected as much wreckage as possible within that small space. I did myself no service. The closet – I cannot call it a room – was then not only dark and cramped, but littered with wooden splinters and shards which poked and cut me every time I moved. My hands were shredded from punching and pummelling. The chamber pot did not break but I hurt my foot on its solid china sides. And so eventually I lay down on the straw pallet, worn out from fury, and I cried in a way that I hadn't since I lost my father.

Then came regret. Incredulity. Why had I not *fought* her? I could easily have overcome her. Why, *why* had I not run?

I suppose I had not really believed she would carry out her threat. (If I learned only one thing that day, it was that my aunt could always be taken at her word.) I suppose I had thought someone would stop her. I suppose I had been *afraid* to run away, there in unfamiliar territory. I couldn't even have been sure of finding my way out of the house. And if I had, it was *London* beyond those doors, not Cornwall. What would I have done in a strange, barely glimpsed city? Where would I have gone?

*

Being in that closet was the physical equivalent of the emotional prison I had occupied when Da died: dark, lonely, comfortless, frightening. Minutes and hours passed and I wondered how long my aunt would consider sufficient. 'Til dinner time, surely, at worst. I hoped it would be less.

As time went on, I lost any ability to guess how long I had been there. I could hardly breathe, I could not fully stretch out. No food was brought, though that did not bother me unduly. There was no clue or marker by which to gauge the hour.

Great waves of fear welled up from inside me. It wasn't right for a human being to be so confined! That thought would not leave me alone, fluttering through me like a giant, blind moth. I could not let myself think of the moors, or remember how it had felt to wake at Braggenstones, to the sounds of a small village stirring: birdsong, doors banging, chickens clucking, rain pattering . . .

I began to suspect how Turlington might have been driven to one wrongdoing after another. And I understood why the lovely Calantha might have taken refuge in insanity. Everyone else in this godforsaken household seemed to get by either by conforming – even taking pleasure in the petty rules and mean constraints, like Annis and Judith – or else by being obedience incarnate, like Sanderson. It was in me to do neither of those things.

I would never be one of them. I hated them all – except

Sanderson. I loathed them utterly and so I promised myself that no matter what, I would *not* be a Grace, I would *never* be a Grace; that no matter what they said, I would always remain a Buckley.

I started screaming again, calling upon all the spirits who had ever loved me to range themselves into a mighty army to set me free. But here, in the great stone city, I was beyond their reach.

When Benson came to release me, she told me it was eight in the evening. Dinner was over. I crawled out of the closet and clung to her, unsteady on my legs. I had been in there nearly twelve hours.

'Come, Miss Florence, it is over now. Mrs Grace wishes to see you. She says you are to make your apologies and she says she will forgive you and resume your training.'

'*Forgive me?*' I roared, even though I had thought my voice all used up from screaming. I stumbled.

Benson steadied me. 'Best go along with it, Miss Florence, and do as they say. 'Tis best.' She caught my eye and tilted her head towards the dark space I had just left. Her meaning was clear: *Do you want to go back in there?*

I took her arm and nodded. I would say what I had to say. Whatever lay in store for me I would weather it and I would get by. As soon as I could, I would do better than get by; I would escape. I would go home. But just for now I would submit, and survive. It was only common sense. That was my firm intention.

My aunt, with Annis seated close by like an enigmatic black cat, was waiting for me in her sitting room. Judith was sitting in the corner, embroidering. All three looked exquisite. They reminded me of ferns: ferns always looked so plumy and inviting but were surprisingly coarse and tough to the touch. You could hurt yourself on ferns.

'Have you come to any sort of understanding, child?' asked my aunt coldly.

'Oh yes, Aunt, a great deal.'

'Tell me what.'

Oh, when I think back to all the things I could have said then. It was so obvious what she wanted to hear and it would have been so easy to say it. I honestly don't know what possessed me then; after all, I had already decided that I would play the game and get by. But instead, what I said was this:

'I understand that you be an evil woman with no heart. I understand that your daughters be vipers and your husband a spineless worm. I understand that I am not one of you and I will never be one of you and I am glad, glad, glad that I am not a Grace. I am a Buckley. I will always be a Buckley. I will never be a . . .'

Back in the attic room I went. Once again I didn't run; I was exhausted and confused. But as they dragged me there I remembered that Hawker Grace wanted me at Helicon. He must be away, else they could not treat me like this, I told myself. But he would return. I would not be locked up forever.

Chapter Twelve

I was there for over three days. My aunt refilled my water jug twice but said not a word to me. This time I did not cry out, I did not despair. I merely lay in the dark, waiting. I could feel the house pressing down around me.

Unable to sleep, and lonelier than I had ever been, I cast about in my mind for ways out of the situation. I told myself I would stay just long enough to acquire, somehow, some small amount of money and then immediately travel home. I would marry Stephen – or not; the only thing that mattered was to be back in the world that I knew. I would put aside foolish notions of adventure and education and fine dresses. For what mattered books, compared with freedom and the moors? What mattered wealth, compared with being the mistress of my own days?

And then I did think of Cornwall. In my imagination I returned to my beloved moors, my soul set free under a purple sky strewn with early stars. The smells of a late summer evening danced in my nostrils: warm earth and thick dry grass beneath my boots, gorse-laden air, a wash of faraway sea, the tang of cow dung drifting in from the farms. I could hear the rustle and drift of night creatures and, very faint, the domestic sounds of Braggenstones calling me home: a clank of a bucket, a sudden shout of laughter, the whinny of the weary pony. But, as always, I wasn't ready to go yet. I was running. I was at the great stone. I scrambled up and felt the old, lined surface hard beneath my hands and from up there I could see the sweep of my land: *my* village, *my* moors, and *my* farmhouse – which was how I always thought of Heron's Watch.

In my mind's eye I explored its grounds. The dense thicket of trees near the house – some oak, some elm, some birch – the pool and the silver stream that passed within ten feet of the front door. The swirls of long, unruly grass. I peered through dirty windows, at rooms all dark and disused, and before my wondering eyes they were transformed: swept, furnished, populated. I heard laughter and a piano. I heard a key rattling . . .

But that was not at Heron's Watch. That was here. But I was happy at the farmhouse. I did not want to come back. Where was I? I did not want to remember.

The key turned, the door opened. 'Florence?'

Who was Florence? I had forgotten that it was meant to be my name. I was Florrie Buckley again, and soon I would be drinking broth with Nan.

'Cousin Florence?' It was a girl's voice, whispering. A square of grey light appeared before me. It was immediately blocked by a head and shoulders peering in. 'Are you awake? It's Calantha. They don't know I'm here but I've brought you some grapes.'

I sat up, suddenly interested, and bumped my head.

'Would you like to come out for a few minutes?' she went on. 'You could take a turn about the attic. If you like, I'll open the window and you can lean out and breathe.'

I scrambled out in haste, afraid I was imagining this, or that someone would come and I would miss my chance. In the attic all was dark. Calantha held a white taper and the bobbing flame threw eerie swirls of dark and light about the place. It was night, then.

'How long have I been here?'

'This is the second night. I would have come before but the wind was blowing the wrong way. Never do anything risky when there's an easterly. Here, eat these.' She thrust a huge bunch of purple grapes into my hands and I smiled. It seemed an odd thing to bring, and yet strangely perfect, since hunger was still the least of my concerns and grapes were refreshing and sweet.

'Thank you.' I looked at the mad girl as I walked around and around the attic, relishing feeling my legs again. She was wearing a long white nightgown, with her blonde hair loose over her shoulders, and she looked more beautiful than ever. She stood on tiptoe and struggled with the catch of the window.

'Here, I can do it,' I said. I was taller. Calantha took the grapes again and I let in a rush of air. It was humid and heavy, but welcome nonetheless.

Calantha sat on the floor, leaning against the wall, and absent-mindedly started eating the grapes. I paced around and around, hungry for movement, but after a while I sat down opposite her. Pacing and getting to know someone did not go well together.

'Thank you,' I said again.

She nodded. Sanderson, she told me, was very upset at my treatment, but he believed I had been locked in my room and was being taken regular meals. She, on the other hand, because of her unusual role within the family, was often overlooked – thus she heard and saw a lot. 'This is a bad house,' she said. 'It has unhappy air.'

I snorted. 'I can tell that at a hundred paces.'

She cocked her head in a query.

'It's what we used to say at home, when someone said something we all could see. You know, like, "Looks like rain," when the sky was black and boiling.'

'I don't think it's going to rain,' she said seriously, 'but I'm glad you feel the air because I've told them so often and they don't believe me. They need this house, they want it so much, but it's bad for them. Bad for all of us.'

'Why is it so bad? Is it very old? Has it an unhappy past?'

'It's not so old. But it's the pinnacle of all their hopes, you see. It's modern, it's fashionable, it's expensive . . .' She popped another grape in her mouth and I wondered if there would be any left for me, not that I minded. 'It's their symbol of all that they are and want to be. But they are its slaves.'

'How did you come to live here? Sanderson said you're my grandfather's nephew's . . . something.'

'I suppose so. My father died and my mother left. Hawker took me in. You know, he's doing that now. Gathering in the lost sheep. Any odd fragment of a Grace comes to light and he'll collect them in. I've been here a long time now. I'm eighteen, you know.'

Like Turlington, she seemed younger. Was it something about being a Grace? Perhaps if you couldn't grow up the way you wanted to, you didn't grow up at all.

'They call me Calantha Grace, but really I'm a Robinson.'

'I'm a Buckley.'

She smiled, and reached forward suddenly to shake my hand. 'Nice to meet you, Buckley.'

'Calantha's a very pretty name. I've never heard it before.'

'It's Greek. It means beautiful blossom.'

'It's perfect for you then. I wish I looked like you.'

'Oh no, don't wish for that. It's too hard.'

I couldn't ask what I wanted to, which was if she was really mad, so I asked, 'Where is your mother?'

Her lovely face clouded and for a moment I cursed my damnable curiosity. 'I don't know. After Father died there was no one to make her stay and take care of me so she left. I was on my own a while . . .' She cast her eyes up to the rafters as though counting. 'Two weeks, or six months. Then I came here.'

I was horrified, but I couldn't stop myself. 'Why did your mother leave you?'

She shrugged. 'She thought I was mad. I kept embarrassing her. Saying strange things at the wrong moments.'

I snorted again. 'Then they'll think *I'm* mad, soon enough. That's all I've done since I got here!'

'Yes, but you're from the country. I don't have that excuse.'

'Do *you* think you're mad?'

'I think *they're* all mad. But the doctor said that thinking everyone else is mad is a sign of madness.'

I made a face. 'Well, I think they're all mad too.'

'I'm glad. And I'm glad you can feel the sad air. Don't let them know, though. They won't like it. And you have trouble enough.'

'I won't.'

'I should go. It wouldn't do to be caught. I hate to lock you up, Cousin, but Dinah Grace is a cruel woman. I'm afraid of her. Everyone's afraid of her except Hawker. But she's afraid of him.'

I shook my head in wonder. 'Surely all of London can't be like this? I thought it was city folk, but now I think it's just the Graces.'

'It's a curse to be a Grace,' she said, picking the last grape off the bunch. Then she spread her hands wide. 'But I don't know what to do about it.'

'No more do I.'

I wanted to cry as I returned to the closet. Calantha threw the grape stalks out of the window. 'Now they'll never know!' she beamed. 'I'll bring you some more tomorrow night and we can talk again. Unless the wind's in the east, because if it is, I'll have to stay in my room, or it's not safe.'

I caught her hand as she was about to shut the door. 'Can't I just run away? I could leave tonight! You could come with me!'

She looked as if she were considering it and my heart drummed, not knowing quite what I hoped her answer would be.

'I want to,' she said, 'therefore it must be wrong. That's what I have learned. That you must never do what you want and always do what you don't want. And if you go, they'll know someone let you out, and they'll guess it was me.'

I looked at her pale, lovely face and sighed. 'I'll stay a while more. Then we'll see.'

She nodded and closed the door. 'I'm sorry,' she said as she turned the key.

True to her word, Calantha returned the following night. At least, I assume it was the following night. I had passed the intervening hours in the same sort of sleepless daze and spent as much time as I could away in Cornwall. By the time I heard her voice again, it might have been hours or days. I remembered Calantha saying she had been alone for *two weeks, or six months*, and felt a real chill of fear that life at Helicon would destroy my own sanity. I crawled out and our odd little interview proceeded along similar lines to the previous. I gulped down the night air and tried to imitate her nice way of speaking while she sat in a pool of moonlight and nibbled away at the orange and piece of chocolate she had brought for me. Then we took our leave and she shut me up again.

Chapter Thirteen

I was released the following day. Benson was sent for me again and could hardly look me in the eye. 'Nearly *four* days, miss,' she muttered, and shook her head as though ashamed of her own complicity.

'Benson, there was nothing you could have done. I see how it is here. Don't worry, I have survived.' And it was true. I had.

I went before my aunt and this time I said what was expected of me. I did not mean a word of it, and I think she knew it. But what could she do? Pleasurable though it might be to keep me locked up, it was not advancing her quest — that of transforming me into a Grace. Time was slipping away and I was still a *dis*-Grace.

So the days continued in the vein of the first. Lessons, scoldings and rules. I was taught the minutiae of a young lady's toilet and dress. Fashion, it seemed, was every bit as important — perhaps *more* important — than respectability.

I was not yet sufficiently fashionable to be seen, however.

I now wore my own clothes, not Judith's cast-offs, thanks to a discreet dressmaker who came to the house and took my measurements, returning days later with armloads of gowns. But my manners and speech still did not pass muster. While my aunt and cousins absented themselves each afternoon for the fashionable three o'clock parade in Hyde Park, I was provided with fat books and endless magazines and told to study.

I had dreamt that my new life would include an education, but this was not what I had been imagining. These venerable tomes were written by such interesting authors as 'A Lady' and explained how to do everything from greeting a person of higher rank to greeting a person of lesser rank, to distinguishing which of the two a person might be, should any confusion exist. They expounded (with helpful sketches) upon the different forks, spoons and so on that might be found at any given meal and in what order they should be used.

I would not be allowed to receive or pay visits for a very long time. However, I learned that when this hallowed day came, I should pay between three and six such calls in a day, and never before that oh-so-fashionable hour of three o'clock. I learned that on departing my hypothetical hostess's home, I should leave two of my (equally fictitious) husband's cards on the hall table but not the drawing room table and *certainly* not in the card basket. (In which case, why *have* a card basket, I wondered?) And if *I* were the gracious hostess, I should never offer my caller a choice of seat (which seemed rather *un*gracious to me) but should direct them with a graceful wave of my hand.

Quick as my brain was, it could not digest such tiny and pointless details in such quantities. It was also theoretical since I had no opportunity to practise. I said as much to my aunt, in defence of my apparently dull intelligence, and it was the first observation of mine that she ever heeded. She then staged a series of 'visits' in which my cousins and I took it in turns to offer and accept tea and practise small talk. Sanderson was commandeered to pose variously as a family friend, a distant but desirable acquaintance and an unwelcome visitor, that I might demonstrate the correct protocol in each of these circumstances. He was eternally obliging and never joined in the criticism and scoffing I received from Annis and her mother. Judith was softer in her guidance, but perpetually flanked by her mother and sister as she was, I could never be quite sure whether I could count her as a friend. She was in awe of them, I soon realised, if not a little frightened; she survived by emulating and pleasing – and she was much better at it than I was.

My diction, of course, came in for a rigorous overhaul and I was made to repeat almost everything I said four or five times for that first month. I had to say 'you' instead of ''ee' and 'those who' instead of 'them as' and 'I am' instead of 'I be'. I was trained to curb my slanting vowels and rolling 'r's, though they were not so easily vanquished. Most of what I said, I learned, was better not said at all. They were exhausting days.

I could go on. But for the love of all things rational I shall not. It was during one such morning of educational play-acting that my grandfather returned. I heard the front door slam, and loud voices in the hall.

Aunt Dinah and Annis looked at each other. 'Hawker is back.'

My 'lesson' was suspended. We all sat like statues while the cacophony in the hall raged and then died down. Booted footsteps passed outside our very door but no one moved to greet him.

'He does not like to be disturbed immediately upon his arrival,' Judith explained, leaning towards me. Her excessive love of talking about people did occasionally have the happy effect of answering one of my unvoiced questions.

The others were listening with heads cocked. I risked whispering, 'Then when . . . ?'

She shrugged her pretty shoulders. A far-off door banged and I flinched but my relatives relaxed a little.

'Enough for today,' said Aunt Dinah, rising and gathering her things. 'I shall go and see Mrs Clemm. Girls, occupy your-selves. Florence, go to your room and ask Benson to change your dress for the blue poplin. Then stay there and read something improving. Or, if you wish to read in the garden, you may, but keep your shoes and clothing *on*, if you please. Do *not* sit on the ground. On the bench. And walk properly, as we have shown you.'

I was so astonished to be granted this permission that I just nodded, not even minding the barrage of instructions. We all left in a flurry and I rushed to change.

I would never have thought that Florrie Buckley could consider sitting in a walled square of manicured garden, trussed to the hilt in finery, an act of freedom. It had only been a week but already I had almost forgotten how it felt to have salty wind blowing in my hair.

When I was called for luncheon I did my very best to behave properly. My grandfather did not join us at the table. But as the meal drew to an end, a maid came and spoke to my aunt. 'Mr Hawker wishes to meet Miss Florence, if you please, ma'am.'

My aunt rose immediately. 'Very well. Florence, come with me. Try to remember all you have learned since you came here. Do not speak unless spoken to and allow me to—'

'If you please, ma'am.'

The maid spoke quietly but the very fact of an interruption infuriated Aunt Dinah. She glared at the wretched girl. 'What is it, Casey?'

'Begging pardon, ma'am, Mr Hawker said he was to see Miss Florence alone.'

'*Did* he now?' snapped the lady of the house.

'Yes, ma'am. He was most . . . clear about it.'

My aunt looked as though she could have torn up the carpet. Then she collected herself, visibly swallowing words, and sighed.

'Very well. Florence, go with her. Casey, I don't wish to see you for the rest of today. If you should see me coming, please remove yourself.'

'Yes, ma'am. Please come with me, miss.'

I left the room, inwardly full of glee. How wonderful to see her thwarted.

My grandfather received me in his study. It seemed everyone in this house had their own bedroom and sitting room or study. I'm surprised they could bother to take meals together. This was a vast room, which made Aunt Dinah's sitting room appear a mere trinket box compared with a packing trunk. His desk was like a mountain plateau, his bookshelves reached the ceiling, his furniture might have been the oversized, opulent choice of a gentleman giant . . . but the man himself was not large. In fact, he was minute.

He perched on a pointed oaken throne like a wicked child. He had the appropriate amount of hair for his age, which was to say very little of it, but more than some. It was soft and silver-grey and neatly combed. His ears stuck out a little from his head and he had big, round blue eyes with a chill in them. Despite a sweet smile, I knew at once he was not a man to be taken at face value. I looked at him and thought, *He is full of hate*. I understood why everyone feared him.

'Well, come here, girl,' said this *pisky*, beckoning vigorously. He had a surprisingly deep and resonant voice. I could imagine he would make a splendid singer, though I could not imagine him taking joy in music, perhaps only in his own ability. I walked across the room and he continued beckoning until my skirts were touching his desk and then he leaned forward, scrutinising me as though assessing whether I were a forgery or not.

'Ah, yes, yes,' he said at last. 'It's Florence, then, is it?'

'Yes, Grandfather.'

'Oh! Don't call me that. Call me Hawker. Everyone does.'

When they're not calling you Lucifer, I thought. 'Yes, Hawker.'

'You have the look of your mother about you. It's not obvious, mind you. You don't have her colouring or her features *or* her beauty and yet . . .' He paused, looking almost soft for a moment.

'You were my mother's father,' I murmured, wonderingly. It seemed so very incredible. Whether or not either of us could feel it, this close bond between us existed.

'Well, I'm aware of that, girl! Don't you think I'd remember something like that! Now then, how have they been treating you?'

I opened my mouth then stopped. Closed it again. Did he want the truth? I thought of the strange, unspoken alliances and contracts between the members of this family that I sensed, but could not define or understand; I wondered who was in alliance with Hawker, if anyone, and whether I should be more afraid of him than all the rest. It seemed my thinking was answer enough.

'That's how it is then.'

I nodded. 'That is how it is, Grand . . . Hawker.'

He chuckled, like a gleeful imp. 'Grand-Hawker! I like that! I think everybody should call me that. Suitably deferent, is it not? I suppose that makes you my Grand-Florence!' He chuckled some more and I felt confused. This was apparently the devil incarnate, yet he appeared to be taking a liking to me.

'Nevertheless, Grand-Florence, let us verify that we mean the same thing by "that's how it is". Unspoken understandings more often than not prove to be erroneous in my experience. All too often I have thought myself in fine sympathy with someone only to discover that we have had each other wrong all along. That is why I like to check each and every fact and each and every impression. My daughter-in-law is a hard task-mistress and uses you abominably ill, is that so?'

Was this a trap? 'I do not mind hard work, Gra— Hawker. I am used to working hard. I am very *good* at working hard. Only . . .'

'Don't think I don't notice you avoiding my question and trying to lead me astray! It won't work because I have a brain like a perfectly run counting house. Every fact, every figure, every query, every coin is stored in its place and never lost. We shall return to it directly. But you interest me. Only what?'

'Only I am used to working hard at things that either interest me or be – *are* – necessary. There is much to learn here. I love to learn, only . . .' He was still watching me intently. 'Forks and spoons, sir? The brightness of a smile? The correct amount of pleasure to be conveyed in a glance . . .' I gave up trying to express it.

'You think it trivial and meaningless. And what else?'

'Dull, sir, very dull.'

'Where did *sir* come from? Call me Hawker, I tell you. Grand-Hawker if it pleases you. At what did you work so hard at before? What do you find to be *not* dull?'

'In Braggenstones, sir— Hawk— Grand-Hawker, that be – *is* – where I be – *come* – from, I worked very hard in the fields. We had little; it was work enough to make it go round. It did not interest me overmuch, but it was necessary to keep us alive. As for what I be – *am* – interested in, I had two teachers in Braggenstones. One was a schoolteacher and she were kind enough to teach me reading and writing and geography and the old myths and such, and poetry.'

'The other teacher?'

'She were a wise woman, s— Grand-Hawker. A charmer, we call 'em in the country. She knew the qualities of plants to heal and nourish and she taught me. And she could . . . well, she could do a great deal else besides.' I remembered what

Calantha had said, and thought it best not to start talking of Old Rilla's spells and potions.

'In the country, is it the usual thing for an old woman such as that to take a pupil?'

'I were – *was* – the only one.'

'Why did she teach you then?'

'I don't rightly know, s— Hawker.' My efforts not to call him sir (for he seemed more of a presence and less of an imp all the time) was interfering with my ability to concentrate on my speech. 'She saved my life when I were – *was* – but eight, after my da died. Perhaps she felt kindly towards me.'

'Presumably she saved a great many children's lives, or she wouldn't have made much of a healer. Why else?'

I bit my lip. 'It may be Old Rilla saw something in me. Some gift perhaps. Or maybe she was old and wanted someone to pass on her learning to and only I was there.'

'Gift? What kind of gift?'

I was growing exhausted. The man had told true: he was relentless in his pursuit of facts, like a hound on a scent.

'I could do some things, sir— Hawker! God damn me, why do I keep calling you that? Damn and blast it all to hell.' I was horrified. I had cursed a number of times in front of my aunt and cousins, inflicting various punishments upon myself including slaps, extra hours of study or sharply chiselled derision, but this was different. I held my breath.

He guffawed. 'Well! I can see why Dinah says she has her

hands full with you! You've used that language with her, I suppose? You must have had your fine cousins in a faint! She says you're a demon in a dress, a hissing, scratching she-cat!'

'They call you Lucifer!' *Oh God*. Again, my mouth. It may be my very worst enemy in all the world.

'Oh, I know that! Believe me, girl, if it didn't suit me for them to think it, I should not allow it.'

'Can you control people's thoughts then? What they say when you are not with them?'

'Naturally I can. Now tell me, what can you do?'

'Can you promise you won't say this to the others? Please? They do not like me and I do not think this will help.'

He nodded.

'I see spirits, Grand-Hawker. I can usually tell what people are thinking and feeling, though it has been much harder since coming here. Sometimes I know what's to happen afore it do – *does*. And I never get lost. At least, I never got lost on the moors. I don't think I would have that gift in London for it all looks the same and there is no sky.' I waited for him to scoff or look at me with disgust or disbelief. But he merely nodded again, collecting facts.

'So you are a *special* girl!'

I felt tears come unwelcome to my eyes. 'Oh, that is what my nan used to call me.'

'Hmm, well she is gone now, and you are here.'

I could not dispute it.

'Very well, let us return to my question after a long and circuitous digression, little witch. My daughter-in-law misuses you harshly, does she not?'

'Yes, Grand-Hawker, I feel she has been most cruel to me.'

'In what particulars?'

'She says many unkind things and makes her hatred of me clear. She slaps and mocks me. She has locked me up for days on end in a tiny attic room and she does not let me go outside. She will not let me take my shoes off.'

'Ah. Well, staying indoors and wearing shoes is what young ladies do, Grand-Florence.'

'So my aunt tells me.'

'She is right. In that, at least. So I suppose you are very unhappy and wish you had never come to us?'

'Yes. I am sorry if that sounds ungrateful to you, but if I could return to Cornwall today, I would.'

'Yet you cannot. That is certain. Let me tell you something of myself. Blood is more important to me than anything. The Graces were once great, very great, but as the decades have passed we have declined, both in number and status. And, I sometimes think, in quality. That nasty, skinny, weasel of a granddaughter of mine, for instance. What kind of a Grace is *that*?'

'I dislike my cousin Annis too. She seems an unnatural sort of girl to me – no compassion or gentleness. I never met such a girl before.'

'Annis? Oh, I don't mind her. I speak of Judith. A sorrier human being I doubt there ever was. Unformed. Weak. Anyway, blood matters. In whatsoever time is left to me I plan to rebuild the Grace family, and restore it to its former state. You are part of that, so you cannot leave. It will be my legacy to the world when I die.'

'To the *world*?' I smiled, wondering how bereft the world at large would be if the Grace clan were to vanish entirely.

All trace of smile and warmth vanished, as suddenly as the sun disappearing behind thick cloud. 'Yes, to the world,' he snapped. 'Do not make the mistake of underestimating this family, Florence. *Your* family. It heats my blood to think of who we were and what we have lost. I want to make you understand, Florence. Part of your becoming a Grace will be to learn about your heritage. And with your love of stories, your fine sensitivity, I have hopes for you. So I will teach you our family tree myself. I will make you proud to be a Grace if it kills me.'

I shall never be proud to belong to such a cold, quarrelling, inhuman family as this, I thought, but still his blue eyes were fixed on me, making me uncomfortable. I curtseyed.

'Be off with you then, girl. We shall meet tomorrow and I shall tell you some tales. I shall not interfere with Dinah, you know. She must discipline you as she sees fit. But I shall make sure you begin receiving a formal education at once, not only a social one. And you will start to go out and about sooner than

Dinah decrees. I should not wonder if you go mad with boredom stuck in here all the time. I cannot promise the society will be to your taste, but at least it will be variety for you. Now go. Back to your aunt.'

'Thank you, Grand-Hawker.' I curtseyed again and made to leave but as I reached the door he called after me.

'I will make you love me, Florence. I will make you love your family. You are a Grace now, forever and ever.'

I curtseyed again, held my tongue, and thought inwardly, *I never will.*

Chapter Fourteen

That night I slept but little, as usual. I still could not get comfortable without Nan snoring softly next to me. Somewhere in the middle of the night I gave up. I no longer dared go outside but I had pulled a chair close to the window and formed a habit of sitting there, holding my orange stone, until I fell into some sort of comforting reverie. I must have been staring into the dark and disconcerting night for an hour or more when I heard a sudden noise. I tensed.

From the other side of the house, which faced the street, one heard nothing *but* noises, both sudden and continuous. I had never known such a din as was London: shouting and wheels rattling and building and banging and trains leaving and babies crying. In those days I did not even know what half those noises were. It seemed that London was in a continuous process of being razed and reconstructed, rather like my life.

But on this side, overlooking the garden, it was usually

quiet; the strongly built house muffled the roar. And this was a noise rather different. Out of place and very near. A clatter. Then a horse whinnying and a man's voice, loud, then suddenly silenced. I was on my feet, staring intently into the night. I could see nothing. When a small, soft light flared in the stable block, I reached for my shawl without even knowing I had done it. I was poised on my toes, ready for flight.

Then I saw a man's shadowy figure in the garden. If he was running away, he was doing a poor job of it; he was moving towards the house, not away from it. I watched until my forehead bumped the windowpane and I could lean forward no further. The figure had run directly underneath my window. I held my breath for a moment and then . . . I heard the door. Muffled swearing. A thump. And silence. The intruder had come into the house!

I threw my shawl around my shoulders, set down my stone on the windowsill and grabbed a candlestick. Silently I opened my door and ran barefoot along the corridor. I climbed down one set of stairs, oh so slowly.

I was about to start my way down the next when I thought I heard murmuring voices. Were there *two* of them? Then I heard one set of footsteps on the stairs. Was the accomplice keeping watch in the hall? Silently I ran back up to the landing and crouched behind a large chest in the corridor.

Peering through the banisters, I saw the dining room door opening below me. I knew that a great deal of valuable art was on display there. There were also silver candlesticks and rare china and a considerable number of those useless trinkets that the wealthy appeared to love. I waited. And waited. It seemed the thief was in no hurry to complete his mission. I wondered what to do. Wake Aunt Dinah? Hawker? But the thought of visiting either of these personages in their bedchambers was a sheer impossibility. I could raise the alarm, but it would alert the intruders too and they would be gone; I had seen how long it took people in this place to get up.

While I debated I saw a faint glow appear around the top of the door, as if a lamp or fire had been lit. And was that the sound of a fork, scraping on a plate? Had the thief paused for a light repast? I frowned. I slid back down the stairs, one by silent one, keeping a sharp eye for the companion below. But I saw no one. I clutched my candlestick more tightly and inched my face and one foot around the doorway.

I saw a man with his back to me, seated before a small fire, warming his hands and bent towards the flames. A decanter of port and a bowl of stew sat on the table next to him and a hunk of bread beside them. As I watched, the man took a great slurp of the stew, dropped the spoon back and returned to brooding over the flames. The paintings, silverware, china and trinkets all appeared to be in place. A suspicion came upon me.

I pushed open the door a little further. I stepped into the room. Making sure there was nothing blocking my escape should I need to run, I spoke, my voice startling in the night's silence.

'Either you be a very poor thief or you be my prodigal cousin Turlington,' I said, the high adventure bringing out my old way of speaking.

The man jumped as though he had been shot. He leapt from his chair and spun round so fast he nearly fell in the fire. A glass of port in his hand spilled on his trousers and he swallowed the rest in haste. I knew him at once. A shock of black hair like a crow's wing still fell across his pale face and he wore the same confused, defiant expression I remembered from the Beresfords' stables in Truro. He was still slender, but more manly now, and very tall. He stared at me as though I were a ghost. I became creepingly aware of my loose, wild hair, my bare feet, my shawl all askew and the fact that I was brandishing a candlestick. This I lowered. There wasn't much I could do about the rest.

'You must be my cousin Florence.' Understanding cleared the clouds from his face and he smiled. And what a brilliant smile it was; it wrought him into some entirely other being. 'We have met before, have we not, long ago now? Although, it was Florrie I had the pleasure of meeting then, was it not? Florrie Buckley? What a strange twist of fate that we should be *cousins*.' His mouth twisted wryly.

I felt something crackle between us. My old ability to read a stranger in a few words spoke to me. *Kindred*, it

whispered, though I was unsure what that word meant. *Broken.*
Lonely.

I hesitated for a moment, feeling the weight of those words,
then stepped forward to shake his hand and matched him smile
for smile. 'Aye, Cousin Turlington. 'Tis me. Florrie Buckley.
Or Florence Grace, as I must now be known.'

'And don't you look charmed about that? Come here, Florrie Buckley, let me see you.' He gently disarmed me, setting
the candlestick down on the table, and took both my hands to
stare into my face. 'Yes! There you are. Just as I had remembered you, except *even* more beautiful. A wild thing among us.
You poor, poor girl. But they will not best you, I think. Oh,
welcome, Cousin Florence, if it is not too late and too thin to say
as much.' And he picked me up and swung me round so that
my bare feet left the ground and bobbed through the air. Then
he pulled me close into a hug.

I yielded to it as though slaking a thirst, yet the definition of
humanity is perhaps 'never satisfied' for as soon as one need
was met, it set up another in me: to melt into his arms and stay
there forever. Unaccustomed feelings, at fifteen.

It is the relief of friendship after a hard, lonely week, I told myself
as his arms tightened around me. *This is what kinship should feel*
like, only the others are so strange and cold. This I told myself in
order to allow myself to stay there another minute and another,
even though it did not feel like kinship and it was improper and
it was the middle of the night and he was my cousin.

We released each other at last, but hung onto each other's hands, grinning like children. 'At last, a kindred spirit in Helicon,' he said, shaking his head and smiling. 'Come! Sit!' He pulled a second chair up to the fire.

A tremor gripped me. He had used that word, *kindred*. It felt like a word of power, something from a myth. My instinct was not wrong. Then I grimaced.

'If my aunt should find me like this, dressed as I am and out of bed in the middle of the night, with you – or, in truth, without you – she will have me locked up in that tiny hole in the attic for God knows how long. Months most probably.'

His eyes twinkled. 'You mean *un*dressed as you are? Shameless and appalling?'

'That's what she said last time.'

He looked truly saddened. 'What is the woman thinking?' he murmured so softly I could hardly hear him. 'What a despicable mind she has. You're naught but a child.'

I wasn't sure I cared to be considered a child, but before I could object he resumed his sparkling manner. 'You mean you make a regular habit of entertaining young men in the middle of the night?'

'Oh no, last time I only went into the garden to take the air – alone – and apparently *that* was enough to bring the entire clan to its knees!'

'I'm quite sure it was. So then, what are our options, Florrie? You can stay as you are, and risk a flogging. We can go to your room and talk there, but then you risk being burned at the stake, for I am a man, as you perceive, and if I were discovered in your impregnable fortress, all would be lost. What else?'

'I could go and dress, boots, bonnets and all, and then, when I am dressed in seven-and-forty layers I might be fit to return here and have a little conversation with you . . .' I laughed aloud at the ridiculousness of it. It was good to find someone else at last who also found it ridiculous.

'I'll tell you what, Florrie. If you will stay and keep me company, dressed as you are *or* in seven-and-forty layers, whatever you see fit, I will undertake to save you from imprisonment should we be discovered. I will offer my life in exchange for yours if necessary. Trust me, Aunt Dinah will not want another quarrel with me – we have plenty. And if we are *not* discovered, think what a delicious secret it shall be.'

So I climbed into the chair on the other side of the fire. With my legs drawn up beneath me and my shawl wrapped snug about me and the flickering light, I was as comfortable as I had ever been in that house.

I could not help but like Turlington Grace, if only because nobody else seemed to, besides Sanderson. Like him, I was set outside the mould; not only here but in Cornwall too I had been different. He expressed himself physically, like me, with ready embraces and smiles and frowns that chased each other swiftly, like clouds on a windy day. He was sensitive like me – I could see it in his fine features and troubled eyes. One way or another there was no doubt that his return was the most interesting thing that had happened in Helicon since I had arrived. And it was twice now that he had held me and twice that I had had that strange feeling: warm, sharp and unsettling.

He refilled his glass with port and returned to his seat. I watched him while he ate. In truth I could not take my eyes from him. He ate and drank and gazed at the flames with an intensity I had never seen. Occasionally he threw me a smile as though checking I was still there. It was a smile full of sadness, relief and comradeship. There was even a dash of gratitude in there, as though I were doing him some great service just by being at his side. This reminded me of home, where I had been so prized by Nan, by Lacey, by Old Rilla. It was good to feel appreciated again; it felt as though things had tilted back to their right order for the while. His hair was long over his shoulders; the wing at the front perpetually fell in his face and he swiped at it repeatedly and pointlessly. His eyes were dark and reflected the firelight. His long frame was hunched as I remembered it, yet there was a strange beauty and even elegance to him; if I had known then of such a thing as a gir-affe, I might have made the comparison. At one point he passed the heel of bread to me without a word and, also wordlessly, I tore off a piece and passed it back.

'This is fine, is it not, Florrie?' he asked, drinking back the dregs of his stew from the bowl and wiping his mouth with the back of his hand. I agreed that it was very fine.

'It's rare I come back to congenial company. In fact, I try not to come back here at all if I can help it.'

'Why are you here now?'

'Well, I had to meet my wild cousin again, did I not? I had to see that you were managing acceptably here. Are you, Florrie?'

'You came back to see me?' I said unbelievingly. 'How did you know I was here?'

'Sanderson wrote to me.'

'And that is why you came back?'

'Yes! *And* because I ran out of money and hunger is no man's friend. But that is not so poetic as a long-lost cousin. But tell me, Florrie, are you?'

'Am I what?'

'Happy here.'

'No. I believe I can be honest with you, Cousin Turlington. I'm very unhappy and there is no one here but Sanderson whom I can count as a friend. Everything is strange to me. There is too much food and not enough air. I cannot understand the people or the customs, or the values I am to adopt as my own. I believe I will never feel like a Grace, nor do I wish to. What do you think of that, Cousin?'

'I am not a bit surprised. We have transplanted you from one life to another – you are a creature from Faerieland dashed down to earth. You are a wild pony dragged from the moors and made to walk to the bit. You are a dash of moonlight, captured against the laws of nature. They have done you a cruelty, Florrie Buckley, but I'll wager they're demanding that you thank them.'

Oh, the relief I felt. I had started to think I would go mad for want of a single soul truly sympathetic to my plight, and now I knew myself again: I had a kindred spirit, no less! What a gift he had given me with those few words. And I was not averse to hearing myself described as a dash of moonlight.

I remembered my suspicion when I was locked in the attic that we suffered from the same thing, he and I, and took the chance to ask him about it. 'I have heard that you behave very badly indeed, Cousin Turlington. Do they drive you to it, with their pettiness and their insufferable cruelty? Is it . . . the only way to be one of them yet *not* be like them?'

A look crossed his face, so dark that I feared I had already lost his goodwill. But it was not directed at me. *There are bad memories deep inside him*, I thought. But his face cleared; I could already see that he was very good at rousing himself from sadness. I suspected he was equally adept at finding his way back into it.

'Why do I behave as I do? Why, Florrie, I'm not sure. Does any of us ever know our own reasons? Have you ever had a fever, Florrie, a delirium? Yes? Well, that is what it is like to be me. That heat and surging are in my blood all the time; they do not abate, it is my nature. And indeed you already know that any deviation from the fold is very sternly viewed here. There is no attempt at understanding, at sympathy, only the necessity to fit the pattern, to become just like them. And I can't.'

I knew exactly what he meant.

'The trouble is,' he continued, 'the worst of it is that I end up hurting people, which is exactly what *they* do – the thing I despise the most! I don't mean to, I just can't help myself. I see an opportunity to hurt *them*, to kick out at everything they stand for and it feels so delicious and delirious to do it . . . but I don't see the consequences until it is too late. I am not surprised they cannot love me.'

'Sanderson loves you.'

'Oh yes, Sanderson does, he is the best of brothers. But he cannot understand me, you see, for our natures are so very different. I think perhaps you understand me, though, Florrie. You know what it is to want to be free, do you not?'

I nodded slowly, remembering with bittersweet sharpness the tang of the early morning air over the moors, long grasses bending under my bare feet, horizons silver and bright. I started to tell him of my moors then, to describe the tiny purple heather bells and the sudden blue and brown pools that waited in the wilds. I glanced up at him from time to time to see if he was bored, this fine, restless gentleman, by my talk of the country, but he listened closely, never taking his eyes off my face.

'I wish I had a place like that,' he said. 'When I was in Madeira I felt something of the sort. You should see the island, Florrie, it is beautiful.' He spoke to me then of peacock-blue skies and rearing cliffs, of floating, white-sailed ships, tiered farmlands and sugar cane in rows. It was like listening to Lacey reading poetry; I could have stayed there all night.

'Are you just now come from Madeira?' I asked when he ran out of description.

His face clouded again. I could not help comparing him over and over again with the Cornish weather. He was every bit as changeable and fey.

'Not just now. It is a magical place, Florrie, a true enchanted isle, yet without a twin soul to share it with it is as lonely as the vilest of slums. To whit, that is exactly where I stay when the loneliness overcomes me. Now I am back in London but unwelcome at Helicon so I am residing in a nasty little apartment in the Devil's Acre.'

'The Devil's Acre?' I shivered at the name.

'A place you are too good ever to see, Cousin. It is the opposite of Helicon in every particular. There is no luxury, no ostentation, no fine dining, there are no Graces!'

'But there is freedom, of a sort?' I guessed.

'You see, I was right. You do understand me.'

We talked, my cousin Turlington and I, until almost six in the morning when the servants came to lay out the breakfast rolls and prepare the grates. Only then did I slip back to my bed to lie for a short time, my head whirling, before readying myself to go to breakfast and pretend to meet Turlington for the very first time.

Chapter Fifteen

'You look more than usually stupid this morning, Cousin Florence,' said Annis as I poured water into my coffee cup. 'Bad dreams, I hope? That is, I mean, I hope you did *not* have any?'

'Oh, careful, dear Annis,' said Turlington, reaching across the table as if to remove something from her face. She sat frozen with horror. 'You have a little . . . Wait, I don't want you to cut yourself, it's so nasty and sharp . . . Oh no, 'tis only your tongue, dear, carry on.'

The breakfast room was as full as I had ever seen it. Only Irwin was absent, for he worked long hours at his bank and rarely joined us for breakfast on weekdays. Hawker was present. Turlington was returned. And Calantha was there too, making a total of eight Graces around the table. Surely the world could have need of no more, whatever Hawker might have thought?

For once I found no difficulty in keeping quiet. I was tired, and afraid of revealing that Turlington and I had met before. And I was fascinated, almost frightened, by the complex currents and cross-currents that flowed between the various members of the family.

My aunt was a furious, frozen statue. Her hatred of Turlington was evident, yet she said not one word to check or criticise him. Curtailment and criticism being two of her greatest accomplishments, I could only assume that the presence of Hawker was in turn checking *her*. She was accordingly sharp with both her daughters, presumably needing to vent her frustration on someone.

They were more intensely themselves than ever, that is to say Annis was beautiful and cold, and Judith resembled a high-pitched parakeet flapping and squawking in an attempt to divert everyone. (A parakeet was a bird that I had encountered only two days ago – Judith had three of the noisy little flying emeralds: Pettigrew, Patterson and Porridge.)

Hawker was in high spirits. The heir apparent was back and had made many promises before breakfast. Hawker was confident that he had at last pummelled him into a reformation.

Calantha glowed. Turlington teased her like a big brother and did not tiptoe around her existence as everyone else did. I liked him for that, too.

As for Sanderson, I had never seen a man so emotional. His brother was home and he could hardly speak for the joy of it. Yet his joy was threaded through with fear; every time Turlington said something controversial, which was often, he darted nervous glances at Hawker and Dinah.

This is not the first happy reunion he has seen, I understood suddenly. *He is waiting for the abrupt end.*

Nevertheless, a week passed, and another and another, and my life at Helicon was transformed for having Turlington there. He had none of Sanderson's compunctions about keeping life smooth, considering Dinah's wishes or following the rules. He would snatch me from my studies in the afternoons when the others were out. He would take me for walks around London or to the stables, where I met Mnemosyne, Turlington's black, snorting mare.

'Mnemosyne,' I murmured, stroking her lovely smooth neck. It had a sheen as fine as any of Annis's dresses. 'The goddess of memory. Why such a name, Cousin?' Just then, her neck snaked suddenly towards me and I leapt back to avoid her big white teeth sinking into my arm.

Turlington did not remark that I knew the name. He never patronised me. 'I tell her all my secrets. She remembers them but loves me still. Best of all, she never tells them.'

'No wonder she's a bad-tempered brute if she knows all you get up to!' I laughed, rubbing my arm for its narrow escape.

At last I saw what lay outside the four walls of Helicon – the great city of London. I saw square white houses much like ours and others built of red or yellow brick, ornamented with cupolas and bell towers. I saw the dark, shiny leaves of trees I could not name crowding over the walls and through railings. I had never considered there might be plants in the world that did not grow in Cornwall, wild. It added to my sense of wonder, and my sense of being out of place.

Seen through Turlington's eyes, London wasn't merely a noisy, relentless desert of brick that stood between me and the countryside, but a place of adventure and interest. The river! A broad, silver, salty stretch upon which there was as much activity as there was on the streets. London Bridge! A construction so mighty and solid it looked to me as though it must have grown up out of the riverbanks, but I learned that it had been built only twenty years ago, replacing an older London Bridge. That had been there six hundred years, Turlington told me, but had been demolished to make way for this vast span of granite that looped once, twice and five times across the river. I stared and stared. Six hundred years! And then gone. London was a powerful place.

Turlington had something of that same power about him. Wherever we went, his tall figure drew admiring glances. He seemed to have an extra, uncompromising vigour that others lacked and his presence gave the days a fierce glow.

Yet he was destructive like London, too. He regularly fought with Annis, who kept her contempt for us both very thinly veiled indeed. At first, I loved to hear her pulled down, but Turlington didn't know when to stop. His words would grow more and more deadly – like an axe whirling about an opponent until it found its mark and Annis's white skin whitened still further. At last, Turlington would set down his wine or whisky and stalk from the room, disgusted with himself. I couldn't help running after him, Annis's eyes narrowing as she watched me go. Turlington would burst from the house to walk off his unrest in the maze of London while I followed – watchful, uncertain – until he remembered me and became my bright, brilliant guide once more.

The highlight of that time was an afternoon concert. I had told Turlington of my fascination with the piano and my secret wish that I might play it one day.

'Get Sanderson to teach you,' he said. 'He's very accomplished. Not me. Torturous beast, the piano.'

I had already learned that Turlington was impatient; he was not the sort of character to trace the arduous paths of self-improvement. If something did not come easily to him, he abandoned it. Nevertheless, the generosity he showed me made me *hope* that the darkness that troubled him might be gradually fading away.

After this confession of mine, Turlington found me a piano concert in a small theatre in an out-of-the-way part of town where we would be unlikely to disgrace the family; as far as Aunt Dinah was concerned I was still unfit for human consumption.

'It's really not the best,' he frowned. 'I'm no expert, but seems to me the fellow's thumping somewhat. I'm not sure Schumann was meant to sound *quite* like that . . . I'm sorry.'

But I was transported. The mere fact of being in a public

place of entertainment thrilled me. I drank in the stage, the ornate lamps and the tasselled curtains with avid eyes. I enjoyed taking our seats among a crowd of music lovers who nodded polite greetings, then studied programmes, adjusted skirts and listened intently. I smiled and nodded in response to several people and no one seemed to find anything disturbing in my behaviour. *The rest of London is not like Helicon*, I thought.

And then, when the *music* started! Knowing still less than Turlington, it sounded wonderful to me. It was the first time I had ever spent that long – indeed, any amount of time – listening to one piece of music after another. Of course I could not tell them apart, I could not judge whether the programme was fashionable or uninspired; I knew nothing. But that pianist's hands rippled up and down the keys with a dexterity that seemed nothing short of magical to me and music poured out into the hall, touching something within me that had been frozen since I came to London. With Turlington tall and warm at my side, I felt safe to cry. He put his arm round me and did not fuss or ask questions; he only held me tight against him and wiped my cheeks with his sleeve when I was done.

We tumbled out into an afternoon that was grey and smoky and disappearing too fast; it was time to hurry back. But before we set off I could not help but throw my arms around him. 'Thank you, Turlington, oh, *thank* you,' I said in a muffled voice as I buried my face in the place where his neck met his shoulders. 'I can never thank you enough.' It had been one of the best experiences of my life, there in that oh-so-unhappy existence.

He smiled at me with a sort of wonder; he was not used to pleasing people. 'You are my thanks, Florrie,' he said, looking confused, and we went back to Helicon together.

Chapter Sixteen

The library at Helicon was a pleasant, shady room at the back of the house. It had long windows looking onto the garden. Because of the position of the rhododendron bushes and because the room did not sit square but faced at a north-easterly angle, the bright sunshine of that first summer in London fell past it rather than into it, creating a realm of dusty tranquillity. There was a large oak desk with many drawers and an ornate design of acorns and oak leaves carved around its borders. There were bookcases filled with books. Brown leather spines winking with gold, spines of blue and cream and grey cloth on board, books tall and short, fat and thin, all waiting for me. I took a dizzy, delighted turn about the room and saw poetry, novels, books on botany, history and science . . .

I was first taken there by Hawker, who seemed to enjoy my dazzlement before insisting we turn to the business at hand — that of committing the history of the Grace family to my overburdened brain. I was disappointed that, with all those books, we were to continue to pour our energies into that same endless theme, the greatness of the Graces.

But it was respite from Dinah's pinion eyes at least, and Hawker's tendency to tell the family stories with as much reverence and drama as if they were tales of gods and angels reconciled me. I was seated at the desk and instructed to take whatever notes I needed to aid my memory while my grandfather sat in an armchair of midnight-blue velvet with bronze studs that was several times his size. Turlington sat in the chair's twin, cradling a tumbler of amber whisky, though the stories were nothing new to him.

'Soon, you will be going into society as a Grace,' Hawker said. 'Of course you must know your family. You know Dinah, Irwin, Annis, Judith, and my two heirs, Turlington and Sanderson. Any questions?'

I raised my eyebrows. Questions? Only a thousand or more. Why were most of the Graces so lacking in compassion? Why was Annis like a little drop of acid, all done up in fancy lace? Had Irwin always been affable to the point of imbecility or had marriage to the indomitable Dinah rendered him thus? And why did no one ever talk about Calantha?

'Facts, girl,' warned Hawker, as though reading my mind. 'Names, ages, occupations, the sort of thing that might come up in polite conversation.'

I sighed. That was nothing interesting at all. However, I had been at Helicon almost a month and while my head was stuffed full of cutlery and conversation, my relatives were not quick to share personal information so there was much I did not know. 'I should like to know all those things, if you please, Grand-Hawker.'

'Your cousin Judith is nearest to you in age. She is sixteen. If she were another girl, I would have you become friends, but she is a vapid sieve with a head full of inconsequence that comes showering down, via the dubious asset of her mouth, onto whomsoever is close at hand. She thinks of nothing but gossip and young men and she is her mother's pawn.'

'I . . . see.'

'Annis is eighteen. She is a clever girl. She has learned her mother's lessons well but she has a mind of her own. She is handsome too and will make a good match very soon, I am confident of that. She knows to do her duty. I have time for Annis.'

I was dismayed to hear it. I now had yet another reason to hate her, for some time over the previous weeks my orange stone had disappeared. I remembered leaving it out the night that Turlington had arrived and I had been too tired and distracted to think of it the following day. When I realised it was missing I asked Benson but she knew nothing of it. Without it I felt more sapped of my old sense of power than ever. I suspected Annis of stealing it, just for spite, but I could not prove it, of course.

'She is . . . she is . . .'

'What, girl? Spit it out!'

'She is not a *kind* girl. She is sharp and spiteful and serves only herself.'

'She is a pestilent sheath of poisoned arrows,' put in Turlington from the corner, flinging one leg over the other in his eternal quest to find comfort.

'She serves her family. That is what counts. You would do well to emulate Annis, Grand-Florence.'

I'd as soon em . . . emulate (it was a new word to me) *Snow White's evil stepmother*, I thought.

'Irwin is a banker.' When he said it, he wore the face of a child on a day of pouring rain. 'I should be grateful. He has a talent for making money and as well he does, given the rate that we all spend it. If it were not for Irwin, I suppose we should all be in the poorhouse by now. Turlington is profligate to a degree that makes the wildest rakes of the Regency look like biddable young fellows. Dinah has a strategy to advance our toe-hold in polite society and it seems to involve substantial investment in clothes, furnishings and parties. I should be grateful to Irwin. He holds the financial position of the Graces in his hands. Yet he is the most *un*remarkable of my children,' he sighed.

'Although I fathered *seven* children,' he continued, looking bitter, 'the current generation boasts only two male heirs.' He shook his head as if at a loss to understand how such a thing could have come to pass. 'And neither one of them is worth the paper you're dripping ink on.'

I looked down and hastily replaced the quill in its stand. I disliked that he spoke so hurtfully in front of Turlington but my cousin's lips had curved into a sardonic smile.

'Turlington is my first heir.' He gestured at my cousin as though he were the illustration of a point and nothing more. 'He is twenty-two years old but as you see, he does not wear his years like a man taking his place in the world. He still thinks he is having a young man's fling with life. His personal fortune is long gone and that is why he has come back to us, you see. Frugality does not come easily to Turlington. He refuses to marry, he will not work, but he likes splendid horses and fine wines and every kind of amusement. He has not the character to make his own way in the world, therefore we find him here, lolling in the library, where I hope at long last he may absorb something of the great privilege that rests upon him. He is the eldest Grace of your generation. It is an honour that Annis would know what to do with. A pity she isn't a man. But Turlington? He hasn't a clue.'

Now Turlington's eyes darkened and his lips pressed together. I saw again that fierce hurt I had noticed the night he returned. Why could Hawker not see it and speak more gently? Or perhaps he could, and did not care.

'I am a great disappointment as you see, dear Cousin,' said Turlington lightly, draining his glass and getting up to refill it. 'Better for everyone had I not been born, yet I am here as you see, inconveniencing everyone and holding back the entire clan from greatness.'

I could not bear it! 'Why take him back then, Grand-Hawker, if he is so bad as all that? Why not cast him out again as you did my mother, and everyone who displeases you?'

Turlington's face softened as he watched me.

'Turlington is the eldest Grace, therefore he is invaluable to me,' Hawker said shortly. 'Your grandmother, my wife, was Rosanna Clifton. She died fifteen years ago now. Turlington is the eldest son of *our* eldest son, Clifton. When Clifton was alive it seemed the Graces could not dwindle or dissipate. He was handsome, clever and charming.'

'He was callous, heartless and cruel,' added Turlington.

Hawker ignored him. 'He was the most sought-after beau of his season. He knew the prize that he was and did not rush to marry. When he married, he chose Belle Turlington, a young lady of impeccable credentials and surpassing beauty.'

'My mother,' said Turlington softly, though I knew that, of course.

'They quickly had a son, Turlington, and everything looked promising for our family. But Belle died during her second confinement.'

'I was three,' added Turlington.

'Clifton married again—'

'Less than three months after my mother was laid in the ground,' said Turlington, with hatred in his face. I started to understand. I had never known my mother, but that she was beloved of my father I had never doubted.

'He did the *right thing*!' cried Hawker in a tone that told me this was not the first time they had had this conversation. 'He was a Grace! He had a duty! We all missed your mother, but he had to have other sons!'

'Oh, and he did that, didn't he?' Again he looked like a sulky boy.

'Do you not love Sanderson?' I asked him sadly.

'Of course I do. It would be impossible *not* to love him. Aside from the indecent haste with which he was created, Sanderson has been the best comfort of my life.'

'Clifton was married again,' repeated Hawker, 'this time to Cassandra Sanderson, another excellent match. Oh, she was no Belle. She was beautiful in the way of a still life compared with a forest scene. All the same, she was an excellent match and a good second choice. They had Sanderson very quickly. He is now eighteen and is as you have found him.'

'He is a lovely, kind gentleman. Why do you not . . . that is, Sanderson will do anything you ask of him, Grand-Hawker, will he not? He takes his family duty seriously – like Annis.'

Hawker sighed. 'I suppose he will. And yes, he is fair to look at and he behaves himself and will make a good match when the time comes. There is some hope in that.' He grew a little vague. *He is bored by Sanderson*, I realised. If Turlington was too rebellious, then Sanderson was too easy, and so Hawker viewed him with the same illogical disdain in which he held Irwin. Indeed, Hawker was not a straightforward man.

'So much for Clifton and his progeny. My second child was Irwin. My third, another boy, Edgar.' *Edgar*, I scribbled on my sheet, with another arrow from Hawker and Rosanna. 'Edgar died in a hunting accident when he was twenty.'

'I am sorry,' I murmured.

'The tragedy is,' he mused, 'that it happened just weeks before he was due to be married. If he could only have waited until he was married and fathered a son or two first. But he did not. So much for Edgar. Then the girls started coming. My fourth child was Bianca.'

Bianca, I wrote obediently, and drew a circle around the inconsiderately deceased Edgar.

'Never mind about her.' He shuddered. Turlington sniggered. I put a little question mark next to her name.

'Then there was Elizabeth.' His face softened again.

'My mother.'

'Yes. A beautiful girl, sweet-natured, warm-hearted. Then she ran off with a . . . well, she ran off with your father.'

'Seems to me that with all this –' I waved a hand over the already complex record of death and tragedy – 'my father should have been the least of your worries.'

'Well. Perhaps you're right at that. But I did not see it then. I freely admit, Florence, that disinheriting Elizabeth was a mistake. I regret that she died without my seeing her again. But there had been . . . other improprieties. I feared I was losing control over my children. I could not see a way to have a man like your father here.'

'You did not know my father.'

He ignored me. 'After Elizabeth came Mary. They were the best of them, Elizabeth and Mary. But Mary died too. She was always sickly. And finally, there was Antonia.'

'Also passed on?' I asked, horrified at the tragedies that had befallen this family on a regular basis.

'Worse.'

'She ran off with a Cornishman too?'

'Oh worse, worse. God.'

'God?'

'She decided He was her saviour. Not just as something to say on a Sunday to keep the vicar happy, you understand. But as something real! She is in a convent.'

'Genuine faith and conviction,' laughed Turlington. 'You can imagine how upsetting they all find it. Tell her about Bianca as well,' he added. 'You may as well.'

'Oh, very well. Your Aunt Bianca, Florrie, is a lady of easy virtue. That is to say she is a whore. She has not been driven to it by harsh circumstance. No, she took to her profession like a duck to water. She will never enter this house again. Now I ask you. Four daughters and this is what it's come to. Elizabeth and Mary both dead. Bianca and Antonia alive but utter disgraces. I honestly do not know which of them is worse.'

★

My daily lessons in etiquette continued. Dinah and her daughters shared the burden of coaching me and we remained at odds throughout. Yet I learned, one small victory at a time, to curb my wayward vowels, to walk in a ladylike fashion and how to hold a fork (indeed, how to hold a great variety of forks).

Annis never took respite from making it clear how she despised me. Nevertheless, she took her duty seriously, as Hawker had promised.

'It is for *us*,' she hissed when I tried to thank her, thinking that my bending might create a little harmony.

And in that spirit she did, I concede, make me contained and graceful where before I had been gangly and awkward. She hammered the dents out of my speech and she had me practise – for endless hours – harmless, meaningless conversation.

For a time my accent came and went like the sea mists depending on who I was with. With Turlington and Sanderson I could be myself. Hawker, too, did not care if my speech slipped in his presence. But with the others, gradually, inconsistently, it began to fade away and a new Florence spoke in place of the country cousin. I did not know whether to resent her as a traitor or welcome her as a new and elegant ally who could make my life here easier.

With Judith, my education was of a different kind. The subject in which she had been charged to instruct me was fashion. Fashion in clothing, ribbons, musical taste, pet dogs, carriage colours, even *horse* colours! Pale horses were *beyond* the pale that season. One must only have black, or else a very dark bay. (That dictum had reversed entirely by Christmas.) It seemed there were fashions in everything. However, she took it upon herself to broaden my syllabus. Although only sixteen, and meek as milk to look at, her favourite topic was gentlemen.

'Cousin Florence, when the day comes, we shall have to find for you a true Swell. Edward Seagrove, you know, is just such a man, but you can't have him for I mean to have him for myself, if Mama doesn't stop it. I don't see why she should, for he's quite as fine as anything. Checked trousers, Cousin, are the mark of a Swell and Edward's checks are bigger than I have seen *any* young man wear. And *don't* embroil yourself with a broad-brimmed hat! *Those* have not been *au courant* since the forties, you know!' (It was, at this time, 1850.)

I had no intention of getting embroiled with any sort of hat, but on she chattered, sometimes pointing out young men on the street as illustration, for she lacked any real-life specimens. Small wonder my thoughts turned often and inexorably to Turlington.

Our friendship continued to deepen and was the cornerstone of my days. Sometimes we took Calantha with us on our secret outings. The three of us were like children playing truant, giddy with liberty. Sanderson knew all about it and he looked sick that he had to miss all the fun. But Sanderson was a proper, polished Grace, therefore he had to pay calls and attend the three o'clock parade.

'You see, brother, it doesn't pay to be good!' pointed out Turlington with glee. 'We are reaping the rewards of being an embarrassment.'

'I know it,' Sanderson groaned, green with envy as we recounted stories of hearing a band in Vauxhall Gardens, of penny poetry readings (the worse the poet, the more entertaining the event), of sneaking off to the zoo, to see the great wonder of that year: the hippo.

Judith was wild to see the hippo since 'the talk is *all* of it!' as she often told me when she returned from Hyde Park in the afternoons. But her mother would not hear of a Grace going to such a place as a zoo, so Judith had to content herself with poring over sketches in the newspapers. I had seen three different sketches of the beast in three different periodicals and each was entirely different. I longed to correct Judith, who assured me that it was 'a fabulous beast with scales and wings, much like a dragon, dear Cousin, except rounder'. But I smiled and kept the secret.

With all of our wanderings it was a miracle we weren't found out by the family, but we were lucky; we only once happened upon someone who knew them. It occurred when we were leaving the Royal Academy. Turlington froze when he heard his name called, but he looked relieved when he saw a pretty young woman who greeted us kindly. He introduced Selina Westwood, the vicar's wife. I had often heard my relatives speak of the Westwoods, who were frequent visitors to Helicon, though I had not been allowed to meet them.

'Sanderson has told me so much about you, dear,' she said, shaking my hand. 'I hope I have the pleasure again soon.'

'Mrs Westwood,' said Turlington, 'I wonder if we might prevail upon you to . . . er . . .'

'I never saw you, Turlington,' she smiled. 'I have heard how it is. I am glad you are showing Florence our wonderful city. But continue in secret, by all means!'

'She is *lovely*!' I breathed, looking after her as she hurried off. 'And so pretty! I never thought a vicar's wife could be so pretty.'

'Pretty enough,' shrugged Turlington, 'but too damned saintly for my taste.'

And it was true that Turlington could not be described as saintly. Sometimes being with him was like being friends with a crate of explosive waiting to blow open a new mineshaft. Mealtimes were fraught as he fidgeted and flung himself about. He did try for the charm and acquiescence of his brother, but the contemptuous comments kept leaking out. Sanderson and I watched in misery as he poured glass after glass of the good red wine and the good white wine and the good Madeira down his throat, until Hawker or Dinah would slap him back and put the bottles away. Even then he continued to eye them as if the solutions to all the mysteries of the universe were settled in their winking depths.

I would sit in silence, feeling his discontent mounting like a thundercloud and wish we were in Braggenstones, just

Turlington and me. I imagined he could feel peaceful there, and I could look after him better there too. I wished for Old Rilla's garden, for practical ways to heal his wounds. I longed for violets. Violets were for protection; they also prevented drunkenness.

One night, Turlington got up from the table in the middle of dinner and left the room.

'Charming,' Annis commented with arched brows.

He returned a few minutes later and handed her a bracelet. 'Why not wear this, Cousin? Your arm looked a little bare this evening and I know how you like to drip in ornamentation.'

Sanderson and I looked at each other in utter confusion.

Annis exploded. 'How dare you go into my room and go through my things! Mama, Hawker, see what he has—' But she stopped when he held up a second object. My orange stone.

'I was astonished to find this amongst your baubles. It looks exactly like the stone that Florence brought with her from Cornwall, a thing of absolutely no value to anyone but her. The *only* thing, in fact, of any significance to her from her former life.'

All heads turned in Annis's direction. She coloured vividly. Turlington dropped the stone on the table in front of Hawker. 'Stealing a stone from an orphan,' he sneered. 'I can see why you are so proud of her.'

Annis opened her mouth but no words came out. Her

mother looked mortified before Hawker's icy glare. It was Irwin who reached out for the stone and said quietly, 'Is this yours, Florence?'

I nodded.

'Here you are, then,' he said, handing it back to me. Thus my stone was restored to me. I was gladder to have it back than I could have imagined.

I never learned if Annis faced any consequences for the incident, or Turlington for entering her room like that. I was grateful to him, of course, but he made a worrying hero. As happy as such deeds made me, I always feared something bad would happen, that he would be disgraced again and sent away.

What happened was worse. When he had been home just five weeks, I came down to breakfast one day and saw his chair empty and an array of grim Grace faces. He had vanished in the middle of the night, taking Mnemosyne, all his belongings and an emerald necklace of Annis's. He was gone.

Chapter Seventeen

Oh, the betrayal that I felt. I felt bereaved, even. *How could he leave me like this?* I fretted all that day and for many to come. *How could he leave me?*

As true an affection as I had for Sanderson, he was too rule-bound to be relied upon for comfort and company. Our time together was rewarding when it came, but it was snatched in the gaps between other priorities.

It was Turlington who had sought me out no matter what, who had made me laugh and laughed in return. It was Turlington who had shared my deep disgust at the hypocrisy of the world in which we moved. It was Turlington who had taken my hand when we talked, or hugged me when something funny or shocking happened, granting me the great blessing of physical human contact in a world where, suddenly, there was none.

And no word for me. No means to communicate with him; no address. He knew how lonely I was. Yet he just vanished, quite literally a thief in the night. I felt as if he were lost at the bottom of the ocean.

At first I was sure there must be some final message, some reassurance. But there was nothing. I had to face the fact that while he had been at Helicon I had been a comfort and a distraction, but that I was only a child and he a man of two-and-twenty; there was a wide world out there that beckoned him. Hawker swore that if Turlington ever came home again, he should not be allowed within the walls of Helicon.

Without Turlington, I felt anew the wound of being severed from the natural world. He had shown me the very best of London, but the fact remained that the air was thick and choking, the din incessant. I could not hear the whispers of the gentle, wild creatures, nor of my own heart. I could not breathe air that smelled of heather and ocean, nor see starlight. Without Turlington, the only thing that stopped me missing Cornwall so much I might go mad was being fully, relentlessly occupied.

Lessons, lessons, lessons, of one sort or another, from morning 'til night, filled my mind, pushing Cornwall to its very edges, making home seem at best some sort of beautiful faded dream. In fact, the only thing I did *not* learn was the piano, though I longed to still. Everything else was considered more important. I could not have said what made me ache so to learn it. While Annis and Judith warbled their arpeggios, I felt no yearning to sing. I had no reason to suppose I had any particular talent. But every time I heard the piano played I would shiver, and feel something inside me thrill in response. So I continued to gaze at the beautiful instrument (which Sanderson had told me was a grand, made of fiddleback mahogany) and to stroke its satiny expanse whenever I passed it, then go and practise conversation with Annis, or learn French verbs with my new governess, who arrived a few days after Turlington left.

Miss Grover (I never did learn her given name) was above forty, already greying, and as unromantic a figure as I ever saw. But she was intelligent and earnest and kindly complimented me as being both able and enthusiastic. We rubbed along well enough together, though I frequently lamented Lacey with her bright dresses and her dancing curls.

Aunt Dinah thoroughly disapproved of my keeping in touch with a provincial schoolteacher from the back of beyond. She complained about it to Hawker. It then became apparent from Lacey's letters that some of hers had never reached me. I suspected my aunt of stealing them, and I complained to Hawker about her. Finally he decreed the correspondence could continue, but only twice a year. Any more, he said, was unnecessary, improper and would prompt him to end it altogether. I wrote to Lacey, explaining, and she responded faithfully – six months later. And every six months thereafter.

Perhaps it was as well. Whenever I heard from Lacey and read of the seasons and the local children, of trips to Launceston or Fowey, of news of neighbours and friends, it filled my mind for days and pulled at me, making me feel so wrong for being away from there, so taut and pulled at an angle and ill-fitting that I could hardly breathe. It made Cornwall real for me, and I could afford for nothing to be real, here, except the Graces and Helicon and one day, when I was ready, society.

When I had been at Helicon three months I was permitted to attend one of my aunt's famous dinner parties. She hosted three a week. Given what I knew about the family's strained finances, it seemed lunacy to me, yet when there were guests my aunt spared no expense.

Long before I was allowed to attend, I was aware of the whirl of preparation that went on below stairs every Tuesday, Thursday and Friday. These were the days that my aunt was particularly scratchy and difficult to please. I learned that her dinner parties were the way that she hoped to win back the regard of society. It was not only the food which mattered but what they wore, the way the dishes were presented and the way the table and dishes were decorated. There must always be a novelty, so that the guests would talk afterwards and the dinners would gain a reputation, so that eventually *everyone* would crave an invitation to one of Dinah Grace's parties.

Come five o'clock, my aunt and cousins would disappear to dress. Earrings might be changed four or five times. The choice of a hair ornament – a delicate butterfly, a glittering pin or a curl of ribbon – could provoke the most heated debate. I couldn't help myself – my love of pretty things overpowered my rationality – I longed for the day when I could add diamond raindrops to my ears and silken butterflies to my hair. It came in October.

The only guests were to be close family friends, and Hawker decreed that it was time for me to meet someone outside the family. Naturally, the risk of presenting me to their nearest acquaintances caused Aunt Dinah immense anxiety. I was a wild card, an unpredictable, undesirable fly in the ointment.

I should like to report that at my first dinner party I comported myself to perfection, to the stupefaction of my aunt. However, that would not be true.

The other guests included the vicar, Mr Sebastian Westwood, and his wife Selina, whom I had already met in Piccadilly with Turlington, but of course could not say so. There was also Mr Andrew Blackford, a scalpel-shrewd man of thirty, who had made a fortune through judicious investments in the railway, and the Coatleys: Mr, Mrs and Miss. Mr Blackford was clearly 'a prospect' for Annis and Miss Anne Coatley was a glistening jewel of a girl whom the Graces were considering for Sanderson in the manner of jackdaws eyeing up a shiny bauble.

I entered the room with my heart drumming as though I'd

run from Tremorney to Braggenstones without pause. The assembly of finely dressed folk stood close about and at first I could not discern family from stranger. The air smelled of lavender cologne and pomposity and onion soup.

I marvelled, though, when I saw the table. It was laid very plainly indeed, white linen and silver, but its great length was studded with six massive silver platters. Piled up on the platters were jagged rocks of ice, grey-white and glistening in the candlelight. Each more than three feet high, they were scattered and strewn with flowers, berries and nuts; vibrant blue chicory, deep pink phlox, brick-red sorrel, the ethereal green of hazel and dark purple blackberries with their white flowers. It looked like a fairy feast.

In Cornwall we would never have eaten blackberries so late in the month; everyone knew that the devil spat on the bushes on the ninth of October, so after that they could bring only bad luck. But I found I did not mind the prospect of the Graces enduring a little bad luck so I said nothing about this. I would stop Sanderson eating them, though.

Spying me, my aunt detached herself from the group and took me round one guest after another. The introductions went without mishap. I curtseyed and murmured polite greetings and remembered everyone's name without effort.

Benson had taken the greatest of pains with my appearance. I wore a pale lemon dress with gold and pearls at my throat and a little lace doily on the coils of brown hair at the back of my head. The bodice was brocade and the skirts were satin and lace. At first I hoped I might pass muster.

We took our seats and I saw that there were beautifully lettered cards propped up at each platter of ice and flowers. *Chicory – for the coming-true of dreams. Blackberry – for the telling of truth.* Liberties had been taken with the meanings, but I supposed all that mattered was a pleasing effect. Aunt Dinah explained that the guests would change place with every course so that they could sit near each platter in turn and the fine ladies be entertained by the secret meanings of the flowers. I began to understand something of the thought and planning that went into a Dinah Grace dinner party.

As the soup was dribbled into patterned bowls I had ample observance of the guests. The vicar, I quickly saw, was someone to whom Aunt Dinah displayed the greatest deference. This surprised me. I would not have thought a religious man would have possessed any of the attributes that my aunt prized. But I soon saw that I was wrong. Mr Westwood was extremely elegant, from his immaculately pomaded brown hair, to his gold-tipped cane, slender as a willow wand. He was also learned and not reticent to display it. The gentlemanly talk of the 'Eastern Question' and Russian expansion was all beyond my understanding but he was at the heart of it and I gathered, from the 'hear, hear, sir!'s all around the table, that his insights impressed everyone. His wife Selina, twenty years younger, fine-boned and pretty, behaved gently and sympathetically, and poured oil on any ruffled waters throughout the debate. She smiled at me often from her place between her husband and Sanderson.

All in all, the vicar was no man of God that I could ever have imagined. He was nothing like wild-haired, wild-eyed Billy Post, who roamed Cornwall with his gaze fixed beyond the horizon, preaching hell and fury with thumping fists and a thwacking staff, and flinging himself to the ground to demonstrate prostration before the power of the Almighty. (He also preached chastity and purity of thought while tumbling every village girl of suitable age and pleasing appearance.)

Mr Westwood asked me my religious persuasion more with the manner of someone asking my preference for claret over Madeira than someone concerned for my immortal soul. I had rarely gone to church in my life, not from any objection to it but because I found God as I knew Him on my moors and in my plants and in the rising and setting of the sun each day, so I said as much.

'Oh, how *charmingly* naive!' muttered Mrs Coatley, a lady in a violet gown straining over a joyous bosom, to her daughter. 'It must be very hard for you, dear, coming all this way, and adjusting to life in the civilised world. Why, it must be like the world made anew for you. Do you know, I have heard of explorers who lived in the jungle for many years – the Amazon, you know, or the Congo or one of them – and when they came home they no longer liked to sleep in beds! They had gone quite native, you know, and slept on the floor. It must be just like that for you.'

My time at Helicon had wrought wonders. Instead of firing up that London seemed eminently uncivilised to *me*, I chose instead to remember that her remarks were kindly meant.

'The world made anew, ma'am,' I echoed. 'You have put it very well.' Her round face, which shone a little with the reflected violet sheen of her dress, broke into a sympathetic smile.

'I mean,' she murmured, 'imagine coming from *Cornwall*!'

'*Cornwall!*' echoed several guests in tones of wonder, as though saying, *Faerieland*.

Her interest seemed to set an example to the whole table and soon I felt like the hippo at the zoo.

'I must say, Hawker,' drawled Mr Blackford, 'she really is uncanny. Quite a jewel in the raw. Your lovely granddaughter . . . Your *eldest* lovely granddaughter, of course, has already told me quite a lot about her . . .'

I could well believe it. Annis looked less than happy to hear me described as any sort of jewel, no matter how raw.

'Quite uncanny, I must say,' he concluded. What does a word like 'uncanny' *mean* in a remark like that?

'You have visited Cornwall, have you not, Mr Coatley?' asked Selina Westwood, perhaps to spare my discomfort. Sanderson touched her arm, as though grateful for her tactful intervention.

They all deferred to Mr Coatley as though he, not I, were the expert on Cornwall and the good gentleman – who had until then slumped at my side in his grey suit like a hefty slug – roused himself and straightened up.

'I have,' he conceded, in a surprisingly light and tremulous voice, 'though it is no time I wish to remember.' He paused on this troubling note to take a draft of wine. 'It was a business trip,' he continued, closing his eyes against the memory. 'I made some considerable investments in the railway at that time, as you know, Mr Blackford, following your excellent advice.'

Mr Blackford nodded. 'They are out-of-the-way parts but I suppose even there people must get about. More to the point, with all the resources in that county, *we* must get to *them*. Trains between Truro and Penzance just two years hence.'

'Truly, sir?' I could not help but cry. How good to hear the familiar names. How I wished I could tell Lacey.

'Resources they may have,' resumed Mr Coatley, 'but I would not go back there for all the tea in China. Not on a train, not in a coach, not if Pegasus himself should fly down and offer to bear me.' He glared at me as though holding me responsible.

'You did not have a pleasant stay in Cornwall, then, sir?' I surmised.

'Pleasant? Pleasant! That is not the word to use, no. It was abominable. How to describe it? It is damp and dismal and dreary. It is confounding and cantankerous. There are tides where there should be no tides. And waters are calm where they should flow. It is the most contrary, bedevilled, pernicious, hostile landscape in the British Isles if not in Europe, of *that* I am sure!'

I could not think what to say. I saw Sanderson and Mrs Westwood exchange an amused glance and I bit my lip to stop myself laughing.

Breathing a little heavily after his outburst, Mr Coatley took another large swill of wine then stared down at his plate as though close to tears.

His daughter took this opportunity to present me with a burning question of her own. 'And is it true – for Papa said as much but he does tell fibs to tease me, you know – oh, pray tell me, is there a mine called Ding Dong?'

'Aye, Miss Anne,' I replied. I had made great progress with my speaking but talking of Cornwall recalled my old manner of speech and suddenly I could not shake it off. 'It be high on the Penwith Downs.'

'Oh Lord!' giggled Miss Anne, holding a hand prettily to her mouth. 'Why do not they simply call it Plink Plonk? Or Doodad? Oh, how *hilarious*! What a quirky folk they must be!'

'Lordy Lord, Cousin Florence, how you do set us in a grin,' said Annis fondly, her eyes sparkling.

'While I was there,' said Mr Coatley all of a sudden, sitting up very straight again, with an expression of horror, 'I heard a story – a true story, you understand. The previous winter the wind had come up so strong and fierce – it happens often like that in those parts – a young lady blew away. She was recovered, with only minor hurts, a few miles away, but was from that day on a nervous recluse and did not venture out of doors for the rest of her days.' Shocked murmurs rippled around the table.

Feeling I must defend Cornwall, I said, 'Not all gentlefolk dislike Cornwall. Why, this very year Mr Wilkie Collins, the popular novelist, you know, paid us the honour of a visit. He even took a trip down Botallack mine, which is a fine, deep mine – though I believe he went only halfway.'

Lacey had shown me the account in the local paper.

'Lord, I heard about that,' said Blackford. 'Though whether anyone here would consider Collins a gentleman I can't avow. They charge ten shillings for the pleasure of going down the mine, you know.'

'*Why?*' wailed poor Mr Coatley. 'Why would anyone pay it?'

'Seems an odd way of exploiting the industry to me,' said Blackford, wiping his mouth with a white napkin.

''Tis a hard living in the mines, sir. Surely they can make a little extra money if people are interested to see?'

'A hard living,' he laughed gently. 'Oh yes, we investors hear all about how hard it is. Interminably. Yet wages have almost doubled this year alone!'

'But also the prices!' I exclaimed.

'Wild and untamed,' murmured Mr Coatley, as though I were a stretch of moorland.

'A compassionate heart,' suggested Selina Westwood gently.

'Hear, hear,' said Sanderson, smiling at her.

'That's enough, Florence!' said Aunt Dinah. 'Ladies, gentlemen, shall we change seats?'

With every course, the guests shifted a couple of places to their left so as to be near a different ice pyramid. Elegant, ladylike fingers reached out to steal blackberries, accompanied by playful laughter as though they were doing something *very* wicked. They placed the pretty pink flowers upon elegant, ladylike hair, in the hope of attracting great sums of money. Whosoever sat by the blackberries had to hold a white flower and promise to speak the truth to any question she was asked. I counted three answers that I knew to be lies, from my aunt, Annis and Judith respectively.

When my turn came I told a few of my own. Miss Coatley asked how I liked life at Helicon and I told her it was very pleasing and a privilege. Judith asked me if I had ever kissed a boy and I said no. (I had kissed both Stephen and the pedlar's son, Joe.) Her mother rapped her hand with a fork. Then Annis surprised me completely. She asked if I was in love with Turlington.

'What?' I asked, quite forgetting where I was.

'Are you in love with Turlington?' she asked loudly and

clearly and Hawker, who had been conversing with Mr West-wood and ignoring the trivial chatter, laid down his fork to listen. The expression on his face was not encouraging.

'Well, Cousin?' Annis prompted.

'Of course not!' said I.

'No? Oh well then.'

'He is my cousin,' I added, 'and I am but fifteen!'

'Oh, but Judith has been in love with someone or other since she was about twelve,' said Annis lightly. 'And people marry their cousins all the time, you know.'

'Not in this family they don't,' Hawker stated. 'I don't hold with all that, Annis, as well you know. I don't care what's accepted, it's a bad idea, and means bad blood. The Graces are not to intermarry and dwindle, they are to cast their net wide, spread their roots, extend and augment themselves. If you have any ideas that way, girl,' he added to me, 'you can forget them. That will *never* happen.'

I had never once formed the thought that I was in love with Turlington. Marrying him had never crossed my mind. Yet, to be told he was forbidden, before I had ever known I wanted him, was somehow disappointing. It was like being given a present and having it snatched away before I could open it. *That* in itself was confusing, given that he had run away from me and I was angry, and sure I could never forgive him. I was shaken, too, by Hawker's sudden, fierce attention. But I have never done well with following rules.

'Oh well,' said Annis again, with a shrug. 'He's in Madeira again anyway, didn't you say so, Sanderson? So I wouldn't worry, Hawker.'

'But there's nothing to worry *about*!' I wailed, my voice rising. My aunt glared at me and I knew I had somehow strayed again into inappropriate behaviour.

Annis smiled sweetly. 'If you say so, dear.'

In Madeira again? I hadn't known. So far away. But what on earth had made Annis say that? If she wanted to embarrass me, she should have said Sanderson; he was sitting opposite me and it would have caused greater awkwardness. Had she seen something in my friendship with Turlington that she had misunderstood? Or had she understood it better than I? It felt like the devil's work, and I hadn't even eaten the blackberries.

'And you, Mama,' continued Anne Coatley when her mother's turn came to clutch a flower between her many rings. 'Are you in love with the dancing master at the academy?'

Mrs Coatley beamed. 'Why, certainly I am, my dear! For he has the finest mustachios I have ever seen and *quite* the most elegant way of twirling a lady. I hope this doesn't offend you, dearest,' she added to her stout husband.

'By no means! Dear ladies must hold a candle for someone or other,' he responded generously.

That is how I should have answered. I should have made light of it, undisturbed. But how could I have known? Surrounded by finery though I was, I had a sudden, fierce grief for life at Braggenstones, which had been hard but, for the most part, harmonious. An occasional feud flared up to be sure, but these were rare, and regretted. I would have given anything to be back there again. I remembered arriving at Helicon and my premonition that I would never be happy there. I thought of the long years stretching ahead of me with despair. What sort of independence could I ever hope to gain from this family? What freedom from these people who spoke with such authority of the mines they had never seen, the mines that had killed my father?

Tears pricking at my eyes, I reached for my glass and knocked it over. Red wine spread across the white cloth and dribbled onto Mr Coatley's leg. An army of servants hastened forward to repair the damage and Annis grinned. I dared not even look at my aunt.

So much for my first dinner party! Let me draw a curtain then across that glittering table. Let me skip over all the coming firsts – my first ball, my first dress fitting at Inglewilde's of London, my first morning calls (paid and received) after all that laborious coaching. For I have recalled quite enough what I suffered since Nan's death had catapulted me to Helicon. Let me cease reiterating all I had lost by those changes and re-emerge nine months later, in July of the following year.

Chapter Eighteen

❦

1851

The Great Exhibition at Hyde Park had opened on the first of May. It was – only a hermit could be unaware – a great collection of artefacts demonstrating the variety and brilliance of our industrial society. Life in Helicon was so inward-looking and blinkered that I longed to go – and for this reason I kept my mouth firmly shut and said nothing about it. For once my desire was shared by Annis and Judith, so I let them beg and plead with their implacable mother, knowing that if they could not sway her, I certainly could not. However, implacable she had remained.

It was frequented, Aunt Dinah ruled, by 'the dribbling mob' and we were likely to be tainted, tarnished and otherwise rubbed up wrongly by the 'plebeian atmosphere' sure to prevail at such a venue.

The end of July saw Judith's seventeenth birthday. My sixteenth had passed the month before, unmarked except for some modest gifts. Only Sanderson troubled himself to buy me something – a pretty muslin scarf – but the coins given by my uncle and Hawker were very welcome. Money of my very own at last! I would save it, I told myself; I would save all my birthday coins, year after year until one day, if it should take until I was five-and-seventy, I would escape to Cornwall.

Judith's birthday, however, warranted a Dinah Grace dinner, for Judith was becoming prettier all the time and had learned to curb her preference for verbal meanderings a little better. Her mother had invited two eligible young gentlemen, knowing that no gift could make Judith so happy as the chance to flirt. One was the fashionable Mr Seagrove, who had retained Judith's admiration by constantly adjusting the checks on his trousers and the slenderness of his umbrella in perfect unison with the changing fashions. His skill in this field was unparalleled.

Even so, Judith joined me in the library the morning after the party with a subdued air. She flung herself onto a window seat, while I laboured over some lines of verse of which Miss Grover had asked me to make a précis. After Judith had sighed repeatedly and gently knocked her pretty brow against the window a time or two, I deduced I was to ask her what was wrong. I laid down my quill and did so.

'I am so unhappy with Mama,' she lamented. 'I long more than anything to see the exhibition yet *still* she says no, even though Mr Seagrove has said he is willing to take me and a more fitting escort there could not *be*, as you well know. If *he* will be seen there, what can possibly be wrong with *me* being seen there? And yet Mama refuses and I am denied. I shall simply pine away for want of the opportunity to see it! She is always telling me to improve myself, yet now that I wish to attend a milestone in the making, she forbids it. I do not understand her. But *you* understand me, Florence, I know you do!' cried Judith, suddenly sitting up and hugging her arms around her knees. 'I love Mama, naturally, but she can be difficult to please, can she not?'

I could not deny it.

'Is there no way, dear Cousin? Mama goes to Hammersmith on Friday, you know, and I thought . . . well, I simply thought . . . but no, I am sure it could not be done.'

'What did you think?' I was intrigued, for it sounded very much as though a mischief were brewing in her pretty, docile head.

'Well, I know that you long to see it too. I only wondered whether you and I might somehow . . . Oh, it's impossible.'

It was entirely possible. I knew the way, I was not afraid to try it and the entry fee would not take much of my birthday allowance.

'Let us go on Friday, Judith,' I said at once. 'Let us seize our chance. What time does your mother go to Hammersmith?'

'I believe she leaves at eleven in the morning and will not be back before dinner.'

'That is ample time!'

But before she left on Friday, my aunt issued us such a flurry of tasks and instructions as to confuse an army into submission. If we went to the exhibition, how then would we complete the list of reading and embroidering and bonnet trimming that was required of us? And if we did not, how would we explain it on her return? Even I was tempted to acknowledge that the outing was ill-starred, so imagine my surprise when gentle Judith poured out a stream of impassioned and rambling justifications that amounted to 'to hell with it'.

Then there was the chaperone question. For two such finely dressed young ladies to walk to the exhibition, unaccompanied, was not the thing at all. On *this* point Judith was persistently nice, and Miss Grover succumbed easily to our urging, also tempted by a trip to the already famous display. She was an ideal chaperone, looking older, wiser and disapproving.

We set off in high spirits, our holiday mood reflected by the crowds in the streets. I felt cheerful, and not only because of the adventure. I had grown steadily, if cautiously, fonder of Judith during my year at Helicon. Annis, apparently, had lost interest in seeing the exhibition with her sister, yet I was touched that today Judith wanted *my* company.

Judith would not hear of taking Calantha. Our lovely cousin remained a source of embarrassment to my aunt and her daughters, which made me sad. Calantha was content to wave us off, however, since it was a Friday, and she disliked Fridays almost as much as she disliked easterly winds.

Around Hyde Park was a circle of buildings-in-progress, destined for the Italianate style, if they were to match those houses already complete. We traversed this chalky Tiber, with its clouds of dust, and at last we reached it, the Great Exhibition.

When we arrived at the Crystal Palace, I stopped short and gawped, all my Grace ways forgotten, a callow country girl once more. The palace itself, also known as the Great Shalimar (a name I liked very much), reminded me of nothing more than a giant summerhouse, like the one in the garden at Helicon but on a mighty scale. Its countless panes of glass glittered in the summer sun and the effect was breathtaking. Inside this fragile-looking yet vastly imposing construction, I saw things I could not name: machinery and technologies unimaginable.

We found Mr Seagrove at the third palm tree to the left of the main entrance. He greeted us all most cordially, but it was clear that it was Judith he wished to see and that her interest lay in the reciprocal direction. Somehow, although the intention had been for him to escort us all, he came to steer her off to see the Koh-i-Noor, whose famous lustre was as nothing compared with her dark eyes, he promised.

How Miss Grover was content to let her go I do not know, except that although a large diamond is a fine thing to see, there were many other things besides and Miss Grover was a scholarly woman. As for me, I had rather not listen to Mr Seagrove's slick compliments more than I had to. So Miss Grover and I found ourselves drinking in a veritable oasis of intellectual pleasure.

We saw everything from locks and trees and musical instruments to the newest fashions in interior decoration – I knew that taste for fussy ornamentation would soon be found at Helicon. I could only marvel at a new kind of image called the daguerrotype. I had only just become used to the wonders of portraiture, now here were exact replicas of faces, frozen at a particular moment. How I wished I had such a keepsake of Nan, or my parents, or of one inch of home. How valuable a technology this would be.

The afternoon wore on. Miss Grover and I had now parted ways on account of her longing to look at a display of buttons, an unexpected passion which I could not share. It was the happiest I had been in nearly a year. I had not known I could feel such freedom in London. Oh, there was no tang of sea salt hanging on the air; no whipping wind to stir my blood. Instead there was a rustling ocean of people, a mountain of machinery, and bracing gusts of grease and pepper. But in that crowd I was alone. I gulped down great drafts of that fusty, humid air just because it was mine to breath in my own way.

I caught the eye of folk who knew me not, neither as Grace nor Buckley. I shared shy smiles of wonder with men, women and children. It gave me a pleasing sense of kinship with my fellow humans.

I stopped before a wonderful piano of Indian satinwood, hoping I might hear a demonstration. It was pale gold in colour and adorned with fretwork scrolls, gilt medallions, acanthus leaves and little carved dolphins. It was staggeringly pretty. I had still rarely played the piano at Helicon, bar a few stolen and unmelodious notes, but the longing had never gone away. I had asked Sanderson if he would teach me and he was most willing and patient. But my other lessons continued and my social exposure increased and I did not like to practise in the evenings, when the family was in the drawing room and Annis mocked my efforts.

'Ah, Collard and Collard,' said one old gent, peering through a monocle at the name on the piano. 'A fine company. Collard Senior was apprentice to the great Clementi, you know.' His companion harrumphed with interest. I had no idea who the great Clementi might have been but I liked the sound of him, so I turned my head to hear more.

And all of a sudden the world tilted on its axis for I saw then the most astonishing sight of the whole exhibition. It was my cousin, Turlington Grace.

But he was in Madeira! We had not seen him in almost a year. I had not received so much as a note to mark our friendship and soften his absence. I had asked Sanderson, once or twice, how he fared, for I could not suppose the brothers sundered. He had only nodded and said Turlington was well, and I continued under the assumption that he was in Madeira. I had almost forgotten that I *had* another cousin. Almost.

'Turlington!' I cried. My voice barely sounded, so tight was my throat and so hard was my heart pounding. He was tall in the crowd even though he wore no hat. I started pushing my way towards him.

'Turlington!' He half turned his head, snatched it round again and ducked into the crowd.

'*Turlington!*' I roared, attracting the astonished attention of several gentlemen. I was furious. How could he ignore me after everything? I did not deserve to be cut, not by him. 'Turlington!' I bellowed again, giving chase.

He moved quickly, sinuously, through the crowd but I moved faster. Manners be damned, I was still Florrie Buckley. I was almost upon him. I reached out a hand. One fingertip touched, or dreamed it touched, his black coat, when a small elephant tumbled out of the crowd and knocked me sideways. That's what I thought had happened anyway. In fact, it was a matronly lady with hips as solid as the armoire in my bedroom. I knew not what had sent her flying into me but a gentleman caught me and helped me to my feet and by the time we were all dusted down and apologies and thanks exchanged, Turlington was gone.

I stood there and burned with tears. This felt like the greatest cruelty a Grace had dealt me yet. My aunt and Annis had never pretended at friendship, therefore there was no betrayal. But *this* . . . The colour and vitality leached from the day.

Miss Grover found me and we found Judith. She was engaged in a passionate embrace with Mr Seagrove and I don't know which of us was more furious. Miss Grover's objection revolved around matters of propriety and virtue. Mine was sheer outrage that my cousin should have this opportunity to see splendid, fascinating things and that she should waste it in favour of romancing with one of those most odious of creatures, a stupid, stupid *man*!

We were home before Aunt Dinah, by a wide margin. Miss Grover was alight with intellectual stimulation, and Judith starry-eyed with love. I alone was subdued. I sought out Sanderson and was fortunate to find him by himself in the drawing room, idly tinkering on the piano.

'Where is Turlington?' I demanded.

He looked up in surprise. 'Where is he?'

'Yes! Where in the world?'

'Well, I don't know exactly, just at the moment. He travels, you know, for his business . . .'

'But is he still based in Madeira?'

'I believe, officially, he is based in Madeira.'

'Officially! But he is not there in truth, is he? He is in London!'

He reddened. 'You've seen him?'

'Yes! At the exhibition. But we did not speak. He ran away when he saw me! He darted off into the crowd like a common *thief* – which I suppose he is – and left me running after him and calling—'

'Calling him?' His blue eyes were fearful. 'No one heard you, I suppose?'

'A great many people heard me, I suppose! I'll wager no one knew what I meant, though. You Graces and your stupid names. Why didn't you tell me he was here, Sanderson? Why does he not want to know me? Did he tire of having a common little girl cousin for company?'

'Oh, it's not that at all, Florrie. Quite the contrary. But you mustn't breathe a word of this to anyone, promise?'

'Of *course* I promise!' I howled, all wild with impatience. '*Tell* me!'

But at that interesting juncture the door flew open and in burst avenging Athene, brandishing a spear, otherwise personified at Aunt Dinah, rattling her chatelaine.

'You wicked, ungrateful girl!' she shouted. 'How could you take Judith to that place? How *could* you?'

Unsure exactly what she knew, I said nothing. Did she know Judith had been caught kissing Mr Seagrove? I was still at pains to protect her if I could. In my ignorance I stood there mumbling until she dealt me a ringing slap across the cheek. Her sapphire ring split my skin and my brain shifted from side to side within my head. Then she frogmarched me to the attic, her anger making her surprisingly strong.

But when we got there, I fought back. I had not been locked up now for many a long month. I would not go into that little room again. And though my aunt was fuelled by righteous indignation, I was younger and stronger after all.

'I *won't*, I tell you! I *won't!*' I shrieked. After a few exclamations of 'wretched girl!' as I pushed and kicked her, she let me go. She stared at me hatefully, a curl of long dark hair dangling over her forehead from the tussle. I stared back, willing her to lay one more finger on me.

'And if you are going to lock me up, you must lock up your precious Judith with me, if going is such a crime,' I fumed. 'What is so wrong with it anyway? All sorts of respectable people were there, we learned a great deal. What is the *matter* with you?'

'Lock up Judith? What a nonsense. As if she would have gone without you to lure her there. I will not have you corrupting my daughters.'

'Corrupting . . . but it was her idea!'

My aunt laughed and I realised that in her wonder at my audacity, she was quite genuine. Suddenly I understood. She was not simply *assuming* her daughter's innocence over mine. Judith had laid all the blame at my feet . . . But why?

'Thank heaven Mr Seagrove happened to be there,' added my aunt. 'At least she had *some* measure of protection.'

Unable to grapple me into the attic, my aunt amended her punishment. I was kept to my room for the next five days with orders to speak to no one. I hardly felt deprived. I was disenchanted with all my cousins: Annis, naturally and always; Judith with a sharp sense of hurt that made me realise I had been even fonder of her than I had realised; even Sanderson, for his complicity and eternal amiable determination to keep the peace at all costs. As for Turlington, I hated him worst of all.

One afternoon in the midst of my solitude I heard a soft tap at my door. I opened it quickly, expecting to see Calantha, but it was Sanderson. I pulled him inside and closed the door.

'I am sorry,' he said, standing in the middle of my room looking troubled. 'Sorry for all of it.'

'I am so cross with you,' I replied but hugged him at once.

'What a mess,' he said. 'What a travesty to have you confined once again.' And he told me what had happened.

As soon as my aunt had returned, Annis had told her about the outing. Annis then hastened to 'stand up' for her sister, saying I had coerced Judith. Anxious to deflect her mother's fury, Judith had tearfully agreed. She had not wanted to go, she was afraid of the nasty crowds, but I had harried and coaxed and badgered her until she was quite worn down. There was no mention of Miss Grover.

I saw now that I could not easily defend myself: any counter account I could give Dinah would not have the ring of truth unless I caused trouble for my governess. Until today I had always thought Judith harmless but I realised I had underestimated the danger that her weakness posed to me. I would not make that mistake again.

'There is so much in this house that displeases me,' Sanderson suddenly groaned. 'Sometimes it is very hard, Florrie, to play the game and go easily amongst it all. But I desire not to add to it, not to be one more person set against other people, to be one constant, at least. I tried to speak to our aunt for you. I tried to tell her the blame did not lie with you. But she did not believe me and there was little I could say without making things worse.'

'I understand,' I murmured, sinking down on the bed. I loved Sanderson. I admired his determination to keep the peace in a house that was anything but peaceful, yet my heart sank as I understood anew he could never be the champion I needed. My thoughts flew suddenly to Turlington. How I wished he were here now to give Annis the benefit of his tongue. *He* did not value peace. *He* was not afraid. But he had run away from me at the exhibition. I had no one.

'Are you all right in here, Florrie?' asked Sanderson.

I reassured him on that. 'It is nice to be away from them all,' I admitted. 'And it is so much better than being in the attic.'

'I still cannot believe they did that. All that time I thought you were here . . .'

'I know. You told me. And before that Calantha told me.'

His face darkened at her name. 'And I am so worried about Calantha,' he said.

'Why? Has something happened?'

He paused for a minute, then shook his head. 'No. Only because she is so very vulnerable, you know, being the way she is. But I did not come here to dispirit you further, Florrie. I came to tell you about Turlington. I'm sorry I did not before. I knew you would want to know. But he asked me not to and I have a long habit of keeping his confidences.'

'But will you tell me now?'

'I will, Florrie, though it is a tale neither edifying nor even particularly unusual.'

'Nevertheless.' I patted the space next to me on the bed, but Sanderson, ever proper, brought my one bedroom chair beside me and sat on that.

'The short of it is this: he sold Annis's necklace and went back to Madeira. He was determined to make his fortune and become independent once and for all. He invested in shipping and sugar both, and things went well for him for a time. He wrote to me of intentions to pay back the wrongs he had done and to live a good, prosperous life. You should not think he forgot you, Florrie. But Turlington is – has always been – very troubled and inconsistent. He wrote to me that he wanted to change, but he knew it would not be easy for him. The drink, you know, has never been his friend.'

'I know it. I've seen it.'

'And I. Many, many times.' Sanderson ran a hand through his curls and for just a moment his youthful face looked old and grey. *Loving someone who will not love himself will do that to a person eventually,* I thought, the insight suddenly flashing upon me.

'Anyhow, he has the highest regard for you, Florrie. No one could doubt it. But he wanted to protect you, I think. He knew life here was hard for you. He thought corresponding with you might create one difficulty too many. He hoped to renew your friendship when he felt more deserving. In truth, I think it may be the first unselfish thought he ever had!'

'He *hoped*?'

'Well, yes. He had a slight setback – a shipment of sugar went down in a storm. He did not lose *all* his money, but he lost heart and spent the rest on drink. He is not good at withstanding the blows of life, Florrie, 'tis not a skill he has.'

'And he needed to come to London to squander the rest?'

'It seems so. He feels safer here. It is his home after all. He knows people who will help him – myself of course, and other less . . . respectable folk. Believe me, Florrie, 'tis best you don't see him now. Even I keep my distance. But I like knowing he is near – nearer, anyway – and so does he. We are only half-brothers but we are close nonetheless.'

'I want to see him.'

'Dearest, he will not. Please, if Hawker knew he was close, he would hunt for him and Hawker is relentless, as you know. He may even call the police. Say nothing. Do nothing to rouse his suspicion. For these darknesses of Turlington's do pass, you know. And his intentions to do better are always very sincere. I live in hope that the next time, if he can only have another chance, he will succeed. And then we could all be so happy.'

I looked at my dear, good cousin, who so loved my aggravating, bad cousin, and I sighed. I think I was growing up a little, for there was a Florrie inside me who longed only to stamp and yell and *demand* to be taken to him. But there was another Florrie – Florence, perhaps – who acknowledged that Sanderson had known him far better for far longer than I. It was this Florrie who sighed and said, 'Very well, Sanderson. I shall not bother you with it.'

He nodded, and let out a deep breath. We sat in silence for a while, reflecting. I had new sympathy for Sanderson. No wonder he liked to keep life uncomplicated where he could. No wonder he rarely showed what he felt, preferring to appear genial and charming at all times. He was guarding some difficult secrets on behalf of his troubled brother, who brimmed over with enough passion for both of them. I wondered if *I* would ever be able to seem as peaceful and constant as Sanderson. These thoughts must have shown in my face, for he smiled and squeezed my hand.

'I am not so good as all that,' he said sadly. 'But life is hard, and I find acceptance is a great balm.'

'I would not know,' I muttered. 'It has always eluded me.'

The next days crawled by and again I felt Helicon pressing down around me, vast, heavy and filled with unhappiness. There were long years before me here. And what lay ahead? The only escape permitted me was to marry and live the same life in a different house. And I could not imagine myself making any such marriage as might please my aunt and Hawker.

And yet, I *was* changing. In my captivity I was brought simple meals but nothing more. Once, it would have seemed ample. Now I had grown accustomed to the constant consumption of 'treats' and soon felt hunger grumbling in my belly. When I ran my hands over it, it was soft and curved where it had once been hard and flat. Once, I would have considered the stifled outings and petty gossip of the Grace ladies' daily life no liberty worth having. Now, I missed being a part of *something*, even if it was nothing I valued. The sweep of moor and valley that had once been my natural habitat now felt like a dream from another lifetime, and without them I felt myself to be floating alone in a callous black sky. I found myself pacing the room, bored with no conversation of any sort to sweeten the hours. I had never known boredom in Braggenstones. Oh yes, I was changing. I was becoming one of them after all, despite my vow that I would always be a Buckley. I was losing my old self and what was to replace her but this flabby, powerless rag doll?

'I'm not a Grace, I'm not a Grace,' I muttered over and over. But I wasn't sure I believed it any more.

Chapter Nineteen

❦

What followed was a state of low spirits I can hardly bear to remember. For almost a month, I was cowed and dark and dull. What had shifted in me during those five days? Even when I was released from my room I spent a lot of time alone. My aunt, still upset over the Great Exhibition, could not bear to have me near for a time. Calantha came often to sit with me without speaking – to me anyway, although she sometimes murmured to companions only she could see. I found her presence comforting, though I could not quite summon the energy to tell her so. I hope she sensed it.

Whether Hawker believed that I had led Judith astray or not I could not tell. He was often absent during that period. When he was at Helicon, he seemed to be everywhere, bullying, hectoring and throwing us all into a confusion of activity. He wanted to see the returns on Irwin's investments. Dinah needed to find favour with this, that and the other family. Sanderson must marry. I must learn to behave properly once and for all . . . Impossible demands and we all twisted ourselves into ships' knots trying to satisfy them. If we had ever stopped to think, no doubt we would have thought some of his demands strange but at the time, with Hawker marching among us, blue eyes ablaze and his shouts of frustration making us jump, they seemed imperative.

Even with Calantha he was brusque. He had always been something approaching gentle with her, making me suspect that perhaps he had a better nature tucked away in some small pocket after all. But now every time he saw her staring into space he would snap at her. Whenever she said something startling and strange, he would cut her to shreds, no matter who was present, and make her cry.

I spent secret hours yearning for life in Braggenstones and counting my birthday coins, though the sum was always the same. Memories of Cornwall sprung up bright and precious, forcing me to yield anew to homesickness.

One of my favourite memories to ponder was when I gave Nan the parcel Old Rilla had given me on my first visit.

When I had returned that day, Nan was cross with me, until I distracted her with the unexpected gifts. As I untied the cloth Nan's mouth opened slightly. She put out one hand to touch the eggs, smooth and brown. It was not as though we'd never had eggs before. But six! All for us! Then I gave her the hawberry brandy. 'That's for you,' I added. 'That's her present to you.'

'For *me*?' She uncorked the bottle and took a suspicious

sniff. I knew what she was thinking, wary old bird that she was. She was wondering if Old Rilla had sent her a magic potion to put a spell on her. But the smell that curled from the open bottle evidently pleased her. She corked it again and nodded. 'That be very kind, aye.'

'She said only to have a thimbleful at a time,' I remembered, but Nan gave me a look which gave that instruction short shrift.

We weren't accustomed, in Braggenstones, to moments of relaxation, to enjoying things for their own sake. But that evening, after all our chores were done, Nan cut two brick-shaped pieces of beech mast sticky and poured a dose of the hawberry brandy for herself which could not fairly be described as a thimbleful and we settled ourselves beside a small fire savouring the delicious and unaccustomed delicacies. I have tried a great many exotic foods since then but I don't think anything has ever made me as happy as that first taste of Old Rilla's sticky, enjoyed with my Nan.

Another memory: every spring, Hesta and I were dispatched by our families to the hill, where the thick green hedges were, and the primroses grew all around like a pale gold ocean. Our job was to gather the dainty flowers, which I had always thought were called 'princesses' when I was little, for tying into bunches and selling at market.

Our primrose days were an idyllic part of that life. In London there is ample scope for young ladies of good breeding to whisper together sharing gentle confidences, bending ringlets over embroidery or sitting in corners at parties. It was not like that in Braggenstones. So when Hesta and I had the chance to spend a whole day together away from everyone else, it felt like a holiday. We would drop down in the middle of the yellow sea and pick flowers and talk all day long. We had lengths of twine ready-measured to secure a fistful of stems together and carried two giant baskets each, in which we laid the posies. White clouds scudded overhead, spring breezes ruffled our hair, birdsong could be heard all around us. We felt like fairy maidens on some magical appointment.

We would walk home in the late afternoon, baskets brimming over with the fragile yellow blooms, the sky turning pink and cold above us. By then we would be shivering after our day amid the brisk March breezes and dreaming of prosaic things – a fire and some hot soup.

Memories like this made it seem impossible that I could ever grow reconciled to my lot at Helicon. In my distance from them I forgot the long, hard days of labouring in the wind and rain, of going hungry, of being cooped up in the cottage during a season of snow. I forgot how my neighbours had annoyed me with their endless preoccupation with money and cleanliness and the tiresome march of chores. I only knew that there had been minutes, hours, days in Braggenstones that were luminous and full of wonder compared with life at Helicon.

★

I was so listless and withdrawn that Sanderson worried about me. He told Aunt Dinah it was high time I learned the piano properly – a valuable accomplishment for any young lady. He would teach me himself, he insisted, it would cause her no expense. He knew I had always longed to learn, and hoped it would lift my spirits.

It did not. Like Turlington, I was not a natural musician. The sheets of black notes dancing across the staves baffled me and my fingers were numb and clumsy on the keys. When I tried to see the patterns in the chords, as Sanderson urged me, I would picture Turlington instead. I imagined him hunched and miserable somewhere squalid. I remembered he had told me, that first night at Helicon, that he had stayed in the Devil's Acre: *A place you are too good ever to see*, he had said.

There had been a time when I would have been overjoyed to sit at the beautiful grand piano with Sanderson, when I would have admired the fretwork music desk and the brass music holders, when I would have examined the handwritten vellum label – John Broadwood & Sons Ltd – with excitement and reverence. That time had passed. I had been at Helicon too long. My spirit was broken, or so I supposed.

But Old Rilla always said that life had a way of hunting you out when the time was right. 'Nature's timing, mind, not yours,' she used to say. Just when things seemed blackest and worst, she taught me, something would come to carry you through, usually through a series of the most unlikely events. So it was for me.

One day I received a note from Selina Westwood, the vicar's wife. She was sorting through her attic looking for suitable things to send to Africa, she wrote. I would do her a great service if I could spare an afternoon to help. My aunt could not forbid it. As neither Annis nor Judith had any interest in handling the dusty relics of a clerical family, she charged Willard, a sour-faced footman with a drooping lip, with chaperoning me. I walked to Mrs Westwood's pleasant home in Marylebone with Willard trotting behind like a mangy dog.

I was there but an hour – Mrs Westwood could have easily cleared the attic herself. I think she had only sent for me to distract me. I suspected that Sanderson had put her up to it; they were friends of a sort and I knew he had great faith in her ability to comfort. But although I liked her very much, she was too close to the family for me to confide in her.

Nevertheless, I set off back to Helicon with a sinking heart that my reprieve was over so soon. To rectify this I took a different route from usual. The strategy worked a little too well and soon I was lost – no streams or trees or spirits to guide me here. I said nothing to Willard; I disliked the man and, besides, I would as soon be lost as find my way to Helicon.

I soon found myself in a small cobbled street with pretty houses crowded together and shops that somehow reminded me of home. A grocer had several neat carts laid out before his premises and the sight of brilliant red tomatoes, deep green ruffled cabbages and dependable old dirty-white potatoes with the brown earth still clinging to them leapt out at me like the memory of something lost. I found myself hungering, both literally and metaphorically, for a return to all that was good and simple and wholesome.

And there was a cheese shop, with great wheels of pale, primrose-yellow cheese glinting in the window. The shop boasted a woman's touch, for flowered curtains framed the display and the window frame was painted a bright white. Gold lettering above proclaimed the shop to be *Speedwell Cheese – Purveyor of Cheeses to the Duke of Busby*. The name and legend brought a smile to my face for the first time in weeks. On impulse, I went inside.

A young woman behind the counter looked up and smiled. She had blonde hair, green eyes and a wide mouth. We greeted each other, then I stood awkwardly, for I had no idea why I'd come. I had no money, save the shilling I always carried in case of the unexpected.

'Would you like to try a sample, miss?' asked the girl. She came out from the counter holding a china platter with small pieces of different cheeses laid out in rows. 'This is Cheddar and this is Gouda. This is Parmesan and this Camembert.' I selected a piece at random, feeling even worse. She was so nice and it seemed wrong to take free samples with no intention of giving them any business. Though I did not know how I would explain to Aunt Dinah that I had spent my emergency shilling on cheese . . .

While I wrestled with my difficulty the doorbell jangled again. The girl smiled, then her expression turned to one of fear. Before I could ask what was wrong, someone seized my shoulder, pulling me off-balance. A strong arm in a rough black sleeve clasped me around the chest, pinning my arms and leaving me helpless. A sweaty, sour cloud enfolded me.

'Where's the money?' demanded a grating voice in my ear. I smelled whisky fumes and tooth decay. 'Give me the money and nothing will happen to the young lady.'

'We don't keep it on the premises!' gasped the girl, looking in horror at a spot a little to the left of my chest. 'Please don't hurt her, she has nothing to do with us. There's no money here.'

I slid my eyes sideways to see what she was looking at and glimpsed the blade of a long knife. The thought crossed my mind that if I were killed, it would make life much simpler for everyone. That frightened me more than the danger I was in.

Suddenly I was released and the man sprang at the girl, sending the china tasting platter flying through the air. It shattered against a wall – cheese everywhere – and the door flew open again. Willard had heard the commotion.

'I'll call the constable, you rogue!' he shouted and disappeared.

Meanwhile the villain had manhandled the girl to the counter and pushed her behind it so she was pinned between wall and man. He was tall and broad, with long, dark hair straggling over his shoulders and blue, bloodshot eyes glittering in an unshaven, tortured face. Here was a man who had lost everything. I felt a strange kinship with him, though I knew that he had gone far beyond me to a place of desperation where he no longer cared about anyone. That made him dangerous.

I stood in an agony of indecision. What could I possibly do to help? With the counter slammed shut behind them, he was ransacking the shelves above, waving the knife wildly in the direction of the shop girl as he did so. China, glass, accounts ledgers and other items rained down around her, catching her on the shoulders and feet. I couldn't help trying to reach them, rattling the counter in vain, though I don't know what I thought I could have done. He towered over us both and he was drunk and wild . . . I tried anyway, throwing myself at the counter in the hope that I could somehow break through, and all the while he was ransacking and knife-waving as well as roaring at me and making occasional slashes towards my face with the knife.

At a footstep behind me I turned in relief, hoping to see the constable. Instead there stood a slight young man of around twenty with fair hair and spectacles and a scholarly air.

'What on earth is going on?' he demanded in outrage.

'Walk away, young gent!' roared the would-be thief. 'Walk away and keep walkin' and then walk some more for luck. Forget you ever saw this and keep your life.'

'Absolutely ludicrous proposition,' said the gentleman in cultured tones, to my utter astonishment. 'Come here at once and answer to me! Leave that poor young lady alone!'

'Answer to *you*?' The desperate man paused incredulously and laughed. Then, apparently overcome with frustration, he seized the girl again and I gasped. He tipped her head so far back I thought he would snap it off and brought the tip of the knife slowly to her smooth white throat.

'I don't want no trouble,' he said deliberately, and incongruously. 'I just needs some money. Give me what you have and I'll let you go.'

Of course she could not respond.

'She's already told you there's no money in here!' I shouted. 'Don't you think she'd give it if there were?'

The young gentleman laid a respectful hand on my arm and smiled at me. 'Please step aside, miss,' he said, 'and don't be afraid.' Then he stepped up to the counter and said, 'Now that's quite enough of that,' in the tone of a parent separating two squabbling children.

I cringed for him, as the robber reached out a long arm and hauled him bodily over the counter, flinging him against the wall and turning, knife in hand, from the girl to this new vexation. He towered above our rescuer. I could hardly bear to watch and wished in vain for the constable. It was all going to be violent and tragic and terrifying.

Then somehow the young man seemed to step into the

robber's heavy lunge so that the larger man's arm lay draped over his shoulder for a moment, as though they were friends. The next minute the villain was on the ground, seemingly unable to move and the knife was safe in the young scholar's hand. He led the shop girl courteously by the hand into the open space of the shop, found two chairs for us to sink upon, and returned to stand over the villain until the constable came and tried to take all the credit. He was closely followed by Willard, and *he* was soon shadowed by a newspaper reporter with avid eyes. Beyond those sequential details I had no idea what had happened.

I had a confused impression of being asked many questions by everyone. Willard's questions were mostly along the lines of, 'Well, I don't suppose this will learn you, will it?' and, 'Now are you glad you went traipsing about London?' The reporter wanted to know my name and age and what had happened. Only our unlikely rescuer asked how I felt and whether I required an escort anywhere.

After I knew not how long, I allowed Willard to lead me from the scene of the drama and the shop girl – Miss Rebecca Speedwell, I had learned – escaped the clutches of the reporter to dart after me.

'Thank you,' she said, 'for your courage and for not abandoning me. Please, please, come and visit me, if it would not trouble you to return here.'

'I should like that very much. Thank you.' On impulse

I took her hand. I had dropped the habit of friendly, spontaneous gestures of late but this one was not rebuffed. She held my hand warmly and held my gaze too.

'Please come,' she said again. 'I think perhaps we might be friends?'

'I have such need of a friend,' I admitted.

Chapter Twenty

It had been a terrible shock, of course, and I slept very little that night. Yet now when I think back, I bless that desperate robber for the event was a turning point in my life. That moment at knife-point, when I had been indifferent as to whether I lived or died, had jolted me out of my inertia. I did not know yet what I could do, but I knew I must do *something*, in order to live better than of late. I remembered my indifference to life after my father died. Old Rilla had come to me and demanded, 'Do you wish to live a life?' Even at the age of eight I had understood that a person could be alive without really living and I had made the decision then, from the depths of my despair, that I *would* live a life. I felt admiration for my younger self and now, though not without misgivings, I made the pledge once again.

The following day I was in the drawing room with Annis and Judith. They dipped dainty needles in and out of embroidery while I practised my piano scales to the increasing frustration of us all. But today I felt a difference. I noticed the way the light fell through the window and spilled onto the piano lid, highlighting the warm, wave-like grain of the wood. Medullary rays, Sanderson had called those beautiful dark undulations, when he had tried to enthuse me about the piano. A lovely phrase. I could not appreciate it then, but today I could. Pleasure leapt in me. I stopped playing for a moment to lay my hands on the wood and truly appreciate that, at last, I was doing something I had dreamed of my whole life. I smiled.

In the silence, blessed relief that it was, we heard a kerfuffle in the downstairs hall; a sort of altercation and stumbling about. Annis and Judith both paused mid-stitch and raised their eyebrows. I froze. So soon after the previous day's excitement I could only imagine the man from yesterday come to wreak revenge. I heard servants cry out in indignation and then footsteps – one set, manly – striding up the stairs towards us. I wanted to run but I was frozen on the piano seat as the footsteps grew nearer and nearer and the drawing room door was at last flung open.

It was Turlington.

Annis shrieked. 'You hellfiend! Where's my necklace? Give it back!'

I had forgotten that he had stolen her necklace.

He laughed. 'A pleasure to see you too after this long while, and I thank you for your kind enquiries after my health. Your necklace, I regret, is long sold, along with some opal earrings that perhaps you haven't missed yet. Many a fine adventure they have paid for, so thank you, Cousin Annis.'

'I hate you,' she spat. 'Hate you with every bone in my body. Mother will deal with you. What are you doing here anyway? You are banned, you know, from Helicon. You are not to set foot in the house, Hawker said so.'

'And yet, despite that unconquerable blockade, I am here as you see. Crossed the threshold as easily as a blushing bride carried by her groom. As to why I am here? Why, to see Florrie of course.'

As he said it his sardonic manner softened and he crossed the room to drop to his knees at my side and take both my hands.

'I saw the newspaper,' he murmured. 'Are you well, my little Cornish witch? Were you hurt? Frightened? Let me see you,' and he poured his soul into my eyes – at least, that's how it felt to me. His face clouded. 'No, you are not well at all,' he said.

I felt as if I were drowning. Everything came rushing up to meet me and I felt I could tumble forward into his eyes, onto his lips . . . What *was* this strange feeling? Annis and Judith must be watching us, I was dimly aware, and yet I couldn't pull back from him, I couldn't . . . He reached up a hand and touched my face.

'Beautiful,' he murmured, 'more than ever, and yet so sad. But that's not because of yesterday, is it?'

I swallowed. I breathed in hard. I sat up very straight. 'No,'

I answered at last. 'As for yesterday, it was frightening at the time but no lasting harm was done, I believe.'

'Then I thank the God I don't believe in for that. I would have Him watch over you in every moment, to keep you safe.'

'Even though you don't believe in Him.'

'For myself, no. But for you, Florrie, why not? You can be surrounded by gods and fairies and angels and any manner of elementals – strange, lovely girl that you are, with your strange, lovely heart. And I would have them all range about you, if they were mine to command.'

'I'm fetching Mama,' said Annis, appearing disgusted by the scene before her. I heard her voice, calling her mother, fading as she ran down the long corridor. Over Turlington's shoulder I saw Judith's button eyes, big and dark and round in her face, displaying something like wistfulness.

I was aware that his words were weaving spells about me . . . and then suddenly I remembered the exhibition. I pulled my hands from Turlington's and shot up from my stool so quickly he fell back on his heels.

'It was good of you to come and enquire after my wellbeing, Cousin,' I remarked, 'but as you can see I am quite well and you were not so eager to see me once, I believe, so please do not trouble yourself further.'

'Whatever can you mean? Not glad to see *you*, Florrie? That could never be!'

'And yet it *was*,' I said with feeling, and then stopped.

He frowned, took my hand again and led me from the room. 'We'll be in the garden,' he said to Judith. 'Don't join us.'

He strode to the garden, and sat me on a garden seat beneath the fragrant stems of a juniper tree. *To ward off evil spirits*, I thought reflexively.

'What troubles you, Florrie? When did I not wish to see you?'

'At the Crystal Palace last month! I saw you and I called out. You took one look at me and strode off through the crowd – you couldn't get away fast enough. You left me to chase after you like a foolish child. *You ran away from me*. Don't pretend you can't remember. Don't pretend it didn't happen.'

'That was *you*? Oh, Florrie! Of course I remember the day! But I did not *see* you, I swear it! I only *heard* you. Truly, Florrie, I thought it was Annis or Judith! You sounded – you *sound* – just like them! Your accent is all gone. Your tone is haughty. You sound like a *Grace*.'

I was stunned. Then perhaps I had not been snubbed after all? Despite all that Sanderson had told me I had still not been able to recover from the hurt of *that*.

'It was still *my voice*,' I sulked, almost afraid of what would happen if I forgave him. He conceded it, but pointed out that the exact timbre of a voice screeching a name above a rumbling crowd and a medley of other noises was hard to discern. I supposed I must credit that.

'Then Sanderson told me that you'd been in London all

along. I missed you, Turlington, so much, when you left. Why could you not include me in the secret?'

'You missed me?'

'Of *course* I did! You *know* what my life here has been! You *know* how I starve for understanding. I thought I had it with you, but you have cut yourself off from me. I have been inconsequential to you.'

'Inconsequential? No, Florrie, never that. I was trying to do the right thing for once, in a way.'

'Sanderson told me so. And I appreciate that – I think. But still . . . you have left a gap, Turlington.'

His dark eyes flooded with light. 'Truly? My heart bursts to hear it. But your life is hard enough. You had no way to survive unless you changed and adapted. Lord, Florrie, how your easy smile and irreverent ways would have brightened my days this year past, but I had to be unselfish. Leave you in peace to become some sort of a Grace. And by God you have done it and done it admirably. You're a young lady now, not a child, not a changeling, though I suspect you still of being a fairy spirit. You're as proud and elegant as Annis herself, only vastly sweeter.'

'Did you not think that being cut off from you, my only true . . .' Here I faltered for I had been about to say 'friend' but Sanderson was my friend, of course, so what was it about Turlington that was somehow even more important, more visceral? 'My only true *kindred*, would be a cruel blow for me?'

'I do not value my own worth so highly, Florrie, that I could see myself as a loss to you. I knew we had a special friendship, but I did not know it had made such an impression on *you*.'

'Well then, it didn't,' I fumed, loath to tell him that to me he was as vital as the stars and the moon turning about the world.

'And yet it did, I see,' he breathed, tipping my chin with a fingertip, so that my face was looking up at him. 'I am sorry, sweet witch, I did not mean to hurt you. Not *you*. For I truly believe you are the one soul on this godforsaken planet who—' he stopped suddenly and waved an arm prohibitively. I turned to see Sanderson advancing on us.

'She's coming!' he called out. 'You have perhaps two minutes.'

'Then let us have them, brother,' said Turlington, turning back to me. 'What we felt last year, Florrie, was it real then? Despite the fact that I am a man grown and a poor show of one at that, and you a child? Despite the fact that we are cousins? Despite everything? Is it real?'

And all I could do was nod, in agony, feeling the impossibility of everything about my life. It was the *only* real thing, it seemed to me. He took my hands in his and I clung to them.

'I go back to Madeira next week,' he said urgently. 'You will not see me for a while, Florrie but now I know . . . I have hope . . . it will be different. And I will come back. Somehow. I *will* be a better man and then—'

'Don't forget me, Turlington,' I heard myself say through

tears and a haze of emotion so deep it tumbled me. 'Don't go!' But he was leaving and my hands were empty. Our aunt was castigating him, Sanderson was at my side and Turlington just kept walking away.

After he was gone, I tried to sift through the pieces of the puzzle of what had passed between us. Perhaps then Annis was right and I was in love with him after all. And amidst the confusion and darkness of his life it was clear he cared deeply for me. He had promised to return a better man. Because of me? But what then? He was banished from the family. Grace cousins could not marry. So what could there ever be for us but a strange, stretched-out friendship? Yet, if that were all we could have, I still wanted it, desperately. He had said it would be different this time. I hoped that meant that he would write. Yet time passed, and no letter came, and I did not see him again for almost three years.

Chapter Twenty-one

Thank God for Rebecca. If a sunbeam had become incarnate, and been dressed up in a neat striped dress, that personification would have been Rebecca. I was so shaken by Turlington's unexpected appearance and abrupt exit that it was a full week before I could marshal myself to pay her the promised call. Aunt Dinah disapproved – a Grace should not have a social connection with a cheese shop – yet she was hard-pressed to forbid it when I reminded her of the danger I had been in with Miss Speedwell. It would have been inexplicably unmannerly not to go and enquire after her. So Aunt Dinah despatched Willard to trail after me once again.

Rebecca greeted me with her wide, green-eyed smile and took both my hands in welcome. Today a stocky boy of about fourteen was with her in the shop – pressing a broom about the floor and glancing out of the window in a brisk manner, as though daring a thief to enter.

'Adam has been with us since the . . . upset,' she told me, untying her apron. 'My father was extremely perturbed about it. Adam, will you watch the shop, please? I will take some tea with Miss Buckley for half an hour or so.'

'I'll let nothing happen to them, Miss Rebecca,' he declared, casting a protective glance over the cheeses.

I remembered that in all the upset of the robbery I had given my name as Florence Buckley. In those moments of extreme duress, I had reverted to my real self. I explained the error to Rebecca as she led me up the stairway and into a snug parlour decorated in red, gold and cream, where she rang for tea and toast – with cheese upon it, of course.

We sat on a plump cherry-coloured sofa before a small fire that furnished the room with a cheerful light more welcome than warmth, for the day was grey but not cold. We skipped quickly through the usual pleasantries since we were both impatient to be friends. She took a great interest in the story of how I had come to be in London among a new family and with a new name. She, too, had lost her mother at a young age.

'So now it is just Papa and me,' she concluded with a small sigh, 'and has been these ten years. He is a good father only . . .' She shook her head and I could tell there was more to say, but that she was a dutiful daughter and would not. 'But that is enough of me, Florence. How do you find your life with the Graces? I have heard of them, of course! I don't know that I would have dared invite you here had I known whom I was addressing. A Grace! The audacity of me!'

'Then I am eternally thankful for the lapse that made me

give my other name,' said I, licking grease from my fingers in a most un-Grace-like fashion, 'for I am nothing like them, Rebecca, whatever you may have heard.'

'I only tease you. I should have wanted to be friends if you were the Princess of Sweden. My father would have liked that,' she added reflectively. 'He would have pressed you for contacts in the Scandinavian cheese industry. He prides himself on his international selection. Promise me you won't be put off coming here when you meet him, Florence.'

'Of course, but why would I be?'

'Oh, never mind,' she said again. 'Tell me of you.' Clearly whatever she wanted to say was in conflict with her loyalty to her father. I suffered no such compunction towards the Graces.

She listened in such a warm and sympathetic manner, and I was so starved of warmth and sympathy that I found myself going on at far greater length than I had intended, laying out the facts of my life in London with a generous splash of self-pity. But the conversation had the feeling of a heart-to-heart between old friends, rather than a first call on a new acquaintance. It felt as though there had been a hundred such conversations between us before and that there would be plenty to come. I could tell that she was hurt and outraged on my behalf therefore I was astonished when I concluded my tale of woe and she said, 'I think you must learn to love them, Florence.'

'*Love* them?' I echoed. 'But . . . how can I? How can I when I detest everything about them and there is no understanding between us, much though I would wish it otherwise?'

'It will not be easy,' she agreed, squeezing my hand. 'But you are stuck with them for now, are you not?' I agreed miserably that I was. 'Then for one thing, it will simply make your life easier. But for another, and more importantly, they are your mother's family. Therefore, they are yours.'

I mumbled that I was all too aware of it.

'But you have not accepted it. If they are your family, then they are part of *you*. By rejecting them you are rejecting a part of yourself. If you only know and understand one side of you, you're like a bird with one wing – you can't fly. And you *must* fly, Florence, that is clear to me after knowing you but twenty minutes. Some people are destined to walk on the ground but not you.'

I did not answer right away for I wanted to let her words sink in and do justice to her wisdom. I did not like her advice, yet it touched something within me. I wasn't quite ready, however, to relinquish my grudge.

'I'm glad to hear you say it, but since coming to them I have felt my wings clipped and plucked and altogether torn off. It is they who have done this. How then can accepting them bring my wings back?'

'I don't know,' she said with a serious face. 'I only know that it will. Do you ever experience that, Florence? Knowing something that no rational mind can explain and knowing you must be true to it even though you could put no justification into words?'

I stared at her and nodded slowly. 'I used to,' I said. 'I used to all the time. It's been a long time since my instincts spoke to me like that. Except for . . .' I suddenly thought of Turlington. My aunt had done everything in her power to prevent me from following my instincts, indeed to confound me so that I no longer remembered that I even had any. Even so, they had survived and shouted loudly on one particular: that somehow Turlington and I were one.

'Never mind,' I added, not wanting to add another long, complicated confession to my first. 'I am sure there is wisdom in what you say. I have become so entrenched in longing for all that I was and all I have lost that I have not been living well. I realised it after that day, here, with the robber. I want to find a better way.'

Rebecca sat up straight and patted my hand. 'Those things are not lost, my dear, I feel sure of it, they are merely dormant. When the time comes for you to be a Buckley again it will be as if you were never anything else. But for now you are a Grace, and remember, they are proud and powerful. Now, I have a suggestion. Would you stay a while longer? My father is dining out tonight and whilst I have no objection to you meeting him at *some* point, this evening will be more enjoyable for his absence. Do you have a later engagement? Might you send your manservant away, and stay for supper? I shall ask Adam to drive you home in our cart later?'

'Oh, I should love that,' I said wistfully. I wanted more than anything to stay in that warm, easy parlour with my lovely, bright new friend. But Willard was in my aunt's charge to keep me to the line. He had been loitering in the street this long while to take me home. He was in the pay of the Graces and he would not allow it, and I said so.

Rebecca raised her eyebrows. 'But, my dear, what have I been saying? Are *you* not a Grace?'

'So they keep telling me.'

'Then he is your servant too.'

It sounded so simple, put like that. Because, of course, it *was*! It was as if a piece of machinery – one of those giant cogs I had seen at the Great Exhibition – fell into place with a clunk inside my head.

'My dear,' said I. 'You are quite right.'

After I had sent Willard away – no easy task, since giving orders did not come naturally to me – I returned to the parlour alone. Rebecca had some small chores to do before retiring for the day and at her suggestion I took off my shoes and curled up on the red sofa. I dozed and dreamed and watched the pictures that danced in the fire. Here at last was a refuge from it all. My head was lolling and a small ribbon of drool making its stealthy way across my cheek when Rebecca returned with a box of chocolates to keep us occupied before dinner. The twin treats of chocolate and her company roused me quickly.

'My dear, may I impart to you a confidence of my own?' she asked, her eyes bright and eager.

'Of course!' I said, sitting up and wiping my cheek with the back of my hand.

'Well, you remember Mr Ballantine, I suppose? You know, the gentleman who saved us from the robber that day.'

I replied that I could hardly be expected to forget *him*.

'Quite. Exactly! Well, the case is this. I believe I am in love with him.' She beamed at me, her green eyes bright and expectant, a few freckles standing out on her nose as she grew pale with the importance of it.

'Oh! I am delighted! And of course he returns your feelings?'

She blushed a little and looked modest. 'I believe so. He has called every day since the incident and though he has said nothing of a romantic nature, I believe his eyes express an admiration and affection for me that I . . . well, that I enjoy very much.'

'I am certain that he must. You are beautiful and clever and he saved your life! Oh, my dear, I am happy for you. But tell me, how did he do what he did that day? I thought he was sure to be flattened, and then he felled that huge man as though it were the easiest thing in the world. It seems like a sort of miracle to me.'

'I said exactly the same thing. He told me that he lived many years in China as a boy and they have there a very ancient art, a fighting art, which everybody practises in one form or another. Mr Ballantine was lucky enough to learn from an old Chinese master. Those are the skills he employed to save us.'

'How extraordinary. And how fortunate for us!'

'Isn't it? He is the most *courageous* of men! And *look*, Florence, he gave me this!' She showed me an exquisite lamp made of drops of enigmatic green. 'It is Chinese jade, one of his treasures from that country. He says it matches my eyes. Is it not beautiful?'

I admired it. 'Perhaps in a few months we will still be friends and you will be telling me of your engagement in this very room.'

'That we will be friends is not in doubt. Of the other thing I am less certain. You see, there is my father.' Her easy smile disappeared and she looked suddenly tense.

'He disapproves? Of the man who saved his daughter?'

She wrinkled her nose. 'And of every other man. And indeed, every other living being in the world.' All at once her words came out in a rush. 'Oh, do not mistake me, I love him dearly, but he is not a sociable man and is extremely wary of anyone outside the two of us. Florence, promise me again that when you meet him you will not let him deter you from seeing me. He will most likely be rude and unwelcoming and you have enough people like that in your life already, but I do not want to lose you – or Tobias.'

'You will not. That is his name? Tobias Ballantine? How

romantic. Rebecca Ballantine,' I teased dreamily. 'It suits you well.'

She blushed again. 'Is it imbecilic to have had these thoughts after knowing him only a week? Yet what could there be about him that is not of good character, not worthy? He is kind and brave and he is remarkable, as you have seen. But he does not wear his abilities like blazing medals for all to see. He is humble and quiet. He is studying to become a professor at the university and he is passionate about philosophy. He is from what we like to call a good family, but he cares nothing for that. All men are equals to him and he is equally gracious to all. There are not many men like him, Florence.'

'No, there are not,' I agreed, thinking fleetingly of Turlington, who seemed to be gracious to very few. 'But surely your father will not put off Mr Ballantine, Rebecca? After all, our desperate villain did not intimidate him.'

'In a contest between a hulking, drunken brute and my father, as to who might appear more hostile,' mused Rebecca, frowning, 'I believe my father would have the upper hand. However, no, I do not think Tobias would be swayed. It is more a question of whether I could ever bear to break Papa's heart and brave his anger. He is my father after all, and I have had none but him to care for me these many years.'

'Does he never wish you to marry at all?'

'I think not.'

'And you think Mr Ballantine could not win him over, even

with all his worthy qualities? If it is a case of your happiness, could he really be so grudging?'

'How can I make you understand? My dear, when you think about what could have befallen us – and the shop too – if Tobias had not come . . . Well, what kind of reward would *you* have offered, if it was your shop, your daughter?'

'Gracious, nothing I can think of would be enough! But a goodly sum of money, perhaps. My undying gratitude and friendship, certainly. Why? What did your father offer?'

'Cheese.'

I had not expected that. 'A cheese?' I echoed.

'No. A *piece* of cheese. It was less than a quarter.'

Silence fell between us and the fire crackled in the interval. There was really nothing to say except, at last, 'What kind of cheese?'

'I believe it was Caerphilly.'

My visits to Rebecca became the sustaining force in my life. My obligations to the Graces were plentiful, but visit her I did. I insisted that I go without Willard and stay for the whole afternoon and supper besides, every Thursday.

I met her father within the month. He was a tall, thin gentleman, curiously S-shaped, like the initial of his surname. His head and neck were pushed forward, his shoulders sagged towards the rear. His belly also pushed forward, yet somehow his feet dragged behind, as though he were reluctant to make progress in any direction at all. As Rebecca had promised, he was extremely ungracious and curt. However, I could not help but sympathise with him. He did not have the gift of winning people over, I could see at once, and in the few moments that Rebecca left us alone together, the room dimmed without her. I resented his selfishness on her behalf, yet I could understand how diminished his life would be if she left him. He must be very afraid. That said, I avoided his company whenever I could.

This uneasy blend of dislike with compassion was something I began, slowly, to extend to the members of my own family. I fancied it was like learning new passages of music for the piano. Every time Sanderson set me a new challenge, I was daunted; I hated it. I missed the old pieces that I had mastered before it. But as I struggled and frowned over the new one, I grew reconciled to difficult chords or unexpected notes by the pleasure of producing – eventually, effortfully – music. Just so with the Graces: my year of struggling, doing battle with them, familiarising myself with their strange ways had somehow made me receptive to Rebecca's advice. I still did not *like* them, but I felt some satisfaction in seeing more in them than I had done at first.

On one occasion I was walking past my aunt's study when I heard my grandfather's voice, shouting like a madman. As I hurried past, the door flew open and he stumped out like an angry imp.

'Grand-Florence!' he roared. 'Your aunt needs you. In you go.'

He hurried off along the corridor and I went inside with a sinking heart, but for once I had done nothing amiss.

My aunt looked as happy as ever to see me, which was not at all. She straightened some papers on her desk and smoothed her hair.

'Oh, Florence, Hawker wished me to speak to you about whether your friend's father could provide us with some exotic cheese for Friday's dinner. Something truly unusual. The Lattimers are coming, you know, there is a great need to impress.'

I looked at her, surprised. She rarely spoke to me so mildly. I looked closer. Her eyes were red. I would not wish to assume she had been crying, but she looked tired, I realised suddenly, tired and stretched to her limits. Always sweeping about the house, commanding young Graces as she would an army, she never betrayed any weakness, yet her expression as she looked at me now was almost pleading.

My days of making smart retorts were behind me, but I would not have baited her then in any case.

'Of course, Aunt. I would not see her 'til Thursday ordinarily but perhaps Mr Speedwell may need more than a day to consider it. Would you like me to go tomorrow? Or I can send a note if you would prefer me to stay here.'

She looked nonplussed by my obliging tone. 'You may go tomorrow, if you please. The Lattimers have been travelling.

We wish to include foods from as many different countries as possible, the more far-flung the better. Will your Mr Speed-well be able to help, do you think?'

'I am certain of it. He prides himself precisely on his unusual collection.' I paused. I knew that Hawker had been talking about winning over the Lattimers for a long time. 'Is there anything else I can do to help you, Aunt?'

'Heavens no, girl. Friday's dinner is far too important to risk *you* getting involved.' She frowned and looked down at her papers. Then she looked up again. 'Thank you,' she added.

'You're welcome. If you think of anything . . .'

'Yes. You may go.'

I cannot report that this signalled the beginning of many a fond exchange between us, but it did make me see that she had pressures and problems of her own. Suddenly I did not wish to add to them.

My friendship with Rebecca had other benefits besides the provision of cheese to the Grace household. At her invitation, I sometimes took Calantha with me when I visited; it did her no good to be always cooped up at Helicon. Yet there were so few places she could comfortably be taken, so few people who did not notice her oddness. Turlington was one, but he was long gone. So she lived a strange sort of half-life, drifting around the house like a beautiful ghost.

She enjoyed the walks through London with me, and she

liked Rebecca very much, as anyone must who met her. Aside from an unusual conviction that the cheeses were communicating silently with each other, she seemed to like the bright, welcoming space of the shop. Adam stared at her in mute admiration whenever she came.

In the apartment upstairs, while Rebecca and I conversed, she would often wander around the room touching the patterned curtains and the jade drop lamp and the furniture, chattering under her breath to all these things. But that did not unsettle Rebecca any more than it unsettled me and when the time came for toast and cheese, Calantha devoured more than anyone, her lovely face joyous and smudged with grease.

Rebecca also began to act as an unofficial post office for letters from Lacey. Lacey had adhered faithfully to the six-monthly rule in order to preserve our connection. I had sneaked two or three extra letters in the post to her when Turlington had taken me about London, knowing she could not reply. Now our correspondence flew unchecked and I was brought up to date with news of home. It was a mixed blessing, perhaps, for it always made me homesick, but at least now I had someone besides Sanderson to talk to about it. Rebecca listened to my idealised descriptions of my homeland with shining eyes.

'I wish I could see it, dear. Imagine if we could take a trip – Tobias, myself and you. You could show us all your beautiful places. Wouldn't that be magical?'

She and Tobias remained friends – her father adamant that

he would not countenance her courting – but her refusal to stop dreaming was a wonderful thing.

And she would not let me feel sorry for myself. Oh, she grieved for all I had lost, but when I became too maudlin she stopped me.

'I'm denied everything that I am here,' I told her bitterly one day. 'Every source of true comfort, every way of coming to know the world . . . nature, freedom, all are denied me.' She could not argue with it, yet she was undaunted.

'Then turn to your scholarship, Florence, learn to, to . . . wield new wands. There is always another avenue, dear, no matter how many are closed off to you. It is the nature of life that there is always another.' She was so convinced and convincing that I started to feel she must be right.

Under her gentle coaching I began to accept, at last, that I was a Grace, even to turn the fact to my advantage.

'Perhaps, dear, you are more of an asset to them than you realise,' she suggested one wet day in December. 'You have spirit, Florence. You are neither debauched nor acquiescent. You know what it is to be free. In some ways you are more of a Grace than any of them. For this reason I am sure you hold a stronger hand with your grandfather than you realise.'

'I should not like to play it.'

'But if you should need to – perhaps the time will come . . . Stop feeling like the outsider now, the inconvenience. You have been with them over a year. I would not know you had come from a different background if you had not told me. You're a beautiful young woman. In time men will want to marry you. You could bless the family with an advantageous match, or you could refuse, and choose someone they would heartily disapprove of . . . You see the power you have to make a difference to them? You, with all your talents and assets.'

It was a considerable mental adjustment to make. However, things did start to change for me at Helicon. My improved spirits were remarked upon by all the Grace acquaintances: the Westwoods, the Coatleys and many other socialite friends. Dowager ladies encrusted with diamonds almost as big as the Koh-i-Noor petted me on the head and murmured approving, desperately patronising remarks. Several beaux of Annis and Judith asked me to dance more than once at parties. I *should* have been above feeling triumph at the ire this caused my cousins, but I was not.

And my piano playing became something more than a punishment for the entire household; my hours of practice at last fed into my music and began to transform it. This in turn fuelled my optimism. For if the mighty iceberg of my musical ineptitude could begin to melt and thaw, then what else might change that now seemed impossible?

Chapter Twenty-two

But then something happened to test me all over again. I returned home one Thursday evening to hear raised voices in the drawing room. I hesitated in the corridor with a sinking heart. This was nothing unusual at Helicon but every time it happened I shrank from it and wished with all my soul that I was not part of a family so combative and inharmonious. Usually I hid. But today I stopped and remembered what Rebecca had told me repeatedly. *I am a part of this family. I may not like it but I must accept it . . . And I am not perfect either*, I added in a frank admission of my own.

As I considered thus, I realised with surprise that the raised voice I could hear was Sanderson's. *That* was unusual.

'Of all the despicable, inhuman things!' he was saying – nay, yelling; there was no other word for it. 'I will *not* countenance it! I will do everything in my power to stop it . . .'

'But you *have* no power!'

That was Hawker, harsh and swift. Silence.

I was afraid. Always the arguments at Helicon involved Hawker, my aunt and me. Occasionally Judith and Annis.

Never once had I heard Sanderson intervene except in the most reasonable and placatory tones. If Sanderson was angry – *this* angry – something was very bad.

I took a deep breath and went inside.

Everyone ignored me. Hawker was standing before the fireplace; Sanderson was standing over him. He was glowering. His fists were clenched. I had never seen him thus. Aunt Dinah was also standing; her face was expressionless. Her husband sat in an armchair at her side, looking deeply uncomfortable. He was slumped in the chair as though he hoped to sink right through it and disappear. Annis and Judith sat bolt upright on the sofa, wide-eyed, like two matching kittens who had spied a bird.

Hawker continued in a voice as low as it was deadly. 'You have no power at all, young man, not within this family and not outside it. You would do well to remember that. I am not interested in your humanitarian doctrines nor do I care about your personal feelings. The discussion is ended. The decision is made.'

I watched, horrified, as Sanderson took up a crystal decanter from a side table and hurled it at the wall. It burst into smithereens, reminding me of the long ago day I had thrown the butter dish at my aunt.

'What will you do, then?' he challenged. 'Lock me in the attic as if I were a young girl? Banish me, like Turlington?'

'I will do nothing at all,' said Hawker. 'You have made a demonstration of how deeply you care about this, and it impresses me not a whit. You have made a mess. A servant shall clear it. You have robbed your aunt of an ornament – she can take that up with you herself. Your petulant displays will not move me, Sanderson. However, if there are any more, I can always disinherit you. Then you will forever be as impotent as you are now. How would that feel?'

Sanderson looked at Hawker as though he were seeing him for the very first time. 'Can you not think?' he growled. 'Can you not feel? It's not too late for this. Don't do it. I beg you. Aunt Dinah! Irwin! *Please.*'

'It is a bad business, Hawker, in my view, for what it's worth,' mumbled Irwin. I was astonished anew. If Sanderson was peace-loving and accepting, Irwin was a wet rag blowing in a breeze. My whole body crackled with fear.

'Aunt!' Sanderson stalked to her side and took her hand. Kissed it. 'Please. Let sense prevail for once in this house.'

And even my aunt looked unhappy. She cast a glance at Hawker but he was staring at her, his chin jutting, his blue eyes hard and fiery as diamonds. She looked away. 'It must be done, Sanderson,' she said, her voice gruff. And her next words sent a chill through me. 'She is a liability to this family.'

Was this about *me*?

Sanderson made a choking sound and threw her hand away from him, turned on his heel and stalked from the room.

'Sanderson, what has *happened*?' I implored him, catching his arm as he swept past me, but he shrugged me off.

I stared at the others. 'Well?'

But the tableau seemed frozen for the longest while. The only movement came from Hawker, who was drumming his fingers on the mantel. Eventually he roused himself and spoke. 'Dinah, send for someone to clean that up. Florence, go and find your hysterical cousin. No doubt he will tell you all you wish to know. The rest of you, I don't care what you do, but let us go about our day.'

I found Sanderson in the library, standing at the window. His hands, white-knuckled, clutched the frame on either side. A tumbler of whisky stood on the sill, ignored.

'Sanderson, please talk to me. I'm afraid.'

He turned and his face was white too. His eyes were dark. For a moment, despite his opposite colouring, he looked like Turlington.

'I thought I'd try Turlington's remedy,' he said, looking distractedly at the tumbler. 'But I find I don't want it. What difference can it possibly make? What is the point of something that makes things worse, not better?'

'What is so bad, Sanderson? You must tell me.'

'Florrie. Oh, my dear, then they still haven't told you.'

I shook my head.

He wrapped his arms around me and spoke into my hair. 'They're sending Calantha to an asylum.'

I pulled away so that I could see his face, but hung onto his hands. '*What?*'

'It's true. Florrie, do you have any idea what those places are like, what becomes of those who are sent there? Calantha is so gentle and fragile. She will be broken, as surely as if they pushed her from the attic window. And all for what? For the family's pride. What kind of a man am I, Florrie, to be unable to stop this?'

So many thoughts whirled through my head that they blocked each other from finding expression. 'But . . . but . . .' was all I could say for a while.

'She is harmless,' he went on, voicing my thoughts for me. 'Oh, her thoughts may be a little disordered but she is the sweetest soul in this place. She causes no trouble, or very little. Despite her difficulties she is happy. Happier than any of us, most probably, because she is in familiar surroundings and she receives a little kindness and she is safe. But she is not strong. She cannot be ripped from all she knows and cast into one of those hellholes. I have been to see the place, Florrie, when I heard what they were considering. It is . . . it is not . . .' He shook his head. We sank into the blue armchairs on either side of the window.

'How long have you known?'

'Two days.'

'Oh, Sanderson.'

'I did not want to tell you, Florrie. I hoped there was some way to stop it. But you heard Hawker. I am impotent.'

'Calantha,' I murmured. 'Where is she now?'

He shrugged. 'I haven't seen her today. In her room, most probably, on a day like this.' Rain was scattering over the windowpanes and the sky was dark and heavy.

'Why now?'

'Oh, some incident. The Lattimers had called to say thank you for the dinner. Calantha wandered in. I don't know what she did, nothing so very terrible no doubt. Stroked their feathers or talked to their diamonds or whatever she likes to do. Apparently Aunt Dinah bundled her out bodily, there and then, and then she couldn't recover herself because they had seen *her* so uncontrolled. You know how it goes, Florrie.'

'Is there nothing we can do? We can't just let her go there.'

'No, we can't, but we have no authority, no fortune, no voice. We know no one who would go against our grandfather in such a matter. I thought of Selina – Mrs Westwood – but she is a *wife*, all she could hope to do is persuade her husband, and *he* will not step in. I thought of your Rebecca, but she lives with a despot father in a tiny apartment. We are a circle of captives, Florrie, though it strangles me to say it.'

I reflected. It was true that Mr Speedwell would prefer to ingratiate himself with Dinah Grace than shelter her mad niece and risk losing business.

'Can it really be?' I wondered, knowing from my own experiences that somehow it could. 'Can they really lock away another human being against her will, subject her needlessly to something so horrible?'

'It takes only two doctors to sign certificates of insanity. With Hawker's influence . . . it is already done.'

We lapsed into a glum silence. The rain grew heavier, the darkness intensified. And then the library door burst open and Hawker and Aunt Dinah stood before us once again.

'Is this your doing?' Hawker demanded.

'Who else could it be?' our aunt spat, looking one breath away from furious tears. 'You have helped no one, no matter what you think, so tell us what you have done at once.'

Sanderson and I looked at one another. 'Done?' we echoed.

Our utter confusion must have been apparent on our faces for she sagged a little and turned to Hawker.

'You have not helped her escape?' he demanded, scouring each of our faces in turn.

'Calantha?' I asked hopefully.

'Yes, Calantha. But you have not, I can see. Dinah, it was not them. How the devil in his halls of flame has this happened?'

She ran her hands over her face and looked exhausted. 'She must have heard something. You know how she lurks about. She must have run away . . .'

The house was searched, the garden was searched, the stables were searched. Calantha was nowhere to be found. As I went through the motions of taking part, I did not know whether or not I hoped she would be. I was not so naive as to suppose that a beautiful, slightly odd young woman would fare well alone in London. I looked out into the hammering rain and uncompromising dark of a February night and I shuddered to think of her alone out there. And yet, I could not help but hope that liberty counted for something. It was a long night.

After three in the morning Hawker finally threw up his hands in disgust and bade us to bed. I stumbled to my room barely hoping I would sleep, but longing to rest my weary limbs. I struggled into my nightgown, climbed into bed and blew out my candle. I lay, staring into the darkness, my heart reaching out for Calantha. Where had she gone? How would she fare? Would I ever see her again, or was she to be another lost Grace, like Turlington before her?

'Florrie. Have you any money?' whispered a voice in the darkness.

I sat up wildly. Stared around suspiciously.

I felt a bumping underneath my bed then someone scrambled out and lit the candle again. It was Calantha, dressed in her outdoor clothes and clutching her boots.

'Oh dear God!' I sighed in relief, laying a hand on my heart. 'You are well, you are here! You are not a robber! Calantha, where have you been?' I looked at her again and narrowed my eyes. 'And where are you going?'

'That, my dear, I cannot say, for I do not know. I do know where I am *not* going, however, and that is Garfield's Asylum for Women.'

'I heard about it today. It's dreadful, Calantha. But will running away be better? Have you thought about what could lie in store for you in London, all alone? You know Sanderson and I would do anything to help you, but there is so little we *can* do. It is not safe, you could be hurt . . .'

'Yes, I could. I know it is not safe. But it *will* be better than the asylum. Do you know what they do to people there, Florrie? They wrap you up in canvas, they douse you with cold water every day, to freeze out the thoughts they don't want you to have. They dose you with poisons to keep you lifeless and half asleep. They stop you being who you are. And no one ever leaves. Well, maybe one or two.' She paused, considering. 'But can you imagine me ever being allowed back here – the relation who used to be in an asylum? I would be there until I die, Florrie. I had rather die on the streets of London tomorrow than that.'

'Dear God, I don't know what to say,' I murmured, patting the bed. She clambered up next to me and laid her head on my shoulder. I put my arm around her and stroked her hair. We sat like that for a while and then I looked at her. 'Is there any other way, Calantha? If I spoke to Mrs Westwood for you, or Rebecca, perhaps they may be able to help. I know they would wish to.'

'I know that. But the thing is, dear Florrie, I am a little strange. And Hawker is very convincing. You may be sure that the first thing he will do tomorrow will be to go to everyone we know, especially those who may be sympathetic to me. He will lay such a good case for the course he has chosen and convince them it is the best thing for me. He will hunt and hunt; I have seen it when Turlington ran away, before you ever came here. He dragged him back . . . That is why Sanderson was so anxious to keep the secret when he was in London last year. If Hawker had so much as an inkling . . .'

'You knew? You knew he was here?'

'I know a lot of things, Florrie. People don't take much notice of you when they think you're mad . . . You won't stop me, will you?'

I shook my head. 'I can't. But I shall worry about you, horribly. Desperately. Oh God!' I suddenly imagined the long years ahead, never knowing where she was, whether she was well, or even alive, and I caught my breath, feeling dizzy. Another person I cared for deeply torn from me. 'Will you get a message to me once in a while? Maybe you could leave it at Rebecca's?'

She frowned. 'I want to promise. But I don't know where I'll be, what I'll be doing. I'll try, Florrie. I promise I'll try.'

I climbed from the bed and dug out my secret hoard of money. It was so very little. Not enough to get me home to Cornwall and not enough to assure Calantha's future, but if it could help her at all, I would give it. I kept it in a small cavity in the wall beneath the window. It was spidery and dusty and barely noticeable. I had judged it as safe from Annis as it could possibly be.

I weighed my little purse in my hands and looked at her again. She looked, as always, like an angel or a goddess. She was making more sense tonight than she ever had. Was I being wildly irresponsible by helping her now? Should I call for Hawker? Plead her case with the family? Offer to stay with her more and keep her away from visitors? Was I sealing her doom in letting her go? I closed my eyes in despair.

I felt her hand steal into mine and take the purse. 'Thank you, Florrie. I'm going now. Thank you for being my friend and I'm sorry to take your Cornwall money.'

I smiled. 'You are so much cleverer than anyone knows, aren't you?'

'Clever and beautiful and eccentric,' she agreed. 'My days at Helicon were always going to be numbered. Let me go now, and say nothing and remember me kindly, my dear.' She stood on tiptoe and kissed my cheek. 'And good luck to you, Florrie,' she added. 'You will need it quite as much as I.'

She took my money and left. Cornwall was further from my reach than ever.

Chapter Twenty-three

1854

I became engaged, in 1854, to a man named Aubrey Marchmont. And Sanderson finally did as was hoped and proposed to
Anne Coatley, who of course accepted. Annis had by now
departed Helicon – and a far, far better place it was for that –
to become Mrs Blackford of Putney. Life was changing for
all of us.

Only Judith remained unaffianced and, aged twenty, she
grew increasingly frantic to address the fact. After all, her sister
had left and now even my departure was pending, though it
would not take place for some months. Mr Seagrove had long
ago lost interest and now dallied with a young lady whose blue
eyes were, he was overheard to tell her, brighter and bigger
than the Koh-i-Noor. The more frantic Judith grew, the more
reluctant her suitors grew, and so it went.

Three years had passed. I had grown reconciled, to a greater
or lesser extent, to my lot. Spring had followed spring and my

life in Cornwall, the agonies of my early days in London and my deep, burning connection with Turlington had receded and misted over. For a long, foolish year I had still hoped to hear from him but now I accepted that I would not. I had written to him twice, at the address in Madeira that Sanderson gave me, but receiving no reply, my pride prevented me from trying a third time. There had been many moments, at first, when I heard a step in the hall and hoped it was Turlington making another of his unexpected appearances, but I had stopped expecting that now.

I permitted myself to ask Sanderson about him no more than three times a year. Sometimes he smiled and told me some small tale of a voyage to Africa or a victory over a competitor. Other times his face fell and he shook his head, troubled. I tried to subdue my corresponding leap of hope or swoop of dismay. It was like making polite enquiries after a friend of his that I had never met, I told myself. I cared for Sanderson's sake, but otherwise it didn't really matter.

Was I happy at Helicon at last? Never truly happy, no, but there were moments and areas of happiness in my life, like patches of sunlight falling into a shady wood. I clung to these with heartfelt gratitude. Playing the piano. Reading and study. The glorious concerts, theatres, galleries and gardens of London. And my friends, Sanderson and Rebecca. I had found a measure of peace after all, as Rebecca had promised I would.

★

The story of how I came to be engaged to Aubrey is easily told. I had proved surprisingly popular with members of the opposite sex, to my aunt's great astonishment and grudging relief. Aubrey was the fourth young man to pay court to me and the other three were all much worse. But that is being flippant, of course. The truth was, Aubrey was my only suitor who satisfied the Graces' fierce demands of what a Grace consort should be *and* who viewed my 'otherworldliness' as something of a prize. He seemed to feel that it was an honour I bestowed upon him, rather than an inconvenience he could tolerate to be associated with the Graces; for this kindness alone I owed him my loyalty. He was a gentle man with round eyeglasses and he loved piano music, even when played imperfectly by me.

He was five years older than me, looked younger but felt older. He owned a townhouse in Pimlico and a country house in Hertfordshire, and a villa in Italy besides. I would not be short of houses. But we would, of course, spend the majority of our time in London – the centre of all things. I suppose I had always known I must marry – or else stay in Helicon forever. I was lucky to have him, I knew. Against all the odds, to 'capture' (as Judith would have it) a good man, with all my differences . . . I was lucky.

I had maintained an uneasy entente with my aunt. As I grew more accomplished, life became easier and I took pride in that. There was satisfaction in succeeding at a challenge, even one that I did not quite believe in, and especially when everyone else had been so certain I would fail.

Even so, a day of oppressive August heat found me in a reflective mood. I wilted in the garden with a book, my skin damp beneath my clothes and my face flushed with heat. The sky was not even blue, made no attempt at blue, but smoked and snarled in scrolls of grey. I was pensive because I had, only days earlier, returned from Cornwall. It had been my only visit in all these years, and the occasion was Hesta's wedding to Stephen. Marriage was in the air for all but Judith, it seemed.

I was permitted to go to Cornwall with surprisingly little fuss. Hawker saw no objection: I had been performing well and it was a singular occasion, not likely to be repeated. There was talk of sending someone with me, but Judith was precisely as enthusiastic to visit Cornwall as I was to have her there and Sanderson was busy with wedding preparations – or at least Anne was, and not keen to spare him. So I had gone, and come back, and now I could not stop reliving those few short days.

As I shifted uncomfortably on the garden seat at Helicon in the stagnant afternoon, I remembered travelling from Truro to Tremorney with a proper Cornish summer blowing about me, which was to say that bright sunshine and gusting rains took it in turns to stand up and dance in a wide-open sky, blue, white and silver. Sky! Oh, I had forgotten.

Suddenly, joyously, I could breathe again – gulp down huge

buckets of fresh air that smelled of grass and glittered with birdsong. Tears had come to my eyes as I stepped onto the familiar cobblestones of Tremorney's main street. In London I had needed to push aside the vivid, living memory of all this to survive. Now I wondered if the price of survival was too high.

I stayed with Lacey. I remembered the first sight of her, tumbling into the street, her face split with laughter, brown curls bouncing in the exact same old way. I stumbled down from the coach and she caught me in her arms and we crowed triumphantly, like two children who had succeeded in running away from a tedious lesson to go and play.

'Florrie Buckley!' she marvelled, staring at me. 'As I live and breathe! Or should I call you Miss Grace now?'

'I pray you would *not*!' I retorted.

We arrived in Braggenstones after a journey where I knew every twig and stone and frond of bracken. A poorer collection of dwellings I never did see, and poorer still in my eyes for the intervening years, yet familiar in a way that made my eyes ache. As the cart rattled into the small village, people came out to greet me, people who looked familiar and yet strange at the same time. Four years had passed.

Here was Hesta's mother, still thin and pinched, and Hesta's father, still coughing and grey. They shook my hands and I saw that they did not know how to be with me. But it was Hesta I wanted to see and they took me to her, inside the same old stone hut I had played in and eaten in and fallen asleep in a thousand times as a child. In honour of her status as bride-to-be, she had been allocated the only bedroom; her parents would sleep that night in the downstairs room alongside their younger children.

Hesta sat brushing her fair hair, a sweet white dress laid out over a chair at her side. The fabric was soft to the touch. I couldn't help trailing my fingers over it. It might so easily have been me sitting in a similar room, preparing for a similar day, a country wedding. But Fate had sent my course spinning off in a different direction.

Hesta did not move at my greeting. 'I couldn't come out, Florrie,' she said, still staring at herself in the window. 'I heard you come. But I den't want you to get here because then 'tis only three days 'til you leave again. I'd rather keep you all in the future. So I can't look at you, because then you'll really be here, and you'll have to go again.'

Unexpectedly I started to cry. 'Hesta, you fool, I am here whether you like it or not,' I said, kneeling at her side. 'You had better look at me, for I don't want to waste a single minute of our precious time together.'

We looked at one another in wonder at first. Somehow Hesta had moved from childhood to womanhood and I had missed it all.

'You look so *fine*, Florrie,' she breathed, touching my ringlets. 'You look like those fine ladies of Truro. *Finer*.'

But then the awe fell away and we spent the night talking,

bringing each other up to date with every particular of our lives during the intervening years. I stayed with her, in her parents' old bed, while a Braggenstones moon rose full and fair and poured its light on the two of us: the heiress and the bride.

It was strange to me, hearing my own life in the telling. I felt as though I were recounting the adventures of some other girl. So long denied communication with Hesta, with home, I rattled through the facts as I remembered them, as I had told them to Rebecca; 'tis always the same things that snag our memories, make us unable to move past them, forget the hurts. And Hesta grew deeply enraged.

'I en't happy for you, Florrie,' she said, biting her lip. 'I wanted to be happy for you, I wanted even to be envious, but I en't that neither. They be vile, hateful people. Come away from there now, Florrie, come home and let us look after you.'

How a part of me longed to do just that.

'You can barely look after yourselves here, Hesta, we both know how it is. I do Braggenstones a great favour by being elsewhere, one less mouth to feed. Besides, they are not so bad.'

'I'm astonished to hear you say it!' she cried. (I was astonished to hear myself say it.) 'They locked you up, Florrie! They threw out your mother and despised your father, your good father, Florrie, who was known to us all as the best of men.

I always wished *I* had your father! How can you but despise them, Florrie, how *can* you?'

I was helpless to answer her. I had thought I hated them as well. Had I sold my soul for fine dresses and books and piano music? Had I somehow grown dependent on them in spirit as well as in means, the way a cringing dog follows the master that kicks her? But it was more than that, something Rebecca had made me see, perhaps.

When I remembered Judith's expedient betrayal of me after the Great Exhibition, I immediately recalled her face on her sister's wedding day, fearful and lost. When I remembered my aunt hauling me off to the attic room I quickly saw her tense, quick steps and the set of her shoulders as she walked, walked, walked the endless corridors of Helicon, *arranging* things, dinners, people . . . always *arranging* things to Hawker's satisfaction . . . And I could not remember Hawker raging at Sanderson, sending Calantha away, without remembering that he was my father's mother, and he called me Grand-Florence. They were strange people, perhaps they were not even good people, but they were people.

I answered her softly, as though my very voice could disturb the smooth wash of moonlight that held us. 'I have to love them, don't I? They are part of me.'

Hesta's wedding. She looked like the sweet, blushing country maid she was, with fresh white flowers in her hair. My old friend Stephen looked proud and determined. If the words 'good husband' had been emblazoned upon him, his intent could not have been clearer. I shed a tear during the ceremony and I danced every dance afterwards.

And when the afternoon wore on and people were the worse for drink, or were deep in conversation, or nodded off in the shade of trees, I stole away, barefoot, to be alone on the moors at last. And there, finally, I cried my heart out.

What on earth did it mean that this was the place that made me know who I was? That this was the place that stirred my heart and made me feel I was . . . in love? How could a human love an expanse of earth and rock? Life was not a myth where gods mated with swans and humans fell in love with trees and the boundaries of species and form mattered not.

What had I *become*? I had come to feel sympathy for those who had been worse than abhorrent to me once upon a time; I could agree to marry a man I knew I did not properly love. Yet to be alone with the wind blowing about me and a dark grey boulder hard against my back and insects crawling on my skirt made me break open and cry for griefs I could not even name; nothing could have prepared me for this elemental and seemingly undirected passion.

I stayed for hours, until it was dark, then eventually picked my way home again. My feet had grown softer, my middle thicker, my back weaker and my head less sure of its convictions, but I knew my way, over the moors, in the dark, as I always had.

As I returned to the village I heard voices calling:

'Florrie! Florrie! You be out there? Damn that girl! It be our wedding! She have this little time with us and off she run! I thought she'd changed!'

I smiled, and felt a little shameful, as though returning from an assignation with a lover. I slipped into the firelight and took my friends' hands. I accepted a cup of ale and my spirit was all new. Something was going to change when I went back to London, I knew it.

As I looked up at the white walls of Helicon it was hard to imagine what could ever change. My eyes dropped wearily to the page again. Horizons were what I missed the most about Cornwall. Horizons and the sky. In London I could not see out over the curtailments of brick and stone. I heard the nearby church strike four. It had been but ten minutes, but I felt as though I'd been sitting there for hours. Aunt Dinah and Judith were in Hyde Park with Sanderson and Anne. Tonight there would be a dinner. Tomorrow I would visit Rebecca . . . Hawker grew more irascible by the day and still Helicon stood and gripped us in its square, stifling hold.

I was starting to doze – the book was not sufficiently diverting to distract me – when I heard a voice say, 'Florrie Buckley. The loveliest girl on earth, once upon a time, and now the most beautiful woman.'

I did not look round. My brain said it must be Aubrey, for

who else would say such a thing to me? (In fact, Aubrey was highly unlikely to say such a thing.) But of course, it was Turlington.

Turlington, whom I had not seen for three years. Turlington, who had been disowned, disinherited and otherwise detached from our lives. Turlington, who was in Madeira, and barred from this house. I closed my eyes.

'For how many fleeting minutes do we have the honour of your company this time, Cousin Turlington?' I asked without looking up. I remembered his last appearance when I had grown dizzy on the piano stool, and the time before that when I had melted in his arms in the dining room. And the time before *that* in the stables in Lemon Street when he rested his forehead against mine . . . It was better not to look at him and definitely best not to touch him.

I sensed him cross the grass towards me. 'For as many as may be imagined,' he said. 'I am come home, Florrie dear.'

Wearing a sceptical frown I allowed myself one small sideways glance at him. He was hovering near my garden seat. He did not look as he had looked before. I allowed my head to turn a little more.

His suit was glossy, well-cut, fashionable. Turlington had always been dashing, rather than fashionable. His hair was not short but the ends were crisp and purposeful. I narrowed my eyes. He looked a little paler, a little thinner, which made him look as though he had grown wiser, though I expected nothing of the sort. He stood before me, apparently assuming nothing, respectful of the long break in our friendship. He had, in short, the air of a man chastened and altogether changed for the better.

I returned to my page with feigned interest and turned it, though I had not reached its end. 'Welcome back, Cousin Turlington,' I murmured. 'Delighted to see you, I'm sure.'

'Are you? You don't *seem* delighted, Florrie.' Now he came and sat next to me, though not too close. I could feel his eyes burning into my face. 'I am home for good, I tell you. Hawker has taken me back, all is forgiven and I have mended my ways. We were always such good friends, you and I. Have you forgotten?'

I closed my book with a thwack and set it down next to me with a second thwack and I looked directly at him. Again that slightly toppling feeling, as though standing on top of the big grey stone on the highest tor of the moors.

Turlington had ever come and gone, disappearing and re-appearing like a blue moon, but now he seemed to be suggesting that this time might be different. I could not afford to let myself believe that. 'No, Cousin, I have not forgotten. But perhaps *you* forgot, all these days, every day of the last three years. *Four* years, excepting your brief appearance after the incident in the cheese shop. Perhaps you forgot that last time you promised, or intimated, that you would write, that we would stay friends at a distance. Perhaps that is why you did not reply to *my* letters? Perhaps *you* forgot and that is why, forgive me, I really cannot muster the expected delight and curiosity to welcome you with open arms and shower you with questions about how the miracle of your return has come about. We are all blessed, honoured, overwhelmed, I am sure, to have you back. Perhaps it is the most exciting thing to happen to the Grace family in many years. Personally, however, I have better things to think of.'

He flinched slightly, like a dog, and asked almost tenderly, 'Like what, dear Cousin?'

'Like this book!' I told him, picking it up and shaking it at him. He looked disbelieving. 'Like Sanderson's forthcoming wedding. Yes, your brother is to marry. But I suppose you knew that. I suppose you take an interest in *him*. Like my piano practice. Like my *husband*!'

'Your husband?' He looked stricken and seized my left hand. Of course there was no wedding band there; I don't know why I said that, rather than 'my engagement' or 'my fiancé'. There was only the diamond and emerald cluster that Aubrey had placed there, rather fumblingly, some months ago. It crossed my mind fleetingly that I could not remember exactly how long we had been engaged. Well, that meant nothing. We were not schoolchildren to count weeks and days and tell our friends. We were adults. Disconcerting, though, to realise that I knew that I had not seen Turlington for three years, one month, two weeks and five days.

'My husband-to-be,' I amended haughtily. 'Aubrey and I are to marry on the fifth, no the fifteenth, no the *fifth* of May next.'

He raised his eyebrows. '*Aubrey?*' he said.

'Aubrey,' I confirmed. 'Aubrey Marchmont. I shall become Mrs Marchmont next year, on the fifteenth of May.'

'I think you mean the fifth?' he enquired delicately.

'Oh, God damn and blast you all to hell!' I exploded and stormed into the house. I had not cursed like that for many years.

His voice floated after me. 'Don't you want your book, dear?'

Chapter Twenty-four

Over the days that followed, I had to readjust to another Grace living in the house. And not just any Grace, but Turlington. We had not lived under the same roof since I was fifteen years old. I had always told myself that he was my cousin, my friend; someone with whom I had a special understanding, like Sanderson. Now I was nineteen – a woman. An *engaged* woman. And I had to confess that it was nothing like my relationship with Sanderson at all. It was certainly nothing like my relationship with Aubrey.

I knew where he was every single minute. I avoided him as much as possible yet my senses tingled when he was nearby, senses I had forgotten I possessed. It was like waking up after a long, enchanted sleep. We could be at opposite ends of the house and I still felt him. I could be at the piano and he in the stables, but still I felt him. When he was out in the city I somehow knew whether he was near or far, even when no one told me where he had gone. It was as though there was a strand of something spun between us, something intangible yet magical.

Despite my refusal to take any interest in the subject what-soever, I learned the story of how he had come back among us. The whole household talked of little else for a while; without plugging my ears I could not remain ignorant.

Hawker had sought him out, it seemed. This was a surprising fact. Despite Sanderson's engagement, Hawker's concern for the future of the Grace line seemed greater, if anything. 'One line is not *sufficient*!' he kept saying. Poor Sanderson looked uncomfortable, as though his virility were being called into question before he had even married. But everyone knew how strange and obsessed Hawker was. It was just one of the facts of life in Helicon that at first seemed startling and then became like the brickwork.

Calantha and Sanderson had been right when they said that if Hawker set his mind to finding someone, he would. It was only fortunate that when he set his sights on Turlington, his intent was benign: to give Turlington one last chance. Hawker was gratified, therefore, when his enquiries eventually reached their target, and Turlington wrote back warmly. He missed the family. He would like nothing better than to lay the past behind him and return to what was, after all, his home. He had not lived well following his disappearance, he confessed, but he had learned some hard lessons and now believed he was finally the grandson of whom Hawker could be proud. In short, his return might prove a boon for both sides.

The two men met one hot summer's day in a tavern near

Westminster Bridge. Turlington declined ale and wine and drank water instead. His drinking, he acknowledged, was a demon he had been forced to shed. It was not in him, as it was in other men, something to be entertained on a sometimes basis. It took hold of him and ran him and he was too proud, after all, to be run. He described his drinking, now, as close to abstinent.

Hawker noted the ring of truth in his admissions and saw all the obvious differences in him. At four-and-twenty, Turlington was relaxed, well-heeled and poised. He looked like a man who had grown up at last. The days of rebellion for rebellion's sake were over.

He had with him a smart black case, and from this he took two items. One was a beautiful emerald necklace. It was not the one he had stolen from Annis, for that was indeed long gone, but it was the best he could do in the way of making amends. He asked Hawker to give it to her with his sincere apologies, since he doubted that she would ever consent to see him again. The second was a sheaf of letters from his business associates, proving that he was successful in shipping, sugar (or white-gold, as it was known) and wine on the faraway island to which he had been banished. He had at last used his ill-gotten gains to good purpose.

Naturally suspicious and shrewd though he was, Hawker was convinced. Despite countless disappointments over the years, it had always seemed to him that it was Turlington who should be the true Grace heir. He said so to Turlington that day, and to the rest of us, repeatedly, afterwards. He had always felt that something had gone somehow wrong during those fractured years, as though a lever had been pulled, setting Turlington off on a wrong path – a horrible, divine mistake. Now the lever had been thrown again and right order was restored. The oldest Grace, beautiful Belle's boy, would take his place in the family once again and this time, he was deserving.

After two months, it was as though Turlington had always been there. For the others it was a return to normality, for he had grown up among them. It was only I who felt it strange. He was appalled and saddened to learn of Calantha's flight, and the horrible reason behind it, and promised Sanderson and me that he would make enquiries. He did, after all, have a number of connections on the wrong side of London. He was not proud of his past, but it may prove useful in this, he hoped. I prayed he was right for I thought about Calantha almost every day, and missed her still.

His business ventures appeared to be at a stage where they could largely take care of themselves. He had an agent in Madeira, a Mr Cinquentes, whose abilities and integrity he rated highly. Accordingly Turlington's workload was light and consisted mostly of correspondence with Mr Cinquentes. He went into London once or twice a week to pursue other concerns of a charitable nature. Second chances meant a great deal to him, he said. He therefore invested a portion of his income into the lost causes of London – prisoners, fallen women and those who struggled with drink.

To be living in a better way, after so many years, he told me passionately in a rare moment when we found ourselves alone . . . well, I did not know what he had gone through. My heart softened a little. After all, the mark of true humanity was not about being perfect but about overcoming those imperfections in meaningful ways. When I said as much, he looked grateful.

Even so, when he returned to Madeira to take care of some business in person, I said a cool goodbye, assuming we would not meet again for a great many years.

Chapter Twenty-five

Imagine my astonishment then when he came walking through the front door, just as I was walking out of it, not a day early, and not a day late, but exactly when he had promised. He was wearing a greatcoat, proof that it was cooler outside than it had been for a while. It made him look bulkier than his actual build allowed and he seemed to fill the hall. I had not known that I was missing him, or secretly hoping that he would prove me wrong, but the leap in my heart made it clear that I had been.

'Turlington!'

An exclamation of my old delight escaped me and before I knew what I was about, my arms were around him. We had not touched since his return, not properly. Only his hand close to my back if he was taking me in to dinner; his arm near my face when he turned my sheet music; our cursory farewell handshake a month ago. But now he engulfed me in the old way. There seemed to be more Turlington than ever, he seemed to swirl about me in an elemental way and it felt as though he had lifted me up, though he had not.

The thick coat between us was too much to bear, like a blanket on a hot night that must be thrown off; I found myself burrowing in its folds. He ripped it open with one hand, which quickly returned to my hair and pressed my face into his neck. His arms were about me so tightly it was hard to tell that we were two people. It was a whole universe, this Turlington-and-Florrie. I don't know how long we stayed like that. It might have been above ten minutes, for I was on my way to an appointment and I recall I was very late.

At last a step on the kitchen stairs parted us, self-conscious and trembling. A maid appeared but did not seem to notice us. With an annoyed exclamation she ran off again, muttering something about candlesticks.

'Does this means that you've forgiven me, dear Florrie?' he asked urgently. It seemed futile to pretend otherwise.

'You came back,' I said.

'I said I would. Oh, I know I have not always kept my word before but I am changed now, Florrie, surely you can see it. If we can be friends again, if I can dare to hope for that, I would like to tell you everything, if you would listen.'

Of course I would listen. I wanted to know everything of every moment that I had missed during that time when he had been a stranger to me. Hawker was right – that had just been a horrid mistake, a twist of a Fate both capricious and unkind. We had not seen each other or communicated in three years, that was the fact. But we were closer than two people ordinarily are on some deep level I could not fathom, and that could never be changed. That was the truth.

However, now was not the time. I was meeting Aubrey at the Westwoods' to discuss texts for our marriage service. May was only six months away. My burning face fell and Turlington noticed.

'You are going out, Florrie. Let me not detain you. We have all the time in the world now that we have our right understanding again. When you return, or tomorrow or the next day . . . We can go riding if it is fine. We can talk in a gallery or a museum . . . We can talk anywhere at all provided you will at least talk to me again.'

'I will talk to you,' I said. Suddenly all I wanted in the world was to spend my days and nights talking to him, holding him, living life at his side. Annis had touched a nerve all those long years ago, I realised with a surge of horror. She was right. I was in love with him. Whatever that magical phrase meant, whatever being in love entailed, whatever it was, this was it. A sorry realisation when he was utterly forbidden to me and when I was betrothed to another.

'You look more beautiful than ever in that rose-coloured cloak,' he said dreamily, clutching my hand as if unaware that he was doing so.

'And you in that big coat,' I murmured. It hung from him loosely now, after our embrace, and he absent-mindedly straightened it, picked up his gloves from the hall table and laid them down again. He raised his hands in a little gesture of helplessness.

'For the love of God, Florrie,' he breathed.

It was the closest we had come to articulating what had been unspoken between us for so long. *Always*, I realised now, remembering the stable, his scowling face at the dance in Truro.

'For the love of God,' I echoed in a hollow voice, and left the house to meet my fiancé.

Chapter Twenty-six

It was as if I saw Aubrey for the very first time that day. The utter state of shock in which I found myself during our interview with Mr Westwood arose from more than just the lasting effects of my physical proximity with Turlington, which continued to ripple through me as I sipped tea and tried to consider bible verse. It arose from more, even, than the realisation of my feelings for him. It was because I felt that afternoon as if a curse by a wicked queen had suddenly been lifted. I had forgotten who I was. Now it came back to me, with a force so violent and unexpected it knocked me off my internal feet. Everything I had learned, become, gained, calculated . . . all meant nothing. *Nothing*. I was in the wrong world.

And becoming Florrie again, I saw through Florrie's eyes. Aubrey, in particular, looked rather different.

'Hello, my dear,' he greeted me when I arrived. I had always liked his mildly affectionate manner. It had seemed a warm flame in comparison with my family's spiky ways. Turlington had suddenly snuffed out that flame and all I saw now was a watery trickle. Aubrey's gentle blue eyes seemed watery too and his gentlemanly hands, politely taking mine for a moment, felt like the dismal press of rain. I looked at his familiar, inoffensive face and I felt horror, absolute horror. I couldn't marry *him*!

What had I been *thinking*? I suddenly saw myself, vibrant and vital, as I had once known myself to be – as Turlington still saw me – and I understood that the horror was nothing to do with Aubrey, who was a decent man after all, but with myself, with the castrated, compromised creature I had become. Like a flower pruned back, back, back until there was nothing left of bloom or flounce or roving tendril, only neat, biddable stem. I had pruned myself, or been pruned, into a woman who could marry a man like Aubrey. But that was not who I was. A horrible mistake had been made and all I wanted was to run away.

I sat in a convulsion of fear while Aubrey and Mr Westwood chatted away and the Westwoods' maid brought tea. Selina came in from her morning calls and joined us, shooting me quizzical glances from time to time. I could not catch her eye. I should cry, if I did.

'Marriage is a very great step, is it not?' she murmured, during a lull in the conversation. 'Such a big undertaking for two young people. Understandably it unleashes all manner of fears but God guides us forwards and gives us the means to confront those fears, all in good time.'

So, then, my terror was writ large upon my face. For so long as she attributed it to the nerves of a bride-to-be all was well. I sat very still, but on the inside I was racked with fantasies of flight. I was a doe in a forest, catapulted to speed by the crack of a twig. I was a cormorant plummeting from a cliff, borne on the plunge of gravity. I was Florrie Buckley again, sprinting barefoot over the moors. Tears came to my eyes. Good God!

I rose abruptly, and went to the window. It had been years since my emotions had been ungovernable like this. I could not let them see. But Aubrey was behind me, his hands on my arms, seeping through my sleeves; I fancied I could feel droplets trickling downwards. He then did an unprecedented thing: he placed a kiss on top of my head. As I was nearly his equal in height, this necessitated him rising onto his toes to reach. I did not turn, was only aware of him bobbing up and down and the sweet, caring gesture, which made me want to slap him hard across the face. I groaned inwardly. The castle that I had built was starting to come tumbling down. With Herculean effort, I forced a lightness into my voice.

'I am well, dear. Only look at that robin! How sweet.' Thank God there was a robin. Otherwise I would have had to say, 'Look at those pleasing bricks.'

'Good girl,' said Aubrey. 'It is particularly hard for a lady, I understand. But we shall be very happy.' He dropped his voice then. 'I shall be most considerate, Florence, most delicate, please be assured.'

Oh Lord, he thought I was afraid of the sex act. If he only

knew how the very thought of such a thing instantly hurtled my thoughts towards my cousin . . . Well, I was a bad fiancée, no doubt a bad person. Any other young lady in England would have been glad – relieved – to have Aubrey for a husband.

'Would you care for more tea, Florence?' asked Mr Westwood in his disapproving voice.

'Perhaps a little tot of brandy?' suggested Selina.

Liquor? In that state? I very carefully took a deep breath and released it. I used a strength that astonished me to steady my voice and stem my tears. I turned to them all with a smile.

'Nothing at all, thank you. But I confess I have just remembered a shocking thing.' Six eyebrows lifted. 'I have been sitting here this afternoon with something troubling me and have just remembered that I am promised in two places at the same time. I am also supposed to be with Rebecca at the cheese shop. She is taking inventory and I promised to help her. How disgraceful of me to let her down.'

'I am quite sure your friend will understand,' said Mr Westwood. 'You will be a married woman soon, you have responsibilities now beyond those of girlhood loyalties.'

'But Florence is so tender-hearted,' said Aubrey. 'Would you like to go, dear? I shall walk with you if you like. We have reached a consensus, I believe, provided *you* are happy with the choice, dear?'

'Entirely happy, Aubrey.' I had absolutely no idea what had been chosen. 'But there is no need to walk with me. Stay;

I know you have been looking forward to this time with Mr Westwood.'

I don't know how I got out of there, nor how I bundled myself through the streets to Marylebone. Nevertheless, arrive there I did, to be confronted by the unwelcome sight of Mr Speedwell curved over the cheese counter. The inventory was a fiction, of course. I fidgeted on the pavement. Rebecca was probably upstairs, but the thought of having to speak to her father, in my heightened state, was a challenge too far. I could not have one more polite conversation.

So I set off and walked, briskly, until my feet were hurting and I was in some dark, close-leaning part of town I did not know. Lost again. I should have to hail a cab to get back and then how would I explain myself? Even so I kept walking.

In this rebellious, reawakened frame of mind I found myself stopping outside a tavern. No well-brought-up young lady would ever enter a tavern alone. But Selina had said 'brandy' and the thought was in my head now. I was unlikely to encounter anyone who knew the Graces here – wherever it was.

I went inside and peered into the lounge, where three other 'ladies' sat. They straightened like lionesses scenting prey. I could sense that they gauged me as ladylike and vulnerable and anticipated a bit of fun at my expense, if not a chance to rob me of my finery. I stormed into the lounge and the glance I flung them put an end to that.

I ordered a large brandy and threw it back. I ordered another and sat in a corner to nurse it and brood. Taverns. Guaranteed privacy from all things Grace. Why had I never entered one before? And there I sat for a long while, buffeted by the thoughts and feelings that were tumbling about in me, trying to prepare myself for my return to Helicon, trying to imagine what on earth I was going to do. And then Fate took a wicked hand in things. A gentleman came in. I could tell from the fur-ruffling, slavering interest of the lionesses.

He approached me and I looked up, dreading to see Mr Blackford or Mr Seagrove or anyone else who would report me to my aunt and Hawker. But it was Turlington.

'God is good,' he said, sitting beside me.

'Is He now?' I asked. I drained my drink without thinking and coughed with the fire of it.

'Another brandy, Florrie?' he queried in amusement.

I couldn't help but laugh. 'No. The two I've had have done their job.'

'And what job is that?'

'They have eased the shock.'

'What shock have you suffered?'

'You, Cousin. You are the shock.'

'Good.'

When he said it, all my senses narrowed down to a single focus. Turlington, dark and enigmatic, sitting before me. The red flock wallpaper, stained and faded, the bald upholstery of the chairs, the sudden cackles of the lionesses, all receded and spun far beyond us, like distant planets. If I was behaving shamelessly, or wrongly, or ill-advisedly, I did not care. He reached for my hand and I took it in both of mine, twined my fingers through his as though by weaving them together we might never be parted. I had never known what it was to be connected to another so deeply that it felt as though any separation could be fatal to both. It was disturbing, even frightening, yet I felt more alive than I had since leaving Cornwall. Now that I had remembered that life could feel so powerful I was not about to question it.

'I have thought of you every day that we've been apart,' he began in a low voice. 'Florrie, I'm sorry I hurt you when I didn't write. It wasn't that I forgot or that I couldn't take the trouble. I decided not to, and I did not, even when it was the hardest thing imaginable.'

'You broke your promise on purpose?'

'I did. But it was the promise that was faulty, not the breaking of it. The promise was made in a moment of weakness. I should never have said it. When you were before me with your dark eyes and your fairy ways it was unthinkable that we should not continue our friendship one way or another. But when I was away from you and I could breathe again, reality reasserted itself, for there are two planes of reality, are there not?'

I agreed that there were and neither of us elaborated for we understood each other perfectly. There was the reality in which such intense feelings had only one possible outcome and that was disgrace – unless we married. *That* was a leap too far to consider with our feelings so newly realised. But even if we did, eventually, reach such an understanding, we were Grace cousins. Marriage was forbidden us. Hawker had decreed it. But there was also the other reality, the one in which we could not be separated, and never had been, probably not throughout many lifetimes; in which we were entwined in our souls as our hands were now.

'In that reality which badgered me whenever I left you,' he continued, 'you were sixteen years old. And before that fifteen. The first time we met, you were thirteen. You have always been special to me, Florrie. You have been my guiding star, ever since that day in the stables. To be sure it has taken me a long time to follow your lead, for men are imperfect creatures and I more than most. There could be no hiding *that* from you even if I wished to.

'But whatever good is in me has come about through following your trail of fairy dust. I have fallen off it more than once. More than a hundred times. But each time I thought myself perfectly prepared to surrender to a useless, purposeless life, I would see you, riding off into that Cornish morning, as bold as could be, or sitting at the table in Helicon, all dressed up and looking cornered, like an animal. Oh, how I longed to free you, Florrie. But how could I? How could a man of almost one-and-twenty, as I was when you first arrived, take off a young girl of fifteen? Aside from propriety, I was not fit to have the charge of a young life. I could barely manage myself. I should have done you such harm, Florrie, and so I left. And I made myself *stay* gone, until – if ever such a day came – I could come back fit to be your . . .'

He trailed off and stared into the fire. I simply waited. What he had said had astonished me utterly.

'I did not know if that day would ever come,' he resumed. 'It was not a question of when, it was a question of whether. As I counted the years and you grew older, I was tortured by the idea that I might one day return home and find you altered and lost to me. That perhaps you had conformed after all, and married some sensible young man of good family. But I could not come racing back just to prevent that happening if I would only make you unhappy. So I waited and took the risk. I have come back and found those fears realised – you *are* engaged, yet it does not *feel* as though you are engaged, Florrie. It does not feel as though you are lost to me at all.'

I could not speak, but I did not really need to. While he had been speaking, we had moved onto a window seat so that we could sit closer. His arm had stolen around my waist and my right hand somehow lay across his heart and now I leaned forward and rested my forehead on his shoulder.

'The first time we met at Helicon, Florrie, I thought that your presence might help me to become reconciled to my life and the expectations upon me. You saw how that worked out, of course. You know how it is with Hawker and me. As long as I am part of this family I will always be Turlington second, and a Grace — the eldest Grace — first and foremost. I would have been told to marry. That was never something I wanted. So to do so against my natural inclinations *and* with my heart straining towards you . . . impossible. I could have seduced you and run off — at one time I was quite capable of it — only some saving angel stopped me. Not you, Florrie, not you.

'So what is left to us now, Florrie? I know I'm not presumptuous in supposing that you return my feelings. I can feel it running both ways between us. It is not just our hearts that are meshed, it is our fates. Whatever we do, we do together from now on, is that not so?'

'That is so,' I murmured. He was gazing at me as though I were a goddess, as though I were the single rarest treasure in the world. There was hunger and disbelief in him that he could lay claim to me. I truly felt like Florrie Buckley again — Special Girl.

I looked around the tavern, suddenly seeing it in its full glory as a seedy, depressing haunt of those who had given up on life. Perhaps that is why I had been brought here — despite all my efforts I had been one of them. But Turlington had reached into the deep grey hideout of conformity in which I had buried myself and plucked me out, returning me to the dazzling, coloured world. I turned back to him and laid my hand on the side of his face.

'Thank you,' I said passionately. 'Thank you. You are my . . . redeemer.'

His face was a perfect mixture of incomprehension and tenderness. 'How could *I* ever be anyone's redeemer?' he wondered. 'Yet if I am yours, Florrie, then my life is not a wasteland after all. For to redeem an angel – surely that is a blessed thing.'

'*You* are blessed! I see it! You are the sole point of light in my existence. Everything else turns around you. Oh, what are we to do, Turlington? What shall become of us?'

I started to cry, swept up, I think, in my own fervour. To feel so little for so long, and then suddenly to have this avenue for love open up in front of me, broad and long as the primrose fields . . . it was overwhelming.

'I know what I want to do,' he whispered, wiping my tears away with his fingers.

No need for pretence that I did not know what he meant, or that I was coy and afraid of it. I grinned back at him.

'Aye, I know you do,' I laughed, giddy with the freedom of it. 'But that is not what I meant.'

'I know. And I know what I want to do about that as well.'

'Tell me.'

'I want us to be together, Florrie. That's why I came back, not for Hawker. Not for the family. Let's run away to somewhere no one knows us. Let's go to Italy! We can live out the rest of our days as Mr and Mrs Spragget and grow sun-burned and indolent. We shall feast on fat, oily olives and figs every morning and swim in the sea and lie together every night as the man and wife we truly are, whether or not there has been a ceremony, and whatever Hawker decrees can or cannot be.'

As I listened I grew dizzy. My senses filled with imagining it. I could not help but strain towards the future he described. Passion. Escape from all I loathed about London. Freedom from the Graces. A life of simple, physical pleasures.

Before I had time to fathom it, he was kissing me, and then I gave way wholly, for it seemed that all my life I had been waiting for this sensation. His lips were soft on mine, his tongue was warm, I could feel the heat of his breath on my skin. I felt myself tip towards him, as I always did, but now there was no further to fall, for we had met in that most beautiful of ways. I could have drowned. I clung to him.

We kissed for the longest time, drawing away for fleeting instants to gaze at each other in awe. I learned him, in those kisses: I learned his deep sadness and his fledgling hope. I learned the part of him that longed to be better than he was and the part of him that was already transformed and luminous. I learned him, dark and scorching as he was, and I loved him, and I showed it.

'First kiss, dearie?' trilled one of the lionesses. She might have been speaking to either of us and we laughed, our heads close together.

'First love, miss?' asked another, and I nodded.

'Beware then, young beauty,' she said. 'That will set your life in one direction or quite another, but rarely where you want to go.'

But the kiss still tingled on my lips like snow melting and I felt him deep in every fibre of my body, so there *was* no way to go but forward, now.

Chapter Twenty-seven

Is there any need to state that I did not sleep that night? I lay awake staring into the darkness, wishing he would come to me, wondering what I had done. Suddenly a new future beckoned, one I could never have imagined. Living with Turlington in Italy, a life of freedom and pleasure. Not a snatched hour with him here or there, but a whole day, and another and another – nothing *but* days with Turlington, forever and ever . . .

I lay there and I yearned for him so fiercely I was sure that the force of my longing would summon him to me. I did not think for one instant of the havoc that would be wreaked if we were found together at Helicon. I did not even think of Aubrey. I only thought of Turlington, and my very skin sang with delight. I only knew that I loved him.

The next morning at breakfast I sat quivering like a lurcher, all my senses crackling with awareness of his every move. I could not look at him for surely my eyes would betray me. I listened painfully for any hint that we would have time alone together today. When he passed behind my chair to help himself to more kedgeree he lightly touched my back and I jumped as if I had been shot. I was heartily glad that Annis was not still among us for she would surely have noticed.

When Turlington left the breakfast room with no more than a polite 'good morning' to me, I felt desolate. I stared at my eggs and my eyes brimmed, but thanks to the ongoing preoccupation with Sanderson's wedding, no one noticed. Aunt Dinah was quizzing him on Mrs Coatley's outfit. If she wore a sea-green gown, would she offend or clash? Would lilac be safer? I only vaguely noticed, through my haze of self-absorption, that Sanderson looked faintly ill and that Hawker was watching him like a . . . well, a hawk.

When I excused myself, they barely seemed to notice. I left the room and did not know where to go, but an arm grabbed me around the waist and pulled me into the library.

Turlington! As he closed the door firmly between us and the rest of the world I laughed out loud with relief and delight. I tangled my fingers in the long ends of his dark hair. I drank in his face with my eyes, truly believing I could never look at him enough. I pressed myself to him and felt his warmth and strength.

'Oh, Turlington,' I sighed as I lay my head on his shoulder.

'Florrie Buckley,' he whispered, touching my cheek tenderly, and I felt like my true self again.

'We shall go mad if we don't have time alone each day, shall we not?' he pondered.

I nodded.

'I don't know what to do, Florrie. We need time to talk, to catch up with ourselves, to rejoice in being together. But we cannot do it here. Sooner or later we will betray ourselves. I don't want to meet you in the seedy, disreputable haunts of my youth but they are the only places we can be sure of not being seen by someone who knows us. Safety in obscurity. Shall we meet at the Dog and Duchess again this afternoon? Do you mind, my love, can you bear it?'

I felt I could bear anything – *anything* – just to be close to him and I told him so. We kissed until I could not stand up unsupported and then he slipped from the library. I sank into one of the blue chairs by the window. I reached for a volume of John Clare's verse, but it lay unopened on my lap as I stared through the window unseeingly.

For a week we continued like this, a dizzy, galloping week of secret assignations at the Dog and Duchess and long walks on dry days through the less salubrious parts of town. I had never been in such sorry places, but in truth I scarcely noticed them. We talked, we kissed, we pondered our options. We told each other endless stories of our former lives, those barren lives before we came together. We clung to each other's hands as though contact were a lifeline. I wondered if any two people had ever needed so desperately to be together. It felt as though we had been one since the oldest aeons of time.

I wondered, too, if anyone had ever been so happy. All that mattered was that he loved me, and he did, none could doubt it. So the future, with all its substantial obstacles, receded into insignificance. Every day I could hold him, tell him I loved him. Therefore nothing was amiss in my world. I felt a luminous power coursing through me. I marvelled that no one else appeared to notice it, though I was heartily relieved that they did not. I remembered when I started to study with Old Rilla, and I'd come back to Braggenstones glowing with the ecstasy of expansion, and no one noticed. Here, too, I felt I was living a miracle that none could imagine and so could not see.

At last Turlington came to my room one night. He stood before me in the candlelight, barefoot, wearing only a long white shirt, his hair curling over the collar of his shirt. He looked unguarded in a way that I had never seen him, as though the brokenness of him was now being entrusted to me. Convinced that my ruination, if such it could be considered, was about to take place, I lifted the covers wordlessly, feeling an intense mixture of excitement and fear. He set the candle on the seat of a chair, then climbed in beside me and took me in his arms. But he only held me that night – nothing else. Nevertheless, I melted into him. Even swathed in long white fabric as we were, all the boundaries between Turlington and Florrie, one being and another, man and woman, blurred and disappeared.

I nestled against him, hardly able to breathe. I could feel the muscles of his arms all around me and the drumming of his heart and the hair on his chest in the V of his nightshirt. I could feel the warm, hard swelling between his legs, but I did not reach out a hand as I longed to do. It seemed that Turlington had his own ideas about what tonight should be.

So this was how it was to be a woman, with a man she loved. I stared into the dark, awestruck. It did not compare with the other inconsequential moments of romance in my life. Stephen's childhood proposal in the hen house. Kissing Joe the pedlar's son long ago with primroses all around. And Aubrey, my fiancé. The most he had ever done was touch my hand. As much as I liked and esteemed him, he had never touched my heart.

Aubrey. I pushed him from my mind; he did not belong here in this moment. For love, real love, was the highest law, was it not?

Turlington stayed with me 'til morning. We did not sleep – at least, I did not; he may have done. More than once when I lifted my head from its nook between his neck and collarbone, I saw, in the guttering candlelight, tears glistening beneath his beautiful eyes. At dawn he kissed me softly and slipped away, leaving my body confused and lost for wanting him.

That night we looked set to enjoy an unusually pleasant dinner time. Dinah, Irwin and Judith had been invited to a dance so the company consisted of myself, Turlington, Sanderson and Hawker. We dismissed the servants and served ourselves. There was something very relaxing about being in the company of only men. The conversation roved from topic to topic unchecked. No instructions about behaviour or posture were issued; a few swear words escaped now and then. We laughed more than was usual and consumed more wine.

At last, from Wagner's romantic opera *Lohengrin*, to finance, to an elderly neighbour's scandalously young and beautiful new wife, the conversation reached the inevitable topic, the greatness of the Graces. Thus the first note of tension was introduced as Hawker lectured Sanderson on his forthcoming marriage. I think he had consumed a little too much wine – at any rate he seemed to have forgotten I was there and certainly he had forgotten any sensibility towards Sanderson's feelings – for he began to harangue him about the wedding night.

'You will do your duty, will you not?' he kept urging, drumming his fingers on the white tablecloth. His red wine trembled a little in the glass. 'Will it be your first time? You do know what to do? When you say you will do your duty I must be sure that you know what it is.'

Poor Sanderson looked naturally uncomfortable. He avoided the question of whether it would be his first time (I was sure that it would for he was so very good and gentlemanly) and assured Hawker in a mutter that he knew exactly what was entailed and that he would do it.

But Hawker pressed on and Sanderson looked miserable and Turlington leaped in to save him, as he always did. He made some flamboyant comment about how Sanderson was only half the equation now as he, too, would soon be making Grace heirs to fruit the tree. But then Hawker started badgering Turlington about when *he* would marry, a subject Turlington usually avoided with any number of ingenuities. He made a joke of it and said that he had eyes only for me.

I caught my breath. It was a daring jest – a truth disguised as a jest. Sanderson, gallant in his relief at having the attention diverted from him, agreed that I was a beauty and that it was hard for any man to see past me.

'She's too good for either of you, that's for certain,' growled Hawker, scowling over his wine glass.

'Undoubtedly that's true,' said Turlington, 'but nevertheless, my heart belongs to her. Florrie, will you have me? Dear, dear Florrie, say you will!' He dropped to one knee beside his chair and took my hands.

I laughed, but my heart started to pound. I sat very still as if there was a spell on us. If it could really be like that – if I could really marry Turlington and be public and open about it, if I did not have to abandon the life I knew . . . I had not realised until that moment that I did not really want us to run away together to Italy – at least, not as a permanent arrangement. It had been a beautiful fantasy but the reality, leaving Rebecca, Sanderson – even London! – was daunting. And Cornwall would be even further behind. Perhaps, if Hawker really loved both of us a little, if he had altered his position on cousins marrying . . .

Those hopes were dashed before they had even drawn breath.

'Get up, you fool,' Hawker snapped at Turlington. 'It disgusts me that you even joke about it. You know how I feel about that. First cousins cannot marry. It thins the blood and weakens the mind and the Graces cannot afford that. Consider Calantha.'

I looked up in surprise. It was the first time he had mentioned her in years.

'Her fool of a father went and married his first cousin, captivated by her "bewitching beauty" and all that balderdash and look what happened! One daughter, equally bewitching, raving mad.'

'Oh, she was not,' I retorted. 'She probably made more sense than the rest of you all together.'

'Indeed, young lady? I see your hard-won manners have deserted you the while. Go and find them, will you? Calantha was a lovely girl, I don't deny, but she was a liability. She heard things that weren't there, she saw things that weren't there . . .'

Turlington and Sanderson snickered in a cousinly way. 'So does Florrie,' they said in unison.

I rolled my eyes at them.

'But she has the sense not to show it!' snapped Hawker. 'It

doesn't matter what you are on the inside as long as you play the part you were born to play before the world. And pray, have the kindness not to call her that outlandish nickname in my hearing. Now hear me once and once only, Turlington Grace. If there is any truth in that jest of yours, any truth at all, even one iota, so help me I will flay you from here to kingdom come. You will be cut off from this family forever and no amount of making your fortune or mending your ways or trimming your hair will sway me this time.'

'But would it really be *so* bad?' mused Sanderson, buttering a roll, oblivious of the nerve he was touching. 'I mean, of course Turlington and Florrie – Florence – aren't going to fall in love, that's a joke, obviously, but in theory I mean. It's not uncommon. Many thinkers say there is no stronger correlation between insanity and first-cousin marriage than with any other marriage. They would say your view is an old-fashioned one. Of course, *I* don't claim to know, I'm not a biologist. Still, it seems to me, in theory, of course, that it could be a good thing. They've both been taught the Grace values, for instance. The family means just as much to each of them as to the other.'

'That it does!' interjected Turlington mockingly.

'You *could* say it might work for the family better than bringing in strangers.'

'Enough!' spat Hawker, looking at Sanderson with real loathing in his eyes. I was astonished, and a little frightened. 'It's an abomination in the sight of God and, more importantly, in *my* sight! Florence will make a fine wife for Aubrey. Your brother is a Grace, notwithstanding his reams of faults and oddnesses, and he will marry within the year – or else,' he added, rounding on Turlington once more. 'That's the natural order of things and I don't care about preference or passion.'

He glared at Turlington, and then to my shock, he glared at me. 'I trust there is none of you in this nonsense, Grand-Florence,' he warned, his blue eyes fastened onto mine. 'No fleeting fancy for your dashing cousin? No fluttering breast when he passes by? No private sympathy between the two of you that I should know of?'

I could hardly breathe. 'Of course not, Grand-Hawker,' I said. 'A fancy for *Turlington*? Are you growing feeble in your old age?' I added for convincing effect.

'You're a cheeky young mare and you're dicing, young lady, dicing, you understand me? Don't think that my fondness for you permits you *any* folly or licence. I hold you on a longer rope than most, with your letters from Cornwall and your cheese princess and your spirited retorts – for as long as they charm me. But there is still a rope, Grand-Florence, and it has an end, and you are most definitely on it.'

I didn't know what to say, so I stared at the table, cheeks burning, hating him. Always when I started to love him a little he snapped me back, back to the Grace position of suspicion and reserve. I knew his metaphor was drawn from tethering horses but my mind's eye would insist on seeing a hangman's noose. Held on a rope! I was not indeed. And yet, why then did I hesitate so about Italy?

The pleasant dinner came to an abrupt end after that. When Hawker left us, I sat around the table with my cousins and the three of us felt roundly chastised. There could be no easy conversation between us because of the great secret that burned between me and Turlington, so I reached out a hand for each of them in silent solidarity. Turlington reached across the table and took Sanderson's other hand and the three of us sat like that for a while.

Chapter Twenty-eight

The next morning, Turlington went away. It was a matter of business, he announced to the family at breakfast. It would take about a week. 'And I need to think,' he admitted to me in private afterwards. I felt cold terror at the prospect of being parted from him, remembering all those previous separations that had lasted years.

'What do you need to think about that you can't consider here, with me?' I demanded, furious with myself for feeling so weak and wanting.

'Nothing, in truth. Indeed, my thoughts are all tangles that I need to tease out with your help. But there truly *is* business, my beautiful girl, and I think that neither of us will do badly for having some time apart. Florrie, what Hawker said last night . . . we need to be sure that this is what you really want—'

'You doubt your feelings!' I cut in, irrational. 'Since when did *you* care what Hawker says? I'm *afraid* for you to go away and think. You did that once and I did not hear from you for three years. If you do that again, Turlington, I'll hunt you down myself and then you'll see the wrath of a Grace. You'll wish I were Hawker!'

He laughed. 'My little fury. How splendid you are. A part of me should like to see that. A more rational part does not. I promise you, Florrie, not above a week. I came back last time, did I not?'

I conceded that he had.

'Well, so it shall be. And as you accuse me of doubting my feelings, let me ask you this: if I were to ask you to come away with me today, to Italy, and leave all this behind, would you say yes, whole-heartedly?'

He had me. He had seen my conflict the previous night.

'I wish that damned conversation had never taken place,' I sighed. 'I wish we could have gone on not thinking, burying our heads in the sand. We've only had a week.'

'We have the rest of our lives, my darling. It is only that we do not know what form they will take. But I will be back and we will decide everything. I love you, Florrie, do not doubt that.'

And I loved him. Oh, dear God, I loved him. When he had gone, the house was desolate. And without the burning physicality of him there to blot out reality, my mind wandered over all the obstacles that it had refused to countenance before.

Aubrey, Hawker, family, duty. First cousins, in a family where there was already madness. I knew it was wrong, I knew

I could never have him, yet nothing could stand in the path of my feelings. Like a team of runaway horses they careered towards him, out of control and borne on wings of supernatural speed.

The days became a vain cycle of longing and loss as I did battle with myself and gave myself one stern talking-to after another until I grew tired of the carping, repetitious nature of my own thoughts. Those incandescent moments I had shared with him, so that I walked around Helicon like an airborne goddess, they were all vanished. Dull turmoil took their place as the days passed and I experienced their inverse: hopelessness.

Because I *could not* have him and in the moments that I glimpsed this, a snake of dread wound its way throughout my entire body and being. I could not have him. My light was put out and I became only half of what I should be.

Then some small atom of me would rebel, and cry, *But I love him*, and suddenly shoots would burst out like flowers in the sun until I was ravaged again by lust and tenderness. I ached to touch him, to rest my lips on the side of his neck, that vulnerable, tender place, and let skin rest on skin, vibrating. I yearned for the touch of our bodies, length against length, humming with whatever strange force existed between us.

I had no way to understand this – yet understanding would not have helped me. I had a hundred good reasons not to let that man into my heart, yet not one that could stop him finding his way there. I felt I was going to break open from the power of it – such power, yet nowhere for it to go. For I could not have him. I could not have him. I could not have him. I told myself over and over.

How was there such a fatal breach between what my head knew and my heart believed? How could such things happen? For my heart was enchanted entirely. It did not believe a word that I told it.

The next day I went early to Speedwell Cheese. Although it would be an hour before Adam arrived and Rebecca could join me, I took refuge in her small sitting room, glad to spend time in a neutral place, instead of within Helicon's accusing walls.

I felt calmer here. No matter the rights and wrongs of it, I could see this: there had never been any way that Turlington and I, one day, were not going to come together in the way of two colliding stars; brilliance and destruction would burn as a consequence in equal measure. Old Rilla used to say, 'If it be writ, it be writ.' Well, this was writ.

Why else, out of all the establishments in London, had Fate brought me in my distress to the Dog and Duchess, and Turlington there at the exact same time? Why else did it arrange for us to sit there long hours talking, then return together to Helicon, the most narrow-eyed household in London, without exciting notice?

I knew, too, that it was not over. I did not need to fear that

Turlington would not return. But he was right. The time was coming, or had come, when we needed to think – and act. All I wanted to do was relive our kisses and that one melting night we had spent together. But the longer I sat there, the more reality raised its shaggy head.

I had a fiancé. Whatever else was in doubt, it was certain now that I could not marry Aubrey. My nature was such that I wished to tell him right away, but when I had said so to Turlington, he stayed me. Until we were ready to take action, he said, it was best to leave everything as close to normal as could be. Everyone supported my engagement to Aubrey; when I broke it there would be pandemonium. How would I explain it? Best not to lay myself open to the minute interrogations that were sure to follow – until we were ready to tell the truth.

I had seen Aubrey only once since that day at the Westwoods', and I had behaved like a mechanical doll. Turlington and I did not know what to do with what was now unleashed between us, so we clung to the status quo as if to a lifeline. But it was intolerable to act so false.

Even from our beloved Sanderson we kept the secret. It was already so complicated; to add another person to the conspiracy would make it worse. I worried, too, about what he might think. I knew he would love me still – judgement and condemnation were not in his character – but would he think less of me in some strange way? He was so pure.

And there was the rest of the family. Every time I went to

meet Turlington, I had to resort to subterfuge with my aunt. It might be imagined that with so little love lost between two people, a lie would not feel like a guilty thing. Yet I found that deceit struck a discord in me that would not rest comfortably. And Hawker! How I quailed when I thought of *him* finding out! It wasn't only fear of the consequences. I did not wish to hurt him. Why on earth did I care for that old devil at all?

And there was something else . . . something I had not let myself acknowledge until now, alone and safe in my refuge in Rebecca's home. It was something about Turlington and me. Not that I doubted our love, not for a minute. But there was *something* . . .

I frowned. Some tiny drumbeat of caution tapping out a warning in my head . . . What was it? I could not tell. When I thought of the way we melted together, the irresistible force that drew us together, that sense of *kindred*, of timelessness, that existed between us, it seemed nothing short of lunacy to question any aspect of it. *But* . . .

Was it something in the way Turlington had said, *That's why I came back, not for Hawker, not for the family*? He had said it without a second's remorse. Without a care for our grandfather's wishes, crazed and prohibitive as they were.

As much as I loved him, craved him, doted on him . . . I had to admit, and he had spotted as much, that the thought of a life which included *only* me and Turlington – even in Italy, even on the banks of a sunlit lake – was a life I found I was not, after all, in a hurry to rush towards. But staying as we were was impossible too . . .

'Tell me at once,' said Rebecca, appearing before me. I looked up, startled. I was so lost in thought I had not even heard her on the stairs.

Rebecca handed me a silver ale tankard full of warm chocolate; she had brought two such with her, I noticed, as I came back to my surroundings. Angel that she was.

'I could see the moment you walked through the door that something has happened. I have been in agonies waiting for Adam and slicing and dicing White Cheshire, wondering what it is.'

I hauled myself upright, having slumped without noticing almost to the horizontal on the soft, comfortable sofa. My chin had sunk into my neck and my skirts stuck up in the air like the arc of a rainbow. Only with such a friend could one be so comfortable.

'Rebecca,' I said when she was seated, 'I am about to bring ruin upon myself and my entire family. I am about to conduct the greatest disgrace a lady in our world can do. I am about to burn the fragile threads of respectability that have bound me here and there will be no going back from it. I will be disinherited. I will not marry Aubrey, and I will hurt many people.'

'It is Turlington, of course,' she said.

I took a sip of my chocolate. It was thick and creamy and

sweet. I imagined what I would have felt as a child to be given such heaven in a cup. 'You have taken the wind clean out of my sails, dear friend. I have not spoken of him for months.'

'And that is precisely why I knew something was going to happen. He has been a constant in your thoughts and words since I have known you. A complete silence following something as momentous as his return to the household was bound to reinforce what I always knew.'

'That I love him?'

'Yes.'

'Oh, Rebecca! This is the most powerful thing I have ever felt! It drives me. But it frightens me too!'

'And he returns your feelings, of course.'

'He does. It is as though there is a force between us bigger than either of us. But I am engaged! Hawker would never consent for us to marry. There is no way for us to be together unless we step out of the world as we know it. I never thought I had much regard for that world, but to walk away altogether . . . Yet we cannot stop, Becky. It is not just a matter of love. We *cannot* stop!'

'Then no wonder you are frightened! It sounds . . . a dark thing, to be so driven.' Rebecca looked thoughtful and chewed her lip while she considered my words. I watched her like an oracle. 'I don't know, Florrie. I think perhaps love has many shades and presents itself in many forms. Not that I am so very worldly as to know. Would that I were a married woman, or . . . or, a lady of the night, to be able to speak from experience . . .'

I burst out laughing at the thought of Rebecca pursuing the old profession. She grinned too. 'But let us not wax philosophical,' she said, shrugging. 'Tell me before I burst, dear, what has happened?'

So I told her all. And she listened carefully, and she did not judge me. I described, as best I could understand it (which was hardly at all), what was happening to me and when I had finally finished she rang for more hot chocolate.

We were silent while the Speedwells' maid, Lucinda, brought us our drinks, and a platter of small pastries. Living in a gastronomic part of town, the Speedwells frequently exchanged cheese for all manner of tasty treats with the other traders. The baker was a particular friend. After Lucinda withdrew, we chewed and brushed flakes of pastry and sugar from our fingers, and stared at the fire.

'Is it anything like this for you, with Tobias?' I asked.

'Something like it, yes,' said Rebecca, frowning. 'But I don't think any of us can gauge our experience by that of another. I think . . . that what we know as love becomes love, for us. For you it is this passion and power, this unmistakable sense of predestiny. Who then am I to say that it is love or not love, only because my own experience is something different?'

'How is it different, Becky? And how is it the same?'

She went a little pink. 'Well, as you know, I love Tobias.'

'No one could doubt it.'

'And I do feel the . . . the longing, to be sure . . . when I think that we might never . . . that Papa will never allow us . . . well, I despair. So I do understand, dear, please do not think I don't. And, then, my love is forbidden too, because of Papa's . . . *ways*! But there is nothing dark about my feelings. I do not feel driven or compelled, I feel free to choose. And of course I choose to love Tobias. Although I also choose to stay with Papa. There is space in my love for Tobias and my obligations. Oh, we want more than parlour visits and conversation twice a week, of course we do. But this is what we have *now* and so we go on. And Tobias is free too . . . even though, of course, because of Papa we are not free at all . . .' She fell silent, clearly frustrated by the sheer impossibility of trying to explain such a thing.

I felt a little cold caution steal through me. I wanted Rebecca's blessing. I *needed* Rebecca's blessing. 'Then you advise me against Turlington?' I asked in a small voice. 'You think that loving him is a mistake?'

'Indeed no! I should never say such a thing! I doubt not for a minute that there is something very special between you, and I long to meet him, Florrie. Only I worry for you, of course. That such a great love should have to mean splitting with your family, unsatisfactory though they are to be sure. That it should mean becoming dependent on this one man who – forgive me, my dear – was known until very recently to be the most unreliable and roguish man in all of . . . well, in all of Europe, most probably. I doubt not that he loves you deeply, Florrie. How could he not? But will he care for you? Is he able to? Will he marry you?'

'We have not talked about it. But suppose he will? We would still have to leave London – can you imagine the *scandal*? Two Grace cousins coming together, defying Hawker, being disinherited . . . I love him so much, Rebecca, that surely I should want to go to the ends of the earth with him? Why then do I feel . . . unsafe at the prospect? Is it what you have said, that he has always been so very . . . turbulent? Do I not trust him now? But I do, I do!'

She shook her head. 'It is all very new, is it not, Florrie? A week since you first spoke of your feelings to one another. I know you have known him many years—'

'And forever, before that!' I interjected passionately.

'If you say so, I cannot doubt it, my dear friend. But those . . . other lifetimes . . . they are beyond human conception, are they not? And in the years that you have known Turlington in *this* lifetime, well, their content does not, perhaps, inspire confidence. I feel sure he has changed indeed, Florrie. But perhaps you need a little time to come to understand that fully. Will he give you that time? Will he be patient with you?'

I hung my head. 'I am sure that he will. But what if *I* cannot be patient, Becky? When he is at Helicon I cannot keep away from him, I cannot think straight, I only want him. It is only now that I have not seen him for four days that I can talk like this at all, and come to realise that . . . there are things in this life of mine that I will miss.'

'What are they?'

'You, of course, and Sanderson. I do not have a great many close friends in London but I think that two of your calibre are more than many people have. I count Selina Westwood, too, as a different sort of friend. And there is my music. It is not that there are no pianos in Italy, of course, it is not that . . . It is the sense of it as a constant, a true expression of myself, which disappears when he is near. I forget there ever was such a thing as a piano when he is with me!

'And my family . . . Oh, Becky, you know better than anyone how I have despised and struggled with them over the years. But Turlington seems to think nothing of it! Of breaking Hawker's heart, stony as it is, of leaving Sanderson, who is not happy, Becky, and I don't know why – I thought I hated them all! Why do I struggle to turn my back on them now?'

'Because you never hated them at all. You were only hurt and frightened. They treated you abominably, but you have found some measure of forgiveness within you and that is a brave thing. You are a caring person, Florrie. Tell me, dear, what do you think Turlington will do if you refuse to run to Italy with him?'

'I don't know. But how can I *not* go, feeling as I do?'

'I don't know.'

I left Rebecca some time later. We had continued to talk, to ponder the troubling pathways of Fate and to come to no conclusion at all. Two sheltered young women, of nineteen and almost one-and-twenty, were not equipped to fathom such a conundrum, we readily admitted. We were both completely out of our depth. Even so, I was glad of her friendship, now more than ever.

I was wandering through Marylebone in the absent-minded state that had become so habitual with me of late when a loud shout roused me from my reflections. I looked up to see a fat gentleman, some distance away, waving his arm with an appearance of outrage. The next minute, a small boy shot past me like one of Judith's parakeets, bumping me as he went so that I stumbled against the wall.

'Sorry, miss!' he threw over his shoulder and sped around the corner like lightning.

The next minute I heard a cry. Peering around the corner, I saw that he had tripped over something, or his own feet, and was sprawled on the road, winded. I was about to go and tend to him when I saw a constable running ponderously in the same direction. Something about the sequence – fat man shouting, small boy flying, policeman lumbering – translated itself into a suspicion. I don't know what made me act without knowing the facts, but I ran to the boy, picked him up – he was small and skinny – and dragged him off the street into the small yard at the side of Speedwell Cheese. He immediately ducked down, pulling at my hand, and together we crouched behind the fence, watching as the constable pounded past and disappeared. The small criminal turned in relief to sit on the ground with his back against a cart and at last he started to gasp and recover his breath. Then he looked at me suspiciously.

'What you do that for?' he demanded.

I wanted to smile but I did not. 'I don't know,' I told him gravely.

'How did you know I didn't steal nothing?'

'I had rather assumed you did. But . . . I thought perhaps you might be sorry.'

He frowned. 'I'm not that sorry,' he confessed, pulling a large gold pocket watch from his trousers. 'I stole this.'

'To sell?'

He shrugged. 'I dunno. No. I don't need to do that no more. I'm at the boys' home now, see, and it's not even a bad 'un. But stealing's what I do. What I *used* to do. I can't sell it. I'm only allowed out with the others.'

'Then how are you out alone today?'

'They sent me on an errand. They said it were a . . . an indication of trust!'

'Trust that you wouldn't steal?'

'Yass. An' the rest.'

'Hmm.'

We both looked at the large, round watch, glinting in the sunlight. He scratched his head. 'I reckon I messed that up. Only it were there, hanging out of his pocket asking to be snatched. I didn't know the copper was there, did I?'

'What do you want to do now?'

'Honest? I want to go back to the home like this never happened. It's the best place I've been, and I've been in . . . ten.'

'You've lived in *ten* different places?' He only looked about seven. He nodded.

'I've lived in two,' I mused.

'Any good?'

'Oh! Yes, the first one was good. This one's . . . complicated.'

He rubbed his hand over his head and his hair stood up in sandy-coloured spikes. 'Reckon I'd be happy if I was rich like you. I think I'll just leave this here. Only it seems a waste . . .'

'I don't suppose you know who it belonged to, do you?'

'Oh yass! Old Jenson's it is. The fishmonger.'

'Well then, suppose I take it back for you. I'll tell him I saw the thief, a big, burly dark-haired lad, that he dropped it in his haste and I picked it up. Then it will be as though it never happened.'

He stood up and squinted at me. He had huge grey eyes, prominent cheekbones and golden freckles over his face. 'You won't tell him the truth, will you?'

'No! Of course not. I thought it could be a second chance for you.'

'Well, thank you, miss. Yes. Thank you.'

I held out my hand. 'A pleasure. My name's Florence. Florence Grace.'

He shook it. 'Jacob Chance. See, I'm telling you my real name. It's an indication of trust.'

'I'm honoured. Might I visit you, Jacob Chance? At the boys' home? See how you're getting on?'

He looked confused. 'If you want to. It ain't very interesting there, and I got no conversation. But if you want to. I'm at the Rising Star Home in Kensington. Don't bring the police round.'

'I promise. Goodbye, Jacob.'

'Bye.' He grinned a cheeky grin and darted off. I set off in search of Mr Jenson, with a feeling as though Fate had come upon me again – and knocked me sideways against a wall.

Chapter Twenty-nine

The day before Turlington was due to return I became as twitchy as a hare. The suspense was so great I could barely breathe, the thought that in just one day more I would be able to fasten my arms about his neck again and kiss him. There was apprehension, too, lest he did not come. And there was even a tiny part of me that dreaded him coming and the changes it would herald.

Unexpectedly, I slept deeply that night, perhaps worn out from the restless mental exertions of the day. I woke to a dusting of snow and my first thought was, *Let it not prevent him from reaching me*. Then I went down to breakfast and he was there.

He was alone in the dining room. Without thinking, I ran to him.

He caught me and kissed me fiercely, briefly, then set me away from him. Not a moment too soon, for the door opened. Aunt Dinah stood there, talking to someone behind her. I took advantage of the hiatus to ask, 'When did you come?'

'Last night, late.'

'And you did not come to me?'

'I hoped you were asleep. And . . . I wish to talk to you, Florrie. There is something you must know.'

My heart sank. From his face I gathered it was not a joyful something. Not another insurmountable obstacle to our love, surely?

Before he could say any more, our aunt and uncle entered.

'Oh, you're back,' said Aunt Dinah without enthusiasm, on seeing him.

'Larger than life, as you see, Aunt. I trust you have been well?'

'Tolerably well. Life goes on busy as always. What's this? Mackerel?'

Shortly Sanderson and Judith joined us and Sanderson's pale face regained something of its old rosy glow when he saw Turlington. *I must ask Sanderson what troubles him*, I promised myself, not for the first time. How had Turlington been gone a week and still I had not found the opportunity? I had been so preoccupied.

'I had a fancy to visit my mother's grave this morning,' said Turlington suddenly. 'Sanderson, will you join me?'

Sanderson looked up, surprised. 'It is Friday,' he reminded his brother. 'I must away to the Coatleys after breakfast.'

'Of course you must, of course. Never mind. Florence, I don't suppose you would care to come?'

'Certainly, Cousin, if you would like some company.' My voice was not quite as steady as I would have wished.

Turlington knew Sanderson was always engaged on a Friday. He had done a marvellous job of arranging for us to go out together and making it seem ever so casual and expected.

We left soon after breakfast and walked to Brompton Cemetery. The snow still fell in the same soft scattering and the streets were unusually hushed. When we were far enough from Helicon he took my hand and I was glad of it. I was seized with a raw fear that I was going to lose him. In the overcast morning, with its fine mesh of snowflakes scattered over tombstone and grave, the cemetery was a suitably sombre setting for such news.

'Have you been here, Florrie?' he asked as we fastened the tall iron gates behind us. 'Have you seen where they all ended up, Morden and Rosanna and Clifton and the rest of them, my mother and Sanderson's, our Uncle Edgar, our Aunt Mary?'

I had not.

'It is worth seeing.' He led me left and right among the monuments without hesitating.

'You have been here often,' I said. I could see him here, brooding, perhaps in his days of exile.

He did not contradict me. He stopped outside a tall, pale grey mausoleum with two angels standing guard, one on either side. Their faces were handsome, their wings outspread, their swords mighty. The mausoleum was imposing, but plain. Solid stone, no embellishments, and above the door, in large, stark lettering, was carved just one word: *Grace*.

We stood hand in hand looking up at it, like two children at the gates of Faerieland. *There it is*, I thought. *The symbol and solid reality of our heritage.*

'There it is,' said Turlington bitterly, echoing my thoughts. 'We used to be in the family plot in St Matthew's, you know, but when this place was built . . . Well, you know how they are about being modish. I feel I've been carrying it around on my shoulders all my life. Though in truth it is not as old as I am.'

'And you wish to set it down,' I said softly. A snowflake landed on my cheek, damp and confiding.

He turned and looked at me with naked longing, whether for me, or for freedom, I could not tell. Perhaps he equated me with freedom and doubtless I had been doing the same with him.

'I would give all that I have to do so. All my life I have been defined by being a Grace. Carved out, like those letters.' He waved a gloved hand at our succinct epitaph. 'Turlington the Grace heir, Turlington the greatest Grace disappointment, Turlington the reformed prodigal . . . I am just a man, Florrie, and I suffer and struggle and I cannot carry it any longer!'

I did not know how to comfort him. Even I had come to accept that I had to be who I was. But I squeezed his hand and waited.

'Look.' Turlington pointed to the paving stone before the door of the tomb. We stepped closer and he bent to brush away the dusting of snow. I saw words carved there too. We read them aloud, together: 'Precious mortality.'

'Precious mortality,' I said again. 'What does that mean?'

'Exactly, Florrie, there you have my thoughts exactly. What does it *mean*? Does it mean simply that human life is precious? I don't think so. Nothing so compassionate for the Graces! For a long time I thought it meant that we, our family, amongst all mortals, are precious. Over there lie the common folk but here, *here* lie the precious. But the last time I came here I suddenly thought, if it meant that, would it not be carved beneath the name? But it's not, Florrie, as you see, it's on the door stone. Where it must be stepped on. I think this is Hawker's way of saying, *So much for precious mortality. We Graces crush it beneath our very boots. For we are Graces, a little thing like death cannot constrain us*. For it was Hawker who had this built, of course.'

'Perhaps you are right. It is a strange tomb. But then, Helicon is a strange house, so why should we be any more comfortable in death than in life?' I gazed at it thoughtfully. Slowly the snow filled up the grooves of the letters so that they became even more obscure. And it struck me that as a Grace, I too was destined for this place.

'I will be buried here,' I said in a wave of fear. 'I will be in London forever. But my mother is not here, with the Graces. She is in Cornwall, with my father – and Nan. My parents are buried in Tremorney and oh, I will be here!'

I turned to Turlington with a sudden sob and he held me

close. In that glorious closeness I felt that my longstanding unhappiness at being dispossessed and transplanted could be buried and soothed.

'Turlington, what was it you wanted to tell me?' I asked then fearfully, my face resting against his chest.

He patted my behind and I giggled, surprised. But he was not being rogueish. 'Plenty of petticoats and padding, I perceive,' he laughed. 'Can you sit?'

We sat side by side on 'precious mortality', and I am not sure what that signified, if anything.

I leaned over and lifted the hair off his neck, laid a soft kiss there, my heart aching with love. He looked at me then and his face was tortured, as it used to be in the old days of his drinking and wrongdoing. My heart clenched. What had he done? Had he stolen something, hurt someone, lain with another woman?

'Whatever is the matter?' I whispered.

He clutched both my hands. 'Florrie,' he breathed, burying his face in my hair. 'Florrie, Florrie, Florrie.'

'I'm here, Turlington.'

'Yes, you're here. But oh, I'm sorry I've dragged you into such a mess. You deserve more than a forbidden love, a choice between your life and your family, or such a sorry wretch as me.'

'Turlington! You are no wretch! Why are you speaking of yourself that way?'

'I have lied to everyone.'

A terrible thought occurred to me. 'Are you *married*?'

To my relief the darkness in his face lifted for a moment and he laughed. 'Married? No! I am not, Florrie, I can promise you that at least.'

'Then what? What has happened?'

'Nothing has happened. Nothing new anyway. It happened many, many years ago, back in the mists of the Grace family tree. An interesting little offshoot, this one, my peach.'

'Turlington! Tell me so that it makes sense or don't tell me at all.'

'Very well. I'm not a Grace.'

I clutched his arm a little more tightly. 'I beg your pardon, my love?'

'I'm not a Grace. My mother lied. *I'm* a lie. There isn't a drop of Grace blood in these veins!'

He lifted his arms out in front of us. We could not see his veins, clad in shirt and jacket and coat as he was, but we contemplated them anyway. He gave an empty, echoing laugh.

'Isn't it ludicrous? Hawker threatens us with disinheritance if we marry, first cousins as we are. But we're not, Florrie! I'm no more your cousin than I am Rebecca's! The only bonds we share are the bonds of love and passion. But if Hawker knew, he would disinherit me anyway! And you too, for loving me.'

I pulled his floating arms back to hold me and stared into the grey air, the crowd of stone angels. Turlington Grace . . .

not a Grace! My cousin, whom I had tortured myself about loving . . . *not* my cousin. The first hope of the Graces, the prodigal who had been welcomed back time after time after time because he was the Grace heir . . . no true heir? It was not easy to comprehend.

And yet, my heart took flight. He *wasn't* my cousin. There was no need for guilt. He was just a man and I was free to love him. There was no sin in it, no matter which belief system you subscribed to.

'Turlington! Oh, the weight that has been lifted!' I was laughing through tears, with a relief I had not known I craved. 'Oh, you're not my cousin! This kinship we feel, 'tis of the soul, and only the soul.'

'Well, and perhaps of the body also,' he chuckled, pressing himself against me and sinking his face into my hair. 'I had not known the cousin matter . . . *mattered* to you so much, my sweet.'

'Nor had I but now I find it did! But tell me, Turlington. How did this come about? How long have you known?'

And now my initial euphoria was tinged with shadow. For I knew before he told me that he had known a long time. Suddenly I remembered our first meeting in the stable in Truro. I had felt so sorry for him, child though I was, without knowing why. I had murmured his name, *Turlington Grace*, and he had echoed *Grace* in such a bitter tone. Even then I had thought it strange. He had lied and pretended to Hawker, to us all, merely to presume a position – and a fortune – that weren't his. *Sanderson's* fortune, in fact.

He sunk his head in his hands for a minute, as though its secrets were too heavy. Then he sat up, shook back his hair and began. 'My mother, you see, had married Clifton Grace, as you know. She was very young.'

'Belle,' I said softly and he nodded.

'Belle,' he echoed, his face tender. 'When her father told her she must marry him, she was in love with someone else. He was an old childhood sweetheart whose family ran a bakery – not poor, not at all, but not sufficiently grand to please the Turlingtons.

'When my father expressed his interest in Belle, you can imagine how their feathers fluffed. As Hawker hammered home to you, Clifton Grace could have his pick of anyone. Many coquettish daughters and aspirational mamas had set their caps at him. To be chosen by him was seen as the greatest honour a girl could receive.

'It is everything that we hate, you and I, Florrie. The ranking of people, one above another on grounds of beauty and wealth.'

'I know, Turlington, I know, but tell me of your mother.'

'Yes. Well, she told her parents of her great love for her old friend but they would not hear of it. They agreed he was a very good sort of man, but he was to bake cakes and pastries for a living, and he was not a Grace. A Grace could open doors for his bride and her family that might never be dreamed of otherwise. Clifton Grace could walk on water.

'Young as she was, she allowed herself to be guided by her family, who told her that marriage rested on a great deal more than affection. She allowed herself to believe that she could do this great thing for her parents, and still find happiness. Deep inside, she knew it was a mistake. But she pretended that she did not know, so that she didn't have to set herself against the family.'

'How very, very sad.'

'Yes. She deserved better.'

'And how do you know all this, my darling?'

'She left me a letter to be opened on my sixteenth birthday, when I was old enough to understand everything. She entrusted it to a dear friend of hers for safekeeping meanwhile. She wanted me to know what her life had been, so that I understood her unhappiness and knew it was nothing to do with me. She said her greatest regret was that I had known an unhappy mother; she feared it would form my character. In telling me, Florrie, she meant to free me from the burden of her unhappiness.'

'But it did not, did it? It left you instead with an impossible secret.'

'The very worst of secrets. And her suffering as vivid a memory as ever. I remember her so clearly, Florrie. I loved her. I remember scrambling onto her lap – I must have been so small – and sitting there in an ocean of white flounces looking up at her dark ringlets with their white ribbons and above all at her face, Florrie. So beautiful. But more than that, so kind and gentle. Then my father would come and pull me down. I remember his boots stamping across the floor, the room shaking, his coarse masculine hand landing on my shoulder, his unquestionable strength wrenching me from her and setting me on the cold floor, his booming voice telling me to be a man and explore the world, not curl up like a sissy on the laps of women.' He frowned.

'I never could understand it. A man, according to my father, was meant to love women, and by love I mean conquer. He had scores of affairs – while he was married to my mother and when Cassandra was his wife. Yet a small boy was *not* meant to enjoy the company of women – even his own mother! Nonsensical!

'Perhaps he was jealous of the adoration she showed me. I was the light in her world. For my own sake, *and* because I was the son of her true love; her letter admitted it. My father would not honour her, yet he expected her to honour him, by God, he did.

'I remember other times. He threw a glass of red wine in her face one evening, just because she was distracted while he told her some boring tale of his exploits. I had started to choke so she turned to me to help. He did not like that. He liked to be the sun around which all other planets turned. Any suggestion that other people mattered too was like shadow on his glory. I remember the piece of meat stuck in my throat, I remember the struggle to draw breath, the fear, my mother reassuring me and patting my back and then an explosion of red in her face, blinding her. She could not help me for a moment and I was still struggling, alone . . .'

'My love.' I kissed his cheek. His face was hard and hurt. *Now I understand you better than ever*, I thought. Tender childhood memories, bitter childhood hurts. No wonder his feelings about the Graces were so tangled and dark.

He drew a shaky breath and laughed. 'So you see, my darling girl,' he said, 'I somehow fell into the wrong life, the wrong family. If my mother had married my father, as she was always meant to, I would still have been *me*, made of her and him, and we should have been happy. My surname would have been Winston, not Grace, and I would no doubt have had some sensible Christian name like John. Instead, I am *still* made of her and him, but I am somehow a Grace, and the expectations of generations of Graces, culminating in that rusty old hatchet, Hawker, all rest upon me, and in here I shall go when I die, when I am not one of them at all.'

'Oh, Turlington. Oh, your poor, torn heart. When we met in Truro, you already knew.'

'Yes. How old was I then? Twenty? Yes. I had long known. My dear mother made a misjudgement in telling me at such a tender age. She had hoped to save me from the effects of her pain, to steer me into a brighter future, but it did the opposite, in truth. But she couldn't have known what a troubled soul I was to be. I believe many an adolescent questions his identity as he is asked to shake off childhood and assume the responsibilities of a man. But to learn that you are not who you are meant to be at all . . . To be able to confide in no one . . . Well, I did not have the wisdom or the nature to digest it. The more I was told, *A Grace must do this, or that*, the more I thought, *But I am not a Grace*! and the whole thing became torment. I drank my first bottle of brandy the night I read my mother's letter. I have drunk many a one since.'

'But how do you tell them,' I mused, coming to understand the depth of his conundrum, 'without betraying your mother's secret, disgracing her memory, losing your place in the world?'

'Exactly so. And then, there is the money too, Florrie, bald as that may sound. I want my inheritance.' He ran a hand over his face and scowled. 'I do not like to think that I am not truly entitled to it. I *feel* entitled. I have served my time in this family, paid my dues. I have suffered long years from their cruelty and petty ways. You know that my personal fortune has grown and vanished by turns. For my own sake I have not cared much. There have been times when I have preferred to live nearly destitute than to try to be a Grace. But I have you to think of now. I have plans for the future, beautiful plans, for the first time. Being the Grace heir means a security I cannot rely upon offering you otherwise.'

'I understand, Turlington, I surely do. And yet—'

'And yet you think to live a lie is a greater disgrace, a greater dishonour.'

'I do not think of dishonour, my love, only of the burden upon you, the dark shadow on your heart. To live a lie so big, so far-reaching . . . must it not cost you most dearly in a thousand small matters of the soul? Does it not poison you slowly each and every day?' I ended passionately.

'You put it in a perfect phrase. It *does* cost me dearly, just so, each and every weary day. And yet do we not all do that, every one of us? Do I know anyone who lives a life of perfect, uncompromised authenticity? Do you?'

'Certainly I do not and you know it.' I brooded for a moment, close against his chest. It was not just that our love had me living a lie. It was everything about me. Well, not everything. My piano playing was real. My friendships. My passion for Turlington. Otherwise . . . my speech, dress, manners, daily habits, constraints, even my plans for the future, were all manufactured.

'I too am far from the field where I was sown, Turlington,' I mused.

'I know it, my sweet, I know,' he murmured into my hair. 'And that is why we understand each other so very well perhaps, and why we always have. We have been cast adrift and pulled into the current that is the Grace family. They have ensnared us in their tangles and dictated so many things about us but they have *never* convinced our hearts and *that* is why we have rebelled in so many ways, great and small.'

'But our love, that is not rebellion?' I demanded, suddenly anxious. 'You do not just want me to hurt Hawker? It is not that I am forbidden?'

He smiled, that slow, lazy, melting smile that I loved so well, and kissed me and laughed and kissed me more.

'There is no life in which I could not love you, Florrie. Not if I were a baker's son called John and you a Cornish girl in Braggenstones, both of us right in our lives and happy, even then I would love you. And if you were a princess and I were a frog, and if I were a duke and you were my laundry maid, and if you were a tree nymph and I were a woodcutter . . . I would love you. I would worship you.'

My eyes filled with tears. We clung to each other. We loved each other so dearly. And we had nothing else.

Chapter Thirty

◁━━◦◦◦━━▷

And so my life slid into a new and distinct phase. Turlington and I could not bid farewell to the life we knew at Helicon just like that; we were simply not ready to face those consequences. Our love, his revelation, these were enough to deal with for the time being. Remembering again when we first met in Truro, I a servant and he the fine gent, it was almost impossible to adjust my understanding to this: that I was more of a Grace than he was.

Our love was the central point of both our worlds and the two of us altered reality as we knew it to make room for it. We continued to meet at the Dog and Duchess or another equally unpleasant hostelry. We walked, when the weather permitted it, around the least respectable parts of the city. I felt safe with Turlington, who knew those parts all too well, but it did not make me happy to be there. Even with the poverty I had known in Braggenstones I had never seen such unhappy lives as I glimpsed here. But while we hoped to avoid being seen by anyone who knew us, our walks also served as a search for Calantha.

Turlington's earlier enquiries had turned up nothing. We asked landlords, urchins, prostitutes if they had seen her – she was easily described. But we heard nothing of her. I never knew whether to feel relieved – I could not bear to think of a life she might lead in such dark, unkindly places – or wretched. What if she had frozen or starved? What if the river had claimed her?

'You know, I believe she was not mad at all,' I ruminated to Turlington as we walked. 'A little unusual perhaps but can the world truly not allow for that? She saw beings that no one else could, and spoke to them, but so did I when I lived in Cornwall.'

'Your moor spirits?'

'Yes. I have not experienced anything of the sort since coming to London where all is stone and man-made, but I do not feel more sane for that. Calantha did not fit the mould, that was her difficulty. No more did you, or I, but I had the excuse of being a country girl and you had the protection of being a gentleman. How I wish we could find her, and find her well.'

'As do I, my love. As do I.'

In the nights, more often than not, Turlington came to my room and I was soon a virgin no more. Never had I known such feelings. The first time he pulled his nightshirt over his head and his dark hair drifted back into place, grazing his bare shoulders, I could do nothing but drink him in as he stood before me. His slender body and long legs, smooth-skinned and luminous in the moonlight, were so cool and delicious I could hardly think what to do. So I pulled off my own nightgown, so that he could admire me too. And admire we both did, until we tumbled towards each other and expressed with our bodies everything that could not be expressed in words. No matter how much we confided in one another, some truths lie in a different realm and must be approached via different roads.

During the days I was exhausted, depleted. Not only did our night-time couplings make for very little sleep, but this new reality took its toll on me. I used Rebecca as my alibi for most of my meetings with Turlington, which meant that I saw her very little in truth, and she had for so long been my primary source of steadiness and strength. I was, too, in a new environment for a large part of my week, one I found dispiriting and oppressive.

Then there was the duplicity: having to remember where I had supposedly been and why, a fiction running parallel to a reality which already took all of my attention. I had to fabricate news when Sanderson asked how things were with Rebecca, for I did not know. Lying to Aubrey, pretending that I was still going to marry him, that was the worst of all. I felt callous and cruel for prolonging his hopes – and indeed I was. It was just that protecting the secret of Turlington and me became all that I could think of during those days. As much as Aubrey's feelings mattered to me, Turlington's mattered far, far more. Aubrey was sacrificed, my own compunctions were sacrificed; I believe that for a while back then I would have sold my soul if it had meant one more kiss with Turlington.

As winter wore on and the weather turned into a vile, spitting beast, we found a new and legitimate way to spend time together. At my request, Turlington had donated a sum of money to the optimistically named Rising Star Home for Young Gentlemen. (They were nothing of the sort.)

I had been, once or twice, to visit Jacob. The owners of the home, Mr Planchard and his brother, Mr Planchard, had received me very kindly. Jacob received me less kindly; it seemed that our initial rapport, forged over flouting the law, had vanished; I found him sullen and distrustful to the extreme. He was only nine years old (older than I had guessed, but he was small for his age and ill-nourished) yet hard-bitten by the world. My heart ached for him, so small and angry as he was. He was scared, I felt sure, though he never would show it. I wanted to help and the best way seemed to be to support the Planchards' venture, rather than to keep targeting Jacob directly.

Now the Planchards had invited us to look around the home and see first-hand the wonders Turlington's money had wrought in these young lives. (In short, they were hoping for a further donation.) I was happy because I cared about the home and because it gave us a reason to go somewhere together without having to pretend we weren't. So one rainy January day the carriage came round and bore us off to Kensington.

Turlington was swathed in his big black greatcoat; I wore a purple cloak over an enormous crinoline of royal blue with purple bows and gold lace. Dresses seemed to become more elaborate with every year that passed. If there was a square inch of fabric not sporting a pleat or a ruffle, some embroidery or lace, an ornamental pocket or some unnecessary buttons, the whole concoction could only be considered very disappointing indeed.

The size of the skirt made it very difficult to get into the carriage. The thing was finally achieved by virtue of Turlington going in ahead of me and pulling me, while a footman poked and pushed at my skirts to coax them to accompany me. Where one bit of skirt would enter the carriage, another would pop out – it was like trying to herd chickens. When at last the door was slammed upon me and my dress, Turlington and I clutched at each other in helpless laughter.

My mirth was wistful, however. I had enjoyed the legitimacy of setting off together while Sanderson and Judith waved us off. I liked solving a trivial, mundane puzzle together. If I married Aubrey, I thought inconsequentially, we would be like that all the time. Then again, if I married Aubrey, we would not now be convulsed with laughter. Aubrey would not be leaning in with eyes that darkened, even while the laughter still simmered there, to kiss me as though slaking a thirst.

We were welcomed by the younger Mr Planchard, who was thrilled to have their generous patron honour them with a visit. He was idealistic, and admitted that it was he who had named the place. His brother was often away looking after other concerns but they both shared a vision of young lives saved, a love of virtue instilled in every young breast.

'For though they might show a preference for theft and cards and wrong-living *now*,' he mused, 'they are still so very young and have been shown such a terrible example early in life. As orphans they have had to make their way howsoever they could. But there is time yet to persuade them of a higher way, is there not, Mr Grace, Miss Grace?'

We were shown around the home, which consisted of three classrooms, two dormitories, a washroom, a small private chapel and an 'easy room' as Mr Planchard termed it. It contained a bookcase, several comfortable chairs, a scuffed old piano and an easel; the boys were allowed to go there whenever they wished to engage in constructive, creative pursuits. It was empty.

There was also a refectory and after our tour we were invited to join the boys for a light lunch. Turlington was about to make our excuses but I said we should be delighted. No sooner had we taken our seats than the back doors of the refectory flew open and forty or so boys aged between eight and eighteen came hurtling in, yelling like furies and flinging their chairs about in a way that suggested they wished to make firewood out of them. I looked at Mr Planchard in some astonishment and he gave a reassuring smile, or at least it would have been reassuring if it had not been so nervous.

'Youthful high spirits,' he explained, leaning forward to be heard over the uproar. 'They have been closeted in their lessons all morning. I do not like to curb them once again, now they are at leisure.'

'Leisure!' laughed Turlington. 'They have embraced the concept most wholeheartedly!'

Sure enough one boy had lain down on the floor and appeared to be sound asleep. Another had run up to the soup tureen and helped himself to a generous portion while the young girl who was meant to be serving tried to rap him on the head with the dripping ladle. A third was demonstrating a complex jig to two of his fellows – and he was doing it on the table, the better for them to see his feet. The dancing boy was Jacob, I realised with some surprise.

'William Mooring! Back to your seat, please, the bell is not yet rung, young fellow!' cried Mr Planchard, but it was like trying to be heard over a gale. 'Jacob Chance! Get off the table! Benjy Gibbs, wake up! Adam Fairley, STOP hitting that boy!' But they paid no attention. I watched in mortification, very much suspecting that these boys had confused kind and honourable with ineffectual and helpless – perhaps, in this case, with some reason.

'Boys!' Mr Planchard ploughed on. 'BOYS!' He resorted to ringing a large pewter bell, but they took no notice of this portent either. 'I am sorry,' he said to us. 'My brother is away ... When there are two of us ... But today he ... BOYS! We have VISITORS!'

'Well, I don't know about you, but I'm hungry,' said Turlington, throwing back his chair and marching into the flowing tide of boyhood. He snatched Jacob from the table and threw him into a seat. He plucked the sleeping boy from the floor and set him, nodding, at the table. He grabbed the bowl of soup from the greedy boy's hands, drank it himself and gave the boy a shove in a tableward direction. Noticing these unusual interventions, the boys started to simmer down and Turlington took advantage of the lull to address them.

'I'm Turlington Grace. I've given some money to this home, to keep you gentlemen in pocket handkerchiefs, marbles and the like. This is good soup, I suggest you try some. Even better, listen to Mr Planchard. I believe he has chocolate for afterwards if you behave.' He strode back to the table and took his seat again. By now all the boys had noticed Turlington in his long, elegant coat and me in my enormous, bright dress. A couple of whistles flew my way but Turlington quelled them with a dark look.

'I have no chocolate!' whispered Mr Planchard, looking terribly guilty.

'I assumed not,' muttered Turlington, 'but we have our result, as you see.'

'But I dislike lying to gain their co-operation. I always feel it is better to address them man to man, truthfully, and wait for their better natures to win the day.'

'You might have had quite some wait, and besides you did not lie to them, I did. I am extremely happy for you to malign me. Shall we eat, Mr Planchard?'

'Oh yes, yes, by all means.'

Lunch was simple but good: soft bread, firm cheese, crisp apples. There was also an apparently bottomless cauldron of excellent chicken soup. The boys fell on the repast like starving wolves and at last I could contain myself no more; I asked if I might sit among them and hear their stories.

'I'm sure they would be delighted!' said Mr Planchard in surprise. 'But be warned, Miss Grace, they are not always . . . *refined* in their ways and speech.'

'You astonish me,' mumbled Turlington.

'Refined? Nor was I, once,' I smiled.

So I went and sat among them and after the initial flurry of rude enquiries – did I have legs or wheels under that skirt? Was Turlington a nancy boy with that blooming great cravat? Was I married and, either way, did I fancy a tumble? and so on – they settled down. We swapped stories while Mr Planchard talked to Turlington about their plans to build a new wing for girls and to plead for funds.

I believed very little of what the boys told me at first. If they were being truthful, I was sitting among more hardened criminals than I would have encountered in London's worst gaols. I believe they were trying to shock me. But I told them my own story and perhaps they responded to the ring of truth in it because then the tales of holding up coaches with loaded pistols, killing six men and robbing banks came to an end. Instead I heard about oversized, undernourished families, about mothers dying in childbirth and fathers starting to drink when nothing else they tried had any effect. I heard about sick baby brothers or sisters, no money for doctors, the need to steal to survive, families halved in size by cholera; commonplace stories, but shockingly personal experience nevertheless, each with different names and details.

But they were funny too. Their early lives may have robbed them of opportunity, respect, shelter, family . . . but they had not taken their ability to laugh at themselves – and others. I found myself talking in my Cornish accent for the first time in years just to make them laugh. I found myself remembering things I had not thought of in a long time – my early enmity with Trudy Penny and the awful things she used to say to me, just to raise a smile in those tough, pale faces.

Jacob said nothing the whole time I was there. He might have been a different boy from the one who had danced on the table. His animation had completely vanished and he looked as sullen and withdrawn as Turlington had looked at that long ago dance in Truro. His sandy hair stood up belligerently and his grey eyes looked like steel. Neither of us gave any indication of our prior encounters.

I asked him a question or two, to try and include him, but he only shrugged. I smiled at him when there was something to smile about, but he appeared entirely humourless, even though I knew he was not. Adults then, or women, or well-dressed people, someone had let him down, broken his trust. I determined to do what I could to mend it.

We came away with Turlington as amused by the visit as I had been moved. He had agreed to give Mr Planchard a further sum. However, he had stipulated it should *not* be used for a girls' wing. 'Can you imagine *girls* around those young hellions?' he marvelled. 'What can Planchard be thinking?'

Instead it was to be spent on employing a new teacher, a disciplinarian to shovel the boys into some sort of order. 'Even if they're only *pretending* to behave,' he pleaded with Mr Planchard, 'they have to do better than that. It will do them no favours this way. Believe me, I speak from experience.'

Until the appointment was made, Mr Planchard begged Turlington's help, once a week. It was true that his own less-than-exemplary past gave him an easy rapport with the boys and his unconventional nature helped him to shock them into obedience if all else failed. They had enjoyed talking with me, too, Mr Planchard told us, delight written all over his face. The feminine influence was something entirely lacking at the Rising Star, since the female teachers he had previously employed had run away very quickly. If I could bear to visit them again, he felt it might do them much good.

So we fell into the habit of calling at the home every Tuesday and spending time with the boys. We missed no opportunity to let them know how lucky they were to be with the Planchards rather than in one of the similar but downright unpleasant establishments that existed elsewhere in London. How much good we did I cannot say but I fancy we did a little, at least.

I loved having a common cause with Turlington. Going there gave us something to think about besides each other. I loved that we now had a bond we did not have to hide from the world and I loved seeing how Turlington rose to the occasion of setting a good example.

Above all, I loved the boys, and especially Jacob Chance. It was one of those irrational yet inarguable things. He was utterly charmless, blank and uninterested. There were dozens of boys more appealing and affectionate. Hostility radiated for a considerable distance around his scrawny frame and he reminded me of a hedgehog, rolled up and bristling. But it was Jacob who tugged at me.

Yet gradually he began joining in conversations, rarely with more than a few words, but they were always well-placed, with a deadly humour. Once, Turlington and I were demonstrating a few dance steps to the boys – a quadrille and a waltz. The boys were crying with laughter at the mores of the gentry.

'This is what you fellows have in front of you if you do as the Planchards intend and follow a gentlemanly path!' Turlington teased them. 'You'll have to waft about and remember your right from your left and above all stay upright and do battle with these infernal skirts. I'd stay miscreants if I were you – far easier.' In just such a teasing, irreverent way, we kept reinforcing that they had choices, that there were forks in the road ahead of them, both with their benefits and their price. It seemed to work better than Mr Planchard's well-meant but unmitigated idealism.

Jacob surprised us all by standing up suddenly and saying, 'I suppose I'd better save you, Miss Grace, and show him how it's done.' He cut Turlington most deftly and started whisking me around the refectory in a spirited jig. It was a little like a country dance I had learned as a girl in Cornwall so I kept up with him tolerably and we broke apart laughing after two rounds.

Jacob rubbed his knees ruefully. 'You're not wrong about those skirts!' he told Turlington. 'Lord, Miss Grace, what are they made of? There's something in there that hurts!'

'There are steel bands in the cages,' I told him.

'Cages? What are you, a linnet?'

'Sometimes it feels that way. It's what they call the hoops that hold the skirts out.'

'My ma had a linnet once.'

'Where is she now?'

'Oh. Long gone.'

I did not know whether he meant dead or lost – both were common stories here – but it was time for lunch and in the enthusiastic press for sustenance I found myself seated away from him. But the next time we visited, I noticed him at his classroom window, watching out for us; his guarded expression relented slightly when he saw us. Such are the miracles that can be wrought by a swift dance, shared laughter and a small confidence.

'Anyone would think you were pleased to see me, Jacob,' I told him later.

He gave his characteristic indifferent shrug.

Chapter Thirty-one

February relinquished its grip on the city and March took its turn at last. Suddenly London wore its best muslin: birds twittered, flowers bloomed, clouds scudded and breezes danced. It was charming. And I was as close to happy as I had been since I came to London. I had Turlington, I had Sanderson, I had Jacob, I had Rebecca. I had my music. Annis was gone and Aunt Dinah, thinking me engaged and soon to be someone else's problem, left me pretty well alone. Life at Helicon then was tolerable and the compensations were more in number than I could ever have dared to hope at one time.

But deceiving Aubrey was growing increasingly intolerable. The fact that it was made easy by his gentlemanly reluctance to exert any pressure on me made it only the more poignant. We had long since postponed the wedding. Turlington had suggested it: 'It will give us some time,' he had said. Aubrey, though disappointed, had been understanding. I was young yet, he agreed — but nineteen years old — and Sanderson's wedding was looming. Perhaps Helicon would not best be served by another so soon after.

Now I was learning who I was when I acted against my own best principles – and I did not like it. I pleaded with Turlington to let me break my engagement but he insisted we must not ruffle the waters yet.

I did not know what he was waiting for. I knew the inheritance was important to him, but it was hardly as though I had been born to the lavish life of a Grace. I told him that whatever we had to share would suffice. I also pointed out that since Hawker was in rude health, that fortune would likely be many years away.

Or perhaps he was waiting for some resolution that he could not yet muster, or for us to agree on our course of action. For he still wanted us to run away to Italy while I still felt seduced and mistrustful in equal measure by the scheme. I had always been fanciful, imaginative, sensitive. Yet I was also a country girl, with a pragmatic streak a mile wide.

At first I, too, had assumed we would be forced to walk away from our lives in order to be together, but now I felt differently. Yes, Hawker would disown us; that would happen whether Turlington admitted the truth of his birth or not. And I would be castigated either way, either for loving my cousin, or for loving a pretender. Hawker's wrath would not be slight, and I dreaded it more than Turlington, since I was troubled by my strange affection for the old despot. But whatever he may have thought, Hawker Grace did not own London. There could still be a place there for Turlington and me. I found it harder than I could have imagined to contemplate turning away from Sanderson, who was unhappy, from Hawker, who was old and, I felt sure, unsteady in his mind, from Rebecca, who was still forbidden to marry, from Jacob, who was blossoming in our friendship, albeit at his own glacial pace. What if Calantha should be found and need a friend? And I *longed* to stop lying.

But Turlington begged restraint, and he commanded my loyalty utterly so I stayed silent. One thing was true: with Sanderson's wedding so close it was not a good time to create the greatest rift the family had ever known. If Turlington and I were banished, Sanderson would be bereft. So I agreed to keep lying – for Turlington's sake, for Sanderson's sake – and something in me curled up very small.

As Sanderson's wedding drew closer there were dresses to be fitted and fussed over and flowers to be approved and re-arranged and a million small inconsequences that naturally meant the world to Anne. I tried hard at last to put aside my own preoccupations to be a true friend to Sanderson. The more time I spent with him, accompanying him on errands and helping where I could, the less I could ignore what I had seen for some time.

'You are unhappy, my dear, dear cousin,' I ventured one

evening as we strolled by the river at dusk. *What on earth could it be?* But it was difficult to ask. We had not been alone together at leisure for some time and Sanderson so rarely showed any cracks in his charming, easy manner that this was unfamiliar ground. A beautiful April evening whispered around us; cherry blossom clustered in connubial abundance and birds fluted romantic songs through veils of fading sunlight. All was soft and lovely and hopeful. The wedding was in three days and nature seemed entirely prepared for it. Sanderson did not.

My heart ached to see him so drawn and tense, he who had only ever wanted a peaceful, happy life for everyone around him – even when those people seemed absolutely set against peace and happiness.

He was quiet a long and thoughtful time. 'Do you ever think that our lives are very odd?' he asked. 'Why am I asking? I know you do! You tell me often enough and I tell you that things are as they are and resisting never made anyone happy. But perhaps submission does not either.'

'You have also told me many times that it is not a question of submission but of acceptance. The one carries the taint of failure and shame, whereas the other is an appropriate response to man's place in a greater scheme of things,' I quoted him.

He sighed. 'Indeed. I have said that. Someone very wise said it to me. It is hard to tell the difference sometimes, though, is it not, Florrie?'

I shrugged. 'I'm not sure if I've ever experienced acceptance to compare the two.'

'That's not true! You have not fought for a long time but I do not think of you as someone who has submitted either. I thought you had risen to your fate, don't disillusion me now!'

If he only knew.

We had reached a place where a stone wall ran beside the water and we stopped to lean our elbows upon it and gaze at the tide.

'We were not talking about me,' I said, evading him, determined to get to the bottom of his unfathomable mood. 'You are to be married in three days, dear. What troubles you? Don't you love Anne?'

He sighed. The last rays of the evening sun glinted on his golden curls. 'Anne is . . . all that is admirable. She is lovely to look at and she is mannerly, thoughtful and intelligent. She has a sweet nature. I am lucky to have such a bride.'

'She is a good woman, yes, but that doesn't mean you necessarily love her,' I said. 'Aubrey is also good and intelligent and . . .' I trailed off as I realised what I was saying.

Sanderson looked shocked. 'Are you saying you don't love Aubrey? Why, Florrie! I had no idea!'

'Oh, I . . . It's not that. Well, that is to say . . . Oh, Sanderson! I don't know. What *is* love anyway? I always thought that as I must marry, I would stand the best chance of happiness with someone kind, someone I could respect . . .'

'You thought? And now? What do you think now?'

'Well, what do *you* think? Do you . . . do you desire Anne?'

I felt a little flushed. I had never spoken of such things with Sanderson. But Sanderson answered me seriously. 'No, I do not.'

'Oh,' said I, falling silent.

I thought of the tumbling nights with Turlington and I felt sorry for Sanderson. I knew that he would have with Anne what I would have had with Aubrey. Sanderson would never know that sweet ecstasy to which I yoked myself nightly. He would never know days lit up by the memory of the dark hours.

I tucked my hand through his arm. No doubt he would do well enough. No doubt I would have. But there would be no passion and surging. Such a life was not good enough for my dear friend. In fact, I thought it was not good enough for *anyone*, though most people seemed happy enough to embrace it.

'And for the love of God why *must* we marry?' he went on. 'I mean, would it much trouble humanity if the Graces were greatly reduced in number? Just who exactly would care, apart from Hawker?'

'Have I not been saying that for years?'

'You have. And I have counselled you as best I knew how. But I find that advice sounds well and good in the abstract, when the dreaded event is years away and theoretical. It is altogether different with three days' buffer between now and the rest of my life.'

'So it is . . . *dreaded*, then, Sanderson? The prospect makes you *very* unhappy?'

'Yes.'

'Then do not marry her, Sanderson! It is not too late!'

'She is a lovely girl, Florrie! How could I humiliate her like that? It is not in my nature.'

'I know. Nor do I wish unhappiness for Anne. I do not say it lightly. But can you really pay for her happiness with your whole life? That cost is too high! Is it that some people are put on the earth to have happiness delivered to them, while others must provide it at every cost to themselves? I cannot believe it. Who would arrange such a lottery? You are not only here to make Anne happy, or Hawker, Sanderson. You matter too!'

'Thank you, Florrie.' He pulled me to him and laid his head on my hair. 'Thank you for caring about me but, well . . . I do not think I can ever be happy, so I might as well give happiness to others. In fact, doing so makes me happier than I would otherwise be. So you see, I am not as altruistic as you think me.'

'But *why* can you not be happy? To be sure it's an elusive state but I'm certain you have just as much chance of discovering the secret as any of us. There is no special obstacle for you.'

He patted my hand and began to walk again, eyes fixed on his feet. I kept pace with him, slow and heavy. I had the thought that our walk was funereal. I knew he was not going to answer me.

'Oh!' I said softly, stopping in the street. He looked at me in surprise. A sudden knowing had flashed upon me in the way that sometimes happened. Sanderson was in love with someone else. *Oh, poor Sanderson.*

It must be someone very unsuitable, or he would not be marrying Anne. I wondered who on earth had captured the heart of my good cousin, but I would not ask. This was a long-harboured secret, I guessed, and it felt too precious to broach now.

I started walking again. 'Just know, dear,' I added, 'that if you broke off this engagement, even now, I would support you, and you know Turlington would too.'

'Just ignore me, Florrie. I am sure these are the usual nerves of a bachelor before his wedding, on which Hawker has lectured me time and again. It's strange, it's almost as if he's never believed I will go through with this, and I cannot think why for I am nothing if not conscientious. I'm hardly the sort to let people down and hurt and disappoint those dearest to me. I mean, I'm not *Turlington*!'

I smiled painfully.

'Florrie, we shall talk a week after the wedding and I'm sure you shall find me the most delighted of men. All will be well and we shall laugh at this conversation on the riverbank. But dearest, I wish to say the same thing to you. It is not too late for you. If you do not wish to marry Aubrey, if it would make you very unhappy . . . you know you have a friend in me. You do know, don't you, Florrie?'

'I do, dear.'

'Florrie . . . I do not wish to pry. I don't wish to make you uncomfortable, but is there . . . is there someone else?'

Oh, how I longed to confide in him and tell him of my unquenchable longing for his brother who was not his brother. But he had troubles enough. Knowing that Turlington and I were about to break up the family might influence his own decision, for then it truly would all rest on his shoulders. So I swallowed down the words.

'Florrie?'

'Oh! No, it's nothing like that. And you, Sanderson? Dear friend, is there someone else for you?'

'No,' he said. 'No, it's nothing like that.'

Chapter Thirty-two

Sanderson married Anne that Saturday, as planned. They made a beautiful, bright couple with their matching golden curls and impeccable manners.

The wedding breakfast was lavish, and made wonderful for me by Sanderson's kind inclusion of Rebecca, who would not normally have been invited to such a grand affair. Her frustration with her father's selfishness was growing. It was becoming impossible, she said, not being able to share her life with Tobias. The structures that had held them hitherto – their platonic friendship, their polite visits – were too small now. Something would have to break and, she said with uncharacteristic ill humour, she very much feared it would be her father's nose.

After the wedding, Sanderson and Anne went to Italy for two weeks, then they returned to live with us at Helicon. Spring edged into summer and two notable things happened. The first was Sanderson's announcement that Anne was with child. Hawker was elated and questioned her daily on her condition, which embarrassed and irritated her. Mama Coatley, who visited every day, was forced to have a word with him.

The second was that Tobias asked Mr Speedwell for Rebecca's hand in marriage and his blessing. They promised to live nearby, even in the apartments above the shop if needs be, and to work in the shop and see to Mr Speedwell's every need. Both blessing and hand were denied.

These events made me reflective. Love crossed, love denied; people made by circumstance to stifle feelings and live lives untrue to their hearts. I did not want Turlington and me to be like that.

Meanwhile, we continued to see Jacob regularly. The new teacher had been appointed, so our visits were now considered special treats rather than part of the routine, but somehow Jacob had attached himself to us. We took him for outings every Tuesday – to the Royal Academy, to watch the performers in Vauxhall Gardens, to Covent Garden, to Hyde Park to see the great parade of fancy folk.

Seeing Turlington and Jacob together gave me real hope. I saw how Turlington stretched to become his best self for the boy and I saw how he responded to Jacob's admiration. My heart swelled with love for the two of them. This was a lovely thing we were doing; a true thing. When I saw Turlington laugh at something Jacob had said, and Jacob's face flush with pleasure and admiration, I could not believe that Turlington would really walk away from the boy – and vanish to Italy as he claimed he would. It was a luscious, sensual picture he painted of our imaginary life there but I did not trust it. It felt like running away. It felt insubstantial, like a cloud. It felt selfish.

Soon enough it was Midsummer's Day and my twentieth birthday. There was a small gathering at the house. Rebecca was not invited but I would be seeing her later. Mr and Mrs Blackford favoured us with a short visit, but my cousin Annis gave me no gift. Judith gave me a bonnet trim she had knitted herself. It was rather pretty. Sanderson and Anne gave me a magnificent cream leather-bound journal. Hawker, still expansive and happy about Anne's pregnancy, gave me a diamond bracelet – quite the most lavish piece of jewellery I had ever seen. As ever, my inner response was to calculate how much I could sell it for, how much it would swell my Cornwall fund. But then I remembered that my future lay with Turlington and Cornwall had not figured in any of our plans. Perhaps I did not need my secret hoard any more; I wasn't sure how I felt about that. Turlington gave me a pearl and opal choker with a long, delicate strand of gold streaming from the centre to reach to the top of my décolletage, where a single coy pearl nestled. Aunt Dinah gave me a card.

Aubrey arrived, and gave me an emerald ring. Not an engagement ring – I already had one of those – just a generous gift. He drew me into a corner and, quite uncharacteristically, pulled me close and kissed my cheek.

'The gift comes with a price,' he whispered.

I smiled uneasily, aware of Turlington's smouldering eyes upon us and of all the many ways in which I was going to disappoint Aubrey.

'If that kiss is the price, I'll gladly pay it,' I murmured, trying to be affectionate, and hating myself.

'It's not the kiss. It's a date.'

'A date?' I queried, though I knew what he meant at once.

'Will you not set a date, Florence? It's surely high time. I *cannot* wait any more, dear, for I long to marry you. Shall we say next month? Why not?'

I groaned. I could not help it; it was sheer agony to hear him speak thus, to realise what I had done by pretending for so long. I had been running, but I had reached a high wall and there was no further to go. No one heard the groan but Aubrey but that was quite enough. Having groaned, I must explain it; it was not the expected reaction to such a request. And no explanation could make sense of it but the truth, so I told it at long last.

'Aubrey, I'm so sorry, I don't want to marry you, I can't and shan't marry you, I'm so sorry,' I blurted out in one long string of misery.

He drew back from me and dropped my hand, which now bore the emerald ring next to his betrothal band. I covered my mouth in horror. I had heaped bad behaviour upon bad behaviour. To tell Aubrey thus, when we were surrounded by my family, when he must compose himself and override all his inevitable feelings because I had not granted him the courtesy of a private interview . . . I was a monster.

'Aubrey, come into the garden with me,' I begged.

'I don't think so, Florence. I cannot imagine you have anything to say that will gladden my heart!'

'No, I don't suppose so but please, please come anyway.' I took his hand and tugged at it.

Suddenly it felt imperative to be alone with him. I wanted to explain what could not be explained, heal what could not be healed. I wanted somehow to lessen a wrong that had been done and would remain done and could not be changed. And Aubrey, good, gentle man that he was, came with me.

'Excellent! A lovers' assignation on her birthday!' called Hawker in jovial good humour. 'Set a date while you're at it!'

Turlington made as if to follow – I don't know whether anxiety or jealousy drew him – but I threw him a furious frown to stay him.

Aubrey strode ahead of me to the garden and I scuttled in his wake. My birthday dress was rose-pink silk ruched and fastened over an ivy-green underskirt with ivy-green rosettes and decorated with lacing of the same colour down the bodice. Because I had put on every birthday gift of jewellery as I had opened them, I tinkled and twinkled as I hurried along and I felt spoilt, over-privileged and quite disgusted with myself.

When Aubrey reached the centre of the lawn he stopped dead and rounded on me, more furious than I could ever have imagined he could look. Then he glanced up at the drawing room windows and with a sharp hiss marched over to the mulberry tree, under which we could stand with some measure of privacy.

'I take it you have known for some time, Florence?'

I nodded unhappily.

'I take it there is someone else?'

I nodded again.

'It's your cousin, isn't it? Turlington.'

I was startled. Was it so obvious? Had anyone else guessed? I couldn't admit it, after these long months of secrecy, but neither could I deny it.

'Why would you think so?'

'Indeed, who else could it possibly be? You are so close. You do everything together. For a long time I told myself it could not be – a man like that . . . with such a . . . but I see now that I am correct!'

'Aubrey, I—'

He put up his hand, square in front of his chest as if to ward off a blow to the heart. 'Don't worry, I won't tell anyone. I don't pretend to understand what you are thinking, why you have seen fit to toy with my hopes all these long months, why the two of you must be a secret, but I am not a vindictive man. It would not lessen my pain to see you unhappy. Go and be with him, I care not. I deserve better than you.'

'You do. Dear God, I know you do, Aubrey, I am so glad you see it.'

'Only, *why*?' His voice was that of a small child calling after his mama on the first day of school. He pressed his hands flat against his face and for a fearful moment I thought he was going to cry. 'I did not mean that. I do care. I care about you and I care about the hopes I have had for us. I am not a conceited man and yet . . . a man like *that*? Are you . . . *well*, Florence? I will not try to change your mind. I'll be damned if I'll beg! But you do know that our marriage would have been a good one, don't you? You know that you cannot have . . . *that* . . . with *him*?'

Did I?

'Aubrey, of course our marriage would have been good. What you have offered me . . . I know most women would be glad to accept.'

'Most women. But not you. You must always be different, must you not, Florence? You must always be special. But damn it, that is what I have loved about you. I *know* you are better than this. There will come a day when you will wake up and realise what you have done.'

'I fear it is already here, Aubrey.'

'No. For you are not done yet, Florence, there is more to

come. I feel it.' He shook his head at me and his glasses glittered earnestly. 'But why am I concerned for you, now, when you have betrayed and deeply wronged me? Why do I care about you still?'

'Because you are a better man than –' horrified, I realised I was about to say *Turlington* but I concluded – 'than I am a woman. You are such a good man, Aubrey. I should have been lucky to marry you. But the heart does not listen to reason.'

'I don't want to hear about your heart and the great sympathy that exists between the two of you. You have lied to me, Florence, a long while. How could you . . . ? Did you *ever* mean to marry me?'

'Of course I did! I meant it when I accepted you and a long while after. But then he came home and . . . No, it was not even then, not for months, but eventually I came to see . . . and I did not know what to do . . . I agreed to marry you in good faith, Aubrey. If nothing else is good and true, that is.'

'Faith,' he said bitterly. 'I don't know what is driving you, Florence, though I fear I can guess. And if I am right, faith has nothing to do with it. You have chosen your path, that much is certain, and the loss is mine. I only hope it makes you happy. Goodbye, Florence Grace.'

So saying, he strode back to the house, disappearing through the garden doors. A moment later I heard the front door slam and he was gone. I stood staring into the empty space where only a moment ago I had had a kindly fiancé and an assured future. Even in that moment I knew I did not love Aubrey as he deserved to be loved. Even if Turlington vanished again, I could never be so selfish as to try to win Aubrey back for my own comfort and security. But there was a ripple of fear in the air with his departure. The ground I stood upon had never seemed so unstable.

Moments later Turlington appeared. I stood in a trance. He strode across the grass, coat tails flying, and perhaps had never looked so handsome.

'What has happened? You have not told him, have you? Is our secret safe?'

'Oh, *Turlington*!' I cried in anguish. 'Can you not stop thinking about yourself and your secrets for one moment? Yes, I have told him. He gave me a ring and asked me to set a date. And I said I could not marry him.'

Distracted, I realised I had not given the rings back. I would have to send them to him, as soon as possible. I had taken too much from that man.

'But you did not *have* to tell him! You could have set a date! Months from now! Bought us some more time.'

I could have torn his hair out. 'No, I could *not*! I *had* to tell him. Turlington, it's *Aubrey*! A kind man who wants to marry and wants – *wanted* – to share his life with me. It could go no further than this. Indeed, it had already gone too far.'

'But you did not tell him about us?'

'No, I did not, but he knows. He guessed.'

'Well, you could have dissuaded him of that, at least! You could have thought of something, surely?'

I remembered my second morning at Helicon when I had thrown the butter dish at Aunt Dinah because she and I had had no way to understand each other. I felt just the same now. '*Turlington!* Do you have *any* idea what I have just felt in these last moments? I am not fit for scheming and scuttling and salvaging whatever last bits of deception are still to be saved. I felt – feel – wretched for lying to him. Seeing . . . how he struggled between anger and . . . and concern for me! Knowing I was responsible . . . Forgive me if just this once I could not spin out a convenient lie to serve myself once again.'

'I know, darling, I know.' In the face of my anger he backed down hastily. He reached for me but I could not suffer him to touch me and retracted like a spider. 'Your feelings do you credit, of course, it is only that we were not quite ready . . . Do you think he will tell Hawker? Of course he will tell Hawker, his pride is hurt, why would he not?'

I stared at him, helpless to explain. 'Why would he *not*?'

'Well, yes. Why?'

I felt myself look at him as though he were a stranger and in a slow distinct voice that seemed to come from far away I heard myself say, 'Because he is not like you!' and I walked away.

★

That evening, I went in search of solace. I would have liked to play the piano, to choose a new and complex piece far beyond my capabilities and see how far I could progress with it. I wanted to engross myself in the minutiae of quavers and minims, forgetting my cares meanwhile. But my aunt and Judith were in the drawing room, together with Mrs Coatley, and I could not face them just now. I muttered an excuse and withdrew then tried the library as my next refuge. Poetry would soothe me.

But when I reached the library who did I see but Turlington, sitting with his back to the door in one of the blue velvet chairs. I opened my mouth, thinking to withdraw the sting of my last words to him, if I could. But before I spoke, I noticed that a brandy bottle stood, unstoppered, on the table next to him and his hand rested on a full crystal tumbler.

Something made the words catch in my throat. I hesitated. I watched as he took a long drink, almost emptying the glass. His hand reached out and refilled it at once. Then he lifted the glass again and cradled it to him. I felt a little cold. It was not that Turlington professed not to drink at all any more; I had seen him take a glass of wine with dinner – but no more than that, not since his return. At first I had watched anxiously, and so had Sanderson, but the fever for it indeed seemed to have left Turlington. I had all but forgotten about this particular form that his demons used to take.

I swallowed. If I had seen Sanderson take an evening brandy,

I would not have felt dismayed. But here was Turlington draining his second and pouring a third in the aftermath of heated words between us. And Aubrey knew our secret and that disturbed him.

Intuition told me that this was not merely a drink. I sensed that he was turning to it the way I had wished to turn to the piano. Sometimes we do not listen to intuition because circumstances forbid it, or because we are so busy or preoccupied that we cannot fully hear it. And sometimes we do not listen to it because we do not like what it has to say.

I knew that for Turlington, in this mood, one drink would lead to another and ten more. He would darken again and go to that place where I could not reach him. He would withdraw, and his attention, his energy, his love, would all be for the bottle.

But I wouldn't believe that. He had been home months now; he had changed. However, a question stole upon me and I wondered why I had never thought of it before. Our first kiss, in the Dog and Duchess . . . I knew why *I* had been there. I had never thought to wonder the same about Turlington. I realised now that he must have been drinking in secret all this long while. Had the circumstance that I had believed to be Fate bringing us together simply been a collision of his demons and mine?

I took a step towards him and he looked around. I saw, though I did not want to, the guilty flash in his eyes. Then he smiled sheepishly and gestured at the bottle.

'Caught in the act, Florrie,' he said and yes, the darkness was there, that tone of voice I had come to dread.

'I did not think you drank to solve your woes any more,' I said, but I knelt beside him and laid my head against his arm to soften my words.

'Oh, I'm not drinking. It's just . . . well, it's just a brandy or two.'

'Is it so bad that Aubrey knows? He won't tell anyone, Turlington. He said it won't help him to see me unhappy. He has honour.'

'You have a very high regard for him.'

'I do.'

'But not for me.'

I lifted my head and looked at him searchingly. 'Turlington, that's ludicrous. I love you. Am I not the one who has been telling you all along all the light and worth that I see in you? You do not have sufficient regard for *yourself*.'

'We can't all be strong and indomitable and clever and wise all the time like you, Florrie.'

'Like *me*?' I laughed. 'Turlington, you are not like yourself. You *know* what a poor creature I have been feeling myself to be lately. All I can hope is that making mistakes and acting wrongly do not damn us permanently. That we can at least try again and do better. That there can be . . . redemption in living our lives as best we can, despite everything.'

'Redemption! My word, Florrie, you've become very grandiose of late.'

I was shocked into silence for a moment and tears brimmed in my eyes. I had never thought Turlington would say something to hurt me so sharply. 'Is it grandiose to want a better life, to be a better person?' I asked at last in a small voice. 'I lost my way a long time ago but I want to find it again.'

As I said it I knew the truth of it. I did not want to escape to Italy, to a fool's dream and a life of froth. Nor did I want to stay in Helicon where I had never and would never be truly happy. I wanted to find a new way. And I wanted him with me when I did. Unthinkable to be without him. Whatever his faults and weaknesses – whatever mine – they only made me cleave to him more tightly.

'I had better go away for a few days,' he mused. 'I have business . . . I have neglected it lately, I have been so caught up in things here . . . and I don't like you to see me like this.'

'If you are like this, better I see it,' I retorted. 'Where will you go? Will you go away and drink until you feel better and forget to come back?'

For a moment he looked truly angry. Then, like a miracle, his face cleared. He sat up and pushed the half-full tumbler away from him. The relief of seeing him come back to me was overwhelming. I closed my eyes.

He tipped my face up to him and kissed me gently. I could taste the brandy on his lips. 'Open your eyes, my love,' he murmured. 'I am sorry. You are right. I sought refuge in an old friend who has betrayed me once too often and I should know better. I *do* know better. You still want me to come back to you then?'

'Of course. Always and forever.'

'Dear, passionate Florrie. Special, beautiful Florence. As if I could stay away now. I need only go to Southampton. I am long overdue a visit to the office that handles my shipping. The accounts and the ledgers need attention and I've been putting it off. I'll have more peace of mind if I go. What say you to three days? Will you trust me?'

Oh, the relief! He was Turlington again.

'I trust you. Three days I can accept. But not a moment more, Turlington. I shall miss you. I need you.' I kissed him hard as if to transmit to him my love and longing, as well as my belief that there was a better future in store for us than any we had yet imagined.

He laughed when we broke apart and rested his forehead to mine in that old, familiar manner. I felt safe again. Our love had weathered this threat. We were entwined. Inextricably and inexplicably one.

Chapter Thirty-three

The following morning, Turlington kissed me goodbye, seeming quite his usual self. I told no one in the family what had happened with Aubrey. As far as the Graces were concerned, he had paid his birthday visit and departed; I was not in the habit of seeing him every day. I hoped I could find some answers before anyone asked any questions.

I went to visit Rebecca and in talking to her I began to make sense of my inner turmoil. It was, of course, myself I was furious with, not Turlington. Well, perhaps it was both of us. I wanted to have it that he, or our ill-starred love, had turned me into this person that I was not proud to be. But none can make of us anything but what we allow.

How I had treated Aubrey! I had been selfish, driven by desire. I had told myself I was following my heart; that it was a true and noble way to live, flouting convention, disregarding stale etiquette. But in truth I did not feel noble. I had flouted another part of my own heart by disregarding the feelings of others. It was not how my da had raised me. I was not the Florrie that Nan had known.

How had it happened thus? The simple answer was that my feelings for Turlington were so great, so tumultuous, that all else had been swept away in their flood. But I had learned from Old Rilla that the simple answer was only ever the thorn on the very tip of the bush. At Helicon I had moved from a life of following my heart, I realised, to a life where I followed it not at all. I had grown proud of succeeding in a world which I had never valued anyway – a hollow victory. And when Turlington came home, after those long, lonely years, he opened the only avenue I had to follow my feelings, the one shining way to be true to myself and everything else be damned.

Suddenly I remembered a sunlit morning years ago, waiting impatiently for Old Rilla to come home so I could tell her of meeting Sanderson and Turlington at the dance in Truro and ask her what it all meant. *When life wants you to take a step forward*, she had said, *when it wants you to learn something . . . it sends you love*. Well, I was learning – and the lessons were hard. I remembered something else she had said: *It is not for the faint-hearted*. It made me feel a little better to gain some understanding of my own heart. To admit my fears about Turlington – his drinking, his darkness – was more difficult, and did not bring comfort.

'I am no oracle, Florrie,' said Rebecca, looking troubled, when I had told her everything. She poured tea from an elegant silver pot with an ornamental handle. Her father had stomped into the room twice already. Since learning of his daughter's affections for Tobias he had grown more protective of her than ever and twice as suspicious. Maybe he thought I would transform into Tobias while he was absent or perhaps he thought I had hidden Tobias beneath my skirts.

'I cannot see the future, nor what will make you happy; I cannot tell you what to do. And if I did, you would not heed me, that much is certain. All I can tell you is what I see now and that is that you are not happy. Ever since I have known you there has been a sadness about you, a sense that you are pulling in a wrong direction. When you became engaged to Aubrey that eased a little, but there was a cost. A light that I have always admired in you dimmed.

'For what it is worth, I think that marriage would have been perfectly fine – but perfectly fine is not right for you. I think you have done the right thing in breaking your engagement. Oh yes, you should have done it sooner, but you have not been yourself lately, my dear. We all make mistakes. You would not have kept Aubrey in false hope so long if you had perfect judgement, but which of us does? It is done now. The only valid question from here on is the one you are already asking yourself. What next? You know I will support you in any way I can.'

'Dear friend,' I smiled, 'thank you for not thinking as badly of me as I do of myself. I may not forgive myself just yet but I will try to look to the future. You know, Becky, even just the thought that there *is* a future, that it need not be at Helicon, that it can be somehow . . . different . . . is so comforting. I do not know where it lies but I sense it. I have been schooled for a long time now to ignore that invisible thread that lives inside me and uncurls one step at a time, but I shall begin to follow it again, be it ever so slow and unfathomable. And that thought makes me so happy I could cry.'

Rebecca smiled and squeezed my hand. 'I am so relieved to hear you say it. That is the only right way, Florrie. What held true for us yesterday does not always work today. We must follow the thread, this way and that, wherever it may lead, and that will take us into our tomorrows.'

We grinned at each other, well pleased with our friendship and our metaphor and our great wisdom.

Then her face clouded a little. 'Florrie, might I ask you something? I do not mean to be . . . to overstep the boundaries of our friendship, only I have been wondering . . . I worry.'

'What is it, Becky? You can ask me whatever you like.'

'I only wished to make sure, my dear, that you might not be with child. You are already taking such risks.'

'How kind you are to care. No, Becky, I have not that fear at least. He has a . . . well, he takes precautions, and there is a special tea I make. A recipe from Cornwall. But, well . . . what of Turlington?' I wondered. 'How can I make him happy? How can I help him?'

She said nothing and busied herself with pouring more tea, setting cups on saucers just so and wiping at non-existent drips. I watched her closely.

'What is it, Becky? What do you want to say that you worry you should not?'

She looked up innocently, then sighed. 'You're too astute, Florrie, sometimes I think you can read minds. You know I like Turlington, don't you?'

I nodded.

'Well then. It is only that I feel a little cross with him on your behalf. Why should *you* be worrying about how to make *him* happy? Why is he *not* happy? He has *you*! He has your love. Do you know how lucky that makes him?

'And then, you have more to lose in this situation than he does. You have already given him your heart, and your virtue besides, which society rates far more highly. If you are both disinherited, *he* is still a man, with the capacity to make his way in the world. It will be so much harder for you, especially if there is disgrace and scandal about you. He has made you very vulnerable, very dependent on him. He should be all of a care to make *you* happy! And now he questions your regard for him? To be frank, my dear, I could box his ears.'

I bit my lip and looked down at my hands. I still wore Aubrey's engagement ring. I could not take it off yet without inviting questions – questions I still did not have licence to answer. And now Turlington had gone again and my hands were tied for another three days.

'Have I offended you, my dear, upset you?' asked Rebecca.

'No, Becky, it is only that you are quite right and I see it. He does not mean to be so selfish, you know. It is only, I think, well . . .' I trailed off. I did not quite know how to explain it since I had not told Rebecca the truth of his parentage. That was his secret, not ours. But I sometimes thought that secrecy had become second nature to him and he could not imagine any other way to live.

'I am sure he does not. But, Florrie, since you and Turlington . . . *began*, there has been a fever upon you. You have been changed. It cannot be a peaceful way to live.'

'Peaceful? No,' I said. 'Yet isn't love *meant* to change us, make us into something bigger and better than before?' But of course this was not the sort of change that had come upon me, as I had been reflecting only earlier. 'Oh,' I said.

A small and precious memory came to me then. It was nothing remarkable, yet it felt extraordinary. It was simply a morning when I sat outside Nan's cottage, not late, not early, and the sun was hot and strong, promising more force to come. I had sipped primrose tea and gazed up at the moors. Heron's Watch glowered down at me, warning of abandonment and ruin, yet drawing me nonetheless. The sun had danced and gleamed on the surface of the hot tea and I felt I could fall into that elusive, golden gleam and become one with it. *That* was peace. I had not felt it for a long time. I had forgotten there was such a feeling. Now I thirsted for it.

I changed the subject to Rebecca and Tobias.

'I have not seen him these two weeks,' Rebecca said. 'My father has watched over me like a guard dog. I cannot believe even he can be this selfish, but so it is. So I have come to a decision.'

'Which is, dear?'

She cast a wary eye at the door and dropped her voice almost to a whisper. 'I must attend your wedding, Florrie.'

'My wedding? And to whom shall I be wed?' I whispered back.

'In truth it matters not. Father does not know that you have ended your engagement to Aubrey so perhaps he will suffice. I shall set out one day to attend your wedding – he will not stop me doing that . . .'

'And you will return a married lady yourself,' I concluded, understanding her.

She nodded. 'An hour is all I need,' she smiled, 'to change my life forever.'

'And what then?'

'Our desires are the same as ever they were. I still wish to live near Father, to care for him, to work in the shop and share his life. Tobias supports my wishes. We only wish to do so as man and wife. So we shall return home and tell Father what we have done and he will rage and castigate us and he will say dreadful, hurtful things, which perhaps I will never forget. And after that, it is up to him. I will continue to try to be his daughter. If he will let me, we will adjust to the new way of things. And if he does not, I will keep trying. It is very simple.'

'I admire you, I truly do.'

'Then help me by setting a date, dear!'

'Certainly, as soon as you wish! When do you think I should marry, Becky?'

'I think the first Thursday of next month would be a fine date.'

'Then so it shall be. And do you wish me to take a note to Tobias confirming the arrangement? Or would you like me to invite him in person?'

'Perhaps you would do me the kindness of visiting him. It will be best to commit nothing to paper.'

'I shall go directly then. Did you have a time in mind for my wedding?'

'Eleven in the morning, if you please. But Tobias knows that already.'

I had to laugh. 'And will I be expected to attend my own wedding?'

'Naturally you will.' She dropped her voice to a whisper. 'You will be my maid of honour, won't you, Florrie? I need you there.'

'Of course, Becky.' This was one secret I was happy to keep.

'Anyway, my dear!' she said, returning her voice to its

normal pitch. 'Before you go let me give you this letter from your friend in Cornwall. It came a week ago and I have not seen you to pass it on. Forgive me, I should have sent word it was here, but I have been preoccupied.'

I laughed. 'I have been preoccupied myself, Becky. How lovely to hear from Lacey, though. I am in need of news from home to cheer me.' And it did. I read it, and then read it again to Rebecca, who took as much interest in my Cornish friends as if they were her own.

Lacey still taught in her aunt's parlour. Her class had dwindled to three children the year before, causing her to become considerably dispirited. When Lacey was not helping people she hardly knew what to do with herself. But now it had grown again – to twelve – a number that could scarcely fit in that worn old room on the main street.

Hesta and Stephen sent their love to me as always. They had not conceived a child yet but were quite content.

The heather was thick on the moors this year, Lacey wrote, thicker and more purple than she had ever seen it. She had gone up to the tor once that summer in honour of me but had been afraid to stray any further lest the spirits misled her and she got lost. I paused for a moment in my reading. I could see it.

Heron's Watch, the old farmhouse I had always loved so much, was untenanted. Mr Cooper Glendower, the owner, had been heard to say that if he couldn't find a tenant by the end of the year he was going to pull it down. I paused again. I hated to think of that fine old house being destroyed. It had always been as much a part of the moors as the grass and boulders, out of time perhaps, in human terms, yet timeless.

Old Rilla was showing her age at last, Lacey wrote. She was not failing, nothing of that sort, but she no longer walked so far in all weathers; more people were permitted to visit her cottage now, else they would have gone untreated. And the years were starting to show in her face where before they had only lurked in the snow of her hair and the twists in her hands.

Mr Harrowman of Launceston had sought Lacey's company at the West Wivel summer dance and had told her that her school was a very improper, imperfect thing *and* expressed an interest in courting her! Lacey had made short shrift of both opinions.

Her letter made me smile. As I read it I could hear her voice confiding in me. I could see them all. I could feel the spring of heather beneath my feet and fingertips and smell the tussocky grass and the marshy pools. I could see the haze on the horizon and the faint pink-green veil of dawn over the moors. I could see it so vividly I could hardly bear not to be there. I laid the letter down feeling a little shaken. I was no longer dogged every day by homesickness but when it came, it still had the power to pull me up by the roots and blow me from where I stood.

★

I left the cheese shop and called on Tobias in his shabby but cheerful student's rooms. It was good to do something besides think about Turlington every minute. Tobias was delighted at the prospect of his wedding.

'Thank you, Florence, thank you,' he beamed, clasping my hands in both of his and shaking them gently up and down.

'I have done nothing!' I protested.

'You have been our friend, that is everything. And we are yours, you know that, don't you?'

'Thank you, Tobias, I do.' I wondered how much Rebecca had told him.

I declined his offer of tea, since I had already drunk so much with Rebecca that I feared I should turn into a teapot myself, and set off for Helicon. I would talk to Anne, I decided, ask how she was faring in her pregnancy. She was Sanderson's wife, after all, and it would be good to reach a greater intimacy.

Chapter Thirty-four

But when I got back to Helicon, Anne was nowhere to be found. Nor was anyone. A strange pall hung over the house. I hurried from drawing room to dining room to library to Aunt Dinah's study . . . No one. Even the servants were conspicuously absent. I went to look in the garden. No one. I faltered in the doorway. The house – and even London beyond it – seemed uncannily silent. I swallowed. I did not understand it, but I felt something very well known to me: death. The sense of it was so strong that I thundered down the stairs to the kitchen, where I found no one but Mrs Clemm, stirring a pot on the stove as though it had dared her to do so until her arm fell off.

'Mrs Clemm, where is everybody? What has happened?' I asked, my voice ringing in the silent kitchen. She jumped a mile in the air.

'Oh, Miss Florence, you startled me,' she scowled. 'It's Mr Grace. Mr Hawker, that is. He's not long for this world. Hours perhaps. They're all crowded round his bedside wondering how much they're going to inherit.' A large, batter-spattered hand flew to her mouth. 'Forgive me, miss! I didn't mean to speak of the family that way. I meant, of course, that they're grieving and want to be with him in his hour of need.'

I stared at her. Hawker dying? *Hawker?* Was this some cruel joke?

'Forgive me,' she said again and I knew what she had told me was true. The empty house and echoing corridors had told me before she did.

'Of course,' I muttered, flitting from the room on legs that felt to be made of paper, too shocked to find humour or outrage in her insolence.

I took the stairs as fast as my shaky limbs would carry me and made my way to his bedchamber. It was on the corridor above mine; I had never been in there before. I wondered whether I should knock, but I dispensed with ceremony and entered.

Sure enough they were all there, arranged in a ring around a large, canopied bed. Annis and her husband had come; only Turlington was missing. The room was shadowed and brooding. I could not see Hawker for the shield of relatives standing guard, but I could feel him. He was fighting. I made my way to the bed and no one seemed to notice me. There was a low murmuring between my aunt and the doctor, who was stroking his beard and looking grave. It was disturbing to have a stranger there. I had seen him only once or twice before; Graces simply didn't fall ill. Just over Judith's shoulder I could see my grandfather at last, lying in bed looking as tiny as a child, his eyes closed. If I had not felt his spirit so keenly, I should have thought him dead already.

'Grand-Hawker,' I said.

Everyone startled. Hawker's eyes flew open at once. 'She's here, is she?' he said, and his voice was so clear and unchanged that I hoped wildly for a moment that it might all be a mistake.

'I'm here.'

'Finally stopped gallivanting with the cheese queen and remembered your family, have you? Come here.'

I squeezed past Judith to the bedside and took his cold hand.

I looked up at my aunt and was surprised to find her staring at me with all the old dislike. 'Why do you want her here anyway?' she demanded. 'She's not one of us, she'll never be one of us. You're dying and we have so little time with you.'

She's worried that he'll favour me in his will above Annis and Judith, I thought. *Mrs Clemm was right.*

'Quiet, woman!' came the surprisingly strong voice from the bed, and his hand clutched mine as he spoke. 'I'll die when I'm good and ready, and I'll decide who I want to see as well.'

'What has happened?' I asked, gazing from Hawker to my aunt, to the doctor, whose name I couldn't even remember. 'I don't understand. I went out but three hours ago. How is he . . . *dying*?'

My aunt turned her face away from me and would not

speak. Hawker closed his eyes again as though I had asked to hear an old and tiresome tale.

'Your grandfather suffered a massive collapse in the early hours of the morning, Miss Grace,' said the doctor.

Aunt Dinah made a small noise that sounded like *pah!* when he called me that.

'He has been troubled for many years by a tumour on the brain. He has defied all my expectations in living as long as he has.' I wanted to argue but I felt the truth of his words with a sinking heart. Through these last years Hawker had grown increasingly irascible, fiery and unreasonable. I looked at him and it seemed impossible to me that the enormity of him – despite his physical size – could be quenched. But the doctor went on:

'He insisted that no one be told, even though I warned him that a sudden decline was very likely. He has been struggling with severe headaches, memory loss and dark humours for nearly seven years. It has not been easy for him.'

Nor for us, I could not help but think.

'What happened last night was the inevitable, if delayed, outcome of his condition.'

Seven years. Before I came to Helicon. Before Nan died. Is that why he brought me here? Is that why he was so determined to gather the Graces together, why he forgave Turlington again and again?

'Quiet, man,' said Hawker. 'She does not need a full medical report. Now, leave me all of you, I want to see my granddaughter alone. *Florence*,' he clarified as Annis and Judith looked at one another.

'Hawker, I really think—' began Dinah but he lifted his head and fixed her with a look of such fearful rage that she quailed. Then he began coughing and the doctor ushered everyone out.

There were so many of them it took some time. Only Sanderson, on his way out, placed his hand on my shoulder. When we were alone, Hawker rolled his head towards me and fixed his great blue eyes on me. 'Well, miss.'

I gently freed my hand and brought a chair right up to the bedside. Then I sat down and regained his hairy paw, bringing it to rest between mine on my lap.

'Grand-Hawker, I'm so sorry.'

'Oh, sorry. I'm only sorry I haven't got more time. I'm still not happy with how things are. I wanted to leave them in good order but it has been hard to . . . see, always, what was for the greatest good.' He lifted his free hand to his forehead and rubbed it and frowned. 'Calantha, that was a bad business perhaps. Or perhaps not. I cannot tell any more. Sacrifice her for the sake of us all, of the splendid future I have foreseen, the right thing to do. But she was a sweet girl, wasn't she?'

'Yes, Grand-Hawker.'

'You're respectable at last. For a long time I thought you were never going to shape up at all but you'll marry Aubrey and do the right thing. Sanderson . . . well, I never thought he was going to step up to the mark but he has done it. It could be worse. But Calantha . . . she troubles me, Grand-Florence.'

I felt a sudden fury on her behalf, but what could I say at such a time? 'Perhaps she is well, Grand-Hawker. It may not be that bad.'

He closed his eyes and groaned. 'And Turlington. His new ways don't deceive me. He is only ever one step away from disaster, no matter how he pretends otherwise. He will never be the Grace I wanted him to be. In fact, shall I tell you a secret, a great secret, Grand-Florence?'

'If you wish to.'

He tried to lift his head from the pillow but fell back. He darted his eyes around the room. 'They have gone, haven't they?'

'Yes, all gone.'

'Turlington is not a Grace at all!'

I felt my hands turn as cold as his own.

'Did you hear me, girl?'

'Yes, I heard you, Grand-Hawker. Whatever can you mean?'

'Belle never loved his father. She was never happy with us. Like you, Florence, like a caged animal. She had a liaison with some fellow, some sweetheart from her youth. Turlington is his son, not Clifton's. He's not a Grace at all.'

I withdrew my hand. I stood and walked around the room. I felt his eyes on me, watching me keenly. 'Why does that affect *you* so, miss?'

Did he know? If he knew about Turlington, did he know about us? If he knew Turlington was not a Grace, why all that fuss about first cousins marrying and a relationship between us being prohibited? For the appearance of it, I could only assume. It suddenly occurred to me that I could tell him everything. He would be dead before Turlington came back. I paced and paced. All these years, he had known. Turlington had worried and fretted and rebelled and grieved for his lost identity and kept it all to himself, nursed a poisonous secret, damaged his soul – and none of it was ever needed at all.

'How do you know?'

'I caught them together, Belle and the other man. I was furious, Grand-Florence. I beat him with my stick. She was screaming and begging me to stop but I was angry.'

I sank back into my chair and covered my face with my hands. 'Because she had dishonoured your son, dishonoured the Graces.'

'No,' he said softly. 'Because I loved her.'

I stared at him.

'Yes. Young enough to be my daughter. Married to my son. Taller than me by far, prettier than anyone had a right to be and *I* was never pretty. What do you say to *that*, Florence Grace?'

I could say nothing at all. My head was spinning. I thought perhaps it would never be still again.

'But how do you know Turlington was this man's son? Just

because Belle . . . just because she . . . well, he could still have been Clifton's son.'

'No. He was born at a time when . . . Clifton complained to me that she had not performed her wifely duty for some months. He had even tried to take her by force, he told me, but she fought him off like a wildcat. I hated him then, Florence, my own son! But I could not stand to think of him handling Belle that way. I never felt the same about him after that. About any of them. Clifton was not sufficiently interested in women's concerns that he noticed the discrepancy, but I see everything. I told you. Turlington was conceived while she was having her liaison – and not sleeping with my son. So there you have it, Grand-Florence. How's that for a deathbed secret?'

'Why didn't you tell him you knew? Family means everything to you! Turlington is . . . not family. How could you bear to keep him in his place?'

'I loved her,' he murmured again. 'I loved her. When he is near, he reminds me of her. And he is hard not to love, Florence.'

Oh, how I knew *that*.

He fell silent then and I stared unseeingly across the room, between the bed-curtains to a portrait of a woman in an old-fashioned dress on the opposite wall. Gradually my eyes settled on it. His wife, Rosanna. A good wife. Yet he had loved Belle. Oh . . . how could I ever tell Turlington that Hawker had always known? And how could I not?

The air was thick and listless. This was not due to illness, I realised. It had always been thus. It had always been a heavy and joyless thing to be Hawker. I was glad for him that he was to be released from this life. He had not made an art of it. Obsession, pride, and hidden love disguised as tyranny. Perhaps he would do better in the next. But I would miss him.

'Grand-Hawker,' I whispered.

'Mmm.'

'I'm not going to marry Aubrey. I'm sorry.'

His eyes opened again but they were not so blue now. 'It's Turlington, I suppose.'

'Yes. I'm sorry.'

He shrugged. 'Do what you like. The will's made, it's too late to change it. Why should you be sorry now?'

'For deceiving you. For disappointing you.'

'You did that, you did that. Foolishly fond of you, I have been, though, miss.'

I looked at him helplessly and he shook his head. 'Never mind. I don't need to know. I have failed but in a few hours I will no longer care.'

'Oh, Grand-Hawker, don't say that. How? I never thought that you—'

'That I was ailing? That I was in any way vulnerable?'

'I never thought you were quite human, if I am to be perfectly honest,' I smiled.

He chuckled, though it turned into a cough and I held a

water glass for him while he struggled to sip and regain his breath. 'Then my illusion was successful. A beast, a bear, Beelzebub himself . . . As you told me yourself, they always called me Satan.'

'Yes.'

'I took it as a compliment.'

'I thought you might.'

'I have done my best for this family. At least, I have done what I thought was best. I think it will all be for naught now. Turlington gets nothing in my will, you know. He tried me too far. Too little, too late. Some things can be pushed too far – broken and mended, broken and mended, and then broken – irrevocably. But I see in your eyes that you already know that.'

Perhaps I did. I did not like to think it, for I had thought I could be Turlington's redeemer. But if he refused to redeem himself? What then?

'You are not going to try to talk me round, change my mind, champion your lover?'

'No, Grand-Hawker.' But I did wonder with dread what Turlington would do when he heard. These secrets were heavy to hold.

He nodded. 'I have changed my will. In whose favour, would you like to know?'

'I don't wish to know at all, Grand-Hawker. That is the last thing that interests me now. It is entirely your concern.'

'Not yours, miss. I have left not a sou to you.'

'I am not surprised.'

'Then why are you here with me? Why do you care, Florrie Buckley?'

'I really couldn't say. Yet I find that I do, very much. But why do you call me that? I thought it was a name you despised?'

'It's who you always were and will become again, I think. For you will leave now, will you not, Grand-Florence?' And as I sat there it came to me in a flash, calm and momentous both at once, that my destiny now lay far away from Helicon. The spell that had bound me here was soon to break. I was of this family, but I did not have to be defined by it any more. And inexplicably, in that stuffy, shuttered room, I felt a breath of air wash over me, like a moorland breeze. Perhaps he felt it too. His voice, weaker now, and muffled, brought me back to the present, to the dark bedchamber, to all the pressing concerns of life at Helicon. 'You will go back there.'

He meant Cornwall, of course. And I realised that I would. Somewhere over the last two days, I had come to know it even before I was ready to acknowledge it. It had ever held my heart. Even as I sat by my dying grandfather, disappointed in love and disappointed in myself and sorry to see the back of this frustrating, spiteful old man, my heart gave a leap at the very thought. I did not know how things would unfold, how life would take me there, particularly if I was to be penniless indeed, but back I would go, I knew it. Helicon would be like a strange dream and I would be a Cornish girl again.

I did not want to crush his hopes as he lay dying, but neither did I want to lie to him over something so important. I had had my fill of lying.

'Yes, Grand-Hawker, I will.'

He closed his eyes then and his brow contracted as though he were gripped by an inner agony.

'But, Grand-Hawker,' I whispered and his eyelids fluttered open again. Then I spoke words which I had never thought to hear myself say, yet I meant them, every one. 'I will always be a Grace.'

He looked at me with such affecting disbelief that I ached to embrace him. He was still Hawker Grace, however, so I contented myself with resting my head on his shoulder for a moment.

He gripped my hand then and nodded, with something of his old compelling zeal. 'Promise me, Grand-Florence. Promise me you'll keep the name, and that you'll remember.'

'I promise.'

He smiled, then. 'Florence Grace,' he murmured, 'you're a good girl. A special girl.'

Chapter Thirty-five

Hawker died very soon after our startling admissions to one another. He allowed me to call the others back to the room and I was glad, if only because I don't know how I could have brought myself to leave the room and tell them he was gone. Eventually we all emerged, blinking, unable to understand that he would never badger or bully us again.

I wanted to turn to Sanderson for comfort, but his place was with Anne, who sobbed hysterically though she knew Hawker less than any of us. Perhaps that accounted for her sentiment. I felt numb, from the unexpectedness of it, the seeming impossibility of it and the revelations that he had made. No one appeared to need me so I went to my room and stared over the garden.

Florence Grace I was to remain then. After all those years of denying it, and protesting. Rebecca had been right all that time ago. I was as much a Grace as a Buckley and to ignore that fact meant cutting myself off from half of what I was, and half of my power. Though I little knew how it could serve me through the storms that lay ahead.

I could not believe that it was the same morning that Turlington had eaten breakfast with us, then gone to Southampton; the same morning that I had talked with Rebecca, and visited Tobias. There were still two and a half days before Turlington would return. He would return to find Hawker gone. I had no way to send a message to prepare him. I did not even know how he would feel about it.

Those days passed. Aunt Dinah, who had actually wept at the bedside, soon snapped into her habitual orientation of purposeful action. As ever, it was all to honour Hawker. She buzzed about the house making the funeral arrangements, doing everything. I offered to help her. So did Annis and Judith. We were all rejected. Irwin had lost his father. He was pitifully affected, given the disdain in which Hawker had held him. It was painful to see.

The days went by and Turlington came home, just as he had promised. But the time when this fact would have filled me with reassurance was gone. I could not see what lay ahead for us all. Nevertheless, when I heard his voice in the hall, I felt the same pull towards him, the old leap in my heart. I stood at the top of the stairs and watched from above as he looked around, frowning, as though he sensed something.

'Turlington,' I said.

He looked up and his smile gave way to a look of alarm when he saw that I was wearing full mourning. 'Florrie?'

I put a finger to my lips and beckoned to him. I wanted to

talk to him alone, while I could. He bounded up the stairs and we went quickly to my room. I closed the door upon us and threw myself into his arms. He embraced me, tight and warm. 'What has happened, my love?' he asked. 'Why are you dressed so?'

'Oh, Turlington. Hawker has passed away.'

He gave me an incredulous look. '*What? Hawker?* What are you saying?'

'Exactly that. He has passed away.'

'*How?* Did a building fall on him?'

'Oh, Turlington, don't joke! He has had a tumour in his brain these seven years, the doctor said, and he collapsed the morning you left. Before you went, in fact, though he was not found until later. I went to see Rebecca, not knowing, and when I came back . . . he died just an hour later.' I ran my hand over my face; I still could not believe it.

'Well, good God.' He sank down on the side of my bed, holding on to my wrist. He looked bewildered. 'What does this mean for us, I wonder?' he said.

I sat next to him. 'I wonder too,' I said quietly. I did not like to ask him if he was at all sad about Hawker.

'Well, this will change everything, one way or another.'

I laid my arm about his shoulders. 'Yes, I believe it will.'

The funeral of Hawker Grace took place exactly a week after his passing. It was held in St Matthew's but could easily have filled an abbey. The great and the good of London – or rather, the fine and the proud of London – filled the church and spilled out into the grounds. A throng of onlookers pressed their noses through the railings. It was like an occasion of state.

Afterwards his body was conveyed in a black carriage pulled by four black horses to Brompton, where he was laid to rest in the great mausoleum that Turlington had shown me the previous winter. Irwin, Turlington, Sanderson and Mr Blackford were coffin bearers. Four pairs of shoes trampled over 'precious mortality' as Hawker transcended the human condition at last. And the will was read the following day.

The tension, as we all took our seats in the library, shivered in the air like frost. I sat between Turlington and Sanderson and hid my clammy hands in my skirts; knowing that Turlington was about to be disappointed, I was more nervous than any of them. I prayed he would find the strength to withstand the blow.

My aunt's face was like china, cold and white. Her mouth was a hard line; her eyes were coals, glinting darkly. I knew she was worrying about who would get what and exactly how luxurious a life she would be able to lead henceforth. She had scarcely looked at me since Hawker had passed; I felt sure she suspected me of wriggling into his affections and taking something that did not rightfully belong to a country upstart. At least she would be content on that score.

Hawker's solicitor, Mr Diggle, entered the room (lucky no daughter of *his* ever married into the family and bore a son).

He was a small man, like his employer, and he scurried mouse-like into our midst. He took one look at the crowd of assembled Graces and took recourse in shuffling his papers for quite some time. He was afraid.

He went to the window and opened it without asking permission then he returned to the desk and looked at us all pleadingly, as if we might excuse him from this duty altogether.

'Well, go on, Mr Diggle,' commanded my aunt at last. 'We should like to hear the will today, if you please.'

He nodded and swallowed and held up one paper before him like a shield. He cleared his throat. Then he put the paper down and took a deep breath. 'I have here the last will and testament of Hawker Grace, dated the thirteenth of May this year. I will read it to you if you wish but perhaps first you will allow me to paraphrase it in brief. It can be very simply put. Mr Grace has left his entire fortune to . . . to . . . one party. He has bequeathed everything to . . . to . . . er . . .'

'Not *Turlington*!' wailed my aunt. Then, 'Oh! Not to *her*!' She turned to look at me and there was such loathing in her eyes that I closed mine.

'Oh, ah, no, Mrs Grace, no. But rather to a hospital in Suffolk. The, er, West Hill Infirmary and Sanatorium near, er, Ipswich.'

There was a little silence. I could see him visibly shrink, as though from a blow.

'A hospital?' said my aunt in a dull voice.

'Yes, m'lady, er, ma'am.'

'A hospital?'

'Yes.'

'He has not left one cent to a single living Grace?'

'No, ma'am.'

'A *hospital*? Is this a joke? Has he instructed you to say this, and then reveal something different? Is he just toying with us all?'

'Er, yes, Mrs Grace, that is to say no, this is no joke, he has not made any such instruction. But I believe he is, or has been, toying with you all. I am so very sorry.'

'Let me see that!' My aunt leaped from her chair and snatched the will from Mr Diggle's hand. She ran to the open window, her hand upon her heart, and stood, bent nearly double, panting. The rest of us sat like sphinxes, upright, staring intently as we watched her eyes devour the page. At last she turned to us, clutching the wall for support, and there could be no further doubt. Hawker, who had for so long commanded our obedience with his liberal threats of disinheritance, had disinherited us all.

I can hardly bear to remember the storm that followed. My aunt screaming, sinking to the floor, blue in the face, my uncle rushing to her side, standing over her with his hands on his knees, saying, 'My dear, my dear,' imploringly. Anne whimpering over and over again, 'Are we poor, Sanderson? Will my baby be poor?' And Turlington springing to his feet and roaring and swearing and kicking over the chair on which he had been sitting. He sent it skittering across the room. 'That old whore pipe! I hope he's pissing pins and needles in hell. To the devil with him! A thousand plagues on him! If I ever meet him after I die, I'll kick his ballocks into his throat and out the other side . . .'

Sanderson and I looked at each other, shocked. He cradled Anne in an absent-minded sort of way as we watched Turlington storm across the room, hair flying, and deal another mighty kick at a side table on his way to the door. The table shattered. The statuette that had sat upon it flew through the air and smashed. He slammed the door so hard after him that it flew open again. And he was gone.

'I had better go after him,' I said through numb lips.

'No, Florrie,' said Sanderson, holding my arm very firmly. 'Not now. Later.'

Judith was sitting alone, crying silent tears, so I went and put my arms around her instead. It was something to do.

The coming days were all just as dark. Helicon froze, like Sleeping Beauty's castle. As I tried to adjust to Hawker's death, and his last cruelty, I was as stunned as anyone, though not on my own account – he had warned me after all. Besides, I had been poor before, I could be poor again. But the Graces without the Grace fortune? It could hardly be conceived. Irwin, who had worked so hard to invest judiciously and curb the excesses of his relatives. Dinah, who had invested too, in her way, all to make the Graces fashionable again, and sought-after and fine. All to please Hawker. Sanderson, who had never done a wrong thing to anyone. And Annis . . . Hawker had said she was more a Grace than any of us. I would have given any-thing for it all to be a malevolent joke, for a codicil to be found, for Dinah and the rest to have their fortune. But wishing did not make it so.

Life felt directionless. The force that had driven us all, dic-tated our actions so that either we followed it slavishly or cast it off at any cost, was gone. And not only gone but rendered mean-ingless in hindsight. Had Hawker *not* been a driven man with a singular vision, but rather a man whose brain was ill, a mere instrument of caprice? Or – he had said he'd never felt the same about any of them since Clifton had tried to hurt Belle – did he really hate his family that much? I did not want to believe it.

Turlington spent his time in a drunken haze, pouring whisky after wine after port down his throat and refusing to see any-one but me. Much good it did. I was horrified by the ready way he returned to drinking. He did not even give himself an hour's grace to adjust to the new reality, to think about what had hap-pened, to enquire after anyone else. He simply reached for a decanter and was not seen without one for several weeks, it seemed to me.

In vain I tried to plead with him. He was always glad to see me, insofar as the word glad can be applied to someone in so wretched a state. At any rate he would reach for me, pull me onto his lap and whisper his woes into my neck. That gave me hope for a time that our connection was still strong, that I might have some influence over him. But he was gone far beyond me. Everything I said, every plea I made, went unheard or unheeded. And when, once, I said, 'Turlington, it's only money,' he pushed me from his lap, not gently.

'Don't you understand anything?' he cried. 'It's not the money, it's the fool he has played us for all the while. Having us dance to his tune, forfeit our every desire . . . and all for *this*!'

'I think I understand better than you!' I blazed. 'You were waiting for that money, Turlington, you were depending upon it because you don't trust your own abilities. You have *never* danced to his tune, and I cannot think of one desire you have given up. You did not even have to forfeit me! It is done now, it is over. There need be no more trying, no more striving to uphold pointless ideals. We can just be us. Just you and me. We can start fresh. Is that not something to cherish?'

'Cherish,' he muttered, staring into the flames in the depths of the whisky decanter. 'Start fresh. There is no such thing as a blank page, Florrie, don't you know that? We will never unstick our feet from this mire.'

'Well,' I said unsteadily, 'I am sorry to hear you say it. For I intend to do exactly that. Unstick my feet and walk away. I want you to come with me, Turlington, but I don't see how you can if you're too drunk to walk!' and I left the room.

It was horrible, horrible, seeing him like that. As I watched him slide into that distant black place countless different feelings jostled inside me. Seeing him so lost and hopeless was anguish and my heart ached for him and I longed to take his pain away. I felt pity, that he had reached the age of six-and-twenty without finding any better tools for dealing with life's disappointments. I felt frightened: where would such a course take him? And where would it leave me? And I felt a grief that was all my own. While he was drunk and dark and hidden away in the corner of the library, he could not be there for me. I missed his laugh, our conversations, his body pressed against mine. A flawed man? Yes. But the man that I loved, nonetheless, and I needed him to be with me, in this life of ours, with all its disappointments and travesties and all its small beauties too. But Turlington was absent just as surely as if he had left us again, taking a necklace or two as he went.

And I felt anger. Yes, he had had a difficult life; yes, the secret of his birth, especially within this family, would have scarred any sensitive mind. But this was only the end of one story, the story of Turlington Grace, first heir of the Graces. Somewhere along the way, another story had begun, the story of Turlington and Florrie. Despite everything, he had won the love of a woman he professed to love in return. For that is the way of love, to find its way into the tumbled and tattered places of the heart, to steal around boulders and barriers, squeeze through cracks and find a way to flower and flourish, like flowers growing up through the walls of a ruined castle. A miracle. Perhaps the greatest of all miracles. Yet he was behaving as if it were of far less consequence than his inheritance, as if it did not carry the possibility for redemption and a joyful future. But Turlington scoffed at redemption and no imaginable future seemed to hold, for him, half the appeal of a bottle of wine. I felt hurt, shunned, slighted.

However, those were my concerns, and I was determined not to wallow in them. I had spent nearly two weeks begging, pleading and tending to him and it had achieved nothing. Meanwhile, the family was falling apart so I turned my attention to them. Without Hawker's fortune, there was no way we could afford to keep on at Helicon. When my aunt heard this, she screamed and entered a fit of shaking and crying that lasted day after day and didn't look set to end. Irwin was busy from dawn 'til night looking for more modest accommodations, going through the paperwork that Hawker had left, arranging and rearranging what little money was left to us and earnestly trying, in his own uncharismatic, bewildered way, to save us all.

Annis was nowhere to be seen these days. After the will was read she professed herself furious with Hawker and relieved that she had already married, and married well. She also suggested then, spite pouring from her lips as usual, that her mother must have misjudged matters very badly for things to come to this pass. She seemed to imply that perhaps we deserved all we got (or rather, didn't get) for not having been as smart as she in finding independent means. I had snapped that if becoming dependent on the affections of a rich husband was her idea of independence then she had indeed been clever.

We were in the dining room – scene of so many previous battles – recovering from the shock. She was standing near the fire, looking stunning as always. Black suited her. She bit back that *I* couldn't even seem to secure the engagement I had, that she was convinced Aubrey had come to his senses, that she doubted a wedding would ever take place.

I knew it would not; nevertheless, I continued arguing the while, just for the pleasure of watching smoke rising from her skirt, unnoticed by anyone but me. Her crinoline was so beautiful, so enormous, that it was almost touching the flames. I had heard of ladies catching fire thanks to this most impractical of fashions, but had never dared to hope it might happen to so deserving a person. Eventually a little spark jumped onto the hot fabric and Annis felt, then saw, the ribbon of gold flame blossoming from her dress. She gave an almighty scream and her mother and sister joined in. I rang for help and then laughed heartily while three or four servants beat her about until the fire was put out. She was unhurt but her dress was charred and her pride along with it. She was shaken, too.

'What on earth? What on earth?' she kept saying as she clutched at her mother and sank into a chair.

'I believe you've been granted a foretaste of the afterlife, Cousin,' I grinned, not hiding my delight.

She left Helicon and it was a long time before we saw her again.

Judith retreated into herself in a way that was painful to watch. Where she had once been a gaudy little chattering parakeet she was now almost completely silent and she watched her mother's more flamboyant demonstrations of anguish with frightened eyes. Her own marriage prospects, which had receded like a hairline over the last year or two, were now completely bald. She could be no comfort to her mother for she was at heart a little girl still, and needed to be looked after herself.

Sanderson's hands were full with his pregnant wife, who was furious that she had married into the Graces and got herself with heir, only to fall at once upon reduced circumstances. And Turlington was drunk. So there was no one to look after Judith or Dinah but me.

When Dinah took to her bed and refused to eat, I took her soup, three times a day, and sat with her and coaxed her to sip even a spoonful or two. I brushed her hair and washed her face and hands and made her change her gown every day. I had never liked her and her company was no more rewarding now – the servants would not go near her for the shouting and the insults they had to endure. She pushed me away, she threw a hairbrush at my head, she cursed me. She was as rude and hostile now as she had been in my early days at Helicon, when I had hated her for her unkindness.

But I was not a young girl any more. I was a woman. I had lived a life of sorts despite her strictures. I had made my own mistakes and taken my own pleasure where I could, even if I had done much of it in secret. I had won something – I knew not what it was – that protected me from her harsh words and hateful looks. I found that I could not bear to see this beautiful, proud woman reduced to a slatternly, wild-haired wreck. I may not have agreed with her values and priorities but they were hers and I could not see her abandon them. So I kept her as beautiful as I could, tried to protect her dignity as far as I could, even while she lay abed shaking and railing at Fate. I was frightened for her too. *Hard*, I had always thought, about Aunt Dinah. Now I had a new impression. *Brittle. Easily shattered*.

When you serve false gods, what happens if they betray you? I wondered. Without vanity, reputation and wealth, upon what could she fall back?

When I was not tending to Dinah, I did what I could for Judith. I loaned her books that she never opened, and took her for walks in the garden, though I may as well have been towing a doll. I fed her parakeets, since she had grown forgetful and distracted. I tried to make her feel she was not alone but I had no way of knowing if any of it made any difference. And every

day I told Turlington that I loved him and I talked to him of
hope. I even confided my secret longing to return to Cornwall
and my wish that he would come with me. He did not respond
to any of it, just brooded, so I could only hope that my words
were like seeds falling on dark soil, that maybe they would turn
into something one day.

Chapter Thirty-six

❦

I escaped from Helicon one morning for Rebecca's wedding. The ceremony was simple, small and achingly sweet. The only other witness was Tobias's brother John. With Rebecca's permission I had invited Turlington, but he had pressing business with his decanter and did not wish to join me.

Somehow, under a veil and a crown of flowers, Rebecca looked smaller and frailer than she really was. Tobias looked thin and serious. I could not help but think that although they appeared so fragile they were inwardly two of the strongest people I had met. I loved Turlington from the bottom of my soul, but I did not think he was like that. About myself, I was unsure. Rebecca and Tobias had been shocked by her father's reception to their declaration of their love. Now they were doing what was right for them regardless – a practice that did not come naturally to them, good, unselfish people that they were. Their consciences had long dictated that they put other people first. But in their feelings for one another they had found a higher truth to follow. They were putting their faith in one another and the life they were to build together. Of course it made me think of myself and Turlington as I stood beside my friend and held her bouquet and witnessed her vows.

I could imagine what life would be like for a couple like Rebecca and Tobias. Shared beliefs and values, a harmony of personality, a unity of spirit. What a blessed life that would be. Whereas Turlington and I . . . was ours a harmonious, humanitarian union that would enrich us both? Or was it simply a force, driving us together, compelling us onwards, 'til we could do nothing but implode?

The wedding, then, was bittersweet for me. And so it was for Rebecca – for as soon as it was over, they were back to Speedwell Cheese to confront her father with their fait accompli. I offered to go with them but she kissed me gratefully and shook her head. It was something for the married couple to face together. They were the unit who must negotiate the world together now.

I took my leave and set off for Helicon, but only very half-heartedly. So half-heartedly, in fact, that I found myself wandering, after a while, to some of our secret places, Turlington's and mine, in the wrong side of the city. It felt as though I were bidding them goodbye, though I had formed no such intention. I passed the Dog and Duchess and was pleased to keep walking. I reached the river and a place with a small pebbly shore where we had walked and clung to each other more than once. I stood there a long while staring into the dragging tide. There was a small eddy, formed of I knew not what obstruction, and the same rubbish kept coming to the surface in strict rotation. An old woollen cap, once possibly blue, a bit of sacking with a tail of rope, a dead gull . . . and I realised that life with the Graces had been very like this.

There, I had been stuck and stagnant, unable to wash myself free. I kept going round and round, trapped in a pull I could not understand. The same thoughts kept circulating, weary and well-worn: I loved him, I pitied him, he infuriated me, I could not leave, we could not continue, *I* was not a Grace, *he* was not a Grace . . . Where was the way out of this? Where was the way to clear seas and fresh horizons? It felt as though we had been swimming in brown and contaminated waters, as though nothing would ever change. Since Hawker's death, everything had been pulled loose. For the others, I was deeply concerned. For myself, I felt only a great release.

When I returned, my uncle Irwin was looking out for me. 'Ah, Florence!' he greeted me in the hall, great purple-black shadows under his eyes. He was as stout as ever but he seemed somehow to sag within his bulk; the outline was the same but the substance had changed. He did not look equal to that spacious hall with its high ceiling, its gleaming black and white floor, its grand staircase that forked and presented its eternal, pointless choice.

'You look tired, Uncle,' I said, taking his hand for a moment and untying my bonnet. 'Can I do anything for you?'

He looked relieved. 'I was about to ask if you would. Do you have any time to come somewhere with me? Now?'

'Of course.' I retied my bonnet. 'Where?'

'Let me tell you on the way. I'll call the carriage.'

'We might be able to keep the carriage,' he murmured as we set off. 'Perhaps just the one horse – that would have to serve as a riding horse too. Of course, Father does not need Lightning any more. It seems wrong to sell Lightning, but he will fetch a pretty penny for all that he's fifteen. It's a big carriage for one horse, though. Perhaps we should sell it and buy a trap. I do not know if Dinah could tolerate a trap—'

'Uncle, you have been thinking and thinking, have you not?' I interrupted. 'You have been working very hard to find a way through all this and no one has helped you very much.'

He looked uneasy. 'It's certainly all very . . . engrossing. Trying to make a logical assessment, not let sentiment cloud . . . not to let certain expectations stand in the way of what is expedient now . . . Dear, dear, our landscape is suddenly very different, is it not, Florence? I could not expect, you know, Dinah to . . . she married a Grace after all!'

He looked away, out of the window at the changing landscape. Here was a man who was unused to talking about his concerns and having them received with any sympathy. I was quiet a while, then curiosity got the better of me.

'Where *are* we going, Uncle?'

'Oh, forgive me, my dear. Well, the fact is, I have found . . . I believe I have found . . . a house for us. It is in Hampstead. Not central, but a good neighbourhood, respectable. Dinah cannot . . . well, she does not wish to leave Helicon, of course. But we must, and soon. I wondered if *you* would look at it for me, Florence. I know you will not be with us long since you will doubtless marry Aubrey sooner rather than later now, but I wanted a woman's view.'

I took a sharp breath. With all that had happened, I had almost forgotten that I wasn't going to marry Aubrey – or rather, I'd forgotten that I had ever thought I would. When something is held inside so long, the releasing of it is always a little frightening. But it had to be said. 'Uncle, you shall have my view of the house, of course, but I must tell you, I am not going to marry Aubrey.'

He looked at me in surprise. 'Indeed? Why, I thought it quite settled between you! I am sorry, my dear. He has not wronged you, I hope?'

'Absolutely not. It was merely that I did not . . . I could not . . . well, it would not have been the right thing to do, even though it looked like such a good match.'

He patted my hand. 'Never mind. You don't have to explain to me. Even your aunt may not care quite so much at such a time. You shall stay in Hampstead with us. And are you quite all right?'

I was nothing of the sort. But what could I say except,

'Quite all right, Uncle, thank you.' Then a thought occurred to me. 'Oh! Uncle, you have been making your calculations and arrangements assuming I would be married soon. You thought me settled. I do not want to be an imposition now. I can make my own arrangements. I can—'

But Irwin cut across me. 'No, Florence. I had included you in all my thinking for I did not know *when* you would marry. Easier to keep you in the equation, you see. I can't help feeling glad, though it's selfish of me, perhaps. You have been a wonder with Dinah these last weeks and you will be an asset in our new household. Besides, you belong with us. You are a Grace!'

'Thank you, Uncle.' I leaned my head on his shoulder and contemplated the strangeness of life. It was clear I could not depend upon Turlington now, and for the second time, being a Grace meant shelter and an alternative to poverty. I found it easier to accept, this time. Perhaps the growing conviction within me that my true place lay elsewhere entirely helped. Not only was everything different within the family now, but something told me that one way or another I would not be here very long.

'About the house,' my uncle continued, 'I believe it meets our needs, we can afford it, and I consider it not unpleasant. I thought you might not have the same bias as my wife and daughter. They accuse me of gross cruelty in wanting to move them to lesser accommodations and will not look at it. I thought you might be able to tell me whether I am unreasonable indeed or if the house is a fair one, in your opinion, before I sign the papers.'

'I would be happy to. And you are very good, to want a second opinion before committing us all. I am sure that when my aunt recovers she will see that.'

He pressed his lips together and looked out of the window again and we continued in silence to Hampstead. I was privately overjoyed. We were leaving Helicon. I would be leaving Helicon at last.

The house my uncle had found was not only a fair one, as he had put it, but to my eyes, entirely pleasing in every particular. I gave a little shiver of excitement as I stood before it; I could feel the edges of autumn coming in.

'I like it at once, Uncle!' I exclaimed and his eyes flared with hope. Heath View Cottage was unimaginatively but accurately named. It was a square white cottage dating from the days of one of the King Georges. For a moment I wanted to consider it small, as my aunt doubtless would, but I remembered the cottage where I had grown up and I smiled. It was more compact than Helicon, that was all. A tall, blowsy plane tree stood outside the gate, arching protectively over the house, dangling its small green fruits mischievously. Red ivy covered the left-hand wall and wound a few pretty ribbons across the front. It was, indeed, positioned on the edge of Hampstead Heath and

I ached to go walking in the open space beyond. But I was not here for that. I was here to help my uncle.

'Let us go inside,' I said, tucking my hand into his arm.

The interior was equally charming. There were three square rooms downstairs, as well as a kitchen at the back and a scullery. A few drifts of cobweb decorated the corners, suggesting that it had stood empty for a time.

'I thought we might bring two servants. There is a small attic room, where one might sleep. Do you think the scullery might serve for the other? It seems clean and warm. Many households are not fortunate enough to have two servants, I believe?'

'Indeed they are not. We shall manage very well.'

'As you see, it is furnished,' said my uncle. 'That will save us a great expense. Of course, we can still bring a few favourite things, but much of what we have at Helicon will not look well here. Better to sell it, I think. Perhaps just bring such paintings as we can manage, some ornamental things to give the ladies pleasure . . . But it is all very old, is it not,' he fretted, looking around at the scuffed dining table, the bookcase with its chipped corners, the faded settle beneath the window. 'Is it entirely wrong, Florence?'

'Not at all!' I cried, moving from room to room and back again. I saw only the leaves around the windows and the glimpses of wild places beyond. I felt only the air of hospitality about the place, which Helicon, for all its splendour, had never achieved. 'We can be very comfortable here and look, there is even a piano!' It sat beside a window, the fall closed, waiting.

'That is useful,' he pondered. 'We could not fit the grand in here. Though Dinah will not be pleased to see it go. It is signed by Godfrey Lockheart, you know.'

'I know, Uncle, but we have to think about making a new life now, not holding on to mementoes of the days when famous tenors visited us at home. I like this piano.' I did. It was made of figured walnut, with a finely fretted front. Dark damask silk showed through the ornate screen. There were brass candleholders, one on either side, and the wood below them was speckled with wax drippings and dark marks. It was an old and well-used piano. I lifted the fall. The white keys were yellowed and the black keys had unusual rounded ends. I struck middle C. It needed tuning.

'Look, Uncle, candleholders. What a lovely feature. Can you imagine us all gathered here one dark night, singing by candlelight?'

His face softened as he looked at me. 'I think you may be thinking of some other family, Florence,' he said with a touch of regret. 'Goodness, how like your mother you are after all. I never saw it before. Not only your eyes, but a tilt of your head. Her luminosity.'

I glowed. I had always been likened to my father when I was young – our height, my tawny hair a variation on his fiery crop. It was good to feel I had something of my mother in me too.

Upstairs were four bedrooms, two overlooking the quiet street and the plane tree, two overlooking the heath. I sighed as I looked out. A grassy distance with a sheet of silver water between the house and the horizon. Trees. Bushes. People on horseback.

'I thought, one room for Dinah and myself,' said my uncle, 'that bigger one for Sanderson and Anne and the baby when it comes. Oh, that won't serve forever but . . . Anyway, one room for Turlington, of course, and one room for you and Judith, if you don't mind sharing, Florence? I am sorry, I know you are not used to it but there is no other arrangement . . .'

'I'm perfectly used to sharing. My nan and I slept in the same room for fifteen years. I shall not mind if Judith does not.'

'Thank you, child. And do you think perhaps you might be able to encourage the others to look favourably on the place?'

I laughed. 'Honestly I do not, Uncle. I suspect they will be set against finding anything to like about it at all, at first. I worry that my good opinion might prejudice them still further. But I do believe this house is very adequate and amenable. You have found them a good place.'

Three weeks later, after a frenzied period of packing and selling and organising and arguing, the mighty Graces, including parakeets, moved to a cottage ('a *cottage*!' wailed my aunt, as though it were a brothel) in Hampstead.

I had spent the intervening time visiting our new home and cleaning and arranging it to make it as comfortable as possible. The servants, when they learned they were to lose their employment, immediately set about securing new positions and gave us little help. How could we blame them? Yet my aunt damned them for their lack of loyalty to the family.

I only saw Jacob once during this time and I suffered for want of his sparky, resilient humour. When I saw him it reminded me that there was life beyond the Graces. I might have made time to go again, busy though I was, except that naturally he asked me about Turlington and I did not know how to answer him. I said that Turlington was unwell, which seemed passably close to the truth. I hoped that when we moved, Turlington would rouse himself and then I would not need to lie to Jacob; I so badly wanted him to learn that some people could be relied upon.

I did walk one day to Aubrey's townhouse and at last returned both my engagement ring and the emerald birthday ring. There was no need for pretence any longer. I could not bear to see him so I entrusted them to his housekeeper along with a note for Aubrey, apologising with all my heart and wishing him well. A sad little chapter of my life had closed.

Rebecca helped me at the house in Hampstead on three separate occasions, even though she had a new husband now. Love overflowed from her, made her generous with her time, expansive. We chattered and laughed as we worked and I felt almost happy.

But true happiness was pushed out of reach by Turlington, who grew angrier and angrier with me the more occupied I became.

'If you truly loved me, you would stay nearby. You would not be able to go about your days so merry. You would *care*.'

I started to cry and was *furious* with myself, but it didn't matter because he didn't notice. I wiped my eyes with the back of my hand.

'I care!' I cried. 'I care about you more than anything and I have told you so, but you don't listen to me. We are starting a new life, Turlington! We could tell everyone about us now, for we have nothing to lose. There is nothing to stop us going forward into the life we have imagined apart from your insistence on clinging to this old demon. Let it go, Turlington, and hold me instead!'

'Nothing to stop us but money, you mean. My fortune is not so very great, on its own. We would not have a grand life, Florrie.'

'And which of us has ever valued that?'

'You might say you don't care about being poor again, but you will when it happens.'

'No, Turlington, I will not. But perhaps you will. Clearly I am not enough to make you happy. Does it never occur to you that *I* might need *you*? I have been working so hard! How much your company would lift my days, how I long to have you laugh and talk freely with me again. I need to feel your arms around me!'

'The last time I came to your bed you told me I was disgustingly drunk and not to come until I was sober.'

'And so you were and so I did. And your choice is as we see. I did not think that could ever happen.'

'But, Florrie,' he said, his voice softening as he looked at me beseechingly. 'You knew who I *was*!'

What did he mean? Did he mean that this had always been likely to happen, at some point, like a fizzing cannon bound to explode? That I had entered into our love knowing this, that I was somehow betraying him now by not accepting it?

It was a question to which I returned again and again over the following days. I had, I thought indignantly, truly believed he had become someone I could depend on to stay with me and share life with me. At least, that is what part of me had thought. But had there not always been that deeper, older knowing that had whispered and whispered, warning me, though I had not heeded it? Had I not hesitated to cast myself adrift with only him? Had I not distrusted the foundations of that future he kept talking about? Yet despite all that I had clung to him and only him as the source of all my joy. I had not listened to myself – again. And *now* what was I to do? Was I to wait patiently, perhaps interminably, for this phase to end? And then to go through life with him, laughing with him and adoring him, always wondering when this would happen next? It was impossible. And yet what was the alternative? I felt I could not live without him. Although, in a way, I was already doing so.

By the middle of September, we were settled in Heath View Cottage and the leaves on the heath turned orange and gold, reminding me, as autumn always did, of my father. My aunt remained uncharacteristically subdued. Irwin was as busy as ever and absent as often; he stewed and stewed and stewed over our affairs. Judith seemed to look to me for guidance as to how she should be in this new life. If I played the piano, she sang a little. If I went for a walk on the heath, she asked to join me. If I rearranged some furniture, she would straighten a picture.

We did not share a bedroom, however, since there was no need. We had plenty of rooms for our number after all. The Coatleys would not hear of Anne living in a cottage, with no nursery for the baby, so she and Sanderson joined their household. And on the night before we moved, without ever having seen the new house, Turlington vanished again, taking a few pieces of jewellery belonging to Dinah and Judith, but nothing of mine except my heart.

When I found that he was gone, I cried until I howled and I did not care who heard me. I had not realised how strenuously I had been clinging to the idea that somehow all would be as it had been, but better, because we could end the pretence. Even while I knew it would not happen, I had still hoped for it. I had hoped that when we were in Hampstead he would come back to himself, find strength and resilience again; that we could walk miles together on the heath, talking and laying plans. Instead I was confronted with a growing realisation, deep within my body and spirit, that he would never really be with me again. Perhaps he never fully had been.

At least he left me a note this time. In a sealed envelope, on my pillow. He had stolen into my room and seen me asleep one last time. I had not sensed him; it seemed impossible.

My darling,

I am so sorry. I am not good enough for you. I have tried to be, but I failed. You were right about everything. I can't reverse it. I am going back to Madeira, going to start over and try to build up the business and myself once again. If I can do it, I will come back to you. If I can't, you are better off without me. But never doubt, not for a minute, that I love you. You are so beautiful, Florrie Buckley. So beautiful. And beyond me.

T

I was so angry. So angry. The tone of maudlin self-pity, the pretence of doing the right thing, because he wasn't good enough for me, the half-hearted reassurance that he might, possibly, if I was very lucky, return. Or not. And what exactly was I meant to do with my life meanwhile? I was suspended again. Like that rubbish in the eddying river. Or I would be, if I didn't fight very hard to free myself. I was quite tired of fighting; I did not relish the prospect of another battle. But I was not going to spend the rest of my life in stasis, waiting, hoping, and wasting the years. I would *not*!

Astonishingly, no one connected my heartache with Turlington's departure. Everyone was too busy that morning in the whirl of preparation, in cursing him when they found that he had helped himself to their rapidly dwindling possessions. They were in turmoil themselves at leaving the great bastion of the Graces. My aunt and Judith came away from Helicon only with a wrench that put me in mind of barnacles and rocks.

I don't think anyone even heard me cry. And when I emerged from my room red-eyed, on shaking legs, unable to stop the trickling tears, I think they thought I too was unhappy about leaving. I stumbled and nearly fell as I walked down those grand stone steps; Irwin just caught me. I looked back at Helicon through a haze of tears and remembered the day I arrived: *I will never be happy here.* I was right. Oh, I was right. I had hoped that in Hampstead it might be different but now, to go forwards without Turlington was unfathomable. I felt as though I had been torn apart, limb from limb, like a rabbit feasted upon by a hawk. Pointless without him. Only half of who I was. No possibility of joy.

Chapter Thirty-seven

But life is not like that. It is not static or limited; it is not so easily quenched. It was unbearable, at first, to be without him. I felt a craving for him every moment. And it gave me a cold feeling, like iced water running through every single one of my veins, to realise that the man I loved more than anyone or anything in the world was not a man with whom I could build a sane, luminous life – even if he did come back. But I did want that sane, luminous life, nonetheless, and I spent whatever solitary time I could muster thinking about how I might achieve it. Solitary time at first, however, was scarce.

At Helicon we had all been able to rattle about in our own corners without seeing each other for hours if it pleased us. Here, although we were only four Graces, we were together a great deal. My aunt gradually began to revive and take an interest in household affairs, but she still relied upon me, preferring to eat the things that I had cooked, liking me to be with her when she ate them. Judith continued to cling to me like a cobweb and much though I wished, at times, to brush her off, I would not.

Mrs Clemm had not come with us; the reduced wage my uncle offered was not sufficient to tempt her. So Benson and her sister Laura came and turned their hands to a bit of everything, and I did a great deal to put the house in order. My aunt and cousin often trailed around watching me, but I no longer felt like Cinderella, scrutinised by her demanding step-family. Rather I felt like a wizard who could perform magical tasks like cooking meals and removing the dust from objects by means of a magical item called a cloth. They watched me in a sort of wonder.

Although I was rarely alone, my true connections were greatly diminished. Not only was there no Turlington, there was no Sanderson. I missed him just as much in a different way. It might have been different if he and Anne had their own household. But we were not made especially welcome at the Coatleys'. It was as though they thought the Graces had procured their daughter on a false promise. I saw less of Rebecca too; we were further from Marylebone now, making a visit a larger undertaking, and my aunt disliked to spare me. It was not like the old days, when she wished to curtail my freedom; it was that she often found herself in a highly anxious state in this new life and my presence seemed to ease it.

I had little time for reading or music. I was tired often – an emotional exhaustion caused by Turlington's abandonment, the ache of which never really went away. I experienced that odd paradox of feeling lonely whilst being constantly pressed about by people. And yet . . .

I did take a walk on the heath almost every day. Usually Judith came too, but sometimes I went alone. I walked miles then, from one edge to the other, around the outside, where I could see the villages set about it, and across the middle where I watched long-legged, steel-eyed herons fishing in the ponds. I picked blackberries – until the ninth of October anyway, then I stopped; I did not wish any more ill upon the Graces. I picked rose hips and nuts. I went home and made rose hip syrup for the colds that Judith and her mother seemed constantly to suffer.

These frequent glimpses of a more natural world did more to restore my spirits and my sense of who I was, irrespective of Buckley or Grace, than I could ever have hoped. My eyes feasted on beauty: the patterns of the branches and berries in the bushes, the sweep of long grass, the washed-out autumn colours of sepia and silver splashed with vivid sunset shades.

Inside Heath View Cottage I liked waking to autumnal chill. I found spiders in every corner and crack as they came in from the cold. These I welcomed as I knew they brought good fortune; I did not point them out to the others. In the evenings the fire fussed in the hearth. Meals were more welcome after work and fresh air, and when they were eaten for sustenance, not for fashion. I liked the feeling that I was creating a home, even if it was not quite my own.

I liked feeling needed, too. Once my aunt even thanked me! She caught my hand as I was clearing her tray one evening after a little supper, then immediately let it go. 'You are very good to us, Florence,' she said, sounding almost distressed.

'I hope so, Aunt.'

'But I have not always been good to you.'

'Those times are past now, Aunt. We are all very different.'

'Yes,' she murmured. 'We are all very different.' Then in a stronger voice she added, 'You are more magnanimous than I could be. The work you do to make us comfortable here . . . is noted. Thank you.'

I thought about kissing her but I knew that was a step too far for us both. Instead I smiled and said, 'Why don't you join me and Judith on the heath tomorrow, Aunt? It's very beautiful and you have hardly gone out since we came here.'

But she only grimaced. '*Nature!*' she shuddered disapprovingly.

We were adopted by a cat as purplish-grey as evening cloud, with bright, starry eyes. We never found out whom it belonged to, but it would slink into our parlour almost every evening and rest with us a while. My aunt disliked it and closed the windows whenever she saw them open. 'It's *cold*, Florence,' she would say crossly, 'and that nasty animal might come in.'

I would just smile and say, 'Yes, Aunt,' and open them again when her back was turned. As Old Rilla used to say, *You fight a losing battle when you try to keep out what has the right to be in.*

And there were kindnesses. Rebecca and Tobias visited sometimes. So did Selina Westwood. And Aubrey sent a note, begging that if the family or I should need anything at all, I would contact him.

Yes, I cried at night for Turlington. Yes, I missed my friends. And I still felt temporary in some strange way. But even with a million imperfections raining all around, it's extraordinary how beautiful life can be.

I used my rare moments of solitude to lay plans. As a child I had believed that I was powerful, in charge of my own destiny. The conviction had returned full force.

Clearly, no person of sense would consider Turlington a factor in any decision to be made. I felt such sadness about it that I had to haul myself out, like a pony from a bog. But the sense of a future with Turlington had always been cloudy, hard to see. The sense of a future all of my own had so far been glimpsed only in tiny moments, but when they came, they were clear and bright.

The first had been the memory of Cornwall that had jumped upon me that day at Rebecca's. The moment of peace, looking up at the moors. It was a memory, but it felt like the future too. I remembered Old Rilla telling me that time was a vast circle. There had been several such moments and flashes since then. I kept seeing things I did not fully understand: an enormous stone fireplace, a family, though I could not see the faces, the moors . . . over and over again the moors above Braggenstones.

I couldn't make sense of it. I knew I could never return to my old life. My time in London had shown me too much of what was fascinating and precious in the world – poetry and music and art . . . I hoped I was not proud and I did not mind hard work, but a life as a labourer, with no small luxuries and no cultural riches, would stultify me.

I surely could never marry. I could not imagine ever loving anyone but Turlington. He and I had thrown ourselves at each other with the force and passion of two volcanos erupting and I was 'spoiled for other men', as my aunt would have said. Even if I wanted to pretend it had never happened, I couldn't. What sort of a life would that be? So the only family I would ever have would be the Graces, and I could not imagine *them* in Cornwall! And what was that fireplace I saw repeatedly? Such a sizeable hearth belonged in no house within my grasp. Nevertheless, I decided to trust them, these glimpses, and the feelings they engendered in me.

I was content enough in Hampstead. But I knew, once more, what had always been true, though forgotten: my heart lay in Cornwall. For a long time there had been no way that I could be there but now I wondered. I need not be penniless, as I once had been. I remembered my younger self hoarding and counting birthday shillings and found pennies with a desperate concentration. I felt a sort of painful tenderness towards my young dreams. I had things I could sell now: jewellery, some ornaments, even clothing . . . I could create a small nest egg – but it would be swiftly spent.

I considered the options open to a woman for acquiring money and they were few. My rigorous training at Helicon had made me an ornament, fit for little useful employment. However, my early years had deepened my practical streak and if there was some way I could marry that with my accomplishments . . . perhaps I could be a governess or teach piano, or *something* . . . I did not even know how to start making enquiries about such a thing. I thought often about writing to Lacey, asking for her help or advice . . . but it seemed too soon to let her in on my plan, if such it was. It was more of a vague impulse than a plan, and I could not see myself leaving my family with any immediacy. They were still reeling from the shock of their dispossession. Still, I took out Lacey's last letter from time to time and reread it:

Lacey's class had grown to twelve – they could scarcely fit in the room. Hesta and Stephen sent their love. The heather was thick on the moors. Heron's Watch would perhaps be pulled down. Old Rilla was showing her age. The West Wivel summer dance . . . pieces of a puzzle, like a box of daguerreotype images being shaken above my head. I did not know how to order them.

Chapter Thirty-eight

After Christmas, I began to insist that I spent more time away from the house. Throughout October, November, December, I had seen Sanderson, Jacob and Rebecca only a handful of times. My aunt and Judith needed to regain their independent spirit – at least, my aunt needed to regain hers and Judith needed to acquire one – and I wished for a life of my own again. It was a fine January, bitterly cold but dry as a diamond, and I rejoiced to be walking through the city once more.

Rebecca and I began to indulge again in long heart-to-heart conversations. Her passion for these was undimmed by married life; she merely sent Tobias away when we wished to confide. They now lived just a few streets away from Speedwell Cheese, in Tobias's apartments, which still wore their bachelor's costume of neglect, brown curtains and boxes. Rebecca had as yet had little time to do battle with all this masculinity for she had been working so much at her father's shop. This did not signal a reconciliation between father and daughter, however; it was simply that Mr Speedwell had fallen into a decline since her wedding and announced himself unfit to work.

Despite the oddness of seeing Rebecca in such untidy surroundings, it was obvious that she was happy – that *they* were happy. Their delight in receiving a visitor as a married couple was always radiant.

My first visit to Sanderson after an awkward Christmas spent at the Coatleys', when we had had no opportunity to talk alone, was deeply upsetting. Anne, heavily pregnant now, clung to him and was loath to leave his side at all. When she did leave us for a few minutes I lost no time asking what was wrong; he had lost his rosy complexion and some considerable weight along with it.

'Sad news,' he said briefly, with a glance at the door through which Anne had disappeared. 'Mr Westwood is dead.'

'Mr Westwood! But how? Surely he was not fifty?'

'Six and forty. He was struck with pneumonia over Christmas. He never fully recovered and last week, he died . . .'

'Leaving Selina a widow,' I finished softly, realising that the death of a rather cold and arrogant churchman was not sufficient to explain his haunted demeanour. All at once I understood his secret. I remembered a hundred small comments, sympathetic looks, quiet conversations between them. All had gone entirely unnoticed by anyone because they were both so good, so beyond reproach. He was in love with Selina Westwood. The vicar's wife! It would have been torture for someone like Sanderson to love a married woman. It would have been torture for her to have those feelings for someone who was not her husband.

He nodded and leaned his forearms on the mantel and his head upon his arms.

'Oh, Sanderson,' I murmured, putting my arms around him and leaning my cheek upon his shoulder. 'I am so sorry.'

'You have guessed then?' he said in a small voice, turning his head to look at me.

'Only this very minute. That is, I guessed there was *someone*. But I should have known. You are so close, the two of you, so alike. You have always had such great respect for her judgement, and she for yours. Oh, Sanderson.'

He stood up straight again; he seemed hardly able to find comfort in any position. 'I thought she would never be free. And Hawker expected, *insisted*. Then within a few short months of my wedding he was dead, and I might have made a different choice, but it was too late by then. Now Selina is free – and I am not. My wife is a tender creature, our baby is nearly with us and they need me . . .'

'My dear, dear friend. Oh, how I wish I could help you.'

'It is agony, Florrie. I am more angry than I ever knew I could be. But you know the man I am. I could never turn my back on Anne and the child.'

'I know.'

'And here they are very jealous – of everyone. They dislike

me to visit my family, Selina, of course, anyone at all. It is like Helicon all over again, but without you.'

At that moment Anne returned and the rest of the conversation concerned the weather. I left with a heavy heart.

At the Rising Star Home, yet more distress awaited me. The younger Mr Planchard greeted me at the door with a worried look.

'It is good to see you. How are you, Miss Grace? Did you pass a happy festive season?'

'Happy enough, thank you, Mr Planchard, and you?'

'Oh, very fine, very fine. And your cousin? He has still not returned?'

I had told them that Turlington had been called away on business for an unspecified time. For a minute I could see him, his face bright with laughter over the antics of the boys, and I swallowed. I told Mr Planchard that his business would likely detain him quite some months.

'The boys will be sorry for it,' he said, crestfallen, 'but glad to see you, certainly. Miss Grace, if I could ask a favour, will you see Jacob alone first? There has been some . . . trouble over the last few days.'

'Of course. But what kind of trouble? Is all well?'

'I fear not. There has been a small . . . business . . . and he has taken it very much to heart, very much. I am surprised, to be honest how badly. After all, it ended well.'

He showed me to a small sitting room and said he would fetch Jacob from his lessons. 'It won't harm to interrupt him. He barely attends to his schooling now anyway.'

'Whatever has happened to throw him off like this? He was working so hard, taking his lessons so seriously.'

'It was an incident with the police. He was held and questioned for the theft of a gentleman's pocketbook.'

'He has not gone back to those ways. I won't believe it, I really won't.'

'Of course he has not. But he was in the area, and with his reputation . . . the constable needed to . . . eliminate the possibility. But they found the real culprit and brought him here to explain to me what had happened. Very decent of them. As I said, all's well that ends well. But Jacob has been . . . brooding ever since.'

'I will talk to him,' I promised.

'Thank you, Miss Grace. Poor Jacob will be so glad to see you.'

But poor Jacob was *not* glad to see me. I had a long wait before he dragged himself in, and this from the boy who had never needed prompting to skip a lesson. Mr Planchard withdrew with an expression more puzzled than ever. The Jacob who stood before me, head angled away from me, hands dangling, was the old Jacob, sullen as could be.

'Jacob,' I said, 'whatever is the matter?' Beneath a blanket of seething resentment, I saw, or perhaps felt, great hurt. I ached to hold his skinny little frame again and take it all away, but I knew better than to try.

'What do you care?'

'I care very much, of course! Jacob, Mr Planchard told me what has happened. It must have been a terrible ordeal. Only, it is over now, dear, and no one who loves you would believe that you'd done such a thing. I wish I had known. I would have vouched for your character to the police . . .'

'*Would* you now?'

'I certainly would, Jacob! Whatever is wrong?'

But his old intractable silence was in place. I sat and waited, gazing at his thin, set neck, the shoulders rigid with antagonism. I could understand that he was angry the police had not believed him at first. It must have cast a near blow at all his efforts to change. But surely he had never had such great affection for the police that this would hurt him so much? He seemed to feel . . . betrayed. He appeared angry with *me*, but I knew I had no part in it. Someone else he trusted then. Not the Planchards, clearly. Otherwise there was only Turlington but Turlington was in Madeira . . . Ah.

I bent towards him and took his small arms, gently but firmly. 'Jacob,' I said softly, 'I can see that something very treacherous has happened. But I don't know what it is. I cannot make you tell me, but I can't help you if you don't. Will you not trust me?'

'Trust!' he snorted. *That's* a fool's game.'

'Who has betrayed you?'

His big, sad eyes looked so confused. 'I'm meant to keep it a secret.'

'But you know that telling me is the same as keeping a secret. Remember the watch?'

'I remember. But I'm supposed to keep it a secret *especially* from you.'

I sighed. 'It's something to do with Turlington, isn't it? Jacob, it is not right that you should get caught up in his secrets. You are a child.'

'Turlington is here in London,' he said, looking at me steadily.

'I should be astonished. But I am not.'

He twisted up his mouth into a little sideways posy and began his tale. 'Mr Planchard had sent me on an errand. I was just near the park when I saw him – Turlington – walking along. I knew it was him, even from a distance. You know how he looks, so tall, that big coat.'

I closed my eyes for a minute. I knew all too well.

'I ran after him. I hadn't seen him for so long and I didn't want to lose him. He had a surprise to see me, Florrie, but not a good surprise. He said he'd just got back from Madeira and not to tell you. I only thought he wanted to surprise you, Florrie, at first, but he kept on and on, not to tell anyone he was here, and I knew there was more to it.

'Just then, a gent started shouting fit to rouse London. He'd been robbed and then I don't know what happened; there was a sort of a flash — I think it was someone running by really fast. Then the constable grabbed me and I realised he thought it was me — they'd seen me running after Turlington, see. I was so relieved he was there to explain. But he wasn't.'

'Oh, Jacob.'

'Just vanished, like he'd never been there! I said I'd been running to catch up with my friend and the constable said something all sarky, like, about invisible friends. Then he asked me his name and, of course, I couldn't say. I'd just promised. Then the constable said how interesting it was that I just happened to be there at the scene of the crime, but of course it wouldn't be me, what with my sparkling reputation and all. He started dragging me off. I kept looking round for Turlington. I kept thinking, *He wouldn't let this happen if he knew, he must have just stepped away for something, he'll appear any moment. He'll come back and explain and I'll be free to go and carry Mr Planchard's message and get back in time for lunch . . .*'

'But he didn't.'

Jacob hung his head. 'I was so angry, Florrie, I did myself no favours. They held me for hours, asking me questions and questions, and I was . . . well, you know how I get, Florrie.'

'I certainly do.'

'Well, I was like that, so then they suspected me even more and I *still* kept expecting Turlington to come and put it all right. How stupid can you be! The only reason I got out of there was because they caught the one that did it. A girl it was, turns out. The constable apologised and brought me home. I couldn't look at him, Florrie. I couldn't accept his apology, even though Mr P. told me I should be gracious and a gentleman. But I wasn't really angry at *him*. I know why they thought it was me and he was all right really. Not every copper would apologise to the likes of me. It's Turlington.'

At last I felt safe to hug my wounded young friend. 'I'm so sorry, Jacob,' I muttered into his sandy hedgehog of hair. 'I had no idea about any of it.'

'I know, Florrie,' he said, all muffled in my shoulder. And we were friends again.

'And now can you put this behind you, Jacob?' I asked, setting him from me once again and looking into his face. 'Now that you've told me what happened, and I understand?'

To my dismay his face clouded again. 'I don't know, Florrie, it's not as easy as that. I've started to feel like the old me again, like maybe that's all I can ever be.'

I was dismayed. These were exactly the doubts that had plagued Turlington, and ultimately driven him away from me. I could not bear to hear the same thoughts from someone else I loved. It was the question that haunted me now as my future lay in wait, yet to be defined. Could a person truly decide to be different, better, and then live accordingly through every up and down? It was not easy, I well knew. Turlington had not risen to the challenge. But I was determined to, and even more so now. I would be happy for my own sake *and* to show Jacob that it could be done.

'But it's not, Jacob! You know that already. Please don't let all your wonderful efforts go to waste. It was very noble of you to say nothing about Turlington and protect him – but *he* should have protected *you*. He is an adult with many privileges and you are a child. So he was wrong in this, do you understand? Sometimes people are wrong, even adults, even our friends. That will keep happening throughout life, but we can't just throw away our chances when that happens. Do you see, Jacob, do you?'

My voice rose, impassioned. If his delicate faith in mankind had been fatally damaged at this early stage, what would become of him? I felt I was watching a young life teetering in the balance.

He raised an eyebrow at me. 'I'll try, Florrie. It's not that easy, though. I ain't been brought up to think I'm decent. You won't say anything about Turlington, will you? You won't, I don't know, go looking for him?'

'Jacob, after what you've told me, rest assured I feel I never want to see him again.'

I left the home and let myself out through the iron gates, deep in thought. I turned right past the sighing trio of pines . . . and felt a hand close around my arm.

'Oh, *Turlington*!' I exclaimed before I had even properly seen his face. 'How could you? How *could* you?'

He looked surprised that I was so unsurprised to see him. But as soon as I had learned he was in London I knew he would be lying in wait for me somewhere, one day.

'Shh,' he beseeched me, even though the street was empty.

'Don't "*shh*" me!' I cried, pulling away wildly.

'Florrie, please!' he hissed, looking around. 'Come with me, to my rooms. They are not very fine, to be sure, but we can talk there in private . . .'

'Why can't you talk to me in broad daylight? Why is keeping your stupid secrets always the most important thing to you? Turlington! You stole from our aunt and Judith when they had just lost everything! You left me again! You allowed Jacob to be *arrested* . . .'

He hung his head. 'I am not *proud* of it, Florrie.'

I rolled my eyes. 'My, what a fine moral compass you do have. Turlington, I am so angry with you that I hardly know where to put myself.'

'Then please, put yourself in my rooms, so that we may talk, even if only for you to tell me all the many wrongs I have done you.'

'I don't know that I have the inclination or the time.'

'Then walk away.'

I looked at him. His face was haggard. It was clear that he had not slept. There were dusky patches beneath his eyes.

Infuriated and wounded though I was, I could see his pain, too, and ached to make it better. Would it ever be any other way? The decision was made before I answered him, before he even asked. Of course I would go with him.

He led me without speaking along a series of streets and alleys that grew narrower and darker and dirtier until we were in the heart of the Devil's Acre. Even after our exploits in that salubrious area the previous summer, I was completely lost. His rapid steps and stiff posture made me tense.

We came at last to a narrow doorway where a small, thin girl with a dirty face and blackened, once-pale hair lay stretched out in the doorway. She reached for us with a feeble hand but Turlington stepped over her and disappeared into a stairwell that reeked of turnips. I could not help myself. I emptied my meagre purse into the girl's lap, for all the good it would do her.

I followed him. Up, up we went, clinging to a splintered wooden rail that sagged beside a disappointed-looking staircase. The wood was rotten through in places, leaving dark gaping holes like decayed teeth.

At the top of the stairs, he pushed open a narrow wooden door. No key, but the door was so obstinate and sticky that the tussle to open it was sufficient deterrent to intruders. Turlington's 'rooms' were little more than an attic arbitrarily divided into two areas by an ancient Japanese screen. The roof was low and dipping and one small window sufficed for the whole. The smell of turnips persisted.

'Oh, Turlington,' I sighed as I looked about, taking in the one small table and chair to the right of the screen, the one narrow bed to its left. *Oh, Turlington.* It seemed to have become my refrain.

'I know it's not much, Florrie.' He said it as though he were a new suitor, lowly positioned in life, and wishing to make a clean breast of it.

'*Not much!*' I exclaimed. 'Turlington, it's ridiculous. You're a wealthy man – or at any rate, not a pauper. Why are you living like this? What are you doing?'

'The business is precarious, Florrie, I have not managed it well of late. I am no pauper, you are right, but I wish to hold on to what I have, in case . . .'

'In case *what*? In case you should find yourself living in a slum? If you're saving it for difficult times, Turlington, I think they are here!'

'Oh, it's not so bad, Florrie. The company hereabouts is . . . lively. There's always someone willing to lend you a coin for a drink. The area is quite central, you know. And you forget, I think, that this is what I am used to. I have lived here many a long year before you set me on the straight and narrow. I'm only sorry I could not stay on it.'

'It may be what you are used to, Turlington, but is it what you *choose*? Out of all the different lives you have known – Madeira, Helicon, here – and all the different lives you have yet to sample, *this* is what you choose?'

'Well, it is not that, precisely, Florrie, only . . .' He shrugged and spread his beautiful hands.

I wanted to stamp, I was so frustrated, but I think I might have fallen through the creaking floor. 'What is it you *want*, Turlington? You can decide and then make it happen. You can!'

'All I want, Florrie . . .' He looked at me, eyes dark, then looked down.

My heart started drumming. I could not help it. I reached out a hand to touch the side of his face, to tilt his chin upwards. He held my gaze again and I trembled. All the months of hurt and loneliness, of hard-won understanding and forging my own path, were lost, for a moment, as the air between us tingled and the silence intensified.

'All I really want is . . .'

'Yes?'

'Is for the pain to go away. I just want it to stop hurting.'

'Oh.' I felt myself droop. What would I have felt if he had said something different?

'But . . . I think that might be *life*, Turlington. I think that might just be the way it is. Only, there are other things too. Can you not think of those?'

He frowned. 'But they are just what *makes* it hurt, Florrie! Like you! Loving you . . . being with you . . . it was a good thing, such a beautiful thing. But with it came such terror. What if you were hurt? What if I lost you? What if I lost your love? It *hurt*, Florrie!'

He sounded like a frightened child. I stroked his face again. 'I know, my love, I know. But is this better?'

He considered. 'It is . . . a little easier, perhaps. That's all. But I am grateful for that ease, Florrie.'

I started to cry. 'But, Turlington, I'm going back to Cornwall. I don't know how exactly but I'm going to go and live a beautiful life there. Won't you come with me? You would love the countryside, it is wild, like you and me. Sanderson could visit us. I could make you happy, I know I could! There's so much happiness waiting!' I suddenly heard Old Rilla's voice as I pined and starved for my father and repeated her demand now. 'Don't you want to live a life?'

'There's so much fear. And so much hurt.'

'So you're going to cower in here and live out your days avoiding all of it?'

'The price of happiness is too great, Florrie.'

'Too great even to be with me? Am I not worth it to you?'

He didn't answer, but I had known all along that Turlington and I would not go to Cornwall together. It was not what I wanted, it was simply what I knew.

I don't know how it happened but we came together then, falling into each other's arms with the inexorable force of a waterfall crashing onto rocks. Beautiful, powerful nature. Hands seeking skin without recourse to thought. Lips falling onto lips, arms winding around shoulders, waists, the only real, unsullied happiness to be found in all of this terrible mess.

We lay together a long time and the result of it all was me, curled in his arms with my head on his chest, a tear running down my face at the impossibility of it all: of being with him in any real way; of turning my back on such loveliness and someone I loved so hopelessly.

At last, as the shadows gathered, we stirred ourselves. Turlington lit a candle and it flickered over his sad face. He gazed down at me.

'Are you hungry, Florrie?'

I said that I was. He got up and paced about the apartment as though he hoped a loaf or two might have magically appeared while we slept. I already knew that there was no food there. The shelves were all bare.

'I have nothing to offer you,' he admitted at last and I nodded. I knew it very well.

It was a long walk back to Hampstead. Turlington escorted me to the edge of the Devil's Acre and I made my own way from there. The afternoon hung close about me like a cloud. I would not be home before dark.

'My darling Florrie, you know where to find me,' he said, taking my hands.

'I'm not sure I'll be able to find my way there again,' I replied gently, and we both knew I was not referring to the geographical challenge of London's more heartbroken areas. 'But Sanderson will always know where to find *me*.'

He opened his mouth as if to protest but I shook my head. 'No, Turlington. You cannot stay hidden from your brother forever. He loves you. He needs you too, for he has his own troubles. At some point you must contact him. You can't keep disappearing from the lives of those who love you.'

He gave a shrug that was neither agreement nor refusal. 'God bless you, Florrie, and may all those strange beings that hover about you bless you too. I love you. Please don't let this be goodbye.'

I was silent for a few moments, marshalling my thoughts. In these last hours with him I had realised that I knew a great many unwelcome things. I *could* still be with Turlington – if I abandoned my new-budding dreams, if I chose a defeated life here at his side. Turlington was never going to change. I could spend the rest of my life waiting but he would never choose happiness. I, however, was determined to do just that. And he would be left behind. It felt too cruel to bear, too cruel to say. Yet I knew these things were so. All my troubles since arriving at Helicon had come about through not listening to my heart's true wisdom, at first through necessity and then through habit. It was time to act differently now, or it would all have been for nothing.

'It must be goodbye, Turlington.' I pulled my hands from his. 'I wish you well always and I hope that one day you yet decide upon a different life. But I cannot wait for it. And I cannot join you here.'

He looked stricken. 'Florrie! You cannot mean it!'

'I do.' I nodded firmly then I turned my back on Turlington and the rookeries and walked away, back to Hampstead and whatever awaited me there. As I walked through the deepening cold I remembered the day after the party in Truro; the day we had met. I remembered labouring through the sea mists over the moors, then emerging into sunlight on the breast of the hill. I remembered standing, then, for a long time, with the swirling grey at my back and the bright hillside before me. Thus it was now.

Chapter Thirty-nine

❧

As I walked away from Turlington, I came to understand that we had said our last goodbye. With every step I grew sadder. I also grew more peaceful. For the next week I complained of a mild malaise and kept largely to my room. My aunt was alarmed and brought me broth on a regular basis. I did not explain that my illness was of the heart and not the body. I sipped the broth and gazed over the heath. The end of such a love merited reflection.

A desultory snowfall. A great deal of rain. Long evenings. The usual array of January weather suited my mood and re-inforced my inclination to keep to the house. My aunt worried that I had exhausted myself looking after them all and was going into a decline. I was not. I simply needed to be still, so that the knowledge that Turlington was not going to be in my future could catch up with me entirely. I needed to be clear, once and for all, on that point.

For I *still* could not remember his quick wit, his intelligence, his gorgeous laughter without my heart catching. I would think, *but surely* . . . I could not remember our eager confidences, or his hands on my body at night, without longing for him . . . I knew the wreckage he always left in his wake, I knew the painful reality of having him next to me yet a million miles away . . . And yet our time together, before all of that, had been so beautiful. It was not something I expected to find again.

I tried to tell myself that my soul had it wrong when it beheld him and whispered *kindred*. But it had not been wrong. It was just that it did not mean what I had thought it meant. It did not translate into a liveable reality. I remembered what Old Rilla had told me, all those years ago. *Love is a strange and mystical force. To think of love and marriage as one and the same thing is like thinking that the sea and a bucket of water are the same.* Perhaps our business with each other lay outside of this lifetime – how could I know? All I really knew was that my heart would never be the same – yet this life still mattered to me, even flawed and bespoiled as it was.

I found the note he had left me when he last ran away from Helicon, still tucked away among my possessions like a shred of defiant hope.

You are so beautiful, Florrie Buckley. So beautiful. And beyond me.

Tears blurred my eyes but I tore it into tiny strips and threw it out of the window. They fluttered like a small handful of feathers about the garden to lie on the grass or catch in the bushes where they softened and grew transparent under the massing drizzle.

As the week wore on, I felt all the tragedy of our situation. The end of such a love merited grief. But as it came to a close I drew a line beneath it all. A week was all I could afford to live thus. It was done. Now to life.

During that sad, suspended week, the news had reached us that Anne had given birth to twins: a boy and a girl. The boy was named Coatley, according to custom, and the girl was Elizabeth, after my mother. Sanderson had produced two new Graces but Hawker was not here to see it. I longed to visit them, but I had other things to do first.

I wrote to Lacey, telling her that I wished to return to Cornwall. I told her that I had a little money, enough to take myself there and live for a short while but that after that I would need to support myself. Did she have any ideas or advice?

I got dressed and went downstairs. Aunt Dinah was relieved to see me about, though disappointed to see me gather my cloak from the hook. I reconciled her to my outing with promises of a selection from Speedwell Cheese. My aunt was partial to cheese.

Through a frosty, swirling, sooty sort of a morning I walked to Rebecca's new home and posted my letter on the way. When I arrived, a letter from Lacey was waiting for me on the mantel in the sitting room. She could have written to me at Hampstead now but in all the turmoil I had forgotten to tell her as much.

Tobias ushered me in, guiding me solicitously over crates and boxes. My skirts caught a few and they toppled. Rebecca's attempts to tidy had not yet extended to the hall. 'I like books,' she had said to me, bewildered, 'but I think there are more books than bricks here!'

I perched on an uncomfortable chair that only a bachelor could have owned, opposite an oddly shaped sofa with stuffing escaping from its left-hand haunch. While Tobias went to make tea and call Rebecca, I opened my letter and devoured it. And nearly dropped it.

My dear Florrie,

I must be brief since a mountain of correspondence awaits me, and countless other affairs . . .

I must share with you some sad news. My dear Aunt Sarah, so long my friend and stalwart, has passed away. It was very sudden – a stroke last Thursday – and the doctor says she was fortunate that it was so decisive and swift. I know you have memories of her, both from your time here as a pupil (how long ago that seems!) and from your last visit to Cornwall for the wedding. She always spoke fondly of you.

And now to my second reason for writing. She has left me the house in Tremorney, Florrie! It is not so unexpected, really, but the implications make my head spin. I can expand my school. I can do it from here if I wish, or I can sell this place and do it elsewhere. Or I can go elsewhere and let this house to tenants. In truth I know not! But I have so many choices, thanks to dear Aunt Sarah.

Now, Florrie, I know that you have been in London a long time and perhaps Cornwall feels like another life to you. But you have had a considerable change in circumstance, I know, and you said in your last letter that it has been a time of reflection for you. I have a proposal for you, dear. If I am to expand my school, I will need another teacher. If you wished to return, but found yourself short of means, you could come and live with me in Tremorney and help me run my school. With your London education just think what an asset you would be! Oh, Florrie, I must not continue on the subject now because I do not wish you to feel that I am trying to influence you (though I am!). <u>Only think what fun we should have!</u> I say no more.

I shall close, Florrie, and write to the other four hundred (so it seems) people to whom I need to impart the sad news of Aunt Sarah. I miss her. The house is lonely.

Ever yours aff.

Lacey

PS It seems that Heron's Watch is, after all, to be destroyed. Mr Glendower has not found a tenant. His own home is in Falmouth and he rarely comes to this area. The weather, of course, is hard on stick and stone and he says that maintenance is an expense and a nuisance that pays him no dividends. It seems very sad; it is such a beautiful old place and it has been there so very long. But who on earth would want to live somewhere so wild?

When Rebecca came in, she found me laughing quietly to myself. I handed her the letter and she read it.

'I have just today written to her, asking if she has any idea how I might support myself in Cornwall,' I smiled when she had finished. 'It seems that making a good decision puts wheels in motion, does it not?'

'Florrie, it is uncanny. It is the solution you have been looking for. I do not want to lose you, my dear friend, but your heart has never been here.'

'London is a splendid city after all. Despite everything, I could never be sorry I came. But I think it is time to leave now. And you will never lose me, Rebecca. We shall keep in touch, always, as Lacey and I have done. And you will visit, will you not, with Tobias? As we always dreamed?'

'Where must I visit?' asked Tobias, appearing with a large tray laden with teapot, cups and dainties. The china twinkled in the gloom of the wintry day. He set it down next to the lamp with the jade green drops, which Rebecca had placed determinedly in the middle of the sitting room as if one thing of beauty would encourage the rest of the room to follow suit. Gradually the tide of bachelorhood and scholarly chaos was retreating.

'We must go to Cornwall, my darling. Florrie is returning home.'

I walked home in a daze. Suddenly I was stuck no longer. One thing after another was becoming clear to me, unfolding at a pace I could hardly match. My thoughts and the world were dancing a deft jig. Before leaving my friends I had begged

Tobias for paper and quill and penned two further letters. One was a note of condolence to Lacey. I also told her that with all my heart I accepted her offer.

The other was to Mr Cooper Glendower, requesting the tenancy of Heron's Watch. I boldly wrote that I could pay for three months' rent in advance (though I had no idea what sum that would be) and that I had a steady income as I had newly acquired a post as a schoolteacher in Tremorney (even though I had no idea if Lacey could pay me). But the words were dashed off and the letter sealed before I could hesitate. I added a postscript to my note to Lacey, asking if she would please see the letter into his hands; it would be quicker than asking her for his address and then sending it.

Rebecca accompanied me to her father's shop. He no longer shut the door in her face when she approached, merely walked up the stairs leaving her alone in the shop when she visited. Things were improving.

We took our leave and I gave Rebecca my letter to post, in case my audacity left me. That it did, halfway to Hampstead, but matters were out of my hands by then. What preoccupied me now was how to tell my aunt that I would be leaving. I tried to assure myself that I had been in London nearly six years so what mattered a few more weeks or months? But now that I was really going, now that I knew it in my heart and my soul, I did not want to wait another day.

Nevertheless, there would be matters to arrange, my

jewellery to sell, goodbyes to be said. I would not want to leave my aunt and Judith in the vulnerable state they had occupied of late. I thought there was improvement, but I needed to be sure. I would not abandon them before they were ready.

Thus engrossed, I barely noticed the paved miles fall away beneath my feet. I was so absent-minded that when I reached Heath View Cottage I thought for a moment that I approached the wrong house, so fine was the carriage drawn up outside. No one who could afford a carriage like that visited the Graces any more. But there were the red ivy, the dancing plane tree. This was the place. And here was Judith running out to meet me. She seized my hands over the gate and squeezed them so hard it hurt.

'You will never guess who is here, Florence!'

'The Duke of Busby?'

'No! But almost as grand! He is a fine gentleman from the Lake District. Apparently he owns half the mines in the North Country and has a vast estate called Bellmere. He is here with his wife!' Her dark eyes danced and some of her old irrepressible energy was back.

I frowned. 'But why are they here? What do they want?'

'Oh, I shan't tell you, Florence, and you never shall guess it! You must come in and see for yourself!'

'I should dearly like to, but you are holding me trapped outside the gate!'

'Oh, so I am. Silly me. Come in.'

She stepped back and opened the gate for me with a flourish. I walked up the path, pulling off my gloves, and stepped into the dim, flagged hallway. I set down the cheese on the hall table; something told me that this was no occasion for cheese. I hung up my bonnet and cloak and went into the sitting room.

At first I saw the gentleman, standing by the piano. He was middle-aged and handsome, with a full, dark beard and side-whiskers and a great deal of satin trim about his costume. He turned to me with a smile when I walked in. His hand rested on the shoulder of the woman who must be his wife, seated before him as though for a portrait. She wore a ruffled gown of champagne and tangerine that offset her peachy complexion and echoed the warm glints in her golden yellow hair. She was exceptionally, ethereally beautiful. A beautiful blossom. It was Calantha.

For a moment I was so astonished I could not move. Then she stood up to greet me, I jumped forward and we came together in an awkward, happy, wildly excited embrace and a crush of skirts.

'Florence!' she squealed. 'How beautiful you look. How that green becomes you. I'd forgotten how tall you are! Are you well?'

'Entirely well, and I have no need to ask how you are for I can see! You look radiant, Calantha! Oh, I'm so happy I could cry. I never thought I'd see you again.' In fact, I did cry, just for a minute. But I soon enough composed myself to meet her husband, Mr James Hanborough.

Genuine, I thought as he shook my hand. *Solid and kind.*

In something of a dream I squeezed between my aunt and Judith on the sofa. My aunt did not say a word, merely stared at Calantha as though a bird of paradise had swooped through the window to land in our house. She looked quite pale and stunned. Doubtless she was remembering the long years of ignoring Calantha, and supporting Hawker's decision to commit her to an asylum. Florrie aged fifteen would have delighted wickedly in this reversal of fortune, but now I took her hand.

They had been waiting for my return before Calantha told her story, so that she did not have to tell it twice. What had happened was this:

When Calantha fled from Helicon, she went on an impulse back to the house where she had lived with her parents. She had a vague hope that it might help her turn to the future. She stood outside the house in the slanting drizzle of a dark blue February afternoon, the gas lamps along the street fuzzy and orange in the rain. The tall townhouse was closed against the day; the weather was cheerless and bleak. Nevertheless, she could not move. She heard a disembodied voice urging her to stay.

My aunt fidgeted on the sofa; how she hated such talk. Mr Hanborough, however, with his square hands and manly beard and air of worldly pragmatism, looked not in the least disconcerted.

Calantha found herself drawn slowly forward, she said, towards the house. The street was quiet and dreamlike. Suddenly the door to her old house flew open and a woman appeared on the top step. She shielded her eyes against the wet and called out to Calantha.

'Mabel? Is that you? Why are you so late?'

'I have no idea who Mabel was,' Calantha said, wearing a faraway expression, 'and the woman was quite unknown to me too. But the strangest thing was that I was quite ready to admit to being Mabel, to step into her shoes and take her place in her life. I lifted my hand and walked forward across the street, but slowly; I could not have hurried if I'd tried. And the next minute, a carriage came hurtling round the corner and nearly knocked me down.'

'It *did* knock you down!' interjected her husband. 'You were lying in the street. My heart stopped. I thought we'd killed you because of my infernal impatience!'

'No, James.' She stroked his hand and continued. 'The horses came within a whisker of me to be sure but what really happened was that I was roused, at last, out of my trance. I jumped back, lost my balance and fell. But of course the good people inside the carriage – James and his sister Gwendoline – saw a figure falling in the street and imagined me mangled by hooves, desperately injured or worse.'

James Hanborough shuddered. 'I relived that night over and over for days!'

'The woman in my old house,' said Calantha, 'came rushing out shrieking "Mabel! Mabel!" James and Gwendoline leapt out of the carriage and ran to my assistance – I was oblivious to all this for I had fainted – and carried me inside. James was convinced he had killed a young lady called Mabel. The woman must have been expecting someone she had never met for she didn't realise I was a stranger. Gradually they noticed that I had no injuries, except for scrapes on my arm and ankle. Then I revived and admitted that I was not Mabel. I've often wondered why she was late and hoped that they found her.'

'So if she wasn't Mabel,' continued Mr Hanborough in his deep voice with its pleasing Northern inflection, 'who was she? Naturally my sister and I were all of a care to restore her to her home.'

'That's when I had to admit that I didn't have one,' said Calantha. 'I told them all that I had run away. I didn't explain why, for I didn't want to put the idea of an asylum in anyone else's mind.'

My aunt winced, but Calantha told her tale without rancour or resentment, rather she seemed lost in the wonder of it. 'I made it perfectly clear, however, that I could never go back.'

'I wanted to know what this beautiful, tragic young lady intended to do without a home and all alone in London,' scowled her husband, dark brows drawing together.

'They asked if I had any money,' smiled Calantha, 'and I showed them the five shillings Florrie gave me.'

My aunt and Judith looked at me in surprise. Mr Hanborough came over and kissed my hand. 'Thank you,' he said.

'They said it was not enough and that I needed a better plan than wandering the streets and hoping. They insisted I come and stay at their hotel.'

'We were only in London for a week, but we had to keep her safe. We thought perhaps we could find her a suitable situation before we left. The short of it as you see is that I married her. We did not find any possibility in London that was good enough for her, nor safe enough. By the end of the week Gwendoline and Calantha had become fast friends and I was falling in love with her. We asked if she would come and live with us at Bellmere and she said yes.'

'Lakes and mountains and mists and kind people,' said Calantha dreamily. 'Naturally I said yes. James and I married some months later and I am the happiest of women. Of course, I did not know how rich they were when I accepted their offer or I should have been quite afraid.'

'I'm a practical man,' he explained to us. 'Money I've plenty of, but imagination and magic, none. She lit into my life like a . . . like a . . .' This practical man was at a loss for words to describe how it had been, but seeing her beautiful and glowing under his protection, it was easy to imagine.

They told us then that Mr Hanborough had recently come

to do business with a London banker who wished to participate in an ambitious new scheme involving all the major mining areas: Cornwall, Wales and the North.

'I receive applications for investment all the time,' he said. 'It's rare I involve myself; I prefer to put my money towards charity these days. But my assistant puts the occasional application past my nose if he thinks it has particular merit. I was more than impressed by the intelligence and circumspection in this application. There were no high-flown phrases, no rash promises, and not a single detail had been neglected. I had never seen a proposal so well thought through. I thought this might be a gentleman worth helping so I came to London to meet him. The short of it is, I invested. I went home again and when I told Calantha all about my meeting . . . Well, perhaps you can imagine who this intelligent, thorough, impressive man of business might be?'

I had a suspicion. My aunt, it was plain, did not.

Calantha rose and came to sit nearer my aunt. She took her hand gently. 'Aunt Dinah, the clever banker's name is Irwin Grace.'

My aunt frowned, but oh, the qualities of that frown! If ever a frown painted a portrait of a long marriage, that did. Clever and impressive were clearly not words she associated with her husband.

'And do you know *why* Uncle Irwin was so eager to secure investment in such an ambitious project?' Calantha continued.

'I . . . I imagine, the reversal in our affairs . . . the need to consolidate certain matters . . .' muttered my aunt vaguely.

'All that and more. Since Hawker's death my uncle has been working tirelessly, Aunt, as you must know, to secure a new fortune for the family. But his particular incentive has been to buy back Helicon, knowing how very much it has always meant to you. With the money James has invested and if the business unfolds as they hope over the next six months, you can go back.'

Judith squealed in delight. My aunt gave a sort of sob and buried her face in her hands. Mr Hanborough took a turn about the room and tactfully gazed through the window.

'I want to make it clear,' he said in a low voice, after a few moments, 'that when I found out that my new colleague was part of the family who had despised and shunned her, the family that had been prepared to send her to an asylum, I wished to retract my support and have nothing further to do with him.'

My aunt looked up at him fearfully through her fingers.

'James! You promised!' said Calantha in a reproachful voice.

'I know, my dear, don't worry, I won't. I only wish to state that I *wished* to retract my support,' he reiterated, very calm, looking at my aunt. 'But I did not for two reasons. One, the discovery did not alter the merit of your husband's proposal. And two, Calantha told me that your husband spoke up for her in the face of great opposition *and* she begged me to help you. She has held no grudge or quarrel. Yet I want to make it clear . . . that she is not mad. She is not eccentric. She is fey. And lovely. And different. And kind. I am proud to bring her among my friends and associates and she has never once let me down or disgraced me. Quite the contrary, she—'

'James!'

'Yes. Well. I just wanted to make it clear. That said, I am very happy to work with your husband, Mrs Grace, and I am glad to play my part in restoring you to your rightful home. Best wishes to you.'

'Well done, James.'

I sat quietly and smiled at Calantha and thought, *I am free.*

Chapter Forty

Within a fortnight I received notes from Mr Glendower and Lacey. Both were extremely brief. Mr Glendower's said he would be happy to take on a tenant as it would save him the bother of dealing with the place. He named a rent that seemed to me to be entirely moderate and expressed a hope that I did not have a London lady's romantic notion of Cornwall. He warned me that the house was lonely and neglected, the country godforsaken.

Lacey's said merely, *Come at once.*

After selling my jewellery I had the fare for my journey and six months' rent. What would become of me after that I did not know but I placed my situation in the hands of God – or the gods – or the spirits – or any force better able to handle my affairs than I myself. I sold, too, several possessions I would not need in Cornwall but which had some value – a bronze bust of Athena that Sanderson had once given me, and some fine clothing.

I packed a box of clothing that would be useful in Cornwall: two warm cloaks, two pairs of boots, two bonnets, two shawls, two blouses, two skirts and two dresses, all the plainest and stoutest I owned. They were not especially plain or stout, to be sure, but I must clothe myself and did not want to waste my finite means on such things. I sent the box to Lacey in Tremorney and asked her to tell no one I was coming; I was not ready for that yet. I could not simply take up a place in the community as if I had never been away, as if the Graces had never taken me in, as if there had never been Turlington. It was a new Cornwall that I was going to, irrespective of geography.

I packed a valise of a size I could carry with a few more personal, less practical possessions – hair ornaments and dance shoes and ribbons and gloves (I could not bear to part with everything of beauty). Optimistically, a sheaf of sheet music. Two volumes of poetry. It was surprising how few books belonged to me rather than the household: there had been no need to buy any when the mighty library of Helicon was at my disposal. Lastly, and most precious, my old orange stone. The valise was ready to leave long before I was.

Calantha and James returned to Bellmere. Promises to visit were not made lightly as the distance between us would be so very great. I would not see her often but I was so glad to know her happy ending.

Next, I went to see Jacob. 'You're going, aren't you?' he said at once.

'Yes, Jacob, I am.' I could not help smiling. I was going to a life that did not yet exist but I would make it, and in it I would live life on my own terms, be both Buckley and Grace. I tried to convey some of my wild hope to Jacob. I had big plans for that life.

'All right for some,' he sulked.

'All right for you, too, I hope, Jacob.'

'How so?'

'Because, if you would like it, I wish you to come with me.'

His face was, as is commonly said, a picture. He could not have looked more shocked, disbelieving, flattered, frightened, excited and forlorn, all at once, if I had suggested making him the Prince of China.

I willed him to say yes, but he didn't.

'I can't, Florrie,' he said, and his manner was no longer sullen, but decided.

I knew in that moment I would not dissuade him, but I had set my heart on him going. I tried to stay calm.

'Jacob, let me tell you everything. I have told you how I loved my home. To many it is not beautiful but to me . . . why, I have missed it every day since I left, even on the days when I did not know I was missing it. It is wild, and challenging, and difficult, and not always easy to get along with, but always easy to love. Like you.

'When I was a girl, there was an old farmhouse by a pond, on the moor. I used to walk miles out of my way just to catch a glimpse of it. It was called Heron's Watch and I thought it the most beautiful name and the most beautiful house imaginable. I intend to go and live there for as long as . . . well, as long as my money may last, I suppose. I must be completely honest with you, Jacob. It will not be a wealthy life, it will not be a life of privilege. In fact, it will be a life of hard work. And a great deal of rain.

'But it will not be so hard as my life was when I was a girl and it will not be as hard as that of many. My friend Lacey has asked me to help her run her school. You would like her very much, Jacob. There would be lots of children around, friends for you, like here. And there will be many other good things: outings and books and country dances and haymaking and harvest suppers and trips to the sea and the markets and Truro, which is a grand town for Cornwall, though it is like a crumb where London is a loaf of bread. And there will be you and me, Jacob, a fresh start for both of us, away from all our mistakes . . . We would have fun together, would we not?'

'Yes, we would, Florrie. It sounds as if you are asking me to be your . . . to be your . . . son.'

He uttered the last word painfully, as though it were shameful in him to think such a thing, as if he had dreamed it so hard that it was too private, too important to be admitted.

'Yes, Jacob, that is exactly what I'm asking you. Although I am a little young to have such a fine son as you. Perhaps you might prefer to think of me as a somewhat flawed but well-meaning big sister?'

His eyes shone for a bright, brief instant. 'No, Florrie, I would think of you as my mother. But . . .'

'Oh please, Jacob, don't let there be a "but".'

'But I don't deserve to be your son. And I don't deserve that life you talk about either. Don't you know? I've started thieving again. I ain't been to school in days now. I hit Silas Pinner clean across the head with my slate the other day because he annoyed me. I've gone back to me old ways, Florrie. It's too late.'

'Oh, I already know all of that. Mr Planchard told me. He wasn't telling tales, you understand, he is simply worried about you and he knew I would understand.'

'Do you, though? Understand? 'Cause I don't.'

'Well, yes, I think so. I think you're still hurt and angry about what Turlington did and I think you're a little shocked. So shocked that nothing makes sense any more. So shocked that you're thinking all sorts of dark things, perhaps that you must be very unimportant and unworthy of regard indeed if he could turn his back on you like that, so why not simply act accordingly? I think you miss him, even though you're angry with him. I think you feel sometimes as if there's no hope planning a fine future because horrible things like that can come at you from sideways and nothing's ever going to get better.'

'You've felt it too.'

'Well, yes, I know something of these struggles, believe me. But it's not so, Jacob. You will recover your equilibrium and with it you will rediscover your power to choose and you'll start to believe again that you can be anything you decide.'

'But it's different for you, Florrie. You were brought up right. You may have been poor but you had ones that loved you and taught you right from wrong. You may have been strange but you weren't *bad*. I was rotten, Florrie, and Turlington was rotten and even though I grew up in the rookeries and he grew up with fine clothes and fancy manners, we're the same, him and me. And look at him now he's all grown up. That's what I've got to look forward to – letting people down when they need me the most. Going months, maybe even years, on the straight and narrow but it's all just pretending because nature's stronger than all of it. I can't come with you, Florrie, I'd let you down. I wouldn't like it, neither, all that mud and fog and all. I'm a town rat. Leave me here and forget me, Florrie.'

'Jacob! I can't bear it! Can't *bear* it! You mustn't think like that! Turlington is *nothing* like you! I've made some poor choices lately and so have you, but if we see it and we want to change, we can change.'

'Not always.'

'We *can*.'

He shook his head obstinately. I fell silent, exasperated. I started talking about my plans again, taking care to make them sound as tempting, yet as natural, as possible.

'I'm happy for you, Florrie,' he said, when I at last ran out of things to say. 'It sounds like you'll have a good life and your friends will be glad to have you back. I wish you all the luck. Do you mind if I go now?'

'Back to your lessons?' I fired rather sarcastically.

He just looked at me. I knew what he was thinking: I was leaving and it wasn't my place to take an interest in what he did any more.

'Of course you can go,' I conceded. 'But please think about what I have said, Jacob. I want you with me. It won't be the same without you. It will never be too late to change your mind.'

In the doorway he paused and looked back at me. 'Do you think Turlington loved me even a little, Florrie?'

'I know that he did.'

'And he loved you, that's for sure.'

'Yes. He did.'

'So you see, it *is* hopeless. If even loving someone can't make you do the right thing, nothing will.' And he disappeared.

I sat there for a long time fighting down tears and a rising fear that I would never see that skinny, belligerent child again. I wanted to go after him. But what could I say that I had not said? I could not hound the boy. I could not kidnap him.

★

At last I rose on hollow legs and went to make my second goodbye – to Rebecca and Tobias. I was offered cheese on toast and tea, in the old way; the preparation, presentation and consumption all took on a ceremonial air.

'I always knew this day would come,' said Rebecca. 'I think anyone who ever knew and loved you a little must have guessed that it would. Oh, my dear friend, how I will miss you. When do you leave?'

'I'm not entirely sure. I had planned to go . . . well, tomorrow. But Jacob will not come with me and I have not seen Turlington since we said goodbye and I am so worried about him. I thought perhaps I should try to see him again, see if he is well . . .'

'To what avail, dear? He will be as he always is, that is to say handsome and confused and confusing. He will probably look a little haggard and very dishevelled. He will profess his undying love for you and may promise to change – and half of you will believe it and half of you will not.'

'I know! I know you are right, Becky. It will not help me to leave with a lighter heart. But oh, to think of him there, alone, in such squalor . . . Perhaps if I tried to talk to him again, perhaps if I gave him some money . . .'

'You must do no such thing!' cried Rebecca in outrage. 'Must she, Tobias? Why, Florrie, that money must last you indefinitely! Turlington can make his own money – there is no reason he cannot do so. But for a woman – alone – in

Cornwall . . . it will not be so easy. Do not you let pity sway you, Florrie. You will have troubles enough without taking on his as well.'

'She is right,' added Tobias. 'Pity is the worst thing you can feel for a man, Florrie. He has not lost a limb. He is not bereaved. Your pity is not for a specific tragedy but for the situation of his life in general, and that he has created himself.'

I bowed my head. 'What we had was not what you have,' I said.

'But you will have it yet, Florrie, with someone,' said Rebecca. 'In time, you will see.'

We talked for a long while and made an emotional farewell. I knew that our friendship would survive the test of distance, as my friendship with Lacey had done before that. Even so I felt strange for a moment, remembering that first day we had all three of us met, when Tobias had rescued us from the robber and Rebecca had asked to be my friend.

I had had my fill of emotion and the dizzying sting of parting for one day. My final goodbye, to Sanderson, would have to wait. Instead I went home and took a long walk over the heath. I was walking considerable distances again, I realised suddenly. I still did not have my old strength, but I was no longer Helicon-corseted and soft. The air was clearer here, though it did not smell like Cornwall. I saw the outlines of distant buildings, softened by the pinkish-yellow haze of an almost-spring afternoon. The ponds glinted coldly in the changing light. I felt spring on my skin and saw buds on trees, sticky, swelling, jovial. It was March, life was waiting.

I went back to the cottage and wrote a letter to Jacob.

Dear Jacob,

This will be a short letter since I have already said everything there is to say. I only wish you to know that my offer to you is open, now and forever. There will never be a time when you are not welcome in my home. I enclose a sum of money so that if you ever choose to take that journey, you will not be without means. Of course, I cannot stop you spending it however you choose — I simply wish to make it possible. There is no address as such. The house, as I have told you, is Heron's Watch. It overlooks a tiny hamlet called Braggenstones. The nearest town or village that you would recognise as such is Tremorney. You would need to travel there and then ask someone to take you or guide you. <u>Do not</u> go up on those moors alone, even if the directions sound simple. I write all this in the fervent hope that you will change your mind. Dear Jacob, it was not that Turlington did not have a better nature, it was that he so rarely chose to use it.

With love,
Florrie

I thought of writing to Turlington also, but decided against it. We had said our final farewell and there was nothing to be gained by repeating it. My energy and attention were all for the future now.

The following morning I slipped Jacob's letter through the door of the boys' home. Then I waited a further two weeks. I had not thought that at the end I would find it so hard to leave. At last I went to the Coatleys' to seek out my dear cousin for the last time.

'Florrie,' he said, holding me tightly. 'When you came to Helicon six years ago I never thought this day would come. We shall be so far apart. What will I do?'

'You must send me a fine, fat letter every week without fail. I shall do the same, Sanderson, never fear. And you must visit me whenever you wish. Bring Anne and the babies . . . although I cannot quite see Anne in a half-ruined Cornish farmhouse. But she is welcome, I mean it.'

'You are kind, Florrie. I will come to your windswept home on your wilderness hill when I can, but I do not imagine Anne will join me. Her father has prejudiced her against Cornwall a little . . .'

We both laughed, remembering my first dinner party. 'The most contrary, bedevilled, pernicious, hostile landscape in the British Isles!' we cried in unison.

'Does she know? About Selina?' I asked.

His face drained of mirth. 'Perhaps she guesses, we have never spoken of it. Some men – most men perhaps – would be able to separate love from . . . from the physical act, and separate it again from duty. It is harder for me, such is my nature. I do try with Anne, but I suppose she can see I am not . . . enthusiastic. You know, Selina and I, we . . . we were . . . *together*, once. Do you understand me, Florrie?'

'Of course I do, dear.'

'Just once. Before I married. It was still wrong, of course. I have never forgotten it. Can never forget it. She will leave London soon and return to her parents in Gloucestershire. I will probably never see her again. Can life . . . can life go on after such a thing?'

And then and there, all at once, I was glad of everything that had passed between Turlington and me. The coming together and the loss. Because it meant that I could answer him truly. 'Yes, Sanderson. It can. It does. It will. I don't know how, but knowing how is not what we are charged with. It is simply to have faith and to wait.'

'Dear, wild, angry Florrie. When did you become so wise?'

I bit my lip. Could I tell him, now? I had to. Cousin he was, but dearer to me than any brother. 'Sanderson . . . did you ever know, guess, about me and Turlington?'

His brows lifted. 'You and . . . ? You mean . . . ? Oh! No. Although, now you say it, I feel I must always have known it. Of course. Of course. Oh, Florrie. When? Are you . . . all right?'

I laughed. 'When? Always and forever. As for when it

became a reality, an *affair*, it was after he came back the last time. I was engaged to Aubrey, Sanderson, can you imagine? I lied to him for months because I did not know what to do but I couldn't *stop*! Turlington is . . . he was . . . oh, you know how he is.'

'I know, Florrie, I know. Like a force of nature, pulling you along. I ask again, are you all right?'

'I am. I truly am.'

He wrapped his arms around me. 'Gracious. Well, good gracious God! Florrie, both of us struggling with a forbidden love, all this time. Oh, *Turlington*!'

'He is in London, you know, in the Devil's Acre. An apartment he lived in long ago, he said.'

'Ah, I know the place. I shall visit him. He is in a bad way then, I imagine?'

'Pretty bad.'

'It is good and right that you are escaping from all that, Florrie. I love him, you know that, but he is not what I would wish for you. There will be someone else for you, Florrie, one day, and he will not tether you to periodic descents into the darkest places of the soul. You belong in the sunlight and the wind, not there.'

'Rebecca said so too. But how can there ever be anyone else for me? I am a woman. I have been . . . well, I have put away those expectations.'

He smiled. 'Then you do not know yourself, Florrie. You

are too passionate to live a life without love. I would wager Helicon – if Helicon were mine to wager – that you are wrong and I am right.'

'Then we shall agree to differ. As for Helicon, Sanderson, will you go back there, do you think?'

'I think Anne will wish to. She is close to her parents but she is a married woman now and does not enjoy coming second to her mother, still, in household matters. So life will go on as it ever did. Except without you. And with Turlington still bumping around the edges.'

'Wouldn't Hawker be surprised?'

He sighed. 'Now that Hawker is gone who will care about any of it? Who will care that Coatley and Elizabeth are the last of the Graces? Irwin cares about security, not conquering the world. Dinah did it all for Hawker. And we were never as important to anyone else as we were to ourselves. All his grand schemes and ambitions, forgotten.'

Chapter Forty-one

For my last journey home I dressed in the finest day dress I possessed. It was a deep-rose-coloured muslin decorated with sprigs of rosebuds embroidered in silk of the same colour. Each layer was quite sheer, but there were three layers, which together amply protected my modesty. There was an under-skirt, an overskirt and an in-between skirt. Each of these tied at the back of my waist in a froth of ribbon. There was, too, an under-bodice, a bodice, and a gauzy blouse with flaring sleeves. It was utterly unsuitable for a two-day journey and the season – it was barely April. It necessitated a warm woollen shawl, which looked a little silly over such a light creation. Still, I needed to honour the momentous step I was taking. For a ball, a wedding, we always dress in our best. It is the sense of ceremony that is important.

I tried to explain this to my aunt, when she exclaimed in dismay over my appearance. But she understood me as well as ever, which is to say not at all. Judith called me to her room and gave me a gift: a hair ornament she had fashioned herself with ribbons and lace and some white satin roses.

'I know you won't have occasion to wear it,' she said a little defensively, perhaps mistaking my silence for criticism, 'only I did not have money to spend and I wished you to have something to remember me by. My embroidery is not so fine as Annis's or I would have given you a handkerchief.'

'Oh, Judith!' I said, hugging her tightly. 'What would I want with a stupid embroidered handkerchief? This is beautiful! You are very talented. And you know how I love pretty things – how thoughtful. You may be sure I shall wear it – they do have dances in Cornwall, you know!'

'Yes, but are there any you would wish to attend?' She pulled a face, a city girl always, and I laughed.

'Indeed yes, and I shall wear this and think of you, dear cousin.'

She wept when I left and I felt a little tug. I had always wanted to like her and now I did. After Annis's abdication she had taken me into her sister's place, a role I never quite fitted but I had done my best. Would Annis reappear in their lives after they returned to Helicon? I wondered. I hardly cared.

My aunt saw me off with shoulders as hard and high as a mountain range. I think she feared I would try to embrace her. I knew better. Instead we shook hands, and she hung onto mine a moment longer than necessary.

'I thank you again for your . . . graciousness, Florence. If you ever return to London . . . please do pay us a call at Helicon.'

'Thank you, Aunt, and if you should wish to write to me, I will be very glad to hear news of you all. I wish you every happiness.'

'Happiness!' she echoed, as she had on my very first night at Helicon, when she had told me that happiness was too much to hope for. Then she relented. 'Perhaps,' she said, nodding stiffly.

Uncle Irwin took me to my coach in the trap. He saw me aboard and gave me twenty pounds. He shook my hand and kissed my cheek. 'If you are ever in need, Florence, I beg you will apply to me. I shall never forget how you have cared for Dinah and Judith. Fortunes go up and fortunes go down but I am a banker, you know, and we can usually lay our hands on some small quantity of money. It is not the most inspiring skill, perhaps, but it is useful.'

The transitions of life are often uncomfortable. We leave one place, person, identity, way of life behind, and turn to another. Human beings are creatures too complex to adjust all at once. Parts of us feel happy and optimistic, while others issue cautions, like leaves chorusing in a gale. And the rest gets caught up in the cross-currents, milling around for howsoever long it takes for the dust to settle. Thus it was for me.

I pressed my nose to the glass of the coach window as I left London, awash with conflicting feelings. I was leaving behind the family that had baffled me, the love that had torn me open, the friends who had sustained me and so many fallen hopes. I was leaving the city that had housed the Great Exhibition, the city where I had attended my first ever musical concert, the city where I had frequented an international cheese shop, a home for orphans, a desperate slum. I was going to a place so remote that the railways still had not extended a practical route there and coach remained the best way to travel. A journey, then, was a fitting way to mark such a momentous change.

Hours passed, rattling, jolting hours where I made a little polite conversation, I can only assume, but none of it memorable. I relished every uncomfortable moment and mile, watching monotonous stretches of road roll by with as much fascination as if I had only just stepped aboard. I was riven with excitement and fear. What if Cornwall was not as I remembered it? What if I had changed too much to feel at home there? What if *everything* had changed?

I spent the night in Norton St Philip, once again, and resumed the following morning. Very early the horses were harnessed, the passengers summoned and I was carried through a changing landscape into my homeland. And once I was there, my fear fell away. I ignored the other travellers and stared at the view, drinking it into my roots like a thirsty sapling, thinking, *I live here again*.

Cornwall in spring. Sudden eruptions of flight through pale blue air as we startled curlews and swallows. Fields as satiny green as party dresses, hedgerows bursting and bustling with life. Little red paths snaking off into bracken – pointless, treacherous enticements that could only have been laid by the fairy folk. Folds of hill and vale, green and brown and purple plaid with the rolling, gusting sky above. I think it had never looked so beautiful.

I climbed down, stiff-legged, at Liskeard in the mid-afternoon. I wasted no time but asked all around where I might borrow a horse. I explained that I wished to leave my bag in Liskeard and ride to Tremorney, where I had a good friend. She would bring me back in her little cart within the next few days, I promised, at which point I would return the horse and recover my valise. There was some difficulty with this, not because there were no spare horses, and not because their owners were loath to trust a stranger – trust was easily bought in this difficult economy – but because everyone advised me to a different course of action.

Oh, how they worried about me travelling to Tremorney alone. I would need to skirt the moors to get there, they told me, and that was a terrible place. All too easy to find myself lured and lost up there. The paths tangled themselves up as if they were doing it on purpose! And this time of day! This time of *year*! Fiendish, unreliable spring. I could find myself lost on the moors with darkness descending . . . Better send word to my friend and wait for her to collect me; accommodation could be easily arranged. Or wait until morning, at least, then someone from Liskeard would drive me there.

In vain I explained that I had grown up in Braggenstones, that the moors held no fear for me. They clearly didn't believe the first part and they discounted the last part as the ignorance of a city traveller. In my frustration I grew autocratic, demanding a horse and flourishing money, simply because they would not listen. I remembered how opinionated and blinkered these folk could be, how it had infuriated me as an imaginative young girl. I realised now that it would infuriate me to the end of my days. So be it. Home was not a place where there were no irritations. It was the place where you suffered the irritations because you knew you would be nowhere else.

They were quite right, of course. Either one of the options they suggested would have been far more sensible than my own plan, which had come upon me quite unexpectedly in the last ten minutes of my journey. Yet now that it was here I was foolishly attached to it and I *would* do it.

Stubborn, I heard Nan's voice say in my head, and I heard twelve-year-old Florrie lash back at her, *Stubborn yourself, you old mule*.

All credit to the good townspeople, despite my steadily lessening cordiality, they remained reluctant to let a fine city lady ride to her death in the wilderness and they put up a good fight. But in the end I realised that, as with all mythical quests, there were magic words that could be uttered to put everything to rights. Being a Grace would do me no good here but there was another name that carried more weight. At last I thought to tell them that I was Dunstan Buckley's daughter. And the matter was settled.

'Whyn't you say so afore?' grumbled an old gent who was suddenly happy to lend me his roan cob. 'All fuss for nothin', that were. This here'm Jester. You mn ave im a week. Longer n at an I'll need to charge you some more.'

'I won't keep him a week,' I promised, taking the proffered rope.

'We remember your da, your nan too. And you, the stories of you running wild up there on that moor. You'm look all different now, though.'

'I am different, and yet I am the same.'

'Your da were a good man.'

'Yes, he was.'

I left everything behind in Liskeard for now, every last piece of Florence, though I knew I would reclaim her soon. But I would be Florrie Buckley again tonight. Jeb Taylor, the old man, gave me bread and cheese for my journey. I offered him further payment but he refused it. He wrapped it in an old rag and tied it with a length of grubby string from the saddle, since he could not spare his saddlebags. I mounted up in the old way, astride, fancying I must look like an orchard nymph with my filmy rose-red skirts cascading down Jester's mottled sides. The gathered crowd looked less than impressed.

'Foolish!' I heard more than one whisper.

'Take a proper cloak at least an bring m back when you come,' called one mystified woman.

It was kind of her and I accepted. If it had been raining, I would have waited in Liskeard, but the sky was blue and the clouds were white and my need was so strong that it out-weighed any other consideration. I rode out of Liskeard at four of the clock and set Jester's nose to the west.

When I came to the place they had warned me about, where it was easy to confuse the lower and upper paths for they wove in and out of each other tricksily, I did not take the path which would lead me safely around the moors and past Braggenstones to Tremorney. I pointed Jester uphill, away from any path, and when he balked, prudent as his master, I kicked him on.

I sang as I rode, old country songs that I had not heard, save for at Hesta's wedding, for many a long year. I passed not a soul for this was not the safe way, it was not even *any* known way; it was simply *my* way and mine alone.

Deeper and deeper into the wilderness we went. On a high, rocky outcrop I stopped to let Jester rest. The whole of Cornwall was spread out around me to north, south, east and west. Curlews calling, frantic and free. A sweet, poignant smell of gorse, the flourishing gold of the flowers. From this point I could not see Braggenstones, but I could see the smooth tail of the valley in which it lay. But I was not going to Braggenstones tonight.

Below me I could see the road that the miners trod on their way home, the road that I had haunted as a child after my father died, hoping against reason that I would see him come home. I could see on the next rise the silvery brook and the clump of trees that guarded Heron's Watch and I thrilled to know that my new home was hidden therein. But I was not going there tonight either.

I took off my shoes and considered them. Pretty, pretty things. But not right for Florrie. I thought about flinging them off the tor and watching them sail away through the air but instead I ate the food Jeb had given me and tied the shoes to the saddle. And then I walked. With Jester's reins looped over my arm, his contented nose bumping at my arm, his horsey smell mingling with broom and bog, moss and fern, I walked, barefoot over my moors.

When I reached the giant boulder from where I could see Braggenstones and Nan's cottage and Tremorney beyond that, it was nearly dark. Countless, fathomless stars spun in a sky drenched with purple. I tied Jester to a small elm tree whipped to an outlandish form by the wind, then wrapped myself in my shawl, and the cloak around that. I knew better than anyone how the weather might change, how I could wake to a hailstorm or drenching rain or a mortal chill. Yet with a deeper knowing I needed to lie on the breast of the land. As an untarnished child I had been safe here, and so I was as a mistake-laden woman. I nestled down in a clump of long grass and I slept.

Chapter Forty-two

I woke early in an opalescent dawn and for a moment I wondered where I was. I opened my eyes to a vast silver and pearl sky, and the thin, dark stripes of waving grass. I truly thought I had strayed into a dream. Then I remembered and almost wept with gratitude.

I rose and walked to Old Rilla's. I had not walked barefoot for a long time and my feet were as scratched and torn as they were dirty when I got there. I paused at the rowan tree and snapped off a twig, putting it in my embroidered pocket and smiling at myself for doing it. I knocked at her door and waited.

Old Rilla was getting older now, as Lacey had said; she was not so swift to answer the door. I took in her tired eyes, her slight breathlessness and her barely perceptible stoop with a sinking heart. I had lost enough people; I was not ready to lose another. But when she in her turn took in my muddy pink dress, my fern-studded hair and bare feet, she broke into a smile which held all the power and radiance of the sun. She reached up tall and hugged me.

'You're home, then, Florrie Buckley,' she said with satisfaction. 'I've some elder root to boil down. Help me.' I went inside and it was as if I had never been away.

I stayed the day and the next night with Old Rilla. I had no particular timetable I was following, just an unfolding sense, moment by moment, of right timing. We worked all day in the garden, talking little. As afternoon leached into night, the rains came: April rain, hard and brilliant. We shut ourselves into the cottage next to a thin fire. I shivered. Even in their reduced circumstances the Graces' fires had been luxurious compared with this.

'Gone soft,' observed Old Rilla, not unkindly.

'No doubt,' I responded easily. That process would reverse soon enough once I took possession of Heron's Watch.

'How was it then?' she asked, and I began to speak. Old Rilla was one of those people – I could tell her everything. Most especially I poured my heart out about Turlington – for two or three hours perhaps.

'How can it be?' I asked insistently. 'How can it be that you feel such for another person . . . and it all comes to naught? How can it be that he feels such for you too . . . and yet you walk away, and he will not come after you? He said – we said – that our hearts were meshed, our fates, that whatever lay ahead we would do together . . . Yet we are apart! How can the soul feel *such* surety, such that you would do anything, *anything* it prompts . . . and yet you are led astray and left alone and each morning you wake alone as if it never was? I will never love like that again, Old Rilla, *never* again. I will never trust that feeling any more. If I ever have it again, I will shut it out and never, ever follow it. It is too hard, too duplicitous. And the pain is too great.'

Old Rilla merely smiled and stoked the fire.

'What is that smile?' I demanded, indignant. 'What is it, Old Rilla?'

She stood, slowly, and fetched an old plate and what looked like a brick wrapped in a cloth. She unwrapped it and my eyes gleamed. Beech mast sticky! She broke off a sizeable piece, put it on the plate and handed it to me. I sank my teeth into it, my mouth watering joyfully.

'Mennan Post, the preacher's daughter, had a baby last week, her first.'

'Mmmmfff?' I said, my teeth stuck together.

She nodded. 'She roared and swore, used language that would have made her father cast her out there and then had he heard it. And she said exactly the same as you. Never again. Never, never again.'

I swallowed my mouthful. 'Completely different thing,' I protested.

She ignored me. 'In fact, almost every woman I have seen through childbirth says the same thing during those painful hours. And why wouldn't they? Agony, they go through. But how many only children do you know? Not many. Nature is stronger.'

'Remember how I could always tell something about a person the instant I met them?'

'Oh, I remember, child.'

'Well, when I first saw Turlington in London, my soul whispered to me then. *Kindred*, it said. And something about that word – I was not even sure what it meant then – made me trust him. Trust in what I was feeling. I thought my heart was safe with him.'

'What else did it say? Was it only *kindred*?'

I thought back to another dark night, sitting by a fire with someone I loved. Me a scrap of a wild girl running around in my nightgown, armed with a candlestick. Turlington breaking into his own home in the middle of the night. Despite myself, I smiled.

'No. It said *kindred*, and then *broken*, and *lonely*. Oh.'

Old Rilla waved her hand as though dispersing midges. 'The beginning, middle and the end of it, all there in those three words. How could you ever be safe with someone who was broken and lonely? Yet how could you ever have avoided what happened, since he was kindred? It was written, Florrie. No judgement of yours could have prevented it.'

'I was young,' I agreed. 'I had no wisdom.'

She shook her head. 'Even then. There *is* no wisdom can protect you from the people you were sent here to love, nor the lessons you were meant to learn. Not every love story has a happy ending. It makes it no less a love story for all that. The next time "kindred" comes knocking at your door – and it will – you will have no say in the matter.'

I frowned. I did not like to think I could again feel so powerless, swept up in a scheme not of my own devising. I knew there was no arguing with her, but inwardly I promised myself I would never let myself believe that feeling of destiny again. In fact, if I ever felt it again, I would run as far away as possible.

The following day I went to Tremorney and presented myself to Lacey. She exclaimed with joy over my return, with dismay over my appearance and with wonder that I had been home for two nights already, 'roaming around out there', as she put it, without her ever dreaming of it. There was no school that day so she took me to Liskeard, where horse was exchanged for valise.

From there we went to Heron's Watch, which was in a sorry state of dirt and dishevelment, much like myself. The key was under the stone nymph by the front door, as Mr Glendower had promised. After so many years of sneaking about the grounds, peering through windows, trying to find a way to get inside, the right of entry was mine. I wondered if the key had been there all the time.

I stood looking up at it in awe. Old and grey, square and

plain, but with a riotous roof, eaved and dipping and crowned with three tall chimneys. Usually things of childhood diminish as one grows older. In this case, the house looked far bigger than I remembered it.

'I wonder how many rooms there are?' I murmured.

Lacey laughed. 'There is only one person I know who would rent a house she has never been inside, without even asking such things. Shall we go in and find out?'

'I'm not sure I'm ready!'

Heron's Watch. Always the most beautiful house in the world, to me. It was not mine, precisely, but it was mine for now. A broad, shallow step flanked the front door and I stood on it and turned around, as I had done as a child. I looked out over the valley. To my right the glade of trees and gushing out of it the silver stream. I did not have to go back to the valley and look up at it, I could go inside it and live there.

At last I turned the rusty key in the rusty lock and pushed at the door. It stuck a little, then yielded and I stepped inside, Lacey close behind me. It smelled damp and disused. A long hallway showed four doors leading off it, two on either side, and a staircase at the far end, mounting to the left. I tried the first of the doors and cried out.

'What's wrong?' asked Lacey, pushing past me. 'Is there a dead fox? They get in everywhere, you know, but can they get out? No. Is it a fox?'

I shook my head and pointed.

'The fireplace?' she frowned. 'What's wrong with it?'

'Nothing,' I whispered and reached for her hand. It took me a moment to be able to explain.

'When I was in Hampstead and I did not know where to go or what to do with my life, pictures started coming to me, pictures that I could not understand. I knew they meant something, but I did not know how they could all come together. One of them was this fireplace! This very fireplace! Every detail exact, even down to that candlestick upon it – though there were no cobwebs in my picture.'

'Well, you always wanted to live here after all! You must have seen it through a window when you were a child. It must have stayed in your memory.'

But I knew it was more than that. I looked around. I had not only seen the fireplace, with its huge, grey stone surround and gaping mouth, but I had seen it from this angle, as one standing before it, staring into the fire. There was no window into this room that afforded that view. In fact, from either window, you could only see it end-on, you could not grasp its sheer size or grand aspect, like that of a banqueting hall of old. Gods could feast here and feel at home.

I swallowed. In thinking of Heron's Watch as an almost-ruin, I had taken on something far grander and prouder than I had anticipated. I did not tell Lacey the other part of the picture. A family around this fire. For that seemed impossible.

Even restoring the place to a liveable condition seemed impossible.

We explored the rest of the house. Three bedrooms and two small attics. Tiny, cobwebby windows, blind and grey, easily wiped clean so that they twinkled under the eaves, looking out over moor and vale and brook, eager as children.

We swept out one room and one fireplace. We beat and aired an old mattress and that served us for the night. Then Lacey left early, and I continued my nesting alone. I swept and scrubbed and washed and polished and wrote a list of supplies I would need. I realised I was no longer anywhere near the sort of shops to which I had become accustomed. I would need to beg, borrow and steal, or else arrange a trip to Truro without delay. Meanwhile I grew used to sleeping again with unveiled windows, with moonlight soaking the room and the cries of owls and foxes raucous about me. Lacey returned that night with my trunk and some food to sustain me while I continued reeling from the magnitude of what I had done.

I had been home a week before I felt sufficient to return to Braggenstones. It had been one thing to go there for the wedding, all caught up in celebration and busyness as we were. But this – real life, continuing, with no Nan, with no real part for me in the village – that was strange and a little melancholy. My neighbours would be my neighbours again, yet I had distanced myself from them by taking the big house on the crag. I was welcomed, of course, and a few, Hesta and Stephen among them, offered me space in their homes, saying I must not live up on the moors all alone. Oh, whimsy enough now, they said, but what would I do when winter came?

But I was undeterred. Old Rilla was a woman alone, and Heron's Watch was five times the shelter of her old cottage; there was no reason I could not do it too. I bought a cow, a pig and some chickens. I started to dig a vegetable garden in the shelter of the trees, as soon as I had brought minimal order to the house.

I began my work at Lacey's school, three days a week. She remained in the old place in Tremorney and now conducted two classes, one from the old parlour and one from the dining room next door. We had eight pupils apiece in those early days; she taught the younger children and I taught the older ones.

It took months for me to regain the physical strength and resilience I had known as a girl. It took as long to grow used to doing without shops and concerts and amenities in ready proximity. I was ill more than once as my being digested loss and gain and everything that had happened. As I lay alone, tossing and turning and coughing in an isolated farmhouse with no Nan to tend me, nor any servants to send for a doctor, I rued my decision to become a Cornish girl again. But each time, dawn came in angelic splendour, tender, humble and bright, glowing like Neptune's own pearls and promising better days. And they always came.

I began to receive letters from Rebecca and from Sanderson. It was strange and lovely – and sometimes sad – to hear news of the city. The weeks rolled by, the days grew longer, life burst into extravagance around me.

Chapter Forty-three

June came. Midsummer's Day. My twenty-first birthday. And with it, a letter from Mr Diggle, Hawker's solicitor, containing the most astonishing news.

My grandfather had, after all, made me a bequest, ordered to be held in trust until I came of age. I was, apparently, the only Grace to inherit any money whatsoever. It was not so large that I could live a fashionable life again – but I didn't wish to. It was, however, sufficient to secure my life if I continued in this modest way. I was able to buy Heron's Watch – Mr Glendower was more than happy to rid himself of this 'leaking outpost' to a person of means. I bought a piano and a horse and cart. I sent off to London for a goodly number of books. My life suddenly became more easeful.

The bequest had an unexpected addendum. My grandfather had also, for some reason, left me his library desk. It was a curious, cumbersome, ungainly delivery to come bumping over the moors. Five separate inhabitants of Braggenstones came up to 'the old farm' to see what had arrived. I think they were very disappointed when they found out.

September. I was back and forth to Braggenstones almost every day. I helped them with the harvest, which was decent, this year. They joked that my return was a lucky charm. With summer spent, Old Rilla came to live with me. She carries on still, bright as a flame, but admits that a life in her lonely cottage is no life for a woman her age. We go regularly to tend her garden and meanwhile we are recreating it in my own, with cuttings and seedlings most carefully transplanted and tended.

And then, one day in late Autumn, an extraordinary thing. I am sitting at the great oaken desk, writing a letter to Rebecca, when I look up to see a stranger in the distance. I squint, and something in me tilts – I know that I know him, yet he is too far to see. I sit quite still, and watch. Definitely not someone from around here. Those are city clothes, though not well-cut, and that is a city walk. That is the city way, to twist the head from left to right, to pause and look over the shoulder as if quite unable to accept that they have landed in such a place.

Past the brook and he is bending to splash silvery water on travel-grimed face and hands. As he straightens and turns to face the house again I see him – in the flash of sunshine on sandy-blond hair. He has grown! He has taken his sweet time! I told him *not* to come onto the moors alone!

I run from the house, barefoot as always. I am laughing, and run over the grass to throw my arms around him in the bright sunlight. It is Jacob, come to live with me and be my son.

I have planted a tree in my garden, quite separate from the Old Rilla garden. It is a hazel tree – always my favourite, the spirit tree, the tree between worlds. And on its branches I have tied pieces of ribbon and thread, one for every member of the Grace family, going as far back into the family's history as I can remember. This way I can keep my promise to Hawker, and never forget.

My ancestors are mostly represented by string and thread, and I have used ribbons for the Graces I lived with for six years of my life. There is a pure white strip from Hesta's wedding bouquet for Calantha. A black funeral band for Annis. A tough hatband in a complicated, multi-coloured weave for Dinah. A piece of sensible brown edging for Irwin. Something lilac and insubstantial for Judith. A rather splendid strip of black satin for Hawker, to which I have stitched magpie feathers; it felt right to do so. A length of pale pink dress trim for Anne. Two pieces of soft yarn for Coatley and Elizabeth, green and yellow respectively. A beautiful bright blue banner for Sanderson and a narrower, more iridescent blue ribbon for me.

I also have a velvet ribbon, emerald-green, the colour of heart's truth, to represent Turlington. But I don't know where to keep it. Some days I tie it to the tree, but he is not a Grace; it feels all wrong and I take it off again. Yet, he was such an

important part of those years, of my time among the clan. So I
roll it up and put it in a box in my bedroom. But that makes it
feel like a lover's keepsake, which is not right either. I don't
regret our liaison now, from this safe distance; I feel grateful
for love shared and lessons learned. But that love, in its extraordinary way, ran its course. Then I move the ribbon to a
lockable drawer in the old desk, but there it feels secret – and I
do not want anything hidden and brooding to fester in this
new life of mine. So the ribbon moves restlessly, from tree to
box to desk to tree again. Turlington's place in this symbolic
world is as troubled and ambiguous as his place in real life ever
was. Yet, when I think of him I try to imagine him happy. I
refuse to dwell on memories of those last, tortured months;
instead I conjure pictures of him laughing, at peace, living
prosperously and well. It seems a small thing to do for the man
I once wished to save. But I have come to believe that we can
only ever really save ourselves – though if we are wise we will
accept help when it is offered. So perhaps this is the most I can
do for him after all: I wish him well with all my heart.

Years have passed now since Florence Grace returned from
London and took possession of the old house on the moor.
The pain of loving and losing Turlington has never been forgotten, but it has faded into the background of my world. I
sometimes reiterate my promise to myself, never to allow that
kind of fateful love into my life again, but as there has been no
sign of such a thing, my resolve is of a theoretical nature. My

adopted son Jacob is a fine, strong young man, who works the land and tends the animals and attends Lacey's school. He has started courting Tarren Mendow, a pretty lass from Tremorney. Old Rilla battles on as ever, invincible perhaps.

Rebecca and Tobias have visited me every year so far. They have two daughters now, Florence and Matilda. Sanderson comes twice a year without fail. His marriage to Anne is better than either of us could have hoped once upon a time. Away from her mother's watchful eye she has come to know her husband for his own admirable qualities, and not only for his being a Grace. He has taken the same pains to get to know her and they are good friends, at least. The partnership brings him comfort and his children bring him joy and so at last I can be content on my cousin's account.

My city friends always spend part of their visit in Heron's Watch and part in Truro – they admire my grand old home and the bleak conundrum of my moors, but it is *too* bleak and *too* much of a conundrum for them. Jacob and I always enjoy joining them for those days in Truro, where we can talk of books and music and the wider world again and hear about fashions and gossip and scandal.

This last Christmas I held a celebration in my home. As I sat at the piano and played the old carols I looked across at the fireplace, its mantel laden with holly and fir and yew. Our Braggenstones neighbours were milling about, gulping cups of the mulled wine that bubbled over the fire, but clustered around the fireplace at that particular moment were Lacey and Old Rilla and Jacob and Tarren. The sight gave me a start. *Family*, I thought. That vision I had seen all those years ago held true. A family does not have to be husband and babies. Other ties are equally as strong.

And that is really the end of my story – or at least, of one particular story: my early life and my time with the Graces. The rest is really just postscript. Or preamble to the next. But when you have watched the heavens wheeling, silent and endless, when you have lived close to the turning of the seasons, when you understand the rise and fall of tides, you come to understand that beginnings and endings are nothing more than arbitrary markers thrust upon the unknowable by timid man. There are many more stories to come.

Epilogue

One spring, perhaps six or seven years after my return to Cornwall, I am sitting outside my house, relishing the sense of winter receding. Dew, not frost, under my feet. The high, clear cry of a hawk and the earth and bracken stirring. I am tying a new piece of yarn – white this time – to my hazel tree, to mark the arrival of Benjamin, Sanderson's second son. The cold spring winds make it a difficult task as they snatch at the wool and numb my fingers. I succeed at last and take my emerald-green ribbon from my pocket. I had thought, while I was at the task, to restore him to the tree again for a while. But as I unroll it, the breeze takes it. I leap to my feet and run after it, but it is already out of reach. I see it sailing high into the sky and bouncing through the air to the moors, and freedom. I laugh and nod. So be it.

I turn to survey my little kingdom. I can just see the red flash of Old Rilla in her new garden, wearing a new shawl. A chicken hurries past, looking flustered. I see smoke rising from two or three Braggenstones chimneys in the distance. They have come through another winter. I turn to go inside when a voice halts me.

'Excuse me, am I addressing Miss Grace?'

An unknown voice. I turn.

A man is before me, cloth cap in his hands. His clothes are poor and patched but he stands with a quiet authority. He is some years older than I, close to forty perhaps, and there are needles of silver in his brown hair. He has clear blue eyes the exact colour of the spring sky. He is tall and broad, and looks like a man used to hard work.

I tell him that I am Florence Grace.

He introduces himself and holds out his hand. I find myself taking it in both of mine, instead of the customary handshake and I'm not sure why. Our contact is warm, and brief. His face is open and bright, his manner at once humble and assured.

He tells me that he is walking from place to place, helping out at farms along the way wherever casual labour should be needed. Do I need any help, he wonders?

I do not. Heron's Watch is not a true farm. We are self-sufficient and a support to the village; there is work to be done, certainly, but there are three of us living here to do it. However, the stranger is very beautiful. I hesitate.

I look into his eyes and see constellations there. My head swims a little.

A gentle man. Warm. Kindred.

I am taken by an unaccountable longing to put my arms

around him. Somehow I know exactly how it would feel to hold him, how we would melt and interweave. So I stand, fighting a feeling I never thought to feel again. Rebecca told me I would, Sanderson told me, Old Rilla told me . . . and I had not believed them. Yet here it is, upon me again.

But I have *promised* myself . . . I know this feeling. I know that instinct is one thing, reality another. I know nothing about this man – whether he is married, if he drinks, if he has a hidden temper. I should thank him, decline, and offer him some food for his journey.

Instead, I follow my heart. It is the only way to live a life.

'Would you like to come in?' I ask.

Acknowledgements

Last year was quite a year! Hot on the heels of all the excitement around *Amy Snow*, I wrote *Florence Grace* and I couldn't have done it without love and support from a huge number of people.

Enormous thanks go once again to my amazing publishing team at Quercus – I LOVE working with you ALL – and especially to Kathryn Taussig, my superb editor, whose skill, judgement and support are second to none. And equally so to my very brilliant agent Eugenie Furniss, who has been with me every step of the way through the process, which means so much to me. Thank you all for everything.

I've once again been blessed with a crack team of trusted early readers whose responses to the first draft of *Florence Grace* have been invaluable in helping me to clarify what I wanted this book to be and holding me to my vision: Jane Rees (Mum), always my first reader, champion and guide; Stephanie Basford-Morris; Marjorie Hawthorne (fellow Madeira traveller!); Ellen Pruyne and Christine Rees. Thank you all.

Acknowledgements

As for my friends, as always, I could not wish for better. I'm so lucky to have you – thank you all.

Especial cheerleaders this time, who really went the extra mile to understand the exciting, challenging and often crazy-making 'second book phenomenon' have been: Stephanie Basford-Morris (who has been a rock, and even personally escorted me from the country at one point), Lisa Mears (who embodies the patience of Sanderson in teaching me the piano), Cheryl Powell (bringer of sunshine), Teresa Sherlock (for great wisdom, especially about the intangible aspects of being an author), Lucy Davies (who understands the joy and necessity of staying grounded), Jacks Lyndon (for generously finding me such lovely opportunities and contacts to promote my work in Wales), Jules Rees, Patsy Rodgers, Rosie Stanbridge and Ludwig Esser (photographer extraordinaire). You are all tremendous. Thank you.

And thank you to the fabulous 'York posse'. Thank you to Cindy Magyar and Vince Magyar for hospitality, friendship and fantastic fun, to Rozz Hancock for warm welcomes and wonderful food and to York Writers for continued support and connection which I value greatly. Could you not all just move to South Wales . . . ?

I'd also like to thank the following:

Nick Rusling at Coach House pianos for taking the time to show me the beautiful and fascinating Victorian pianos in his wonderful warehouse and for being a treasure trove of information.

Acknowledgements

Elaine Uttley at Bath Fashion Museum for my amazing study session of 1850s clothing.

And finally another enormous thank you to my parents, for endless love and support and for being the best parents anyone could wish for.

The following books have been useful and fascinating resources when I was writing *Florence Grace*:

Alison Adburgham: *A Punch History of Manners and Modes*. Hutchinson, London 1961

John Burnett: *Plenty and Want: A Social History of Diet in England from 1815 to the Present Day*. Scolar, London 1979

Daphne Du Maurier: *Vanishing Cornwall*. Penguin Books, London 1972

Judith Flanders: *The Victorian City*. Atlantic Books, London 2012

F E Halliday: *A History of Cornwall*. House of Stratus, Thirsk 2001

Adele Nozedar: *The Hedgerow Handbook*. Square Peg, London 2012

Michael Paterson: *A Brief History of Life in Victorian Britain*. Robinson, London 2008

Q&A with Tracy Rees

The author of *Florence Grace* and *Amy Snow* discusses some of her favourite things . . .

What was the last film you watched in the cinema?

In the Heart of the Sea, starring yummy Chris Hemsworth and an even yummier whale.

What's your favourite album?

SO MANY!!! For the sake of being concise I'm going to say *Long Road Out of Eden* by the Eagles.

Hardback or paperback?

Paperback! Can't explain why they're so magical but they are. And I always hurt myself on the corners of hardbacks.

What did you want to be growing up?

A writer! Really. Also, briefly, a ballerina and a fairy princess.

What's your favourite sort of chocolate?

That's an upsetting question. I'm trying to give up at the moment.

Tea or coffee?

Tea! Morning, noon and night. I'm a total tea junkie and I have different mugs for different varieties.

Heels or flats?
Flats. Better for dancing and for running away.

What is your favourite thing to do with friends?
I don't think I have just one. Country walks, cooking, eating out, dancing, watching films, writing poetry (that's not as random as it sounds – I'm in a poetry group) . . . I guess what they all have in common is talking!

Do you have any guilty pleasures?
Lots of pleasures but none I feel guilty about.

What one object could you not leave your house without?
My key! I always need to know I can go home again after the adventures.

Read on for an exclusive extract of Tracy Rees' Richard and Judy bestselling first novel *Amy Snow* . . .

Prologue

~~~

January 1831

Aurelia Vennaway held her breath as she tiptoed from the stuffy parlour and stole along the hallway. Her mother and aunts had paid her no attention for the past hour but that did not mean she would be allowed to leave. Her mother thought that the weather would keep her inside, that for once she would sit quietly and decorously in the corner as a little girl should.

She jammed her fur hat over fat, drawing-room ringlets and stuck her feet into sturdy boots. Shrugging on her blue cloak as swiftly as she would shrug off her destiny if she only could, she heaved open the door.

It was the kind of day that glittered and beckoned like a foretaste of heaven. The snow no longer fell, but lay thick and silver-white on the ground. The sun dazzled and the sky was a rich, celestial blue. On such a day as this, the whole world might change.

Aurelia sank up to her knees, then squared her shoulders and considered her nonsense of skirts. Gathering them up in great bunches, she lurched like a staggering deer through the snow until her lungs flamed with its cut-glass brilliance.

Last week she had not seen her mother for five days. The metallic smell of blood and the screams that came from the bedchamber were only a memory now and her mother was back amongst the family once more – but harder than ever to please. Aurelia was not sure that she cared to try. The house was brittle and tense.

Sunlight could find no way into the woods beyond the house. Snow-laden branches of yew and wasted, straggle-thin fingers of oak reached for Aurelia. She laid her hands on them, greeting them like old and comforting friends. Her ringlets had loosened into snakes. Screeching jays made the only sound. She swung herself onto a low branch to listen and dream of the time when she would leave Hatville Court and never come back.

She nearly tumbled into the drifts when she heard an unfamiliar cry. It came in bursts, feeble yet grating, insisting she jump down and follow. She felt as though some other-worldly force were playing catch-me-if-you-can with her. It came again – goblin song – drawing her through the trees and into the sunlight.

Finally, she stood on the breast of a hill. Before her, something blue and hairless wriggled in the snow. For a moment the enchantment of the old woods clung to her and she feared to touch the creature. But curiosity broke the spell and she stepped closer. It was a human child, a tiny baby. She tore off her cloak and snatched the baby from the snow. Its skin was as chill as strawberry mousse. She wrapped it up and hugged it close.

Something was distinctly wrong, Aurelia decided, when a naked infant lay alone at the edge of a deserted wood.

'Hello?' she called, staring all around. 'Hello? I have your baby!'

Nothing but silence, and a crow lifting into the air on silky wings. The baby was very cold and weighed almost nothing. Aurelia turned and, as fast as her skirts allowed, she ran.

PART ONE

January 1848

Chapter One

I know they are watching me go. The road out of the village is long and straight. It will be miles before it bends, carrying me out of sight of the upper windows of the grand house. I know what they see: a nothing, a nobody. A small, staunch figure, lonely in mourning black, stiff skirts rustling about my boots, cloak fast against the cold. A crisp black bonnet settled grim upon my head and ribbons whipped by the wind. What a desolate January traveller I must represent.

Frost on the fields and upon the road, the village empty and forlorn, my boots leaving a trail of prints that peter into infinity. That is what they hope I will do – vanish like a melted footprint. If I can, I will oblige them. My reason for being here, the only person I have ever loved, now lies beneath six feet of earth and thick, shadow-green boughs of yew in a quiet corner of the churchyard. She was laid there yesterday.

The air is so cold that the tears are flayed from my eyes, eyes I had thought to be finished with crying for all time. After the biblical floods I have shed in the last three days I thought there could be no water left in my depleted form. Yet it seems that life, and grief, and winter go on. My toes are numb as I trudge the miles that lead me away from Aurelia's grave and from Hatville Court, the only home, grudging as it was, that I have ever known.

Soon enough, it threatens dark. The sharpest sickle moon I have ever seen hangs razor-edged in a grey sky and ahead I see the silhouette of Ladywell, the next village. I have walked for hours.

I stop there because I know I must, although my needs are not the sort to be assuaged by food, or ale or fire. The chill in my bones is nothing to the freeze in my heart and no congenial company on earth could compensate me for the lack of Aurelia. But the next village is six miles yet further and the lanes are awash with shadow. It would be the height of folly to go on; a young woman alone has ever been an easy target for villains. And although I have little faith that my life will ever again feel worthwhile, I still do not wish to throw it away. Aurelia may be gone, but she is not done with me yet. I will carry out her wishes in death every scrap as faithfully as I did when she was with me.

I enter the Rose and Crown. With my second, secret legacy from Aurelia I could afford the White Harte Royal, a hotel of some repute. But news flows between Ladywell and Enderby. If it were heard at Hatville Court that Amy Snow was seen taking a room at the Harte, they would be after me tomorrow in their carriage like the hounds of hell. For then they would guess there is more to my legacy than meets the eye.

The Rose and Crown will suffice. The chat in the lounge may not be the most refined for a young lady with a mind to her reputation but then I am *no lady*; this has been made abundantly clear to me.

I hesitate in the hall. *What am I?* Respectable young woman or guttersnipe? Servant, sister or friend? My role in the tale of Aurelia Vennaway puzzles no one more than me, especially now that I am called upon to conclude it.

'May I help you, miss?' A soft-spoken landlord approaches, clasping his hands as though anxious that his very presence might cause offence. How well I know that feeling.

'Thank you, sir. A room for the night, if you please, and perhaps a little supper – nothing rich – and a warming drink.'

'Certainly, miss, certainly. BELLA!' His welcoming tone leaps to a bellow and a young maid pops into the hall like a jackrabbit from a hole.

'Bella, light the fire in the Barley Room and take the lady's bag there,' he instructs, resuming his normal pitch. 'Might I recommend, miss, that you take supper in the lounge tonight? I would not suggest it except there is a blazing fire there and it will take a while for your room to reach a comfortable temperature. The lounge is quiet – the cold is keeping many at home – and, if you'll forgive me, you look frozen to the bone, Miss . . . ?'

'Snow.'

He looks at me then, understanding dawning. Bella stands with my bag stretching her skinny arm almost to the floor, gazing with frank curiosity until he orders her on her way.

'Begging your pardon, Miss Snow, if the lounge is acceptable I will attend to you myself, ensure you are undisturbed. By the time you are fed, your room will be fit to receive you.'

His kindness brings fresh tears to my eyes and only a supreme effort keeps them there.

I take my supper in the lounge and though I can eat only a little, the warmth and flavour are somewhat fortifying. I do not linger but retire to a small, simple room which is, as promised, tolerably warm. I perform a rudimentary toilette in a daze.

Whilst I walked I conceived the idea to write an account of my time and travels, so as to feel that my life has some substance, some witness. Alone in the silence, Aurelia's absence presses down upon me but now is not the time to give in, not so very early on in my quest. I must be as strong as I need to be.

I begin to write. Really, there is nothing else I can do.

My Favourite Fictional Heroines

By Tracy Rees

How to choose? One of my favourite things about this world is that it is packed with so many incredible books, and so many wonderful characters. I suppose the first and most obvious choice has to be Jane Eyre. I love her fierce integrity, her determination to do what's right according to her own principles – the flashes of temper, spirit and passion that get her into so much trouble at various points in her troubled life – she won't take the easy road.

Then of course there's Scarlet O'Hara. I once missed my tube stop and was late for work (in a new job!) because I was so engrossed in her adventures. She's a much more expedient, less virtuous heroine than Jane but she's always unashamedly herself. Even when she's misbehaving she scintillates – and who wants to be good all the time anyway?

When I was a child one of my favourite heroines was – obvious one, this! – Jo March in *Little Women*. I loved how she would shut herself away in her attic, bristling with indignation about all the injustices in life, then forget it all by plunging into a fictional world. As long as she's scribbling stories, or doing *something* creative, she feels alive. No parallels there! Other childhood favourites were grumpy Mary in *The Secret Garden*, Anne of Green Gables and horse-mad Jinny of Finmory in Patricia Leitch's lovely series. I like heroines who don't get it right all the time, who keep bumping up against the established world and asking questions!

In contemporary fiction one of my favourite authors is American writer Elizabeth Berg. Her heroines are so *real*! Nan in *The Pull of the Moon* and Samantha in *Open House* always stay in my memory. Samantha's fixation with Martha Stewart is just hilarious and Nan's need to walk away from life as she knows it — at least for a while — is very powerful. I always applaud the effort to live a really authentic life, in fiction and real life.